DON
ANDRÉS
and
PAQUITA

DON
ANDRÉS
and
PAQUITA

THE LIFE OF SEGOVIA
IN MONTEVIDEO

ALFREDO ESCANDE

Translated from Spanish and Edited by
CHARLES POSTLEWATE
and **MARISA HERRERA POSTLEWATE**

a/p

AMADEUS
PRESS
An Imprint of Hal Leonard Corporation

Amadeus Press
An Imprint of Hal Leonard Corporation
7777 West Bluemound Road
Milwaukee, WI 53213

Trade Book Division Editorial Offices
33 Plymouth St., Montclair, NJ 07042

Published by Amadeus Press in 2012
Originally published in 2009 by Alfredo Escande

Photograph credits may be found on page 403, which constitutes an extension of this copyright page.

Printed in the United States of America

Book design by Publishers' Design and Production Services, Inc.

Library of Congress Cataloging-in-Publication Data

Escande, Alfredo, 1949–
    [Don Andrés y Paquita. English]
    Don Andrés and Paquita : the life of Segovia in Montevideo/by Alfredo Escande; translated from the Spanish and edited by Charles Postlewate & Marisa Herrera Postlewate. — 1st hardcover edition.
        pages   cm
    Includes bibliographical references and index.
    ISBN 978-1-57467-205-3
    1. Segovia, Andrés, 1893-1987—Exile—Uruguay.   2. Madriguera Segovia, Paquita, 1900-1965—Exile—Uruguay.   3. Guitarists—Spain—Biography.   4. Pianists—Spain—Biography.   I. Postlewate, Charles, editor, translator. II. Postlewate, Marisa Herrera, 1954–, editor, translator. III. Title.
    ML419.S4E83 2012
    787.87092—dc23
    [B]
                                                                2012015027

www.amadeuspress.com

To my wife, Beatriz Font

Contents

Contents

Foreword

I had the good fortune to follow the creation of this tome very closely from afar, and it is a pleasure to accept the challenge of providing a foreword, made necessary by the special nature of the work. *Don Andrés and Paquita* is an accounting in which various aspects of the subject come together simultaneously, some complementing each other, others illuminating a dichotomy. It is a purely historical study, factual and thoroughly documented, yet, at the same time, a subjective testimony of the participants in the story. This book shares with the reader the protagonists' emotional experiences, filled with twists and turns, while presenting the facts with documents, press articles, and archival records of the era. It does so in an exhaustive and detailed manner, showing that it is the fruit of a serious and tenacious investigation.

The aspects of history, both the minute details and what one might call "the big picture," are seen intertwined in circles, or better, concentric ellipses, leaving the reader to find the center of this network of rapidly changing circumstances. The result is an informative procedure wisely laid out in a design much more effective and logical than that of a mere chronological presentation.

Onto the personal testimonies and information that uncover an aspect almost hidden from musical historiography—guitaristic in the case of Segovia, pianistic in that of Paquita Madriguera—are superimposed broader frameworks that weave a comprehensive web of seemingly unconnected individuals such as Agustín Barrios, Teresa Carreño, Pablo Casals, Gaspar Cassadó, Mario Castelnuovo-Tedesco, Carlos Chávez, Mischa Elman, Eduardo Fabini, Manuel de Falla, Federico García Lorca, Enrique Granados, Jascha Heifetz, Miguel Llobet, Salvador de Madariaga, Joan Manén, Aparicio Méndez (ex-president de facto of Uruguay), Anaïs Nin, Manuel Ponce, Henryk Szeryng, Heitor Villa-Lobos, and Margarita Xirgú. The end product sheds new light on sometimes clandestine relationships among diverse creative worlds and their environments.

At the other extreme, we step into a heavily veiled microhistory acquainting us with the affairs of some of the protagonists and their emotional dimensions, such as the tragic case of Beatriz Segovia Madriguera. In that sense the "Generation of '98" [the group of writers that were active in Spain at the time of the Spanish–American War of 1898, when their country lost the last remnants of its mighty empire] tone of the title fits into the thoughts of Miguel de Unamuno for the importance that he gave to the story told "from below"—from the perspectives of individuals.

Alfredo Escande offers the more general reader a fascinatingly informative novel of great interest constructed with the same real life as its characters, and an implicit homage to the city of Montevideo, whose capacity to provide a setting for this dense plot perhaps reveals some of the secret of its enchanting nature. It will lead the specialized reader—musician, guitarist—to an understanding of the full musical scene, one that concerns the private lives of its actors as it does the level of their ideas or their political and cultural context. All of this provides the background that nourished the magic of the interpretations of Andrés Segovia that we hear today in his many recordings. Finally, *Don Andrés and Paquita* will provide the historian or cultural scholar an essential source for all serious study of this very special time and place.

Ruben Seroussi
Tel Aviv, Israel
June 29, 2009

Translator's Preface

I believe that today's work prepares you for the challenges of tomorrow, and so it was with the translation of this book. I was given a six-week summer research stipend in 1985 by my employer, the University of Texas at Arlington, to begin my quest on expanding right-hand technique for classical guitar to include the little finger. After being given this grant I asked that it be lengthened with a one-year sabbatical for the following academic year, which the university generously approved. I then applied for a research travel grant to visit South America and investigate three important previous attempts to use the little finger—by Abel Carlevaro in Montevideo, Domingo Prat in Buenos Aires, and Heitor Villa-Lobos in Rio de Janeiro. Carlevaro invited me to study with him for one month—in July and August of that summer stipend period—with an emphasis on his two-year attempt to conquer the little finger almost fifty years earlier.

My travel grant money was not approved until the end of May 1985, and then I was faced with the daunting task of having to learn to read, write, and speak Spanish in just six weeks. Marisa Herrera was the upstairs neighbor in my apartment building, and for the previous two years of our busy separate lives we never said more than "Hi" and "Bye" in the parking lot. When I learned that she was a Spanish teacher and native of Spain I asked her, "Can you teach me to speak Spanish in six weeks?"

She looked at me like I was crazy, but when I explained the jam I had gotten myself into she replied, "I'll try." She would not accept payment for the nightly three-hour tutoring sessions, saying, "I'm just glad to see that you're interested in my culture." To make a long and tantalizing story short, I took her out to dinner as payment. We fell in love and were eventually married—all thanks to that trip to Montevideo.

In the Uruguayan capital I rented a room with board in the seaside neighborhood of Pocitos. When I asked Carlevaro about his years of study with Segovia in Montevideo, he informed me that I was living just four blocks down the street from the location where Paquita Madriguera owned the house in which she and Andrés Segovia lived for much of this captivating story, the same house in which he studied daily for most of six years with the maestro. He said that Paquita's house was replaced by a high-rise apartment building around 1950, but the builders kindly saved the palm trees that adorned the front yard of her home. From then on during my daily walks I would stop in front of that site at the corner of Juan Benito Blanco and Massini streets, look up at those giant palms, and say to myself, "If only they could talk, what a tale they could tell."

Fast-forward twenty-four years, when I came across Alfredo Escande's recently self-published *Don Andrés y Paquita* while doing research for two articles published in the quarterly guitar journal *Soundboard* in 2009 to commemorate the fiftieth anniversary of the death of Villa-Lobos. I was overwhelmed at the amount of new material on this secret and mysterious part of the life of one of the most celebrated musicians of the twentieth century—and to think that I once briefly lived where it all unfolded. I was also impressed by the quality of the writing and organization of this complex, intriguing, and fascinating story. I contacted Escande by e-mail and told him that he should get it published in English, and I even volunteered the services of Marisa and me to translate the initial chapters for his presentation to a publisher, with the idea that if a publisher was interested, the author could find someone in his country to translate the remainder of the book. After doing the sample chapters, Marisa and I were hooked. It took us the entire year of 2010 to complete the first ninety pages. We then volunteered to travel to Montevideo to escape the interruptions of home life and translate the remaining four hundred pages during January and February 2011.

Marisa and I rented an apartment in Pocitos and worked closely with Alfredo, as we had done for the initial pages, but now in the same city. On our daily strolls, my wife and I walked the same streets and beach of Pocitos—just as Don Andrés, Paquita, and many other protagonists of this chronicle had done seven decades earlier. I had told people over the years that I lost half of a summer in 1985 from the reverse in seasons (Montevideo is about the same distance below the equator as north Texas is above), and I recouped my loss by trading the boreal winter of 2011, the harshest in Texas history, for the beautiful austral summer of the Río de la Plata. And Marisa, a native Spaniard, was able to experience her first taste of South America—in the city that had brought us together by coincidence, good fortune, or plain sheer fate!

But I believe that of all the great things we experienced with this unique adventure, and Marisa agrees, the best of all was making the personal acquaintance of this book's author and his wife, Beatriz. Alfredo and I had only had contact via e-mail and regular mail until Marisa and I arrived in Montevideo on January 14, 2011. We heard each other's voice for the first time when he and Beatriz arrived at our apartment that night to take us out to a Uruguayan *parrillada* restaurant as a welcome and to celebrate my seventieth birthday, a celebration postponed for six days so that Alfredo and Beatriz could share this joyous occasion with us. Alfredo was a pure joy to work with, as we encountered many problems of how to translate this word or that sentence to make it read well in English. I suggested that we add more material at times, which you will see notated in the endnotes as "Trans." (for Translators' Note), to make the text clearer and the subject easier to understand for the English-speaking reader. Alfredo eagerly accepted almost all of my suggestions (nobody's perfect), and as we progressed he encountered new material that we also added. As a result, the bilingual reader who is familiar with the original Spanish version will find this new edition much more comprehensive.

We found Montevideo to be as enchanting as had Don Andrés and Paquita in those years in which they visited it as concert performers in the early 1920s and as residents in the following decades. We met many amiable Uruguayans during our stay, the most memorable being Paquita's youngest daughter by her first marriage, María Rosa, whose voice you will hear as she recounts many details of this story. The food, wine, and overall ambiance of this tiny republic on the world's widest river provided an unforgettable experience for this project, and it is hoped that the readers can capture some of that same charm as they thumb the pages of this tome.

After the translation work and the return home to Texas, I began refining the manuscript, chapter by chapter, to make the text read more smoothly so that readers might travel in the footsteps of the plot without stumbling over a dangling participle or falling into an ambiguous phrase. I wish to thank my two proofreaders, who burnished my manuscript with their eagle eyes— Colin Cooper, with his keen knowledge of grammar, and Ron Purcell, with his personal acquaintance of Segovia and some of the details of this story. My joy in working with these two exquisite figures of the guitar world was tainted only by the sudden passing of Ron on September 7, 2011, exactly one week before Alfredo, Marisa, and I came to an agreement with Amadeus Press for this publication. Hopefully a copy will soon be available to my longtime friend in the Extraterrestrial Library of Guitar Heaven.

And a final thanks to John Cerullo, head of Amadeus Press, for recognizing the value of the fruits of this trio's labor; and thanks to our project editor Jessica Burr and copy editor Barbara Norton, whose suggestions and guidance made a significant contribution to this finished text. Without such a publication team you might all have missed out on the remarkable tale that has fascinated and enraptured this volume's producers in these recent years.

Charles Postlewate
Granbury, Texas
September 17, 2011

In Montevideo, February 24, 2011: (*left to right*) Alfredo Escande, Marisa Herrera Postlewate, María Rosa Puig Madriguera, and Charles Postlewate.

Author's
Acknowledgments

This project would not have been possible without the priceless and generous help of many individuals to whom I owe the most sincere appreciation, first of all to those great ladies María Rosa and Sofía Puig Madriguera, as well as the daughter of the latter, Roxana Delgado Puig. They supplied me all the documentation that remains in their possession after several diffusions and provided me with enjoyable hours of interviews in which they shared their wealth of memories.

My good friend Ruben Seroussi was an invaluable advisor throughout the process of developing and writing these pages, which likewise would not have been completed without the generous contribution of data, information, and points of view that the following individuals provided at various times: Carlos Álvarez Fabiani, Lucas de Antoni, Néstor Ausqui, Ramón Ávila, Héctor Carlevaro, Puri Collado, Sergio Elena, Luis Alberto Fleitas, Angelo Gilardino, Julio Gimeno, Francisco Herrera, Michael Lorimer, David Norton, Martín Pedreira, Eduardo Roland, Raúl Sánchez Clagett, Matilde Sena, Julio Vallejo, and Frédéric Zigante, as well as the Asociación Granados-Marshall in Barcelona. To all I extend my most sincere gratitude. I must also thank Tomás de Mattos, director of the National Library of the Oriental Republic of Uruguay, who allowed me access to documentation that is unavailable to the general public.

Colin Cooper and the late Ronald Purcell provided important support as proofreaders of the English translation and deserve my deepest appreciation. Ron also generously supplied some of the photographs that enrich this volume from his monumental International Guitar Research Archives.

This English edition has been made possible thanks to the magnificent and generous translation and editing work done by Charles and Marisa

Postlewate, who have also honored me with their friendship, one of the best rewards with which the exciting adventure of this book has endowed me.

Alfredo Escande
Montevideo, Uruguay
September 16, 2011

Map of South America

The Coastal Neighborhoods
of Montevideo

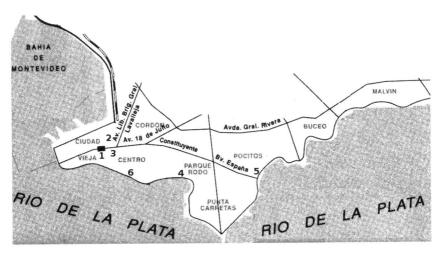

1. Teatro Solís
2. SODRE Studio Auditorium (site of the premieres of the Castelnuovo-Tedesco and Ponce guitar concertos)
3. Palacio Lapido Building (residence of the Segovia-Madriguera family from July 1937 to June 1939)
4. Parque Hotel (residence of Don Andrés and Paquita from April through June 1937)
5. Paquita's house on Massini Street at Benito Blanco (residence of the Segovia-Madriguera family from June 1939 to October 1946)
6. Central Cemetery (final resting place of Arturo Puig, Paquita Madriguera, and Beatriz Segovia Madriguera)

Note: The boulevard running the full length of the Río de la Plata shoreline is called the Rambla.

DON ANDRÉS *and* PAQUITA

Chapter 1

Prelude in London

On October 20, 1980, at 3:15 in the afternoon, Andrés Segovia gave another of his concerts in London's Royal Festival Hall. Among the spectators who filled the hall was a young Uruguayan tourist, a future architect who was enjoying the traditional senior excursion at the end of his studies. Having paid for his ticket plus an additional thirty-five pence for the evening's printed program (featuring a large photo of the octogenarian artist, his face in the foreground and on his lapel one of the many honor pins received during his career), he was guided not only by his love for music and the guitar, but also by the determination to fulfill a promise he had made to a friend.

Outside the theater after the concert, a crowd of anxious admirers and autograph seekers surrounded Segovia, who, standing by the car that was to take him back to his hotel, with some effort signed programs. Finally, somewhat annoyed by the stress of so many people and surely exhausted, the guitarist announced that the autograph session was over and got into the car. From the back of the small crowd, having almost lost all hope of getting the autograph he had promised to obtain, the Uruguayan managed to yell out above all those present, "It's for a friend in Montevideo!"

As if he had heard an incantation, the elderly maestro put his head out the car window and called out, "Who said Montevideo?"

A hand waved above the packed crowd. Without hesitating, Segovia cried out, "Come here!"

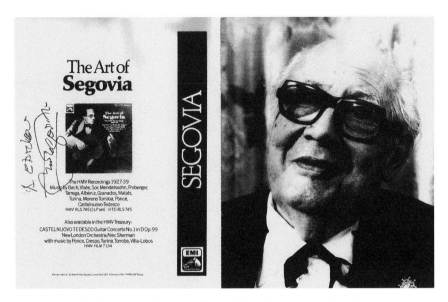

Autographed program of Andrés Segovia's London concert, October 26, 1980.

When the young man managed to get to the car, Don Andrés opened the door, surprising all those present. Those standing nearby, who had been, incomprehensibly, passed over, were able to hear him ask, "What is your friend's name?"

"His name is Carlos, Maestro."

Then, from inside the car, uncomfortable but willingly, Segovia wrote on the back of the program with his habitual large strokes, so personal and recognizable (though now shakier and imprecise), "To Carlos," followed by his famous guitar-shaped signature.

The magic word that in London's evening air exorcised weariness and nuisance from the noble maestro, whose sound had caused Segovia to change his mind and give a young tourist the autograph he had promised a friend—was *Montevideo*.[1]

Chapter 2

Information, Slightly Out of Tune

A ny reader who is only familiar with the biographical sketches (official or not) of Segovia that have been published in Europe and America will probably have been surprised or will have smiled with incredulity upon reading the preceding anecdote. Any guitar enthusiast who is up to date on the information habitually divulged about the Spanish maestro, or who reads articles on Segovia's career published in northern-hemisphere periodicals, is probably as astonished as were the passed-over admirers who witnessed how the mere mention of the word "Montevideo" suddenly awakened the veteran artist's interest on that London evening. In all that has been published in the northern part of the planet about Segovia's life and his artistic trajectory, the references to Montevideo are fleeting, and the various chroniclers pass over his time there as if it had no significance in his life. They tiptoe over it, as if fearing to discover something that may change their own vision of his story. Occasionally some may remember that in this city (who knows by what coincidence) Segovia gave the world premieres of concertos for guitar and orchestra by Mario Castelnuovo-Tedesco and Manuel Ponce. They may even mention the significance that these concertos acquired and the impact they had on the guitarist's career and the repertoire of the instrument.[1]

In 1973, for example, the Spanish musicologist Carlos Usillos, in his one-hundred-plus pages titled *Andrés Segovia*, dedicated just these three sentences to the almost ten years that the guitarist lived in Montevideo:

The outbreak of the Spanish Civil War and immediately following, during the years of World War II, moved Segovia away from Spain and Europe. America welcomed the guitarist, who would return to his native country after an absence of many years. In the meantime, his recordings nourished the passion for the guitar and the admiration for the artist in our country.[2]

Usillos's work does contain some pertinent information in a chronology that the author includes at the end of the book. However, not all of the information is correct:

> 1936: Final concert in Spain until his return in 1952.
> 1938: His daughter Beatriz is born. Married to a diplomat, she will die in Guatemala at the age of twenty-eight.
> 1939–40: The concertos of Castelnuovo-Tedesco and Ponce, dedicated to Segovia, were premiered in Montevideo by the Official Orchestra of SODRE, directed by Baldi, the guitarist from Linares performing as soloist.[3]

To set the record straight: Segovia did not give a concert in Spain in 1936, Beatriz Segovia Madriguera died after celebrating her twenty-ninth birthday, and the premiere of the Manuel Ponce's *Concerto del sur* took place in 1941.

Nine years before Usillos published his biographical work, Sol Hurok, Segovia's artistic representative in the United States, disseminated what appeared to be the official biographical sketch of the artist:

> Andrés Segovia was born on February 18, 1894 in the Andalusian city of Linares. Having gradually gained recognition outside of his native country, Segovia was ready for a full-fledged tour by 1919. He performed that year in South America, where he gained an enthusiastic reception. Subsequent engagements kept him away from Europe until 1923.
>
> The outbreak of the Spanish Civil War forced Segovia to give up his home in Spain in 1936. After living for a time in Genoa, Italy, he moved to Montevideo, Uruguay. From there he toured extensively in Central and South America. After an absence of five years Segovia returned to the United States in 1943 . . . .
>
> When not on tour, he lives surrounded by fine Spanish antiques in his Upper East Side apartment in Manhattan, which he shares with his wife Amelia Segovia, a former student of his whom he married in 1962. An

earlier marriage ended in divorce. A son from that marriage is a painter now living in France. He also has a daughter, Beatrice.

Years later, Segovia would say that his date of birth was February 21, 1893, the date that appears in many other biographical sketches. During the decade and a half that his relationship with Paquita Madriguera lasted, Segovia's birthday was celebrated on November 11. That is how it is recorded in the Spanish pianist's personal diaries and what Paquita's daughters, Sofía and María Rosa, confirmed to the author in various interviews. To add to our confusion, the passport issued by the Spanish consulate in Montevideo shows the birth date (probably provided by the applicant) as November 21, 1893. It is quite evident that these contradictions regarding the date of birth were sowed by Segovia himself, and it has never been clarified whether he did not know or did not want to reveal the true details of his origins. In a scene from the documentary *Segovia in Los Olivos*, filmed by the British producer Christopher Nupen in 1967, the guitarist says, "I do not remember when I was born. They tell me I was born in Linares."

As a small child Segovia was put in the care of an aunt and uncle who raised him. The author received a certified copy of a document (reproduced at the end of this chapter) stating that Segovia's official date of birth is February 21, 1893. This document seems to clear up the issue regarding the date, although it does not clarify the reasons for the erroneous facts about the maestro's life. On October 7, 2009, after the publication of this book in Spanish, Carlos Andrés Segovia sent a warm and congratulatory e-mail to the author. The only reservation the maestro's youngest son expressed was, "The exact birth date of my father, as well as the place at which he came into this world, continues to be, at least for me, an enigma, along with the disparity of dates that you mention."

Segovia's initial tour through South America was in mid-1920, when he made his debuts in Buenos Aires and Montevideo. He returned to Spain, where he married for the first time at the end of that year, and he appeared again in the Río de la Plata (River of Silver) region in September 1921; but in June 1922 we find him in Granada, in the famous Concurso del Cante Jondo (Flamenco Singing Competition). His last wife was named Emilia, not Amelia; and not one but two previous marriages ended in divorce. The painter Andrés Segovia Portillo was the product of the guitarist's first marriage (to Adelaida Portillo), as was his younger brother, Leonardo, who died at an early age in 1937. Beatriz was the daughter from the guitarist's second marriage, to Paquita Madriguera.

The dance of erroneous and contradictory (or simply missing) facts continued to develop following Segovia's death on June 2, 1987. Two days later the Madrid newspaper *ABC* dedicated about fifteen pages to the death of the great Spanish guitarist, with a plethora of testimonials and photos. On page 74 of this edition, under the title "Noventa y cuatro años de genialidad pulsados con sencillez" (Ninety-four Years of Genius Played with Simplicity), and without pointing out any authorship other than "Servicio de documentación" (Documentation Service), there is a biographical review, only one brief paragraph of which is devoted to Segovia's decade in Montevideo. There is not a single allusion to the Uruguayan capital:

> After his first wife died, he remarried in 1935, a daughter being the fruit of this marriage. A little later, while living in Barcelona, the Spanish Civil War broke out. "It was the only period in my life," he would say in his old age, "in which I did not play the guitar." On August 28, 1936, he abandoned Spain, to which he would not return until 1952, and he settled in South America, from where an extraordinary activity would unfold. A widower once again, in 1961 he married his former student, Emilia del Corral—she was eighteen and he was seventy....

Segovia says in his autobiography that he left Spain on July 28, 1938, although there is an evident printing error regarding the year, since he could not have been confused about the beginning of the Spanish Civil War. Paquita Madriguera wrote in her notebook that the departure date was July 31, 1936. Nor was he a widower when he married Emilia Corral Sancho. He was divorced from Paquita Madriguera in 1948, and she lived until 1965. It is possible that "divorced" was not a word that the *ABC* wished to print or its habitual readers to encounter, even in 1987. The stated ages of both husband and wife are also incorrect. On the same page of this newspaper a chronological outline signed S. D. (again probably for Documentation Service) complements the biographical review with the following:

> 1920: He marries the pianist Paquita Madriguera on December 22. Of the two sons from that marriage, only Andrés survives.

1935: After the death of his first wife, he joins the Lusitanian-Brazilian Olga Coelho. They had a daughter who died in Guatemala at the age of twenty-eight, the victim of a lung affliction.

On the date mentioned, he married Adelaida Portillo, with whom he had the two sons mentioned. In 1935, at the time of his second marriage, to Paquita Madriguera, Adelaida had not died, nor did he yet know Olga Coelho. He was able to marry Paquita thanks to the new divorce law approved in Spain under the Second Republic. Perhaps, once again, the chroniclers of *ABC*, or whoever gave them the information, did not see fit to refer to a divorce. Segovia's first wife died forty-five years later, in 1980. He established a relationship with Olga Coelho in 1943; Paquita Madriguera asked for a divorce in 1946. Beatriz Segovia Madriguera (Paquita's daughter, not the Brazilian singer's) died in 1967 at the age of twenty-nine, not of a lung affliction but of suicide—another unsuitable word, apparently, in certain media.

On the same day, the *New York Times* published an obituary under the headline "Andrés Segovia Is Dead at 94: His Crusade Elevated Guitar," by Donal Henahan. Although it too has errors, Henahan contradicted some of the information in *ABC*:

Segovia's first marriage ended in divorce in 1951. In 1961 he married a 22-year-old guitarist, Emilia Corral Sancho, a student of his. Their son Carlos Andrés, now 17, was born when Segovia was 77 years old. A son, Andrés, and a daughter, Beatrice, by his first wife were born more than half a century before Carlos Andrés.

Only the third sentence contains no errors. Andrés, the guitarist's first child, was born in 1921, forty-nine years before Carlos Andrés. Beatriz was born in 1938, thirty-two years before her younger half brother, whom she never met.

An Italian example, from Maurizio Colonna's 1990 book *Chitarristi-compositori del XX secolo* (Guitar Compositions of the Twentieth Century), closes this enumeration of false or absent information. Chapter 4, dedicated to Andrés Segovia, includes a chronology of his life, "compiled by Griselda Ponce de León and published in the magazine *Chitarre* [Guitars] (no. 24, March 1988)." Everything that took place in the "Montevideo decade" is once again omitted, only being alluded to by a few erroneous facts. Stated here, in total:

1935: Following the death of his first wife, he marries the Uruguayan pianist Paquita Madriguera, with whom he would have a daughter, Beatriz, who died in 1967 at the age of twenty-nine.

1936: On August 28, with the outbreak of the Spanish Civil War, he abandons his house in Barcelona, which will be bombed in the aerial raids; in the fire he will lose his extensive library and his archive of letters, documents of art personalities, and his artistic works. He establishes himself in South America and divides his musical activity and residence between Montevideo (Uruguay) and Buenos Aires (Argentina).

Along with the erroneous date of the beginning of the war, Segovia's apartment (not a house) was not bombed, nor did it burn. It was reportedly looted in the middle of the chaos into which Barcelona was plunged during the first days of the Spanish Civil War.

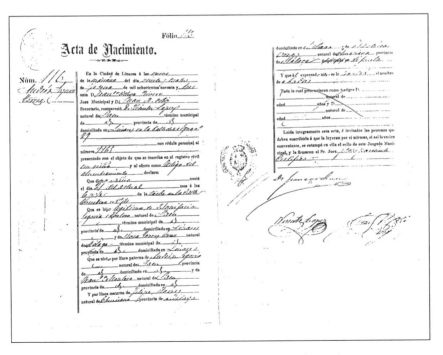

Copy of the birth certificate, with the number 116, entered on February 24, 1893, at the Municipal Court of Linares and stating that Andrés Segovia Torrez [sic] was born at 6:30 P.M. on February 21, 1893.

It is not an exaggeration to affirm that in all of those reviews about the life and career of Segovia that make reference to his ties to Montevideo, there are more omissions and errors than well-established facts. Such was the case in spite of the abundance of sketches and impressions that the long-lived guitarist left in the memories of his contemporaries, as well as in the chronicles of critics, reporters, and researchers of the southern hemisphere. It is valid to ask why nothing seemed to be known about the life of the artist, at least up to that time, that could justify such a vivid reaction as the one he displayed on that evening in London; and why in his known biographies was there nothing that would manifest such an emotional preference for the smallest capital of the Río de la Plata? Perhaps there are reasons that could explain why this important period in the life of Segovia has for so long been shrouded with mystery and at times marginalized with the spreading of erroneous facts, contradictory among themselves and at times deliberately falsified. The object of this book is not to uncover the reasons for these gaps in information, but rather to examine the meanderings of history in an attempt to faithfully reconstruct its true development, with the aid of those aforementioned sketches and the fruits of this investigation.

Chapter 3

Resonances of a Past
in Montevideo

A little more than a year before the event described in the London anecdote took place, Segovia visited Montevideo for the last time. On Monday, August 13, 1979, he appeared at the Teatro Solís with an overflow crowd and great expectations—seventeen years had passed without a performance in this capital by the great Andalusian artist.[1] It was the maestro's first concert appearance following the death of his second wife, Paquita Madriguera, in Montevideo in 1965, and from the time that his only daughter was buried in the same city barely two years later. Below the title "Andrés Segovia Recital" on the program cover was printed, in a smaller font, "In Memory of His Daughter Beatriz Segovia." The Montevideo newspaper *Mundo Color* (World Color) published an account the following day stating: "He also has a daughter buried on Uruguayan soil (at the Central Cemetery) in whose memory he dedicated last night's concert at the Teatro Solís, in the presence of a full audience."[2]

Could a clue be found there that would explain the significance that the name of this city had for Segovia? Indeed there was; but it was not the only one. Other clues later appeared that repeatedly suggested a connection between the Spanish artist and the land of the Río de la Plata—resonances of a past that confirmed this hypothesis. I was at Teatro Solís on that August day in 1979 and have several significant memories of that event. Certain facts and details made me suspect that Segovia had numerous important ties with this city, even though nothing about it was mentioned in his biographical sketches. These ties, coming from different directions, went deeper than his artistic life.

The sharpest of my memories is of a personal experience that took place immediately after the concert in Segovia's dressing room where several Montevideo guitarists had gathered to honor the artist. Strikingly, the small room was packed with people who did not belong to the guitar world—older men and women to whom Segovia spoke with great familiarity, addressing each by name and asking about the children of one or the grandchildren of another. A foreign observer would have thought that it was the dressing room of a concert hall in Spain, or perhaps that the performer being congratulated was as Uruguayan as the audience surrounding him. It was clear that Segovia appeared completely at home in Montevideo, but at the same time, it seemed to have for him certain problematic, and even disturbing, facets.

The other highly significant memory—one that is impossible to avoid—has to do with the sense of exhaustion that Segovia conveyed from the moment he stepped onto the stage on which he had performed so many times in the past. His entrance—slow and awkward—was unusually delayed to the point that the audience grew restless. After he sat down and attempted to tune the strings of his instrument for a few minutes, he left again, heavily, but returned a few minutes later. During the concert, that feeling of low spirits resulted in noticeable problems in properly tuning his guitar and reaching his typical command of the repertoire and the audience's attention. Something disturbing could be perceived in the atmosphere, although it was difficult to find any explanation for it besides the artist's advanced age. Sometime later I learned of another: Don Andrés was awaiting the arrival of someone who had been his close friend, to whom he had extended a special invitation and who at that

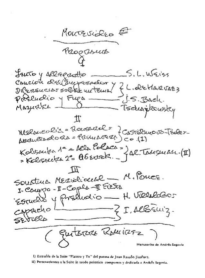

Inside page of the program of August 12, 1979, reproducing Segovia's original manuscript.

moment held, de facto and as an arbitrary appointment by the military, the office of the presidency of Uruguay.[3] The empty presidential box, directly in front of Segovia, caused the elderly maestro to lose the calm and concentration he needed to give his concert. An eyewitness to an incident during the concert's first intermission sent me his account in writing as I was reconstructing this story. His description powerfully backs up what had been my perception regarding Segovia's morale:

> When the first part ended, a scene took place that I was able to personally experience with Maestro Abel Carlevaro and our respective wives. From my spot I could see that Carlevaro, who was among the audience, was heading swiftly toward the exit followed by [his wife] Vani. My wife and I descended the stairs rapidly and got to the reception area of the theater at the precise moment that Carlevaro was entering the dressing-room area. We managed to get through, and a few meters from the door of the first one, we heard the voice of a woman who was mercilessly reproaching Segovia: "How embarrassing!!! What are you doing? Your guitar is unbearably out of tune." She continued, "Why don't you just forget Aparicio and concentrate on your playing?"
>
> He also heard Segovia answer with timidity and hurt, "Why didn't he come? I invited him. He is still angry."
>
> At that moment Carlevaro entered the room and said in a loud voice, "Andrés, you are playing very well."
>
> Segovia, looking dejected owing to the scolding he had just received, said to him, "Tell her, Abel. Tell her that I am playing well."
>
> Meanwhile, my wife and I looked on, surprised and saddened by the scene. With considerable effort, Carlevaro managed to channel his spirits to the point that Segovia appeared to recover his legendary posture. He autographed my program and came out on stage for the second part.[4]

It seems evident that the familiar environment in Segovia's dressing room after the concert, the sensation that the guitarist felt in some ways at home, was offset by bitterness, broken friendships, and old, unresolved resentments. It is probable that the ill-humor created by the absence of his former friend was not the only negative sign of the past that Montevideo persisted in presenting the aged artist, in opposition to his other, pleasant reencounters. It is possible that the disappointment, in addition to the emotional weight of the uncontrollable absences, could have caused his difficulties with tuning the guitar and achieving the level of virtuosity and professionalism his audiences had come to expect. A recording of some fragments of that concert confirms, even if we take into account the poor sound quality, that Segovia's instrument was indeed out of tune. Certain technical inaccuracies in his playing also revealed a state of unease that intensified those errors attributable simply to age-related deterioration.[5]

Another eloquent testimonial regarding Segovia's performance on that occasion also provides a resonance of his forgotten past in Montevideo. On the night of the concert in Teatro Solís, the composer Guido Santórsola recorded on tape cassette a message directed to Segovia, addressing him familiarly as "Andrés." However, the message is harshly eloquent in reference to the poor impression made by the concert, and from the tone of his words one can surmise ties tarnished by bitterness of uncertain origin and long standing. After telling Segovia that he should have already retired, and before advising him emphatically not to play anymore (and venting who-knows-what old differences sown during that remote decade), Santórsola carefully enunciates, in his characteristic Spanish (marked by his Italian origins and his long stay in Brazil), as if weighing every word, "You cannot tune your beautiful instrument. You have lost the sharpness of tuning. You try to tune the instrument, but it remains out of tune. And in that manner you continue to play, disturbing the auditory sensitivity of the listeners."[6]

Going beyond the transcendental meaning of the event that was to mark Segovia's last visit to Uruguay, and of all that this then-young aficionado of the guitar could observe and preserve with regard to the various aspects (the musical and the instrumental, as well as those touching the maestro's stage presence), the important thing to point out is the nature of all these anecdotes. Given what we now know about his rich, profound, and tragic story, it is unsurprising that Segovia would find it emotionally difficult to play once again in Montevideo, especially taking into account that the last time he had done so—seventeen years earlier—Paquita Madriguera and their daughter, Beatriz Segovia Madriguera, were still alive and in the audience. It must have been difficult for Don Andrés to walk out on the stage of the Teatro Solís and feel the weight of their absence and of the many events that the memory of both women brought to mind. But the facts also point to the maestro's strong ties with the citizens of Montevideo and with personalities of Uruguayan life that were not necessarily connected to music, or even to the art world in general. And they suggest the existence of profound problems that were never fully resolved, problems that were part of a private and personal life that had to do with Montevideo and that continued to be significant even toward the end of his life. The development of this book will detail the deep and dramatic plot that continued to weave Segovia's life in Montevideo and its surroundings, and whose tenacious and powerful echoes continued to resound some decades later.

In the days prior to the concert, the Uruguayan press also recounted certain memories that made reference to Segovia's former presence in Montevideo. The music critic Roberto Lagarmilla wrote:

> For the people of Montevideo, the image of Don Andrés Segovia was something very familiar and emotional. During the years of the Spanish Civil War he settled in our capital city. There in Pocitos, his residence became a colloquium of discussions and teachings. We still remember those events in September 1941, when the Mexican maestro Manuel Ponce, author of *Concierto del sur* for guitar and orchestra, visited us. Evening after evening, guitarist and composer polished the facets of this simultaneously dense and transparent work, replete with Latin American melodies and rhythms. It was at the SODRE, on October 4, 1941, with immense and justified success. During some pauses in the rehearsal, Segovia played for us pages of old Spanish lutenists, transcriptions of Bach, and recent works by Villa-Lobos, Ponce, and Castelnuovo-Tedesco. . . .
>
> Tomorrow, Monday, Andrés Segovia will once again be before "his" musical Montevideo. . . . The figure once familiar to us all will once again be in his rightful sphere—the concert hall. Now, more than ever, laden with glory. The man—genial and simple in his greatness—will again breathe our air and receive the emotional homage of his listeners and disciples, among whom, today, there are world-famous guitarists.[7]

A few days before his appearance, Segovia had performed in Teatro Colón in Buenos Aires. The newspaper *Clarín* published a full-page article on August 2, 1979, toward the end of which a suggestive passage is found:

> We were there when a gentleman walked by us, stopped, looked, and proceeded on, but quickly returned and introduced himself, "Maestro, I am

Soler, your admirer. Perhaps you will remember Couture,[8] who enabled me to get your photograph."

Sebastián Soler, one of the preeminent lawyers in the country, the greatest criminologist and a man of great culture, enters into our conversation following his introduction to the Spanish musician. And immediately Dr. Aparicio Méndez, president of the Republic of Uruguay and a friend of both men, is remembered. Among his non-political sins there were some musical pieces composed without the academic rigor that Segovia demanded.[9] We all laughed—perhaps the ruler of our neighboring country will never know just how an Argentinean critic found out about his philharmonic vocation.[10]

The magazine *Mundo Uruguayo* published an extensive interview just a few days after Segovia's previous concert in Montevideo, in 1962. The interview took place in a residence in Montevideo where Segovia appeared to feel right at home; he even welcomed a young guitarist to play for him and gave him a lesson.[11] Throughout the published interview, the most significant paragraphs of which appear below, the reporter seems to understand perfectly just why Segovia was so familiar with the surroundings that sheltered him at that moment:

"Maestro."

"Pleased to meet you."

The virtuoso hand meets mine. Segovia looks out clearly from behind the restless, drooping eyelids and bags below and behind black-rimmed lenses. While I waited for him, I had a delightful conversation with Paquita Madriguera in her modestly elegant and overheated apartment. In one corner of the tastefully decorated room is a kind of shrine to the guitar. The maestro has come in with economical steps and a certain solemnity. With a restrained gesture, he opens his palm and magical fingers to offer me the seat I was already occupying. . . .

Smiles and an interruption by Paquita to inform him that a guitarist will come later from the city of Durazno so that the maestro can listen to him. It occurs to me that this has happened to "Andrés" (as she calls him) throughout his long artistic pilgrimage around the world. . . .

One look at the pipe. He fills it and lights it. One can hear distant notes from a piano, probably from another apartment, being tortured by a beginner. . . . He tells Paquita, "That piano reminds me of when I was a boy and the heat of the summer—hey, similar to that of this room—I listened to studies by Clementi." He puffs and now directs himself to me. "The guitar had no tradition. Tárrega, a great artist, but limited to a small circle of friends. . . . He had a student, Miguel Llobet, also very good, but lazy."

"It's true," remarks Paquita Madriguera. "He always made the same mistakes, and when we pointed that out to him he would say that it was impossible to correct, that it was very difficult . . ."

"However," continues Segovia, "he was very good." . . .

The doorbell interrupts—it must be the young man from Durazno. It was, with various friends accompanying him. There were introductions and so on. The room is arranged so that we can listen to him. . . .

He smoothly concludes the final note and looks anxiously at the maestro, searching for a response. The maestro refills his pipe . . . and proceeds to clinically dissect the young man's performance with the firmness of a maestro who knows what he is talking about. . . .

I hear a couple more playings. Time is pressing, and I say goodbye. Paquita walks me to the door. The maestro continues with terse sincerity, and I listen to his final words: "You need to study music; study hard; broaden your horizons."[12]

Perhaps an introductory summary of Segovia's feelings toward this corner of the planet, "so distant and lost that it cannot even be seen on a map" (as a popular song dedicated to Montevideo describes it), is this paragraph from an interview that appeared in a 1981 Montevideo newspaper:

Interviewer: Have women had a big influence on your life?

Segovia: Yes, of course, but of those who have passed through my life, the ones that have influenced me most, naturally, are my wives. I have been a big womanizer, but the family has been more important than anything else. The women have given me everything in life. My two previous wives, now deceased, and this third one who has given me the happiness of a beautiful boy who makes these, my final years, very joyful. I hardly see my oldest son and I had a daughter who died at age twenty-eight [*sic*] and is buried in Montevideo, a land I adore because I spent some of the best years of my life there.[13]

It is also worth mentioning Segovia's epistolary reaction to an article that appeared in 1976 in a Montevideo newspaper. The artist's almost immediate response was another clear sign of the direction in which a good part of his affection pointed. The interview took up the entire front page of the Sunday supplement, yet there was only a brief mention of Segovia's life in Montevideo:

Interviewer: Tell me about your years in Montevideo.

Segovia: I arrived in 1936, close to the beginning of 1937, because after leaving Spain on account of the revolution I did a tour of Europe, the United States, and various South American countries. We landed in Montevideo and we stayed; that's where my daughter was born, who died in an accident at the age of twenty-eight [*sic*] in Guatemala and is buried in Montevideo. The last time I was in Montevideo was for that purpose.

Interviewer: Why did you choose to live in Montevideo?

Segovia: It's a place I have long enjoyed. When I made my first visit to South America, I left Spain by steamship; I played in Buenos Aires and then immediately in Montevideo, in 1920. I later lived eight or nine years in Pocitos, at 3410 Massini Street on the corner of Benito Blanco. Today the house and garden no longer exist; they demolished them and erected a building. I haven't returned since the death of my daughter, although relatives are still there, the daughters of my second wife, who was a widow; and not long ago one of them came to visit here. . . .

Interviewer: What hobbies do you have besides music?

Segovia: Reading. . . . Also walking, swimming, and, when I was in Montevideo, horseback riding. I had a great property close to Mosquitos;[14] my horse's name was Bicarbonato [Bicarbonate], and he wouldn't allow anyone to ride him but me. We would get up at five o'clock in the morning with my girl and go riding.[15]

A little more than three weeks after this article was published, Segovia wrote a letter to the newspaper clarifying that the period of his Uruguayan residence was more significant than these paragraphs reflected. The letter, written from his home in Madrid, is dated August 16, 1976. There is a brief introduction, and then he gets down to his purpose in writing:

I would also be extremely grateful, if it is not considered out of order, if you would be so kind as to add this supplement to what has already been published. The purpose is to somewhat accentuate the prominence of certain points where my faithful reporter has let her pen slip, barely touching them, no doubt owing to the diversity of topics the interview included and also considering the extensive length of her remarkable work.

In effect, when asked about my life in Montevideo, the words of gratitude that come flowing from my lips are those that I feel and express when I speak about that noble and extremely friendly country, when I remember the friends who surrounded me and who have already passed on, and those who still belong to this turbulent world. And if these words did not come out from my lips, it is possible that it was because, distracted by the rapid flow of so many and varied questions, I did not take advantage of the one opportunity to produce them.

From a personal and artistic point of view, I owe Montevideo undying memories. The most vivid, obviously, is, among the first, the birth of my daughter in the hospital, if I remember correctly, on Tacuarembó Street or nearby. And the most emotional, the place her three Uruguayan half sisters—Paquita, Sofía, and María Rosa—chose for her eternal resting place in the family pantheon, despite the fact that her remains did not belong to that funeral chamber. They were not sisters, but little vigilant and loving mothers who accompanied my poor daughter throughout her short existence. . . .

As for my artistic memories, I recall with pleasure the premiere of the first concerto composed for guitar and orchestra during this era, by Mario Castelnuovo-Tedesco. . . . Years later there was a similar premiere at the festival sponsored by SODRE and dedicated to symphonic compositions by the saintly Maestro Ponce. This time it was the lovely *Concierto del sur.* The group of Uruguayan artists closely surrounded the noble Mexican musician. Fabini, in love with the guitar since his youth, and to which he devoted a bit of his great talent under the name of *Mozartiana*, which at times has appeared in my radio or TV programs. Fabini, I repeat, generously facilitated whatever was necessary to carry out the festival in the honor of such an illustrious brother in the art.

And how could I forget the enthusiastic collaboration of the orchestra, of its director, Baldi, and the other Uruguayan artists, each of whom endeavored to overcome difficult obstacles? Hugo Balzo, Nybia Mariño, etc., etc.

It would not be right to neglect an affectionate mention of Abel Carlevaro. From those afternoons in which my lessons concluded with family tea, his talent continues to evolve—from a well-trained artist to a reflective composer with a prolific pen, and in that aspect a conscientious student of unchanging traditional forms, without the knowledge and practice of which all new contributions would always be feeble.

All of this, and more that I leave in the inkwell in order to avoid an abusive extension, matters in the emotional life of a man and in the memory of an artist, if the former is not ungrateful and the latter is not forgetful.[16]

During that same year, Cédar Viglietti referred to Segovia's significance for Montevideo:

He lived for some years in Montevideo, during the period of the Spanish Revolution. On the occasion of the founding of our Centro Guitarrístico [Guitar Center] we had the occasion to consult with him in his apartment

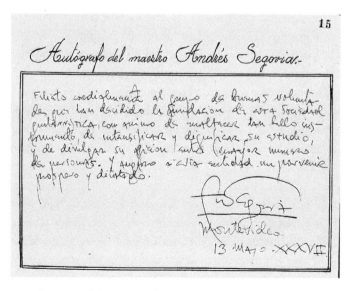

A fragment of page 15 of the minutes book of the Centro Guitarrístico del Uruguay.

on Avenida 18 de Julio and Rio Branco, more than thirty years ago, and we went along with the elder Américo Castillo and his daughter. Warm and understanding, he and his wife at the time, the pianist Paquita Madriguera, received us; he seemed pleased by the idea, endorsing it later by writing words of good wishes on an album for our Center.[17]

In several passages of the book Viglietti mentions the guitarists who studied with Segovia during those years. The one who is best known for his historical consequences, for the public recognition accorded him by Segovia, and for the length of instruction is Abel Carlevaro (1916–2001).[18] But Viglietti also names two other Uruguayan guitarists who later had a long trajectory beyond their country's borders—Raúl Sánchez Clagett and Antonio Pereira Arias. Both were younger than Carlevaro and in an earlier stage of their guitar and musical studies at that time. They also continued their careers in Europe, where they once again came into contact with Segovia:

Segovia with members of his class in Siena, Italy, 1953. At the far left are the Venezuelan guitarists Rodrigo Riera and Alirio Díaz. At the far right are Raúl Sánchez Clagett and the young John Williams.

Raúl Sánchez Clagett was already giving concerts in the Centro Guitarrístico more than thirty years ago; around 1942 he took lessons from Segovia.... In 1953 he went to Siena [Italy] on a scholarship to study once again with Segovia, and later studied the lute with Pujol; in a photograph disseminated in music magazines some twenty years ago of students at the Chigiana Academy in Siena, one can see a group that includes Sánchez Clagett, Elena Padovani [a noted Italian guitarist], [and] a twelve-year-old boy wearing shorts, who is John Williams.[19]

Then, referring to Pereira Arias, the author continues:

Antonio Pereira, born in 1929, studied from the time he was very young with Rapat using a small and beautiful instrument built by his father.[20] Years later he took lessons from Segovia. In 1942, when he was thirteen, he gave two concerts at the Centro Guitarrístico, and at fifteen he gave another at SODRE.[21]

The resonances left by Segovia's stay in Montevideo include two interesting press citings after his death. In the first, a curious item that appeared a little more than two months after Segovia died, the most interesting paragraphs state:

Almost two months ago in Madrid, the sublime Andalusian Andrés Segovia, a universal maestro if ever there was one in the art of the guitar, died at the age of 94. His life was transcendent not only as a performer and teacher. In his navigation through this existence, there was something as important as, or more important than, the unfading art he cultivated and exhibited in the most diverse settings of the world—his democratic faith and conviction, which were manifested in the exile from his native Spain from the moment the Civil War exploded and elevated Francoism to power [not a historically accurate description, as will be pointed out later].

And during that exile he had Montevideo as a broad and generous port for the continuation of his teaching career. Here he lived, played, and taught for a long period in a generous giving of his spirit.... Andrés Segovia was a regular of clubs and cafés, one more coterie in the intense layout of Montevideo, with its cafés alongside the theaters, with its smoke rings illuminating the common dreams. Now—and this is why we start this anecdote off with allusions to the complex plans of chance—a few days after the death of the guitarist, someone (who prefers to remain anonymous) has made an unexpected find in an area close to Malvín Alto,[22] and in an almost desolate area surrounded by garbage dumps: nothing less than his passport, worn away by rainwater and the other ravages of the open.

With the photo of the artist, who at the time would have been 50 years old, the passport states that the document was issued on November 9, 1944, by the Spanish consul in Montevideo, Luis Avilés y Tiscar. It says that it was granted "for North, Central, and South America" and that it is valid until November 5, 1945.

In reference to the personal data, it states his name: Andrés Segovia Torres; profession: artist; place and date of birth: Linares (Jaén) 11–21–1893 [*sic*]; marital status: Married. We learn that the artist lived at that time at 3410 Ramón Massini Street in our then calm and majestic neighborhood of Pocitos, free of the skyscrapers that would change its "belle époque" façade.

Handwritten at the bottom of page 4 is a clarification that stipulates, "Second renewal until November, 1947, in the first added page at the end."

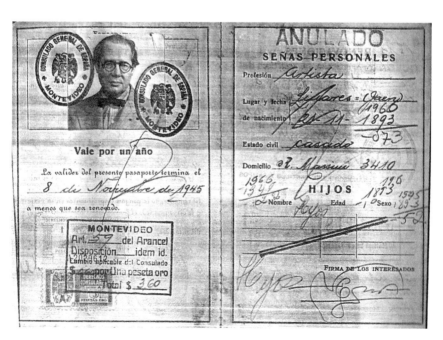

Two pages of Segovia's 1944 passport issued in Montevideo.

Later come stamps of the visas in Panamá, Cuba—the one before 1959—Colombia, Chile, Ecuador, the United States (New York), Argentina, Venezuela. . . .

The worn document is covered with stamps of various origins and colors, and some of the pages are stained and wrinkled. It is testimony to Andrés Segovia's remarkable stay in Montevideo.[23]

The other relevant mention of Segovia's life in Montevideo in the city's media was in a radio program. In 1993, in a commemoration of the musician's one hundredth birthday, the journalist Ramón Mérica interviewed one of Paquita Madriguera's daughters for the popular *Live and Direct*, broadcast on Radio Sarandí's CX8. In the interview with Sofía Puig Madriguera on November 23 of that year, many elements that aided the present investigation came to light and began outlining the true course of history; and in the process some hypotheses were established that would foreshadow the reasons for the lack of prior knowledge. Some of the most important moments follow an introduction by Mérica:[24]

On February 21, 1893, now one hundred years ago, Andrés Segovia was born in Linares, Jaén. This man brought the guitar into the concert halls and made the instrument one of the invaluable and extraordinary bastions of twentieth-century music history. He died on June 2, 1987, at the age of ninety-four. Of those ninety-four years, he spent eleven in Montevideo, Uruguay, married to a colleague—the great pianist Paquita Madriguera. Those years in Montevideo were for Don Andrés an ordinary and peaceful life, with the exception of intensive and incessant guitar practice. He went to the Expreso of Pocitos, the Sorocabana, and at his home he received illustrious men or visitors such as Jascha Heifetz or Salvador de Madariaga. Here Don Andrés also left a daughter, Beatriz, who died at the age of twenty-nine in 1967.

Beatriz, his only child with Paquita Madriguera, is buried alongside Paquita in the Central Cemetery in the pantheon of the Puig Cibils family. But this man left not only these two family witnesses, but also an indelible memory and three stepdaughters (daughters of Paquita and Dr. Puig) whom he treated, loved, and considered his own daughters. One of them, Sofía Puig, was asked by *Live and Direct* to remember Don Andrés on this one hundredth anniversary of his birth.

The interview was recorded at the home of Paquita Madriguera's middle daughter prior to its broadcast on the radio:

Interviewer: I am at the home of Sofía Puig Madriguera, a place full of memories, on the fifth floor of a small street of Pocitos in Montevideo [Achiras Street], where Don Andrés Segovia, her stepfather, sometimes visited, and where are housed a guitar, scores, picture frames, pencils, papers, books, and photos that reveal this genius's stay in this city and in this home. These are also the legacy of Sofía's mother, the great pianist Paquita Madriguera, who was married to Don Andrés Segovia. Thank you, Sofía, for receiving us and for trying to remember at least parts of those eleven years of Don Andrés and Paquita in Montevideo, and, above all, to pay homage, since the memories of the 100 years since the birth of Don Andrés appear to be very quiet.

Sofía: It's true. Thank you, Ramón. I think it is beautiful and very just that you are able to do an interview now, here in Montevideo, in the Uruguay where Andrés lived pleasantly and very happily for a good while.

Interviewer: Why did your mom and Don Andrés come to Uruguay?

Sofía: The Spanish Civil War had begun, and, because we were Uruguayans, the Uruguayan government asked to bring us back to Uruguay, that we leave Spain because of the war going on, and that is why we had to leave.

Interviewer: What year did you come here?

Sofía: We arrived in 1937. Mom and Andrés came first to look for a place to live, etc., while we were in Canada and the United States. Once they sent for us, we very happily returned to Uruguay. . . .

Interviewer: Segovia, in his eleven years in Montevideo—from when to when was he here?

Sofía: From 1937 until practically 1948. And we lived first on Avenida 18 de Julio and Rio Branco, in the Palacio Lapido; later we went to live at the country property we had and still have—it belongs to me—in Piedras de Afilar, in Canelones. We were there for a little over a year, and it's where my younger sister was born, the daughter of Andrés and Mom. She spent her childhood years in the country. Later we came to live in Pocitos, in a large house at Massini and Benito Blanco. Our life was beautiful. . . .

Interviewer: How was Don Andrés's life in Montevideo? Did he go to the bar, did he have friends, did he cook . . . ?

Sofía: The first thing I want to tell you is that his life was not one of a foreigner, because as soon as he arrived the Puig family welcomed him and included him as a member of the family. In other words, he was surrounded by a wonderful family—he who had no history of a large family. Our family was very kind and liked him a lot. His life was very normal. The three of us girls went out to walk along the Rambla [the avenue that runs along the Río de la Plata in Montevideo], the three of us somehow hung on to both of Andrés's arms to be able to walk with him.

Interviewer: Apparently you had a very good relationship, of stepdaughters and stepfather. . . .

Sofía: Yes, very good. We loved him a lot. The truth is that Andrés won each of us over in different areas and aspects, the three of us. . . .

Interviewer: Did he give concerts?

Sofía: He gave concerts.

Interviewer: He gave concerts with your mom, right?

Sofía: Yes . . . he gave several. Two or three times, or four, I believe. . . .

Interviewer: When your mom came to Uruguay married to Segovia, was she already an important woman, a known pianist?

Sofía: Before marrying my dad, Mom was already a great concert pianist and very famous. She was a child prodigy. She was one of those geniuses who are born from time to time. She began playing the piano at a very young age and was already composing at three. . . .

Another important moment of the interview takes us to the breakup of the marriage between Don Andrés and Paquita:

Interviewer: But there was also a moment when Paquita, your mom, said "enough" to her relationship or her marriage to Don Andrés. Why and when did it happen?

Sofía: Look, it happened because Andrés had an affair with a Brazilian woman. And although he swore and said it was just a passing fling—and it was—Mom did not want to accept this challenge. She was very hurt. She believed that she had to act with dignity facing this dilemma, and yet, caring for him very much and being in love with Andrés, she divorced him. And this took place here, in Uruguay, although it was not valid in Spain at that particular time. Andrés tried for a long time to redo the bond. He would come, he would insist. . . .

Interviewer: He returned later?

Sofía: Several times, yes. He would come and stay at the Hotel Nirvana . . . and he would ask Mom, and Mom couldn't. She was never able to get over the previous situation.

Interviewer: In other words, they separated and never put the marriage back together.

Sofía: No. They got together again at times, but never married.

Interviewer: Segovia married again, right?

Sofía: Finally, yes. After some years over there, to another lady . . . a Spaniard. . . . At a very advanced age he had a son named Carlos Andrés. He lives in Spain.

It is certain, as can be seen from this extensive recounting of the suppressed resonances of Segovia's stay in Montevideo, that too many things have remained hidden or simply been ignored. The importance of embarking on a quest to come as close as possible to the true facts, as well as their causes and consequences, is not to be doubted. The ensuing chapters are dedicated to this intriguing, revealing, and extremely interesting journey.

Chapter 4

First Exposition of the Theme

Before we begin a thorough chronological account, this chapter will briefly summarize the story linking Andrés Segovia to Montevideo. Not everything in this volume is completely new,[1] but the story presented here—accurately documented and based on firsthand testimony—will substantially modify a great deal of what is now known about this period, as well as its antecedents.

At least one fairly serious article does attempt to point out the particulars of Segovia's Montevideo period and the reasons it came about: Richard Pinnell's "Segovia in Exile: Protagonists and Projects of the Montevideo Period (1936–1947)." Yet it is not free of errors and important omissions. To precisely establish our coordinates, it must first be said that 1937 is the beginning of the period that can be called Montevidean. It was on the last day of April of that year that Segovia arrived in Montevideo with Paquita Madriguera, who became his second wife in October 1935. He had previously visited the Uruguayan capital in 1920, 1921, and 1928 as part of his successful concert tours during those years; he was also there in 1934 on his first tour in the company of Paquita, although there is no evidence that she accompanied him on the crossing from Buenos Aires. Whatever the circumstances of those earlier visits, Don Andrés arrived in Montevideo in 1937 with Paquita to establish his home—and, though he could not have known it then, there he was to remain for quite some time. Many circumstances converged to impel Segovia to settle in Montevideo with his family and establish permanent residency in 1937.

Pinnell's article is mistaken in at least one assertion: "Segovia's decade in Montevideo coincided with the Spanish Civil War (1936–1939). Like many Spanish intellectuals of that period, he fled the dictatorship in hopes of continuing his career in exile."[2] While there were many Spanish intellectuals who did take refuge in Montevideo from the dictatorship of Francisco Franco, this was not the case with Segovia. When he and his family (Paquita Madriguera and her three school-age daughters) hurriedly left Barcelona, they did so to flee the violence that resulted from the revolt of Franco and his military forces against the Second Spanish Republic, fully three years before the Franco dictatorship was firmly established in Spain. Moreover, Segovia's position was not in opposition to the Generalísimo. According to a letter the guitarist wrote to Manuel Ponce, Paquita—whose family was Catholic and very conservative—suffered death threats from the extremist left (or from those who wished to appear so), and they tried to enroll Segovia himself in an armed faction.[3] Both musicians feared for their safety and that of the girls, and, having already witnessed some atrocities and received news of others, they felt that these developments could put their lives in danger. Since all three of Paquita's daughters were born in Uruguay, they secured diplomatic refuge, enabling them to leave Spain under safe protection. It was through the Argentinean consulate in Barcelona at the end of July 1936 that the four were able to get aboard an Italian ship. They arrived three days later in Genoa, and while settled in that city's outskirts, Segovia received news that his Barcelona residence had been looted, for which he always blamed Catalonian leftists. According to his youngest son, writing many years later,[4] that was one of the determining factors for the support Segovia gave Franco—support that later caused some difficulties in his career—during his years of exile, described by the guitarist himself as open in Europe but discreet in the United States.[5]

The pianist and composer Paquita Madriguera was born in 1900. She had been the favorite student of Enrique Granados and had already achieved a prolonged series of successes in important concert halls in Europe, the United States, and South America when she married Arturo Puig, a wealthy Uruguayan lawyer and politician twenty-five years her senior, in 1922 at the end of a concert tour. From that moment on she abandoned what had been a brilliant performing career to devote herself to her family and the social life in the Uruguayan capital. Paquita gave birth to three daughters by Puig in Montevideo, where the couple settled. She was widowed in 1931 and returned to Spain with the three girls the following year. The return to her native country put her in direct contact once again with the musical world in which she had grown up, and she even attempted a return to the concert halls. Shortly after arriving in Barcelona, she entered into a romantic relationship with Segovia, whom she married in 1935 in the Catalonian capital. Between 1934 and 1936, Paquita accompanied Segovia on various concert tours of Mexico, Peru, Chile, the Río de la Plata region, the United States, France, and Italy, as well as, finally, a long trip through the Soviet Union.

The couple had barely been settled a few days in their new home in Barcelona, following the Soviet tour, when the Spanish Civil War began. They had to flee swiftly, with practically no money or luggage, to Genoa with Paquita's three daughters. The family lived in Italy for a little more than two months under an anxious uncertainty about their immediate future. Having lost all of their material reserves, the family depended on the income Segovia could generate giving concerts, as well as the inheritance money that Paquita and her daughters received from Uruguay following the death of Puig. Some properties in Uruguay (a home in the Montevideo neighborhood of Pocitos, other houses and commercial buildings in the city, and a country estate) would later serve to support a stable life for the family, which for about six months suffered a literal separation before managing to reunite under the same roof in the shelter of the comforting and cultured tranquility of Montevideo.

Paquita Madriguera's daughters were sent temporarily to the United States at the end of 1936, accompanied by their maternal grandmother and two aunts. Paquita's brother—the violinist, bandleader, and composer Enric Madriguera—had been established in New York for some time. In the meantime Segovia went on a concert tour, first alone and then with his wife, to England, North Africa, France, the Netherlands, Switzerland, and Italy. After the guitarist's European engagements were finished, the couple headed to the United States, where they visited Paquita's daughters, siblings, and mother while Segovia gave concerts in several North American cities. At the end of March 1937, the two musicians went to South America, leaving the girls behind in New York. After Segovia's concerts in Bogotá, Caracas, Port of Spain, Recife, and Rio de Janeiro, they arrived in Montevideo on April 30, when they began alternating between preparations for moving the entire family to Uruguay and the concert engagements Segovia had arranged on both sides of the Río de la Plata. Finally, at the beginning of July 1937, Paquita's three daughters arrived in Montevideo, and the family was reunited under one roof—an apartment in the center of the city.

Between September 1937 and April 1938, while the three girls were left in the care of their maternal grandmother (who had arrived a few months after the girls), Segovia made a long and intensive concert tour throughout Europe, accompanied by Paquita. They arrived in Geneva in December, where they stayed for a while. The guitarist's second son, Leonardo Segovia Portillo, had died there a few weeks earlier in an accident. He was only thirteen years old and had lived there with his mother (Segovia's first wife) and his brother, Andrés (Andresito). Shortly after the couple's return to Montevideo in June 1938, Beatriz Segovia Madriguera, Segovia's only daughter and Paquita's fourth, was born.

Still, the couple did not remain in one place for long. Paquita Madriguera had surgery in July, and in October she embarked once more for Europe to meet Segovia on his tour, leaving behind her baby, barely four months old. The two planned to continue on to the United States in January 1939, but before leaving London for New York they were informed that Segovia's American tour had been cancelled owing to the pressure brought against him by "the Jewish circles," as he wrote to Ponce later that year.[6] They decided to return to Montevideo, arriving home at the end of February.

Thus began a period of restricted concert activity that lasted until November 1943, during which Segovia saw his schedule restricted to most of the so-called Southern Cone of South America—Uruguay, Argentina, Brazil, and Chile—and slightly beyond, to Bolivia. This was partly due to World War II, which made international travel both difficult and dangerous, and partly to restrictions imposed by music impresarios on Segovia's appearances in the United States in reaction to his expressed political position. However, this was not a dark or sad period in Segovia's artistic life. Ironically, in spite of the geographical limitations to which he was subjected, a period of intense and rich musical, as well as social, activity unfolded. It was truly a period of creativity regarding new compositions, arrangements, and transcriptions for the guitar, and, perhaps more significant, a period defined by a highly artistic collaboration with his wife. It was also a time of warm family life for Segovia—a family life that marked him forever and whose loss he recalled with regret till his dying day.

For Paquita Madriguera, this would also be a very important period, marking her return to the performing career she had interrupted almost twenty years earlier. Still young—around forty—she began to play again in concert halls, first in Montevideo when the Mexican composer Manuel Ponce visited the city, and then in a number of other South American countries. Paquita's return to the stage in 1941 included solo piano concerts, performances as soloist with orchestra, and sometimes accompanying her husband in the guitar concertos of Castelnuovo-Tedesco and Ponce. Importantly, she also collaborated with Segovia in the preparation of the premieres of these two concertos for guitar and orchestra. As her husband received Castelnuovo-Tedesco's manuscripts and then Ponce's, Paquita rehearsed with him, playing the orchestra parts on piano. The extent to which this influenced the development of both works cannot be overstated: the guitarist was accompanied daily in his own home and whenever necessary by a high-caliber professional artist. The couple gave recitals together on numerous occasions during the following years, even after their marital relationship had deteriorated, presenting these two concertos in versions for guitar and piano.

Following a breakup that caused some rocky times, Segovia went forth with what would become the best-known part of his career, while Paquita alternated family and social life with several concerts a year in the area of her adopted home and Buenos Aires. She died in Montevideo at the age of sixty-five and is buried there in the Cementerio Central (Central Cemetery). Next to her rests Beatriz, the daughter she had by Segovia and who outlived her by a little less than two years.

Montevideo was not only the place where Segovia saw both his daughter's birth and burial, but also the city where a very special romantic relationship and domestic life flourished and bore fruit, the city that played a powerful and positive role in his artistic maturation, and the city about which he reminisced with special affection until his final days. In the end, for Segovia Montevideo would always be—from the time he arrived there in 1937 with the illusion of living in peace—associated with the name of Paquita Madriguera.

Chapter 5

Paquita

Francisca de Asís Madriguera i Rodón, better known as Paquita Madriguera, was born on September 15, 1900, in the city of Igualada, Spain, close to Barcelona. Her parents came from two well-to-do families—the Madrigueras were rich Catalonian businessmen, and the Rodóns had sugar refineries in Cuba. Two of the four daughters to whom Paquita gave birth in Montevideo, Sofía and María Rosa Puig Madriguera, still live in the Uruguayan capital and graciously revealed to the author the adventures of their Catalonian ancestors.

> I am going to begin talking about Mamá Paqui's family, about our grandmother,[1] about the Rodóns. Our great-grandmother's name was Eulalia Canudas Bosch, and she married a Rodón (I think his name was Francisco, but I'm not sure). They went to Cuba and set up a sugar refinery with a partner. It began very well for them. Our great-grandmother Eulalia had several children. Mamá Paqui, my grandmother, was the oldest. Then came three or four children who were in the middle and Uncle Ramón, who was the youngest. Mamá Paqui was thirteen or fourteen years older than Uncle Ramón.
>
> Then came an epidemic in Cuba (I can't say for certain what kind it was, but I think it was yellow fever) and Rodón (the father) and the three or four middle children died. . . . Eulalia was left with Mamá Paqui and Uncle Ramón, who was still being breast-fed. As you might imagine, in those days women did not go to work in factories or anywhere else. So Eulalia

returned to Spain with her two children, having taken one step forward and one step back—that is, it had gone very well for them financially, but with the epidemic everything fell apart. Mamá Paqui and her mother, Eulalia, were very good with their hands, and they started sewing, making those elaborate ties that men wore in those days. They supported themselves and raised Uncle Ramón with those ties.

When they finished working in the evening, they sat on a bench in the village to enjoy the fresh air. This was in Barcelona. And while they were sitting there, Enrique Madriguera—who belonged to a very wealthy family, was very elegant, and played the piano—would pass by on horseback. His family tree could be traced back for generations. I have the idea that they had possessions, and he was the first-born, destined to inherit everything. And my grandmother, who saw him pass by on horseback, so elegant, fell in love and married him at the age of sixteen.[2]

Four generations. Grandma Eulalia (*seated in front*); Mamá Paqui (*standing, second from left*); three of Paquita's sisters, María, Rosita, and Mercedes (*standing from left to right*), and the pianist's three daughters (*left to right*)—María Rosa, Sofía, and Paquita (nicknamed Pitusa). Photo taken in Barcelona in 1933.

Paquita Madriguera inherited from her father, Enrique Madriguera Haase (1869–1939), a musical talent that she shared with her only brother, also named Enrique and a year and a half younger than her.[3] Despite his extraordinary innate ability, the highest artistic level the children's father ever reached was that of a rank amateur, as was the case with everything to which he had dedicated himself: "He played very well, he was a great artist. The family had a business, and they would reproach grandpa for playing the piano when he had to go do things."[4] Between his financially powerful family and the protection of the old Catalonian custom that automatically made the first-born son the sole heir of the family estate, Enrique Madriguera never worked or developed any skill at anything besides playing the piano, horseback riding, and cultivating the refined social rites of the conservative financial aristocracy to which he belonged:

> What I heard when I was young is that, since he was the first-born and was going to inherit everything, he did nothing. The other siblings, on the other hand—one was a lawyer, the other was a doctor—they studied. But just before his father died, the law changed and the inheritance was divided. Nonetheless, grandpa was well off, because when we were there [in 1932] the table was set with the Baccarat goblets—one for water, the red one for red wine, the green one for something else, a beautiful carved goblet for liqueurs—and all the silverware; and that for everyday. With servants and all that. And grandpa played the piano. But I am not sure about the law of the first-born. I don't know if that was one of Mamá Paqui's excuses because he didn't work. I am not 100 percent sure about that. What is certain is that my mother [Paquita] was the oldest daughter of a well-to-do marriage. Then came Uncle Enrique, two years younger.[5]

The entire weight of managing the home (besides Paquita and Enrique, there were four other girls in the family—Carmen, Rosita, and the twins María and Mercedes) thus fell on the vital energy, enterprising ability, and great practical disposition of Francisca Rodón. Soon Mamá Paqui, as her children and grandchildren called her, began to travel, first in Spain and then throughout Europe and America, to publicize the exceptional musical abilities of her two eldest children.

Paquita Madriguera was considered a child prodigy of the piano. She was only three years old when she began her studies under Frank Marshall,[6] and at the age of five she gave her first public concert in the Centre Autonomista de Saint Gervasi as the first-prize winner—by unanimous decision—in a contest for young performers. Marshall himself recommended her later to his own teacher, Enrique Granados,[7] so that he could guide the advanced education of the girl who held so much promise. A Spanish music dictionary described Paquita:

> Maestro Marshall prepared Paquita Madriguera to introduce her to Maestro Granados, and the latter was so won over by the qualities of the petite artist that he offered to accept her in his Academia as an honorary student. Madriguera was then seven years old. Marshall continued the piano

teaching and the maestro Mas y Serracant taught her *solfeggio* and composition. The precocious student progressed so rapidly that at the age of eleven she gave recitals at both the Palau de la Música Catalana [Palace of Catalonian Music] and the Ateneo de Madrid.[8] The first part of her concerts included works by Mozart, Weber, Mendelssohn, Liszt, Beethoven, Albéniz, and Granados, and the second part consisted of her own compositions. The success of those events constituted a definite triumph for the pianist and composer, who received unanimous and passionate applause from the public and praise from the press. At thirteen she did a tour of Spain and then performed at the [Royal] Albert Hall in London, on which memorable occasion the Orfeó Catalá of Barcelona [the choir of the Palau de la Música Catalana] gained renown with the cooperation of Paquita Madriguera and [the famous Spanish opera singer] María Barrientos. It was a complete success.[9]

Many years later, while living in Montevideo, Paquita Madriguera published a book, *Visto y oído* (Seen and Heard), in which she recounted some of her memories of the earliest years of her artistic career. Her writings are brilliantly expressive and will be mentioned often throughout this work, the chosen fragments being essential to gaining an idea of the pianist's experiences, feelings, and way of thinking.

Granados, who from a young age was my teacher, granted me the privilege of having private lessons. He treated me with the confidence he had for his own children. The paternal affection that he felt for me was enriched by the affinity of both of us for the love of music. Numerous times he ate his meals in my presence, and they were served to him on a large tray in his studio-lounge. Because he had to follow a strict diet, he did not participate in the family social gathering during meals. Although I was very young, he would ask me from time to time to audit the master classes that were under his direction. He wanted to put me in contact with the important piano pieces; the maestro wanted to have me listen to the different interpretations of each student and, above all, to instill the criteria that he had about the composer in general and the work in particular.[10]

A little later Paquita goes on to describe Granados:

He was a very fine artist and, in addition, had an enviable gift for words. He created an atmosphere just a few seconds after beginning a story, and his conversation was not only intelligent but often immensely emotional. He would often add humorous sparks and, in general, had a rich palette with which to express himself—a palette that, without fear of exaggerating, he could affirm that he painted what he was explaining. . . . On the other hand, his cultivated spirit was extremely vulnerable [to criticism]. When negative remarks by his fierce opponents reached him, he would take them as being strictly truthful, without thinking that they could be exaggerated or adulterated. These comments would wound his soul, immediately submerging him in a sea of sadness and pessimistic considerations of human kindness and justice.

I remember that when I was eleven years old, and because of my concert in Palau de la Música Catalana of Barcelona, the music critic of the city's most important newspaper took advantage of the opportunity to annoy him. Printed beneath my name in the program was "Student of Enrique Granados." Just minutes before the recital began, with almost all the seats occupied, this critic said, in a loud, stern voice so that he could be heard clearly, "Bah! A student of Granados? Can't be any good. I'm leaving." And getting up from his seat, he headed for the aisle, disturbing all those seated in that row. The next day, my teacher told me this with tears in his eyes and predicted for me a life that would be dark and tormented by the jealousy of others.

He had big dark eyes, a dreamy look, black hair and mustache, long and nervous hands— the hands of an intellectual. He was on the thin side and tall. He was a refined dresser; he liked beautiful things of good quality.[11]

Paquita in 1912. Cover photo for the Barcelona magazine *Feminal*, March 31, 1912. At the bottom it says, "Little Paquita Madriguera y Rodón, performer and composer."

Thus, by the age of eleven Paquita had already earned prestige in Catalonia as a concert pianist and was playing an ample repertoire of the most important composers of the baroque, classical, and romantic periods, complementing works by Albéniz and her teacher, Granados. She did not regularly attend any school and instead owed her general education to private tutors: "My home life, without attending schools and with the teachers who came to my parents' address, surrendered to the arts in body and soul and completely isolated me from contact with the moral misery of the world. I lived on the summit of dreams and fantasy."[12]

In May and June 1912, when she was not yet twelve, Paquita Madriguera began expanding her horizons. She gave a series of public concerts in Madrid in several halls, as well as some private recitals for members of the royal family. As she invariably did until her marriage in 1922, she was accompanied everywhere by Mamá Paqui, who would not leave her daughter unsupervised for a moment. We let the pianist herself evoke, from her maturity in Montevideo, those childhood adventures in Madrid:

> Gonzalo Bilbao, Néstor de la Torre, Bagaría, and others, whose names have been erased from my memory, introduced me in artistic and literary circles, even though I was barely eleven years old. What a free dissipation of gracefulness and ingenuity took place in those cafés! With all the material shared in those circles in Madrid, knowledge that drifted away indifferently among the scrolls of smoke like sugar cubes dissolving in a cup of coffee, they each published their volumes in France, Germany, and England, making good use of the energy wasted in these café gatherings in Spain. I met Menéndez Pidal, Ramón del Valle-Inclán, and other personalities who broadened my mental horizons in such interesting ways. My mind took great joy in sensing each word, every glint of intelligence in those circles. How I would have loved to stay forever in that modern Olympia![13] . . .
>
> On a certain evening, maestro Serrano, Princess Isabel de Borbón's piano teacher, came to my hotel.[14] "Her Highness is very puzzled by your attitude," he told my mother and me. "A musician never comes to Madrid without asking to be received by her. Only you have shied away, so to speak, from that old custom. The princess . . . has closely followed the press's comments regarding the girl's concerts and today told me, 'Since they are not asking for an audience, go tell them for me that I wish to hear the little one.'"
>
> My mother gracefully got out of the jam in which maestro Serrano had placed her and set a date and time to go to the palace of the king's aunt. . . . At midday, it was time to get together with Her Highness. The sun steamed the pavement of the raised Quintana Street, where the stately old woman

lived, and our carriage horse, his head hanging down, infected the scene with the laziness of his slow, heavy movement....

Miss Bertrán de Lys sent my mother, maestro Serrano, and me to a hall where, standing and dressed in a rose-colored silk dress, a rather fleshy lady of average height awaited us. She had a rounded face and a kind, dreamy expression, a rather broad snub nose, and hair that was almost white....

She talked extensively with my mother and showered me with affection, kissing me several times on the face. I played, and afterward she showed us part of her palace. As she took her leave, asking us to come back when we returned to Madrid, she gave me a pearl pin as a remembrance of my visit.

Two years later we returned to the capital, but we did not consider it appropriate to call on her. But once she learned of our presence she summoned us to her palace for lunch, scolding us cordially. "If I find out that you come again and don't come to see me, I will definitely be upset," she said.[15]

In addition to these private recitals, while still a child Paquita gave several concerts in Madrid halls normally reserved for well-established performers. It was in reference to two of those concerts, in the Ateneo of Madrid and the Sala Navas, that the press made mention of the Princess Isabel. Yet the princess was not the only important member of the royal family to invite Paquita in those days of her very special childhood:

An old friend of my parents, Juan Godó, deputy to the Catalonian Parliament, arrived in Madrid along with his daughter Clotilde. They were both personal friends of Princess María Teresa, sister of the king. This lady, through the intermediary of our mutual friend, asked to hear me. The Godós, my mother, and I answered her call. Pale, with a long face and a sweet look, on the melancholic side, with a soft smile, tranquil.... I played for her, but I had the feeling that she remained untouched by the music. However, she took my face in her two hands and, looking deep into my eyes, as if to burn them into her memory, kissed me twice on the forehead. Then she herself hung a gold charm set with a sapphire around my neck. Two months later that woman, so refined and affectionate, died after a difficult childbirth.[16]

After those meanderings through the royal halls in the dawn of the Madrid summer of 1912, Mamá Paqui continued taking the girl round the intellectual circles that struck her with the brilliance of the discussions and the opulence of their settings. Paquita's stories continue to be a relevant source of information for understanding her cultural development and emotional life:

> I went back to the bohemians. Bohemians who knew how to live and were exempt from the "odors of bohemians." Odors repel me; I cannot even stand "the smell of sanctity." Those bohemian artists and men of letters formed part of the social group of Madrid that liked to mix their lavish life styles with flashing intelligence. It is the most interesting fusion that can be obtained. Brilliant minds in luxurious palaces![17]

Among Paquita's stories was an anecdote concerning a private concert played in Barcelona for the former sultan of Morocco, Muley Hafid, who, after traveling through various Spanish cities, visited the Catalonian capital during the final months of 1914. On December 5, the Barcelona newspaper *La Vanguardia* announced: "In order to take the opportunity to try out a magnificent piano acquired by Muley Hafid, the notable pianist Paquita Madriguera played a concert in the Hotel Orient." Paquita recalled that event in 1947:

> My cousin Enrique, an enthusiastic fan of literature and music, and a violinist, arrived home and told me, "I read in the papers that you will play tomorrow for Muley Hafid. How is that?"
>
> "Don't even mention it, Enrique! I haven't slept for two nights thinking about what program to come up with for him." . . .
>
> "How did the invitation come about?"
>
> "Through the mayor of the city. I cannot get out of it."
>
> "Will you go with your mother?"
>
> "When have you ever known my mother to leave me alone? Much less with a Sultan."
>
> The next day, my mother and I went to the hotel where the distinguished royal visitor was staying. He and his party took up the entire first floor. Some young, friendly, distinguished-looking Moors were awaiting us, and they accompanied us to a large, opulently furnished hall. There, sprawled out in an armchair, was the sultan, surrounded by other older Moors. The grand piano was so out of place in that environment; I thought it looked sad.
>
> As I bowed to Muley Hafid, I noticed in his look (although he was careful, since I was a Christian) that he was eyeing my measurements and

perhaps even comparing me to one of those little creatures in his harem. I was just as curious. He appeared fat, almost obese, in his robe. Black beard and mustache, and, judging by his hands and feet, the skin covering his body must have been like that of an elephant or a turtle. He gave out a certain bitter odor, unpleasant to the white sense of smell.

I sat at the piano, caressing it so it would feel the closeness of a friend, and started playing a Beethoven sonata. After finishing the first movement, I looked at the sultan, focusing on his eyes, which had become black onyx—not because of their color, but for the stony expressionlessness. Beethoven would have aroused the same emotion in a pair of paperweights. I abandoned that composer and tried Chopin, with the same results. A Spanish dance by Granados. Nothing! Finally my mother told me, "Play your *Indian Wedding*."

This *Indian Wedding* was a musical scribble, something I wrote when I was eight years old. From the knowledge I had about Indians at that time, I had constructed a dance of monstrous and frenetically syncopated sounds, while the bass notes were sustained by great thunderous trills. It was a crude piece. Muley Hafid smiled with satisfaction when he heard it, showing two rows of extremely white and solid teeth. This grand finale ended the concert, and we left the hotel at a reasonable hour, very happy to be out in the streets, to once again breathe the civilized air of old Barcino [the ancient Roman name for the city].[18]

The Spanish press was now publishing more and more reports of the impact made by the precocious artist's burgeoning career. On April 18, 1914, *La Vanguardia* mentioned a concert played by Paquita the night before in the Palau de la Música Catalana:

The announcement that the girl Francisca Madriguera y Rodón was going to give a piano concert drew a very distinguished audience to the Palau, the best of our concert public, who already knew and admired the talents of this gifted and notable pianist. And during the event, which delighted lovers of

Muley Hafid, sultan of Morocco.

good music, insistent and spontaneous applause cropped up like the end-less wonders of an April musical temperament, but now showing the poetic luxury of the most exuberant spring.

Francisca Madriguera is a child prodigy. She played the Sonata in E-flat Major by Beethoven and left us delighted. This pianist must be [no more than] twelve years old, and even at that tender age she manages Beethoven with surprising ease. . . .

Even more than the sonata, we liked where she showed off her impec-cable technique in the Mendelssohn Variations. As a composer, she made a graceful exhibit of her talent with a *Pastoral, Theme & Variations* and the *Danza de las Brujas* [Witches' Dance]. . . . It is surprising for such clear musical ideas to develop in the mind of a child, without confusion, keeping the appropriate harmonic discipline. . . .

During the third part [of the concert], Madriguera played the prelude from the *Holberg Suite* by Grieg, *Au Couvent* [The Convent] by Borodin, a waltz by Chopin, an arabesque by Debussy, and the *Allegro de Concierto* by Granados. In all those works she displayed good taste and a fine and atten-tive intelligence. To satisfy the enthusiastic audience, she played encores by Ole Olsen and by the composer of *Goyescas* and was offered flowers along with the applause. The girl gracefully acknowledged the crowd, and we saw the radiant joy of a victorious artist in that beautiful head, framed with golden curls.

About the same occasion, the reviewer for the *Diario de Gerona* wrote:

Almost all the newspapers of the capital of Spain are dedicating lauda-tory articles to the Catalonian girl Paquita Madriguera, classifying her as "a true prodigy." She has given several concerts in Madrid, and her fame has spread widely among the select and distinguished public. She has played her own compositions and works by Wagner, Meyerbeer, Bach, and other great masters, eliciting warm applause from a crowd that admires not only the precise execution, but also the remarkable memory of the child pianist, who always plays without music. The day before yesterday she was received by Princess Isabel, and now she has left for Paris to join the "Orfeó Catalá" and give some concerts.[19]

In February 1915 a magazine devoted to, according to its cover, "the arts, letters and sports" began appearing in Barcelona. On the inside cover of the first edition is a list of the members of the editorial staff, where we find Paquita's name along with that of the Spanish writer, philosopher, and art critic Eugenio d'Ors (1881–1954), the composer and musicologist Felipe Pedrell (1841–1922), and others. That first edition of the magazine *Mediterrania* included an interview with Paquita, accompanied by a four-page musical supplement consisting of one of her works—*Cant Religios* (Religious Song), dedicated to Maria dels Angels Mateu i Plà (quite probably the daughter of the person who had given her the piano referred to in the following interview fragments):

Postcard with a photograph of Paquita taken in 1914.

In a tower in Vallcarca is the ingenuous composer about whom I will briefly inform you through a simple interview. She opened the door for me and greeted me with such a firm handshake, with so much energy, that I still feel it; she had on a yellow jersey and wore her hair long, appropriately for her age, enviable, above all, when one lives as she does. We entered a living room decorated with taste and refinement; a rather large piano, a gift and reward offered by Mr. Mateu i Plà, took up a good part of the room. Her big eyes, with a firm and intelligent look, illuminated her beauty and substantiated the lovely creations of a mind enveloped by golden curls. I wonder whether or not I am watching her at play.

Finally, since I was in the presence of an artist, I could not resist asking her to play some notes. I swear that as I listened she disappeared—her art, more powerful than anything, transported me. I would have never said that before me was Paquita, the fourteen-year-old girl.

> *Paquita*: See? That was *L'aplec de l'Ermita* [The Collection of the Hermitage].
> *Interviewer*: Is it your first composition?

Paquita: No, sir. When I was five years old I was awaiting a new baby sister, and to celebrate her arrival I composed *La Non-non* [The Lullaby]. . . .

Interviewer: Who is your teacher?

Paquita: Enrique Granados and Frank Marshall, assistant director of the Granados Academy.

Interviewer: What I can't believe, like I didn't believe of Mozart, is that your first composition was at the age of five.

Paquita: You can believe it. Like you, Mr. Vidiella also didn't believe it,[20] until I composed something in front of him, I forget what it was. You see, I am very absent-minded, and on the other hand I am lazy about writing down everything that I quickly compose on the piano keyboard. Many times at night, when something comes to my mind, I get up from bed and go play the piano. I have composed pieces that way. I think that at night, when nothing gets in the way and the solitude helps you, when you are yourself and not distracted by anything else, I think that is the best time. It was at the age of five in the Centre Autonomista de Sant Gervasi that I played in public for the first time. You know, I arrange the works to my taste. I played a fantasia on themes from *Faust*, which by the way they liked. I won first prize, given to me by a jury composed of Tintoré, Marcet, and Baldés. At the age of eleven I played my first concert in the Palau de la Música Catalana. There I played the following . . .

She showed me her program, in which was printed a picture of the brilliant little artist during her first concert: a cute face, friendly, a child to smother with kisses. In the program was the presentation made by a friend, Francesc Pujol: "Compositions by the girl F. Madriguera i Rodón: *La Non-non, L'aplec de l'Ermita, Cap vesprada d'estiu* [No Summer Evening], *Boda India.*"

With curiosity, my eyes glanced over Pujol's introduction: "But if these pianistic qualities, so well developed under the guidance of her teachers Granados and Marshall, are at all extraordinary in a five-year-old child, her qualities as a composer are much more notable, bordering on the phenomenal. They are the manifestation of an exceptional musical nature, one that

First page of *Cant Religios*, in the musical supplement to the
magazine *Mediterrania*, February 15, 1915.

in all the sensations, the feelings (and we could also say passions, because
who knows what goes through her mind so alert and heart so vibrant),
everything—everything is translated into music. And this musicality is not
the result of patient cultivation and polished discipline, a kind of torture to
which a child prodigy is submitted. No, this musicality is innate; it is like
playing with dolls for the lively Paquita, like the wish to skip, run in circles;
it is a need of her spirit, a need that is translated into vague and fugitive
improvisations when the sensation or the impression felt is not so strong
as to crystallize into a determined concept.[21]

By the time she had reached adolescence, Paquita Madriguera's fame transcended borders. She was barely thirteen years old when she performed in the Royal Albert Hall in London, and she traveled for the first time to Central America and the United States at the age of fifteen, when the start of World War I limited her activities on the European continent. In the States, to which she made a number of lengthy visits beginning in 1915, Paquita had several experiences that would be of great significance for her career. There she was also able to meet several important musical figures, as evidenced in her book. Paquita made concert tours of both the East and the West Coast of the United States, actively participated in rehearsals for the New York opening of the opera *Goyescas* by her teacher Enrique Granados, made a few piano-roll recordings (now available in digital format), and substituted for the pianist Teresa Carreño during the second half of what would be the celebrated Venezuelan artist's final concert.[22]

Paquita and her mother departed for the United States in mid-October 1915. They had a few delays before they were able to leave. The young pianist had given a farewell concert on May 8 in Barcelona's Mozart Hall but returned to play in that city on June 21 and October 8.[23] The success she garnered in her first recitals on North American soil, which took place in San Francisco, served as a springboard for performances in New York City a few months later—although these were not without certain stumbling blocks, as will be seen.

> In San Francisco I had played eight concerts, two of which were in the Festival Hall of the International Exposition.... My success there was great and New York was interested in the fourteen-year-old pianist.[24] There were many contract proposals from that city, and it was necessary to go to the urban Babylonia. Seven days of incessant bustle on the train closed the distance between the two cities, like pins that quickly join the opening from one side of a brooch to the other....
>
> We got to New York, and I began my work there by participating in one of the Sunday concerts that took place in the great Hippodrome Theatre. Immense signs, with my name in large letters, announced my performance. Later I had to play at the Metropolitan Opera House and in many more hearings that were being prepared.[25]

Nevertheless, things did not turn out to be so simple in New York. In her book Paquita reveals that the programmed concerts had to be canceled. The piano teacher Alexander Lambert threw up obstacles to her performances in reprisal for her and her mother's refusal to comply with demands he imposed in exchange for sponsoring her performances in that city. Among other things, Lambert insisted that Paquita be introduced as his student, just a few weeks before her real teacher, Enrique Granados, was to arrive in that same city.[26]

In January 1916 Paquita Madriguera was still in New York, recovering from those unfortunate incidents and now giving some recitals in programs shared with other artists while preparations were under way for the opening of *Goyescas*. On the seventeenth of that month she participated in a concert in the Princess Theatre, where the most important feature on the program was the Catalonian guitarist Miguel Llobet (1878–1938), who had arrived four weeks earlier along with Granados. On the thirtieth she performed in the Hippodrome with the soprano Maggie Teyte, the tenor Giuliano Romani, and the Sousa Band.[27] However, the young pianist's attention was focused on the presence of her teacher in New York and on the expectations generated by the first performance of *Goyescas*. Several pages of her book describe some of the events and characters connected with this premiere. In her own words, the artist evokes her observations as a fifteen-year-old:

> For some time Paris had been proposing the transformation to opera of the piano suite titled *Goyescas*. The job was arduous, but in the end, Granados gave way to temptation and began working on his adaptation for theater. The result was not brilliant, since transforming a work so characteristically pianistic into a piece for orchestra increased the difficulties of execution and created confusion, casting a shadow over the most beautiful passages. . . .
>
> The New York Metropolitan Opera House, in competition with the Paris Opéra, vied for the world premiere, and the conditions of the former were incomparably more favorable. My teacher naturally opted for New York and, in spite of his aversion to the ocean and with profound reluctance (because for him to be away from his mistress meant an enormous sacrifice), he decided to go to the United States accompanied by his wife.[28]

To better understand some of Paquita's marginal notes while relating Granados's experiences in New York, which would end up costing the composer his life, it must be pointed out that both she and her mother were aware of an affair that the composer was carrying on with one of his students in Barcelona, as a result of Paquita's having walked in on one of their trysts

Program for the January 17, 1916, "An Hour of Music" program in New York City.

before a piano lesson with the composer four years earlier.[29] Granados's wife, Amparo Gal, was aware of the affair.

> That was during the time of the war (of 1914–18). The Spanish ships— small, uncomfortable, slow, and ugly, but safe—in addition to flying a flag of neutrality, avoided crossing areas of conflict if at all possible. As a result, they set sail from Barcelona in one of those ships, bound for New York.
>
> The guitarist Miguel Llobet, the Granadoses' traveling partner, told me that from the first day of that journey [Granados] was seized by a profound

feeling of melancholy, losing interest in absolutely everything. From time to time he had a fever and barely had anything to eat; he spent hours lying on a chair on the deck, or inside when he got cold. This languor affected the crossing and particularly his poor wife, who knew well what the reason for it was. . . .

When they arrived in New York, I was already there to fulfill my contracts. I followed closely the development of the preparations for the staging of the opera, its rehearsals and numerous setbacks. I witnessed the honors and courtesies that the citizens of this huge city paid to my teacher. The same with the valuable gifts they offered him.[30]

Granados, Amparo, and Llobet boarded the steamship *Montevideo* in Barcelona on November 25, 1915, and arrived in New York City twenty days later, on December 15. As if chosen on purpose for this story, this same ship was also the one boarded by Paquita and her mother in 1916 during their second trip to the United States. Once in New York, Granados took part in a concert along with the cellist Pablo Casals and recorded several piano rolls for the Aeolian Company, which also produced recordings by Paquita. On January 28, 1916, *Goyescas* was premiered in New York by the Metropolitan Opera. A few days before, Granados composed his Intermezzo, which later became famous on its own. Paquita, present at all the preparations for the premiere, was the first to play it on the piano:

Goyescas was premiered. It was pointed out before that this work would be considered a trial for another one he might compose for the Metropolitan the following year. For a set change, a short interlude was needed, which he composed right before my eyes in less than half an hour. He passed it to me from his work table, saying, "Here, Nana (that is what he always called me),[31] play it; I want you to be the first one to play it, and I want to be the first to hear it."

This Intermezzo was the biggest success of the entire piece and had to be encored in each performance, to the astonishment of the composer himself, who placed absolutely no importance on it. Granados was experiencing the happiest period of his life. Having stabilized his financial situation, he could dedicate himself almost exclusively to composing, and he now had commitments with publishers, theaters, musicians, recordings, etc., etc. His definitive work was on the horizon.[32]

Five days after the premiere, on February 2, *Goyescas* was performed for the second time by the Metropolitan Opera, and after that Granados began to prepare to depart for Spain. Knowing the tragic outcome of his return trip adds a dramatic interest to Paquita's story of the ups and downs surrounding the decision of which ship the composer and his wife should take for the journey to Barcelona. Granados seemed to be in a hurry to depart:

The days passed. My teacher suffered from the cold and the cosmopolitanism of New York—from the fast pace of life and from "time is money." And he thought about Barcelona, about the Sagrada Familia,[33] the sunsets, about "her." . . .

It was a matter of preparing the longed-for return to Spain. The talk began about ships. Those of us who cared about our friends insisted that they return in a Spanish one, but not all his friends were so careful. In particular, the wife of a diplomat, whom I can't recall without cursing her ill-fated meddling in this matter, began to praise the Dutch ships, better and much faster than the Spanish ones: "In a Spanish ship, it will take you at least twenty-three to twenty-five days, while on the *Rotterdam*, for example, you will get to Barcelona in nine days at the most. And those ships are also neutral. I am leaving on one of those and I would love to have you as traveling companions."

"Nine days!" exclaimed the maestro with a brilliant look of feverish joy. "That's it. We're leaving on that one!"

My mother, Llobet, others, and I became frantic. Yes, it was true that the Dutch navigation line was neutral and the ships were better and faster, but on the other hand its route did not offer the safety of the Spanish ones because they stopped at British ports and then had to cross the English Channel war zone to Calais. Once ashore, they would have to travel to Paris, also a war zone! The devil of speed had possessed my maestro, and it defended him tenaciously from our sensible advice. The most powerful reason that operated in favor of his decision was that the date of departure of the Spanish ship coincided precisely with President Woodrow Wilson's invitation to play at the White House.[34]

Granados played a concert of his music in the East Room of the White House on March 7, 1916, for President and Mrs. Wilson and about three hundred distinguished guests, including ambassadors and ministers from many different countries. It was a successful conclusion to the biggest triumph of his career, but ironically, it cost him his life. As described by Granados's biographer, Walter Clark:

> The next day Granados was feted at the residence of the Spanish ambassador, Juan Riaño, who could not make it to the White House concert and prevailed on Granados to perform again at his residence as part of the luncheon. Riaño was incredulous that Granados was not going to take a Spanish vessel on his return voyage. Although the Germans had suspended submarine warfare after the sinking of the *Lusitania*, sailing into British waters still seemed too risky, even on a neutral ship. Granados respected the ambassador's opinion but could not change his reservations because the Dutch line would not refund his money.[35]

The end of the story is well-known. Granados and his wife boarded the Dutch ship and arrived safely in England. Instead of taking the shorter Dover-to-Calais route across the English Channel, they decided to take a longer but safer route from Folkestone to Dieppe on March 24, 1916, aboard the French steamship *Sussex*. The passenger ferry was torpedoed about a mile and a half off the English coast by a German submarine that mistook it for a minelayer. Although Granados did not know how to swim, he and others panicked and, against the captain's advice, left the ship, some by jumping into the water and others in lifeboats—one of which capsized. In one manner or another Granados and his wife, a good swimmer, wound up in the sea together. He pulled her down with him in the frigid waters, and they were among the nearly fifty victims of a ship that, in spite of having suffered severe damage, was able to be towed to the French port of Boulogne.[36]

Starting with the second trip to the United States, later in 1916, Mamá Paqui also took Enric, the other child prodigy of the family, who played violin and soon got a scholarship from the Aeolian Company to continue his studies in New York with the most important teachers. During their stays in that country, some of which lasted more than ten months, the Madriguera family usually shared lodgings with Rosa Culmell and her children. This Cuban-born singer taught in the Granados Academy in Barcelona at the same time that Paquita was studying piano there. One of her students who became famous was Conchita Badía,[37] a well-known soprano who on more than one occasion performed with Paquita in Barcelona concert halls.[38] Several decades later they would both return to the stages of Río de la Plata in a musical homage to Granados. Rosa Culmell was the wife of Joaquín Nin Castellanos (1879–1949), a Cuban composer born of Spanish parents. When her marriage broke up, Rosa traveled to the United States with her three children to settle there. Two of them would be notable in their respective artistic activities—the oldest, Anaïs,[39] as a writer, and the third child, Joaquín,[40] as a pianist and composer.

Anaïs Nin was three years younger than Paquita, but when the two girls shared rooms in the United States, one was already an outstanding concert pianist, while the other had begun, two years earlier, writing the journals that would later make her famous. It can never be proven whether or not Paquita's custom of daily writing down the relevant events of her life stems from those days of early adolescence that she shared with Anaïs Nin. However, these diaries, kept in notebooks by Paquita's daughters, are extremely useful in reconstructing her steps during the 1930s and 1940s.

Paquita's performances on North American stages were making an impact in the Spanish newspapers. A weekly Madrid magazine published an article on September 2, 1917—approximately halfway through the six-year period when she was touring the United States. Signed by Miguel de Zárraga,[41] with the headline "Spain in New York: The Greatest Pianist in the World," this article, written on American territory and inflamed with a certain naïve Spanish nationalism, provides some interesting details:

The United States of America is undoubtedly the land of hyperbole. Here everything is bigger, better and more amazing. It is the country of fabulous wealth and surprising inventions. No multimillionaire can compare to the New Yorker Rockefeller, whose immense fortune, if turned into coins, would not fit into any bank. The world owes to the Americans (among many other inventions tied to world progress) the incandescent light bulb, lightning rods, typewriters, the airplane, the electric locomotive, the linotype, the machine gun, the telegraph, the sewing machine, the phonograph, the armor of the warships. According to them, even their submarine *Holland* precedes our *Peral*, the French *Gymnote*, and the Swedish *Nordenfelts*.

The United States also proudly possesses the tallest buildings, the largest telescopes, the largest hydroelectric plants, the most important aqueducts, the most astonishing train stations, the most sumptuous libraries.

And when they lack the greatest of something, they import it! That something is everything artistic. Musicians, poets, painters, singers. And with the sole exception of the poets, Spain usually has a very brilliant representation here of one or the other. [The painters Joaquín] Sorolla and [Ignacio] Zuoloaga triumphed in New York with all honors, followed by [Eliseo] Meifrén, [Francisco] Pausas, and [Julio] Vila Prades; others who triumphed were [the musicians Isaac] Albéniz, [Tomás] Bretón, Granados, Casals, Llobet, and [the violinist Manuel] Quiroga, as well as [the singers] María Barrientos, Lucrecia Bori, María Gay, Concha Supervia, [José] Mardones, and Andrés Perelló de Segurola.

Pablo Casals was proclaimed—and this is how it was announced— "The World's Greatest Cellist," María Barrientos as "The World's Greatest Soprano." And beneath each of these glorious names, as if the flag were raised, it read, "Spanish." Now it is the turn of a precious creature who is barely out of childhood, although her sixteen Aprils flourish in her— Paquita Madriguera. Another Catalonian, like Barrientos and Casals, who, after being consecrated by Paris and London, has victoriously toured all the main concert halls of the United States, from California to New York.

For the North Americans, Paquita Madriguera is already "The World's Greatest Pianist," and, in a double homage to our country, "The Heir to Granados." But Paquita Madriguera, like Granados, is not only marvelous, a performer of genius, she is also the author of thirty-five very inspired musical compositions relished by the most cultured audiences in Europe and America. Before this prodigious artist, as before all our

PAQUITA MADRIGUERA, ADMIRABLE PIANISTA, DISCIPULA PREDILECTA DEL IN-OLVIDABLE GRANADOS, QUE ESTA RECORRIENDO TRIUNFALMENTE LOS ESTADOS UNIDOS DE NORTE-AMERICA. (FOTO CAMPBELL.)

Photo published in Madrid's weekly *Blanco y Negro* on September 2, 1917. The caption reads: "Paquita Madriguera—admirable pianist, favorite student of the unforgettable Granados—who is triumphantly touring the United States of America."

triumphant compatriots, Spain reaches out, and the borders open to let us through. The conquerors of Art, like those of Science and those of Labor, are the ones that most lift up the people. It is Peace that conquers.[42]

Paquita Madriguera's representative in New York was Antonia Sawyer, who was affiliated with the Aeolian Company, maker of pianos and piano rolls and the company that later awarded her brother, Enric, a scholarship. Paquita made a number of piano-roll recordings for Aeolian's Duo-Art label. The company had a subsidiary in Barcelona, and by September 1917 announcements appeared in the city's newspapers promoting Paquita's recordings, and even public playings of them in Aeolian's hall, located at 35 Paseo de Gracia. These piano rolls were rerecorded on a modern piano in 1992 and compiled on a CD dedicated entirely to Paquita's performances. It is now possible to appreciate her abilities as a performer, with excellent sound quality, in a total of seventeen pieces recorded between 1916 and 1920.[43] The selections consist of various works by Albéniz, Cécile Chaminade, Claude Debussy,

The young Paquita, on the cover of the modern edition of her recordings.

Granados (including the Intermezzo from *Goyescas*), Franz Liszt, Moritz Moszcowski, and Ole Olsen, as well as three of Paquita's own compositions: Serenata, *Danza de sátiros y ninfas* (Dance of Satyrs and Nymphs), and *Caravana* (Caravan).

Along with her musical activity in the United States, Paquita led a very intense social life, which she flavored with concert trips to the Cuban capital of Havana. Her writings give youthful impressions of certain historical personalities of the music world, although they were written thirty years after the fact and are probably filtered by her maturity and later knowledge. Of particular interest is Paquita's thorough description of the guests at a New York reception in honor of Granados in January 1916. She and her mother were in the circle of Fritz Kreisler, Ignaz Paderewski ("the great gentleman, friendly, refined, intelligent, with his lion's head"), María Gay, María Barrientos, and other artists. Also present was the legendary Enrico Caruso:

He was a very nice man. The clothing he wore, according to him, was to make the bankers talk.[44] He was a good friend and proved it by attending all of my concerts. He confessed his incapacity to enjoy classical-period music. Romantic music seemed more accessible to him, and his favorite part of the concert was the third, generally devoted to musicians from my country. That friendly effort was highly appreciated.

Those who heard this exceptional tenor can never forget the quality and power of his voice. The prodigy capable of erasing the impression he left has not yet appeared, and the passage of time—the bargainer of so many glories—has not been able to dull the shine of his exceptional star.[45]

The description of the event is replete with references to other musicians who had been gathered together to pay homage to Granados—Casals, Llobet, the violinist Eugène Ysaÿe, and the singer Lina Cabalieri. Paquita then stops on the name of Manuel Ponce, and we must remember that she is writing from a more recent emotional state,[46] after the years of her relationship with Segovia and his closeness to the Mexican composer:

Who is that being that seems to be bound to the incarnation? His look of kindness, his head of an apostle, his angelic smile! (Do angels smile? I don't think so but if they did, it would be in that manner.) Who is he? He is a musician, a great musician, Manuel Ponce. Among the splendor, the ambitions, the blinding display of the ambiance, Manuel Ponce is the "observant." He is the restraint of passions, the proof of mere earthly value. The outpouring of his entire persona displays it unassumingly. We are nothing; it is not so important to stand out in a crowd and acquire honors as some believe. If you achieve it, you must give thanks to the Divine Providence who willed it. And with his humble and wise smile that understands and forgives, he disappears slowly behind a curtain, that rare alloy of musician, philosopher, sage, and saint. My eyes follow him with intimate emotion, and my conscience is convinced that Manuel Ponce must not wear out the soles of his shoes because his body floats above the ground.[47]

However, the most fervid evocation of this event is devoted to the Venezuelan pianist and composer Teresa Carreño:

> Only one woman could do without such treasures and in spite of it still be the center of attention: Teresa Carreño. The great and precious pianist possessed an accumulation of qualities that formed an uncommon whole. . . . It feels like I can still see her, magnificent, dressed in a pearl-gray suit. But I remember her even more precisely when I recall the day of her final concert.[48]

Teresa Carreño's final concert had a very special significance for Paquita Madriguera. A dramatic and surely unexpected event, which is mentioned in passing, shows the artistic and mental stature that the sixteen-year-old pianist had attained by having suddenly to supplant the artist she so greatly admired. This took place in February 1917, about a year after the reception in honor of Granados:

> It was in New York. She wore a magnificent suit with silver sequins. She performed the works of the first part like a titan even though she was feeling ill before she started playing. I was in the audience. She sent her husband to find me and pleaded that I finish the concert, as her ailment was worsening. She went home, and I never saw her alive again. I share the sad honor of having finished her last performance. The next morning her husband, Mr. [Arturo] Tagliapietra, told me that she had lost her sight, and a few days later she died.

I attended the funeral, which was held in her apartment. That beautiful and helpless figure, with silver hair and wearing the same dress she had on at her last public appearance, was lying among flowers that enhanced her majestic dignity of a silver goddess, around which all the great artists went to pay tribute with great and respectful admiration. The violinist Mischa Elman played two pieces to bid her farewell. Then we went to the crematorium, and a half hour later her daughter, Teresita, carried a small urn with a handful of ashes—a miserable summation of the beautiful essence of such a gifted human being.[49]

Carreño died during Paquita's second trip to the United States. She had traveled, as always, in her mother's company, and for the first time her brother, Enric, accompanied them on this ocean crossing. The manifest of passenger arrivals at the New York port reveals that the Madrigueras boarded the steamship *Montevideo* on September 25, 1916, and arrived on October 13. The previous visit by Paquita and her mother to the United States (which began in the spring of 1915) extended to eleven months, and this second visit lasted almost nine (until at least June 1917), with Enric accompanying his sister on the stage more than once.[50] After spending the summer in Barcelona, Paquita and her mother were back in New York for a third time in November 1917. An article with the headline "Little Paquita Madriguera Plays," published in the *New York Times* on November 11, announced the performance in which she also figured as composer:

Paquita Madriguera, herself hardly more than a child, as indeed she was when she came from Spain a year ago as pupil with Granados, reappeared as pianist at Aeolian Hall last evening in Bach's Fantasia in C minor, a sonata of Grieg, seventeen *Serious Variations* of Mendelssohn, and pieces by Raff, Moszkowski, Chopin, [and] Liszt, as well as some by herself and by her late teacher, who was drowned on the *Sussex*, sunk in the English Channel by a submarine [*sic*; the *Sussex* was not sunk].

Little Miss Madriguera, like some artists a few years her senior, finds a friendly public here among the Spanish and South American colonies in New York. She has gained in those qualities, once precocious, now happily maturing, that gave promise for the future when she originally appeared, and her audience last night was of great size and generous in enthusiasm.

Paquita wrote a long description in her book about her compatriot Llobet, including a 1917 dialogue she had in Barcelona with a friend:

Pilar: Since you mention Llobet, tell me—what is he like? And what is he doing in the United States? Have you talked to him much?

Paquita: Much? We lived for several months in the same well-known hotel in New York, seeing each other several times a day. Let me explain. He is an excellent person; I don't know any sins, with the exception of laziness, which makes up for all the others. He is a musician of superior qualities. When he plays works that do not exceed the limited reserve of his technique, believe me it is a true delight to listen to him; but he has no aspirations. If he hasn't reached the level of fame of other great virtuosos, it is not due to lack of merit; it is because it is more convenient for him to stay where he is. . . . Albéniz, Debussy, and Granados, enchanted by his art, wanted to compose for the guitar, but he discouraged them, claiming that it is a terribly difficult instrument to adapt to music in general, and only those who possess his secrets are able to do it. In reality the problem is that he is lazy and didn't want to edit what those musicians would have written.[51]

This dialogue took place when Paquita was sixteen and did yet not know about other "great virtuosos" of the guitar who had reached "levels of fame," making her evaluations of Llobet possibly unfounded. Segovia's opinions were probably an influence, consciously or subconsciously, in the shaping of Paquita's judgments, written in the mid-1940s after more than a decade of living with the Andalusian guitarist.[52] She continues:

He inevitably makes the same mistakes in the same passages of the same pieces; all because of his lazy unwillingness to work on them with care, because he doesn't practice more than an hour a day; he spends the rest of his time smoking, talking, drawing (he has a good knack for it), and contemplating how his friends work.

I once asked him why he didn't increase his practice time, and he used the excuse that the same mistakes that kept occurring in the works he played were because the guitar was an instrument incapable of technical perfection. . . .

He has moist red lips, a very fine nose, and a look full of mischief when he says something malicious. He makes an "ee" sound when he laughs, and when he sits, he wraps his right leg twice around his left, forming a sort of barrier with them. His curious ability to draw himself in like this is striking, and I have often thought about making him get up quickly, which would cause him to fall, because it takes a few seconds for him to untangle his legs.

He eats a lot and with delight; he turns this material necessity into a real religious ceremony. . . . He is extremely playful and pulls pranks typical of a child. . . .

Pilar: Does he give many concerts?

Paquita: Well, no. He gives plenty, but in private homes rather than in public. He also doesn't like to play a complete program by himself. When his manager urged him to give at least one public concert, [Llobet] came up with a thousand objections. He asked for my collaboration—he wanted me to play two parts of the concert and him only one—but my manager would only allow me to play one part. [Llobet] didn't come to an agreement to play the other two, either, and got the help of a singer named [Giovanni] Martino. This hodgepodge of names was announced at the Princess Theatre in New York.[53] Minutes before the start of the concert, Llobet showed up carrying a small package under his arm and, going up to my mother, asked, "Let's see if you can guess what's inside this package." "I don't know," responded my mother. "Perhaps an afternoon snack?" "Hee, hee, hee. No! Underwear, because I ge-ge-get very nervous, you know."[54]

Between 1915 and 1920, Paquita Madriguera made five extensive tours throughout the United States as well as to Havana and other Cuban cities before including South America on her agenda. According to her book, each of those tours lasted ten months. She remained in Barcelona for most of 1918, and that city's bimonthly magazine *Vida Artística* published a review on May 14, 1918, of

Miguel Llobet, in a photo dedicated "To my good friend Mrs. Rosa Nin. With my most sincere affection, M. Llobet, New York, April 28, 1916."

two of her concerts (one solo and one with orchestra) in the famous Palau of that Catalonian capital:

> The graceful Paquita Madriguera has appeared once again in our Music Palace, following a long absence during which she has definitely established herself as a great pianist before British and North American audiences. She is no longer just the interesting little girl who plays the piano, but an artist who uses her instrument to express the aesthetic emotion that the works by the great composers produce in her. And she is admirable in her expression. Perhaps where she didn't achieve the necessary high level of emotion was in her interpretations of Beethoven, because the works of the colossus from Bonn are too powerful for pianists so young and delicate to penetrate. And the secret of Paquita's art, which is a feminine one, is to suggest, attract, and captivate—not to thrill, move, or subdue. For works like Beethoven's she lacks the strength and maturity—she remains a young girl. And youth is a defect that disappears with age.

Fragment of page 31 of the magazine *Vida Artística* where the notice about Paquita Madriguera appears. The picture is that of the Spanish guitarist Regino Sáinz de la Maza.

The same can be said of Paquita as a composer: she shouldn't rush. She also should not rush into offering works such as Liszt's Concerto in E-flat Major, whose first performance went unappreciated owing to a lack of orchestra rehearsals. Nevertheless, the two concerts Paquita gave were a triumph for her, as an artist and as an adorable young lady.

Paquita played at the Cercle Mercantil (Merchant's Circle) in her native town of Igualada on September 26, 1918. Between December 1918 and December 1919, she gave a series of "farewell concerts" in anticipation of return trips to North America. In December 1918 she played a group of three successive recitals—a cycle titled "Three Farewell Concerts"—given on the thirteenth and the twentieth in the Palau de la Música Catalana and on the twenty-second in the Sala Granados.[55]

A similar occurrence took place in December 1919 with two concerts on the fourteenth and twenty-first, both in the Sala Granados. The cover of the program that grouped them read, "Two Extraordinary Concerts before her Fourth Tour of America." What was actually her fifth tour, on which Paquita and her mother embarked for New York on December 24, 1919, was extended for several months in 1920, and its course would take the pianist to South America for the first time.

Tres Concerts de despedida

per la Pianista

PAQUITA MADRIGUERA

≈ 1918 ≈

Cover of the program for Paquita's
in December 1918.

Paquita Madriguera's success in the United States encouraged her mother to agree with the pianist's agents, who intended to open the doors to new centers in which she could display her maturing artistic talents. The Río de la Plata region showed, from afar, the vigorous growth of Buenos Aires and Montevideo (on a smaller scale) as artistic centers where European

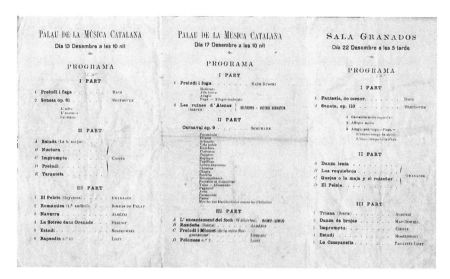

Program for the series of three concerts in December 1918.

musicians, some already known and others just starting their careers, were beginning to arrive. Arthur Rubinstein, the Vienna Philharmonic directed by Felix Weingartner, Andrés Segovia, and a few other artists had already debuted in Montevideo between 1920 and 1921. Mamá Paqui thus decided to accompany her daughter, now almost twenty-one, to this part of the globe with the idea of continuing to widen the boundaries of her musical triumphs under the auspices of impresario Ernesto de Quesada—who, coincidentally, also represented Segovia. As a result, mother and daughter visited Lima, Peru, then Santiago, Chile, and finally both republics of the Plata. In Lima, with Liszt's Concerto in E-flat Major, Paquita was the first pianist to play in the newly inaugurated Teatro Forero, later renamed Teatro Municipal. The young pianist garnered such acclaim from audience and critics alike that she was still remembered with admiration when she performed in those cities again more than twenty years later.

Destiny would significantly play various cards and roll the dice in the southern-hemisphere spring of 1921. Following her performances in Buenos Aires and Montevideo, from June to October of that year, Paquita and her mother returned to Montevideo at the invitation of an Uruguayan family of Catalonian descent. During their brief stay they could rest, and the pianist would give a benefit concert. Shortly after mother and daughter settled down

Program for the concerts in Granados Hall in December 1919.

in the family's home, Paquita fell in love with a relative of their hosts'—a mature, well-to-do widower who lived in a neighboring house. The artistic tours ended abruptly when Paquita decided to stay in Montevideo to get married the following April to Arturo Puig and settle down there with him, in her own home.

One phase of this story appears to close unexpectedly while another opens up. However, none of those involved knew until much later that the seeds for the third stage were already sown. The other card the hand of destiny played for Paquita Madriguera in that austral spring of 1921 caused her first appearance in Buenos Aires to coincide with Andrés Segovia's second concert tour in that city. This would be the second time both musicians would meet face to face, the first one having been four years earlier in Barcelona.

Chapter 6

Segovia

Paquita Madriguera first heard of Andrés Segovia in Barcelona, when she was around seventeen. Her extensive impression of Llobet, recounted in the previous chapter, forms part of the story of how the pianist learned about the emerging guitarist. It was probably between July and October 1917, since she was in New York in mid-June for the funeral of Teresa Carreño and again in November to perform. Segovia, who from his first concert in Granada in 1909 had met with both good and bad luck trying to forge a performing career in several Spanish cities, first encountered Miguel Llobet in Valencia in 1915. Both guitarists met again later that year in Barcelona in November, just before Llobet sailed to New York on the same ship as Granados for the premiere of *Goyescas*. At that time, Paquita was already a renowned artist with a steady succession of concerts and recording sessions in the United States, while Segovia was lamenting his lack of support from Llobet in pursuing a concert career in Barcelona.[1] Nonetheless, thanks to the enthusiastic reception his playing got from Frank Marshall, Joaquín Cassadó,[2] and other personalities of the Catalonian cultural world, Segovia's art bloomed in the region's capital. Between January and March 1916 he gave several important concerts—two each in the Layetana Galleries, the Mozart Hall, and Granados Hall, and one in the Palau de la Música.[3]

By 1917 Segovia had secured fame in Barcelona, thanks to a series of successful performances from previous years. Paquita relates the moment at which she became aware of the singular presence in Catalonia of a

Andrés Segovia at Barcelona's Cementerio Nuevo on December 18, 1915, for the exhumation and transfer of Tárrega's remains to his hometown of Castellón de la Plana.

personality named Andrés Segovia, who was there making music, among other things:

Barcelona, 1917

"Pilar, what is that coming down the Rambla?"

"'That' is Andrés Segovia."

"And who is Andrés Segovia?"

"A young man who plays the guitar admirably well."

"Ah! Better than Miguel Llobet?"

"You'll see, Paquita. Some say yes and others say no."

"I say no."

"Why, if you have never heard him?"

"Because I am a friend of Llobet's."

"What extraordinary artistic reasoning! Let's hope he comes closer, so we can see him better."

A strong young body inclines its defiant head toward the curious stares of bystanders. He wears large, round tortoiseshell glasses. Long hair down to the back of his neck, and black sideburns flowing down his cheeks. He wears a large hat, a scarf as a tie, a black velvet vest, and oversized plaid pants that remind you of a field hand's. His large, soft hand (an unmistakable expression of his ingrained sensual temperament) wields a huge cane.

"Pilar, do you think that in order to play an instrument well one should wear a costume?"

"To wear a costume, not at all. But I think he is right in dressing differently than the bourgeois."

"How do you justify the presence of that large cane?"

"Well, Paquita, that is another matter. There I do not defend him, but criticize him.

Andrés Segovia listens to Miguel Llobet in Barcelona at the end of 1915. *Standing*: León Farré, luthier Enrique García, and Juan Parras del Morral. *Seated*: Francisco Tárrega (the son), Segovia, Llobet, and Eusebio Gual. The photo is by Joan Vilatobá.

He uses that large stick almost every evening on the heads of the Catalonian autonomists, when they gather to parade through the Rambla in support of the campaign in Madrid for economic autonomy of our region. The exalted ones from here yell insults at the government, which leads to police intervention and pro-government Spanish-speakers [i.e., not Catalan-speakers], and a riot breaks out; evening after evening, Segovia takes advantage of it to strike blows left and right. Slashings, stonings, beatings, canings, and insults; women run terrified, dragging their children by the hand, businesses close to protect their windows; the arrested go to jail; and the result is that such demonstrations ruin the intellectual work that the leader of the Catalonian autonomy tries to perform, with so much patience and tact, in the parliament!"

"And what does Segovia care about our political problems?"

"It's simple. He speaks Spanish and reacts against Catalan. I don't think, however, that he hates Catalonia, cradle of his first important successes. Barcelona has been the godmother in the brilliant career he foresees, and he knows it all too well. You aren't up to date about what goes on around here because ten months out of the year you live in the United

States; but I hope that you have the opportunity to hear him and you will see."

"He's unfriendly. I don't like him at all and I vote for Llobet."[4]

Thus ends Paquita Madriguera's description of that first impression that Segovia's persona—from a distance and according to what her friend told her—generated in her spirit. Sometime later the man would appear again in her path:

Gaspar Cassadó came to tell me that Tarrasa wanted a concert with me, him, and Andrés Segovia—the three of us on the same event. "You and I would be fine," I responded, "but it bothers me that the presumptuous Segovia would share it with us."

"Do you say presumptuous, Paquita?" Gaspar inquired. "No, no, Paquita, no. On the contrary, he is very nice, a great artist, and has a cheerful disposition."

"Yes," I interrupted. "Very happy and with a large stick in his hand that makes your hair stand on end."

"Allow me to introduce you to him, Paquita, and you will change your mind."

"I don't care to. I can see in his haughty look that we would never get along; and besides, note that he is the only young musician here that, in a rather obvious manner, does not attend any of my concerts. I find him very arrogant."

A temporary illness kept me from taking part in the concert that Tarrasa arranged, which was carried out by the other two artists, and I didn't have the opportunity then to hear Segovia.[5]

The inevitable personal encounter finally took place in January 1919, when Paquita was eighteen and Segovia almost twenty-six. It is interesting to see how each remembered the event years later. First from the pianist, as she recalled it at a distance of three decades:

Soon one of his recitals was announced in Sala Granados. I attended with my mother. The program drew my attention because it wasn't typically "guitaristic." Its makeup denoted serious and unerring good taste. He walked

A photo of Paquita Madriguera and the Muñoz Lucena portrait of Andrés Segovia, both made in 1918, around the time of their first encounter.

onto the stage. He sat down. He challenged the audience with his look; he seemed ready to offer us a couple of slaps. "Demon, Segovia," I told my mother. "Insolent and unbearable."

If I were spiteful I wouldn't have come to listen to him, but I was interested in distinguishing his artistic merit from the rest, and I confess that I had come with the secret and fervent desire that he fail, so that I could tie the one with the other. Then the concert began, and the first few measures were enough to reveal a superb player. His marvelous tone, clear technique, beautiful phrasing, varied nuances—constrained within the circle of good taste—were all contributions leading to a summation very rarely found. "What a shame that he is so aloof!" I exclaimed.

Among the works he performed, the Andante from Mozart's Sonata in C Major stood out and moved my soul from its very depths.[6] Once the concert ended, I went to greet him, forgetting my mundane pettiness. He was surrounded by admirers, and when I saw an opening I moved forward and, very cordially and sincerely, congratulated him, pointing out the emotion that Mozart's purity had produced in me. He took my remarks indifferently, though he responded with smiles and bows to the compliments others made. Humiliated and sorry for my generosity, I left there convinced of having met "the best guitarist of the time" and the most unbearable human being as well.[7]

A concert program for January 26, 1919, in the Asociación Granados-Marshall is the only documentation available of a Segovia concert with that Mozart Andante in the Catalonian capital around this time. Segovia recounted this first meeting with Paquita in the only volume ever published in English of the autobiography he never finished. Two paragraphs after saying that he remembered playing the Andante, transcribed by Tárrega ("I remember it for sentimental reasons"), Segovia appears to contradict Paquita's impression regarding his air of indifference:

> Among the people that I received in the adjacent small salon after the concert was a beautiful young girl of about fifteen [*sic*]; enormous blue eyes, delicate nose, fine smiling lips, a graceful, slim figure, half child, half woman, a delightful vision. Her mother, portly and elegant, was behind her. Frank Marshall introduced us....
>
> The young girl took my hand in hers. "I just loved the Mozart Andante," she said enthusiastically, "It sounds marvelous on the guitar."

Segovia related that he had heard about the emerging brilliant pianist and her success in London, and that he had been told of her mature talent, despite her age. He added that Paquita Madriguera had studied with Granados since the age of eight and was not only an excellent pianist but also an accomplished musician. He confessed that he was captivated by Paquita, but felt a bit uncomfortable because she was so young and already famous, while he was still trying to make his way in Spain. The guitarist ended by saying that a few weeks later Paquita and her mother left for New York, while he kept thinking of her, as "a mysterious inner voice seemed to tell [him] softly that [they] were destined to meet frequently in the future and form a close and lasting relationship."[8]

Segovia made a similar reference, significantly shorter, in a 1973 interview: "I met Paquita at my first concert in Barcelona in the Sala Granados. She was then close to fame, while I was just beginning. She was a great pianist, with a fine temperament, a delicacy."[9]

He makes another inaccuracy in this interview, probably owing to the passage of so many years. His two first concerts in Sala Granados were on January 16 and February 20, 1916, at which time Paquita was in New York giving concerts and working on the premiere of *Goyescas*. It is more likely that this anecdote took place at one of the other concerts that Segovia gave in Barcelona in this hall or later on. The only concert in which all the coordinates align is the one on January 26, 1919. What is certain, with relation to the present story, is that, as Don Andrés wrote in 1976, shortly after that recital the young pianist and Mama Paqui crossed the Atlantic once again, returning to New York and to the life described earlier.

SALA DE CONCIERTOS DE LA
ACADEMIA GRANADOS
AVENIDA DEL TIBIDABO, 14

CONCIERTO
EXTRAORDINARIO
DE GUITARRA
Domingo, 26 Enero 1919, a las cinco de la tarde

Cover of the program for the concert of January 26, 1919.

Meanwhile, events in the life of Andrés Segovia began to accelerate. His successes in Barcelona (perhaps Spain's most significant musical center of the period) and particularly the friendship he developed with Gaspar Cassadó at that time were determining factors for the direction his career was to take. As Segovia wrote in his autobiography, Ramírez the luthier had told Gaspar Cassadó, the cellist, that he was in Madrid. It was through his friend Cassadó that he met Ernesto de Quesada, who had founded Conciertos Daniel,[10] the sole concert management firm in Madrid at that time. Cassadó introduced Segovia to "the owner, general manager, clerk, and office boy, all in one person—Quesada himself," and persuaded the manager to organize a trial concert for Segovia in Madrid, at his own expense. The guitarist would not have to pay anything, in lieu of his receiving any fee.[11]

The arrangement of some concerts in different locales in the vicinity of Madrid strengthened Segovia's relationship with Quesada, and new ideas on a larger scale, as well as other types of events, began to emerge in 1919. As a test, the enterprising agent wanted to present Segovia at the Teatro de la Comedia, a large and reputable hall, and if the concert was successful with public and critics, Quesada would organize for him a tour of Uruguay, Argentina, and Chile for the next season.[12]

The concert in Madrid was a success, and Quesada, convinced that the trial had been passed more than satisfactorily, immediately began negotiations with his associates in South America. Thus was born Segovia's first visit to

Montevideo. At the same time, a new link was added to the chain of events being forged in new directions in the artist's life. One morning, when Segovia arrived at Quesada's office, he "was stunned by the beauty, garb and grace of a young woman sitting in the waiting room." She was accompanying Carmen Rangel, a Mexican pianist friend of hers, who was looking into possibly giving a presentation concert in Madrid.[13]

The young woman was Adelaida Portillo, who was born in Cuba in 1894, the daughter of a Spanish soldier. Her romantic relationship with Segovia began almost immediately, although he was in the midst of arranging for his first tour outside of Spain. Once the tour was over, the guitarist promised, they would set the wedding date.

Andrés Segovia first arrived at the Río de la Plata area on the last day of May 1920 at the age of twenty-seven. He had left the port of Cádiz in the middle of the month after secretly saying goodbye to Adelaida (who coincidentally was in that city), unbeknownst to her parents. Segovia described his state of mind and the fears that overwhelmed him at the moment of departure: the emotions of the farewell, the sorrow of having to leave his beloved behind, the uncertainty over what could await him across the ocean, the thought of his mother's "precarious future" if his tour failed, and the idea of being seventeen days at sea and arriving in a new land, "without loved ones to meet."[14]

Segovia's first concert took place on June 4 in Buenos Aires, and seven days later it was Montevideo's turn. Quesada's company, through his partner Cirilo Grassi in Argentina, had already done the necessary arrangements and the Uruguayan capital's press was ahead of the event. A notice of the concert appeared in the daily newspaper *El País* on June 3:

> The highly praised guitarist Andrés Segovia will visit us soon. It has been said that he has a passionate temperament, a first-rate technique—a player who knows how to apply his own style to all the compositions he performs, and he is outstanding among the great Spanish guitarists. Segovia will give some concerts in Teatro Solís.

On Wednesday, June 9, two days before the guitarist's Montevideo debut, the same newspaper made reference to the news that had already arrived from Buenos Aires. With the name of the artist as the title, the article says:

Next Friday in the Sala La Lira, the acclaimed concert guitarist Andrés Segovia will make his debut. The reviews that come from abroad are very flattering, showing the young guitarist's beautiful artistic work, and in this respect *La Nación*, of the neighboring capital, says: "The guitar, which is one of the oldest and most popular instruments, has not had many connoisseurs, nor has it been used so that the great composers would dedicate their works to it. Perhaps this stems from the lack of resources for the guitar, its extreme technical difficulty or its character, more suited to the bedroom than to the chamber. Therefore, above all one must admire the bravery and selflessness of those such as Tárrega, Pujol, Llobet, and Segovia, who dedicate their life and truly higher skills to the virtuosity of the guitar.

"Last night the above-mentioned Don Andrés Segovia appeared in La Argentina, a Spaniard, like the others mentioned, and their equal in quality. A young Sevillian, he learned the guitar almost at the same time as the language and displayed his predilection so expertly that, though barely past adolescence, he can be considered a master, as proved by a long and interesting program executed with astonishing perfection. Full sonority, surprising clarity, confident mechanics—his interpretations of the most famous pieces provoked long rounds of applause. And, applauded at the end with real enthusiasm, he had to add *Danza Mora* by Tárrega, *Sevilla* by Albéniz, and *Scherzo Gavota* by Tárrega to satisfy the persistent demands of the full house."

Andrés Segovia's highly anticipated first concert in Montevideo took place on Friday, June 11, 1920, on Paysandú Street, a few meters from the corner of Florida Street, in what was then called the Sala La Lira (in 1940 the name was changed to Teatro Odeón). The next day, *El País* published a review of the performance:

The amiable man from Granada, who performed last night in La Lira hall showing his absolute command of the guitar, reminds us of the mother country, where the tambourine, the drumsticks, the guitar, and women reign. Without any doubt, Segovia is a consummate master in the handling of this difficult instrument. The strings, forcefully plucked, produce a beautiful sound that causes his interpretations to shimmer. Segovia feels what he plays, and the absolute confidence of the left hand, in the service

Teatro Solís just before 1920.

of a rigorous technique, allows one to appreciate for all it's worth the beauties locked in the guitar. Last night the Spanish guitarist won a real triumph in his performance of the well-chosen program. In particular, the second part—consisting of Mozart, Handel, Chopin, and Mendelssohn—allowed Segovia to show his great qualities as a performer. We cannot elaborate on those qualities for reasons of space but will do so at another time.

The guitarist returned to Buenos Aires immediately as his concerts multiplied on Argentinean soil. He played again in La Argentina on June 16 and on June 19 at the Teatro Odeón. Over the next several days he also played in the cities of Rosario and Córdoba, northwest of the capital. In the meantime, it was announced that there would be more performances in Montevideo. On June 17 another notice appeared in *El País*: "The celebrated guitarist A. Segovia, who achieved a noted triumph among us in his performance at La Lira, will soon play his second concert, at Teatro Solís."

Segovia continued to be acclaimed in the neighboring capital, where his numerous engagements prevented him from fixing the date of his next performance across the Río de la Plata. His second Montevideo concert took place on Sunday, June 27, at the Teatro Solís, a much larger hall that could better accommodate the audience, which would probably be much greater thanks to the excitement produced by his previous concert and the news coming from Buenos Aires.

The three-part program included, first, a section with original works for

TEATRO SOLÍS

DOMINGO 25 JULIO

1920

A las 21.15 (9.15 Noche)

GRAN CONCIERTO

DE DESPEDIDA

DEL EXIMIO GUITARRISTA

ANDRES SEGOVIA

Cover of the program for the concert of July 25, 1920.

76

guitar by Fernando Sor and Tárrega; second, a brief transcription each of Bach, Beethoven, Schubert, and Mendelssohn; and third, a section dedicated to Granados (*Spanish Dances No. 5* and *No. 10*) and Albéniz (*Granada, Cádiz,* and *Sevilla*). On the first of July, *El País* announced that the third concert, scheduled for Friday, July 2, was postponed to July 4 at 9:15 P.M., adding: "With this recital Segovia says farewell to our public."

However, owing probably to the artist's considerable success with the public, Quesada and Grassi were able to organize one more recital three weeks later, on Sunday, July 25. The following appears in the lower part of the printed program for the concert of July 4: "In the next week, the famous artists Arturo Rubinstein and Gaspar Cassadó will give their concert."

Regarding the repertoire that Segovia chose for these new concerts, he changed some composers and works but maintained the structure he had used for the second one. On July 4 he played more Sor and less Tárrega in the first part. The composers represented in

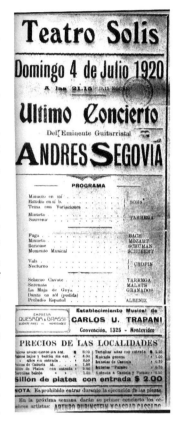

Program for the concert
of July 4, 1920.

the second part were Bach, Mozart, Schumann, Schubert, and Chopin; and in the third part the number of Spaniards increased: again Tárrega, Granados, and Albéniz, with the addition of Malats. Finally, for the actual farewell concert he played Sor's Sonata Op. 22 and Tárrega's *Capricho Árabe* in the first part; Bach, Haydn, Schumann, and Chopin in the second; and Tárrega, Henri Vieuxtemps, Tchaikovsky, and Albéniz in the third.

After returning to Spain, Segovia met with Adelaida Portillo again, and the promised marriage took place on December 23, 1920. A few months later, already expecting their first child, the couple embarked for Buenos Aires in the guitarist's second tour outside of his homeland—a trip that would also be his second to the Río de la Plata. The guitarist played seven concerts in

Teatro Odeón in Buenos Aires between May 26 and July 7, 1921. Alternating with that series of concerts in the Argentinean capital, Segovia crossed the Río several times to perform in Montevideo also. *El País* announced on June 18 that the great Spanish artist was going to give a concert to benefit the Fund for Poor Children a few days later. The concert took place on June 26, providing the framework for the inauguration of Teatro Albéniz.[15] The day of the concert, *El País* published an article entitled "Segovia Inaugurates the Albéniz" that described the repertoire the guitarist was going to perform:

> The eminent guitarist Andrés Segovia, an unrivaled artist who has exalted his instrument with his magical interpretations, will play today at the Teatro Albéniz (formerly the Catalunya) with a very interesting program. [His program will include] Minuet in E, Andante Cantabile, and Theme and Variations by Sor; Serenata by Malats; Allegro by Vieuxtemps; Bourrée by Bach; Minuet by Mozart; Mazurka by Chopin; Canzonetta by Mendelssohn; [and] *Granada, Pavana, Cádiz, Sevilla,* and *Leyenda* by Albéniz.[16]

The next day a review appeared in the same newspaper recounting the great Spanish artist's sensational success:

> The guitarist Segovia had a triumphal return to Montevideo. His talents as an interpreter and the fine musicality of his selections had already conquered the unanimous warmth of the public and critics in his concerts of the previous year.... The persistent and enthusiastic applause forced the artist to perform encores more than once.

In July 1921, Segovia gave three more concerts in the Teatro Albéniz in Montevideo: Sunday, July 3; Saturday, July 9; and Sunday, July 17. According to the announcement in *El Día*, the last was a benefit for the Patronage of the Needle. Adelaida Portillo's advanced pregnancy prolonged Segovia's stay in the Río de la Plata area a little longer, and on September 25, 1921, the guitarist's first child, Andrés Segovia Portillo, was born in Buenos Aires.[17] Segovia's residence of several months in the Argentinean capital in 1921 was also registered in a couple of accounts that are important to note in the framework of this story. Paquita Madriguera narrates one encounter in her book:

We met in the hallway of the Teatro Odeón. He greeted my mother atten-
tively and shook my hand while looking elsewhere. It is in vain, time does
not diminish that Olympian antipathy. He still hasn't attended my concerts;
I respond in the same manner.[18]

A few pages later, Paquita reproduces a dialogue that she had with Segovia in 1933, in Barcelona:

"It has been many years since we last saw each other, right?" he told me.
"Along the way, I calculated the years; eleven, because the last year we met
was in 1921, in Buenos Aires."[19]

"But you saw me in Buenos Aires?" I asked.

"Naturally! In the hallway of Teatro Odeón, don't you remember? You
were with your mother."[20]

Could Paquita Madriguera and Andrés Segovia have ever imagined, during their brief meeting in 1921, that twenty years later they would be together
again in Teatro Odeón in Buenos Aires, this time not in a casual encounter but sharing the stage? To continue with the story: the second piece of
evidence regarding Segovia in Buenos Aires—more precisely, regarding the
timing of events—while providing some interesting details, has to do with a
letter from the other guitar-world colossus of this time, Agustín Barrios, to
his Uruguayan friend Martín Borda y Pagola, dated October 15, 1921:

Dear brother Martín,

Believe it or not, I am in Buenos Aires. I came to this city eighteen days ago,
having been contracted by Max Glucksman to make gramophone recordings. I've already made a series of six recordings this year; so I should tell
you that I signed a contract with the just-named house and am obliged for
a term of five years to record exclusively for the same, a minimum of five
records per year. The recordings in this series, which corresponds to the
category of select records, are one-sided, three minutes long. . . .

Dear brother, taking advantage of the shape I'm in, I am also going to
give two or three concerts at La Argentina. For this purpose I give you the
welcome news that I was fortunate enough to hear Segovia in one of his

concerts given in the same hall, La Argentina. At this concert I was introduced to him by our great Elbio [Trápani, Barrios's Argentinian secretary],
and we are already great friends. Afterward I went to visit him at his home
accompanied by Elbio and Martín. He treated me with much consideration
and affection. I let him hear, on his own guitar, some of my compositions,
which he liked very much. As a result of the sincere and honest welcome
that Segovia gave me, I must tell you, brother, that I feel a great friendship
for this great artist. I am delighted by the way he plays, and I try to imi-
tate him in everything—without losing my own personality, naturally. He
showed a particular liking for *La Catedral* and told me to give it to him to
play in concerts. So I beg you, Pagolita, do me a great favor and send me a
copy of this composition as soon as possible, since Segovia sails for Europe
on November 2. He gave me a lot of encouragement and told me to make
an effort as soon as possible to go to the Old World.

He showed no petulance with me. On the contrary, he showed me
that he felt a special esteem for me (of a kind he had shown to very few
professionals) because, according to him, he saw in me a great deal of artistic integrity. So, brother, I won Segovia over; now I need to win over your
friend Llobet. I forgot to tell you that Segovia promised to give me some
of his repertoire works, among them a *Torre Bermeja* by Albéniz that is a
treasure. . . . Keep with you my constant affection and regards to yours, a big
hug to our old friend Don Antonio, and you receive another big one from
your friend and brother always,

Agustín Barrios
My address is: México No. 953. B. Aires[21]

From what Barrios writes, he probably had arrived in Buenos Aires the
last week of September. Segovia gave a concert at La Argentina on the day
that Andresito was born, September 25,[22] which is probably the concert
alluded to in Barrios's letter. It is also worth noting that Barrios had already
made several commercial recordings over the past seven years, while Segovia
still had not made any. This encounter between the two artists has caused
quite a stir in the guitar world. Another account of it exists, from the Paraguayan guitarist Sila Godoy, but it lacks documentation. It is from a story that
Segovia told to a group of participants in one of his Santiago de Compostela
classes in 1959. According to Godoy:

In a meeting that took place outside the academic site, Hostal de
los Reyes Católicos, he [Godoy]
was a witness of the declarations
Segovia made with respect to
Barrios. The topic came up ...
raised by the followers of the
conflict between Barrios and
Segovia (among these John Williams, then nineteen years old),[23]
who wanted a public statement
by Segovia. The notable Spanish
guitarist, wanting to excuse Bar-

Cathedral of Montevideo in the 1920s,
the inspiration for Agustín Barrios's
famous composition *La Catedral*.

rios, said (a dramatic moment in that bohemian hall, a Spanish tavern):
"... In 1921, in Buenos Aires, I performed in Sala La Argentina, famous for
its good acoustics for the guitar, where Barrios had given concerts weeks
before my performance. He was introduced to me by his secretary Elbio
Trápani. At my invitation, Barrios visited me at the hotel and played on
my own guitar several of his works. Among the ones that really impressed
me was a magnificent concert piece, *La Catedral*, whose first movement is
an andante introduction like a prelude, [followed by] a second movement
of great virtuosity that formed a great piece for the repertoire of a concert
guitarist. I had ten days to continue my tour, and Barrios promised to send
me the work immediately, though I never received a copy.

Long afterward, some good friends of Barrios's told me that Barrios
had sent a letter to Borda y Pagola urging him to send the copy to put into
my hands, and I confirmed to them that Barrios was a sincere and serious
artist, but given the vicissitudes of his bohemian life and the arduous trips
that he always took, he had no way of having his files at hand."[24]

It is noteworthy how several significant events converge during that
spring of 1921 in Buenos Aires. Andrés Segovia becomes a father for the first
time, his presence in the Argentinean capital coincides with that of Paquita
Madriguera, and they have their second brief encounter. During that time,
quite possibly the only meeting between Segovia and Barrios takes place,[25]
and Paquita performs what would be the last concerts of the first part of
her concert career. A few days later she would travel to Montevideo, where

her life would reach a turning point. It is interesting to observe that Segovia still had not earned the preeminent place he later enjoyed in the world of the guitar. This was obvious in Argentinean guitar circles during those years, if we read carefully the first two issues of the magazine *La Guitarra*, produced by Juan Carlos Anido.[26] The feature article of the first issue, published in July 1923, was published under a title that can be translated as "The Guitar Over Time: The Origin and History of the Guitar," by Ernesto De la Guardia. The eight-page lead article begins with a large photo of Francisco Tárrega, on whom the writer focuses in the section about "the modern school." After affirming that Tárrega was not only a composer but also a virtuoso concert guitarist who strongly modernized the technique and spirit of the art of the guitar, De la Guardia asserts that he created a school whose brilliant tradition is maintained by his students. He goes on to observe:

> The glory of Tárrega's school shines today, especially in the art of Miguel Llobet, the most prominent and famous of today's guitarists. . . . Llobet's fame extends throughout the world, and today he is the master of the guitar and acclaimed in all the European nations, especially those with a more elevated music tradition, such as Germany and Austria. Llobet has also toured throughout America to great acclaim, and in Buenos Aires, which he has already visited three times, he is one of the favorite great artists of the *porteño* [Buenos Aires] audience. His magnificent art, which is revealed in his masterful performances and transcriptions with which Llobet has enriched the repertoire for the guitar, his extensive musical culture, and his interpretive personality can all be summarized in the words of his colleague Emilio Pujol: "Llobet is the guitar genius of our century."

After establishing Llobet's international prominence on the guitar, this spokesperson for a good part of the instrument's community in Buenos Aires points out what he considers to be the hierarchy. He begins by mentioning Pujol:

> This last name should be cited immediately following. In fact, Emilio Pujol is a notable guitarist because of his artistic seriousness and fine qualities. Josefina Robledo, Josefa Roca, Daniel Forteá, Domingo Prat, and others also belong to the school of Tárrega. Among us, this famous school for the

guitar is brilliantly represented by María Luisa Anido, the great Argentinean concert guitarist. Miss Anido is still a little girl, as she was born in Buenos Aires in January of 1907. . . . In 1921, María Luisa Anido performed at the Asociación Wagneriana of Buenos Aires, winning a complete and energetic triumph. . . . Soon Miss Anido will be known in Europe, where her concerts will honor the Argentinean art.

The next paragraph indicates where the aficionados of Buenos Aires placed Segovia in the constellation of guitarists:

Among the concert guitarists that do not come from the school of Tárrega, there are a few worth mentioning, especially Andrés Segovia, a concert guitarist applauded in Buenos Aires several times. Of expressive temperament and beautiful sound, he is an artist who is mostly self-taught.

A purely anecdotal bit of evidence that nonetheless shows that Segovia still had not reached a predominant place in the consideration of at least a certain portion of Argentinean guitarists, on page 11 of the second issue of *La Guitarra* is printed the photo reproduced at the beginning of this chapter. The caption reads: "Llobet giving a private concert to a select group of admirers." It appears that the unmistakable figure of Andrés Segovia was not recognized by the editor of the magazine, or perhaps he didn't see a reason to mention him. The presence of Segovia was not mentioned in another photo (also shown at the beginning of this chapter) appearing on page 19 of the magazine's first issue, showing the attendees of the exhumation of Tárrega's remains in Barcelona, despite the fact that the young virtuoso is right in front of the coffin. Undoubtedly, there were other names that enjoyed greater attention from the guitar circles there and in other parts around the world. Segovia was probably aware of this, and it may be one of the reasons he stayed away from Río de la Plata for seven years: he realized that the career he envisaged for himself required conquering audiences of greater importance that would truly make all eyes of the musical world focus on him. It is quite probable that, at the beginning of November 1921, when he embarked on the *Infanta Isabel de Borbón* to return to Spain with a new member of the family and sharing the voyage with another prominent guitarist, Regino Sáinz de la Maza, Andrés Segovia knew exactly what his next steps toward his goal would be.

Segovia's story is well-known in this stage, and it includes some significant milestones. The spring of 1922 found the guitarist in the Spanish capital enjoying family life, as seen in a photo published by the Madrid magazine *Nuevo Mundo*. In May and June of that year, he participated in the First National Flamenco Singing Competition in Granada, organized by Manuel de Falla and Federico García Lorca. This was perhaps the festival of greatest artistic significance to take place in Spain in those days, according to José Mora Guarnido,[27] García Lorca's friend and biographer. Mora Guarnido writes that a benefit concert was held in the Theater of the Alhambra Palace Hotel, where, as a novelty act, Segovia played a *soleares* and García Lorca read his *Poema del cante jondo*. A number of other accounts also cite articles that appeared in the newspapers during that time:

> Music for the guitar had an important place in the days prior to the competition, and the great entertainer was Andrés Segovia. On May 16 "the eminent guitarist Andrés Segovia arrived in Granada, accompanied by his beautiful wife and son. At the request of the Centro Artístico Society, he will give two concerts in the Alhambra Palace Hotel before going abroad," a tour that should be extended due to the success obtained. . . . "Another great success was the second concert (by Andrés Segovia). . . . In the third part, the *Homage to Debussy* by the illustrious Falla was so well liked that Segovia played it as an encore at the end of the program. Given the success, another concert is announced for the 25th. There are complaints by the people who were unable to get in."[28]

Segovia with Adelaida and Andresito in Madrid. This photo appeared in *Nuevo Mundo* on May 5, 1922.

A year later, in 1923, Segovia again crossed the Atlantic, but this time heading to Cuba and Mexico. His first concert in the Mexican capital, on May 4 at the Teatro Colón, was attended by Manuel Ponce, who gave it a glowing review. That was the beginning of a fruitful relationship between the two that generated one of the most important twentieth-century contributions to the guitar repertoire.

The year 1924 saw several significant events in the life of Andrés Segovia. In addition to the birth of his second son, Leonardo,[29] the guitarist made a triumphant debut in Paris on April 7 in the presence of some of the most important figures in the music world—a true accolade for the career of the guitarist. He also made a trip to Munich, where he met up with Miguel Llobet, and the two of them visited Hermann Hauser.[30] Hauser became Segovia's preferred luthier and built one of his favorite guitars.

In both 1926 and 1927 Andrés Segovia made tours through the Soviet Union, and he played in Germany and Scandinavia as well. He also made his first recordings in London in 1927 for the Gramophone Company, sometimes referred to as "His Master's Voice." On January 8, 1928, shortly before his thirty-fifth birthday, Segovia made his American debut at Town Hall in New York City, twelve years after the debut of the very young Paquita Madriguera in this same city. This concert gave Segovia the great triumph that had been missing from his career. The critic Olin Downes wrote the next day in the *New York Times*, "A New York audience has seldom been quicker or warmer with its approval." Lawrence Gilman of the *New York Herald Tribune* enthusiastically seconded Downes's opinion: "Under his fingers the guitar has long

Miguel Llobet and Andrés Segovia with members of the
Munich Guitar Society in 1924.

ceased to be the sentimental vehicle of the serenade, and becomes, when its master wills, the voice of a grace and noble loveliness."[31]

Segovia had managed to put the guitar on the same stages frequented by the best pianists and violinists, who were considered to be the true kings of the solo concert during this period. The road had been paved far in advance by his managers, and it is possible to find articles in the *New York Times* announcing his tour as early as September 1927. Publicity posters proclaimed "The World's Greatest Guitarist"—the same title that New York had conferred upon Miguel Llobet twelve years earlier. The difference was that Llobet, according to Paquita, did not dare play more than a third of an entire concert and was not able to stir up the enthusiastic fever in the New York critics and public that came from Segovia's 1928 performance. The emerging king of the

Poster produced in 1928 for promotional purposes by the
Metropolitan Musical Bureau, Segovia's New York management.

instrument had established a turning point in the history of the guitar in the United States, and his jubilation is revealed in the letter he sent to Ponce from the Hotel San Remo in New York. He said that he had the greatest triumph of his life in New York, as a crowning achievement of an artist's career. He also added that his partial successes in many European cities had yielded in New York to a "magnificent totality" that was unexpected to this extent.[32]

Upon returning in March 1928 from his triumphant tour of the United States, Segovia settled with his family in the Swiss city of Geneva. In a letter to Ponce, Segovia said that Adelaida and the children were doing very well, and that she looked happy, much to his delight, making plans to furnish the nice apartment they had taken in Geneva. Segovia described the apartment, saying that its six rooms were very sunny, that it had a small but very nice terrace, and that it was isolated from the street by some vines crisscrossing the iron fence. He also devoted some lines of the letter to tell Ponce about his two children, Andrés ("splendid, mischievous, witty, handsome") and Leonardo (whose eyes were "still slightly out of tune" but with a "picaresque charm").[33]

With the solid credentials that the successes granted him in the most important cultural and artistic cities of the world, and following a brief tour of Italy in April, Segovia reappeared in the Río de la Plata region after an absence of seven years, now

Program for the concert of July 12, 1928.

accepted and consecrated as a major figure in the guitar firmament. In addition to performing again in Buenos Aires, he gave six concerts in Teatro

Solís in Montevideo between July 5 and August 15, 1928, with a refurbished repertoire integrating new compositions written for him by Federico Moreno Torroba, Ponce, and Joaquín Turina, as well as some of his new transcriptions of Bach.

In the first of those recitals, on July 5, he premiered *Fandanguillo* by Turina and the Sonatina by Torroba for the Montevideo public; on July 10, he presented Torroba's *Suite Castellana*, Albert Roussel's *Segovia*, and Turina's *Sevillana*. In the third concert, two days later, he premiered *Serenata Burlesca* by Torroba and the Sonata No. 3 by Ponce.[34] On July 20 it was the turn of the Sonata in A, also by Ponce—the first one created by the Mexican composer—and Segovia played three of its movements, appearing in the program under the titles "Humoresque," "Andante," and "Allegro non troppo."

This fourth performance in Montevideo had been announced as "the farewell concert," but the resulting success obliged him to set two new concerts during the month of August. In the first, on August 10, he did not play premieres but repeated the Sonatina by Torroba, and on August 15 he premiered *Tres canciones populares mexicanas* (Three Popular Mexican Songs) by Ponce.

Paquita Madriguera, now the mother of three daughters, attended all of the performances by Segovia in the main hall of the Uruguayan capital. She stated in her book:

> In 1928 some concerts were announced in Montevideo. I now dwelled in that city, retired from life as a concert pianist and married to Dr. Arturo Puig. My husband bought me a subscription box to Segovia's concerts. The Teatro Solís was full, and Segovia showed me an artistic development greatly elevated and enlarged in all respects, thanks to the experiences he was internalizing. "Would you like for us to go greet him and invite him to our house, as you have done with other Spanish artists who have visited us?" my husband asked me.
>
> "No, Arturo. One just has to listen to him and nothing else. He is an unbearable snob."[35]

Seven years earlier, Segovia and Paquita had crossed paths briefly for the second time, as spectators at a concert in Buenos Aires. It had been six years since she had settled in Uruguay and dedicated herself to family life. Another five would pass before their respective orbits would next cross in Spain, after she traversed the Atlantic once again.

Chapter 7

Paquita in Montevideo

O ne may well ask what moved Paquita Madriguera in 1921 to suddenly answer the call of love in her heart and settle in a city like Montevideo, where she had recently arrived for the first time almost by chance. A successful young pianist, barely twenty-one years old, with a very promising career ahead of her, she was an artist who could have toured all around a world that finally, after the War to End All Wars, seemed to have entered upon a period of stability and peace. Now she had decided to make radical changes to her life, her family, her social world, and her geographic surroundings. Yes, she had fallen in love with a man who had much to offer her; but what could a country so remote provide a young lady who had alternated living between Barcelona and New York and was adored by the public?

The Uruguay that Paquita found when she arrived there for the first time in October 1921 was a republic with a population of a little more than a million and a half, of which only a fifth was considered rural. However, agricultural activity was practically the only source of the country's wealth, with eight million head of cattle and fourteen million sheep, and during those years the country usually enjoyed, for reasons tied to outside events, a positive trade balance. The Uruguayan peso equaled US$0.80, 10 French francs, or about 0.17 pounds sterling. The city of Montevideo, where about half of the country's population lived (as it still does today), had about 1,200 cars on streets that had been paved with asphalt just five years earlier. The capital had close to 20,000 telephone customers, with service provided by a North American company that had just begun connecting the country with Argentina, Brazil,

Havana, and New York by cable. Although most residents had at least a primary-level education, only about five thousand students were enrolled at the secondary level in Montevideo, and only seven thousand in the entire country. Nonetheless, at that time university-level education had broadened with the creation of new departments such as the Department of Veterinary Science and Agriculture, in line with the country's main productive activity.

On the political front, Uruguayans were living a period known as the "Batllista Reform,"[1] a period that lasted thirty years into the twentieth century. The country had reached a stage of democracy, following several decades of habitual uprisings to settle political differences. A constitutional reform in 1917 mandated annual elections for the different terms of the president, representatives, and members of the National Administration Council.[2] The death sentence had been abolished; the eight-hour workday, mandatory vacation, and a minimum wage for agricultural workers had been established; women had been granted the right to divorce, and bullfights, as well as all forms of animal abuse, had been prohibited by law. A spirit of optimism and true self-satisfaction reigned in some ranks of the population, as reflected in a 1919 textbook:

> The author of this book has visited the main cities of Europe and can say, without fear of equivocation, that Montevideo is one of the most beautiful cities in the world, with an unequaled ambience, a splendid climate, and all of the modern conveniences. Paris, London, Madrid, and Berlin have very cold winters and hotter summers than ours. Few cities offer a trolley service, electricity, and water like ours. All these services are very expensive, but they are good, especially the water.
>
> Our civilization does not have to envy the most advanced country in Europe—on the contrary, it surpasses many of them. It must be because we do not have anything against the foreigners, as it is among the European nations where each country considers the others to be enemies . . . and they try to prevent, with high import fees, foreign products from entering the country. We treat all the nations that send us the products of their labor equally, so we have much from which to choose—the best that each country produces in food, clothing, machinery, tools, etc.
>
> We are a cosmopolitan country; more than half our population in the capital is foreign, predominantly Italians and Spaniards. We dress according to the fashions from Paris, we eat the best food produced by each European

country, we use Italian, German, British and American automobiles, and our shops have the most perfect machines known. We know about the great inventions before many European countries do. The best plowing machinery is used in our fields for threshing and to harvest wheat and flax. Our universities and schools use the best textbooks published abroad, as well as those we write, using European and American models. In spite of all this, our insatiable desire for progress makes everything we have look bad. This defect of ours is less damaging than the opposite, which can be seen so frequently in Europe, where each nation thinks it has nothing to learn from its neighbors.[3]

During those years of Paquita's first stay in Montevideo, there were, of course, those who drew their perception of the country from a different point of view, whether it was the opinion of the most conservative sectors of society and the political parties of the opposition, or the point of view of foreign visitors. A British tourist and famous explorer of the time published a diary of her period in Montevideo in which she gave a very different view of the country:

> After leaving Brazil . . . arriving in Uruguay is a rude awakening. From that Eden one gets to this other country where . . . the most modern fight in the world has begun, an experiment comparable to Russia's, destined to leave the finances exhausted. . . . The efforts to pass legislation in Uruguay—the new laws of progressive social outreach—demonstrate a great valor, while at the same time, if I may say so, a slightly accentuated optimism. I have always lived under socialism . . . but . . . I cannot help but see in Uruguay . . . a fate of backwards feudalism. . . . In Uruguay I have found . . . a great optimism, an incredible optimism. Everything is built for the future. . . . In Uruguay there is a belief that education is the supreme end, when it does not cease to be a means. There are . . . too many teachers, too many college students. The manual laborer has been a lawyer. . . . I have visited numerous schools in Uruguay and was amazed to see that the children knew who were Bernard Shaw or Lenin, but, they don't know the names of the Apostles at all.[4]

In 1922, the year Paquita Madriguera married and settled down in Montevideo, the president of the republic was Baltasar Brum (1883–1923), who had taken office in 1919 at the age of thirty-six. The youngest president in the history of this country, he continued to work for reform, backed by the policy of Batllism within the Colorado Party.[5] This was characterized in broad terms by a strong concern for the collective whole, the separation of church and state, measures of economic intervention, and the creation of state monopolies in the most important areas of production and services. The political opposition, which also existed within a sector of Brum's own party, was most significant in the National Party, one of whose most troublesome leaders was Luis Alberto de Herrera (1873–1959). Several months before Paquita visited Uruguay for the first time, Herrera had written an article in his party's newspaper registering his outright opposition to the reform policies carried out by the Batllist government:

> We were an organized and distinct family. The doors were guarded by the old native customs that are the honor and glory of our Spanish roots. We lived happily with our austere mediocrity. The boss was the workers' best friend. A love of work united them. The children of the old laborer grew up next to the children of the rancher in a close relationship; and it would be like that forever in all walks of life. The poor were less poor than today, although it was not as apparent. We believed in order and the pursuit of happiness, without care or worry. But then came the reformers and, after belittling the old guard, which was, according to them, a sign of backwardness and imbecility, they began to do and undo. They took on the sacred heritage; they sold all the great memories; they squandered what was there; they axed their way through the customs; they broke, with their extravagances, the social organization; they auctioned off the old, used furniture; in short, they came to "redeem" us.
>
> After twenty years of craziness you now have the results of that recklessness. The country has never known such a serious economic situation as the current one. Never has our situation been more precarious. Never has the next day seemed so dark. They broke with the past, embittered the present, and mortgaged the future—for that? ... Moral ruin, political ruin, economic ruin. In the meantime, winter approaches, and the cold blows from the inside out and from the outside in. ... The reformers![6]

As the opposition's spokesman, Herrera had his opinion expressed in the newspaper *La Democracia*, among whose directors and financial supporters

was Arturo Puig Mathó. This presti-
gious lawyer, born on February 23, 1875,[7]
was a political militant in the National
Party, having been a member of the
legislative body as a representative for
the department of Treinta y Tres,[8] and
quite probably supported another position that Herrera (with whom he had
been in law school) expressed in 1915 in
the Chamber of Representatives:

> I represent a department of the cam-
> paign, and my taste, tendencies, and
> decidedly conservative criteria lead me
> to find perfectly reasonable the peti-
> tion that comes from the ranchers to
> all legislators of the country.... As a
> citizen, an agricultural representative,

Arturo Puig.

and a conservative man ... I blame the finance minister, who comes to
revolutionize us ... with this excess of fiscal greed.[9]

When Paquita came to Montevideo for the first time, at the beginning
of Montevideo's spring of 1921, Arturo Puig was a forty-six-year-old widower
who had lost his only child from his first marriage. In addition to his political
activity, Puig was a successful and financially secure lawyer. But in October
1921 he was living alone in his house in Pocitos,[10] with no company other
than his memories.

> Papa's first marriage was to a cousin of his (something quite common at
> the beginning of the last century) named Sarah Puig Aneiros. They had a
> son named Arturo Puig Puig. Sarah became sick after a surgery. It turned
> out that they left a piece of gauze or a clamp inside her, causing an infection
> throughout her body. Since there wasn't any sulfur, penicillin, or antibiotics,
> they discharged her from the hospital. Dad took her to Europe, which it
> was her dream to see, and there she died. Their son also died later, at the
> age of thirteen or fourteen, from meningitis.... That is why he was alone
> when Mama appeared here.[11]

The earliest reference to Paquita's presence in the Río de la Plata region comes from the Montevideo press in the middle of June 1921. On Saturday, June 18, on *El País's* theater and music page, an article appeared under the title "Paquita Madriguera" proposing that the pianist be invited to participate in the inauguration of the Teatro Albéniz.[12] The brief article implies that Paquita and her mother had been in Argentina for some time, since it gives information about the pianist: "[Paquita Madriguera] has recently played a good number of concerts in Buenos Aires and in the Argentinean provinces. It would be a success if the firm Quesada and Grassi presented her to play works by Albéniz for the inauguration of the theater that carries his name." On August 30 *El Día* once again announced under the title "Paquita Madriguera":

> As a note of interest for our numerous aficionados of piano concerts, another bit of news is announced in reference, of course, to the [Teatro] Albéniz. We refer to the two concerts that the pianist Paquita Madriguera, the celebrated student of Granados, will give; she will dedicate a large part of her programs to the works of her teacher, of whom we count so many admirers among our aficionados and amateurs.

Paquita Madriguera's first visit to Montevideo took place shortly after her twenty-first birthday. In fact, on September 16, 1921, *El País* included in the "Theaters, Concerts, and Movies" section another brief article with the pianist's name in the title:

> As announced, tomorrow (Saturday) and Sunday the 18th of this month there will be two splendid concerts at the Albéniz by the celebrated pianist Paquita Madriguera, who has so many admirers among us. Saturday's concert will take place at 9:15 P.M. and Sunday's at 3:30 P.M. There is great interest among our social and artistic circles in this concert.

Since at least the beginning of June 1921, Paquita was in Buenos Aires (this may have been when she ran into Segovia at Teatro Odeón). Her artistic agent was Ernesto de Quesada. Now she and her mother were crossing the Río de la Plata so that the pianist could give some concerts in the Teatro Albéniz in Montevideo during a tour that had been extended several weeks. The weekly magazine *Mundo Uruguayo* dedicated the cover of its 144th issue, dated October 13, to Paquita. The caption below the artist's photo read: "Eminent Spanish pianist who has won great acclaim in her latest concerts."

Mundo Uruguayo, October 13, 1921.

The initial plan for two presentations in the Albéniz was later expanded to a total of five concerts, thanks to the resounding success of those first two performances. *El País* published an interview with Paquita on September 17, the day of her Montevideo debut—half a page long in three columns and illustrated by two photos, conducted the previous evening at the hotel on Rincón Street where the pianist and Mamá Paqui were staying.

Paquita, who by her own admission has "a name that is not vulgar, but very ugly," is young, very gracious, has a big smile, and is very pretty. Her eyes are big and deep blue, her hair blond, abundant, and mussed. She has an air of supreme distinction, a very fine pug nose, and a small mouth. And immediately, one gets an impression of youth and happiness, of a lively and domineering girl who knows her merit—not her merit as a concert player, which is what matters to her the least, but her merit as a woman. Two more details complete the picture: one, her talent for understanding—the interviews no longer tire her because she is used to them and they are the same everywhere; the other, her femininity— she does not want to be photographed with the piano because she is very vain. The other details will come up once this dialogue, which we began just after our photographer found a fine lighting effect to capture Paquita's image, comes to an end.

Paquita Madriguera sonríe.

Music

"My musical personality was formed by two different orientations—Granados, the poet of the

El País, September 17, 1921.

piano who gave me the sense of beauty, and Marshall, the great concert player who created for me the ability to carry it out. The first, whose private playing was fairly extraordinary, was, however, a mediocre concert player, owing to the horror the audience caused him. But that horror was precisely what Marshall took away. And so, I have been at the piano since the age of seven and giving concerts since I was ten!

"Regarding the schools, I like them all, with the exception of the ultra-modernists, whom, I freely confess, I do not understand. But I prefer Albéniz and Granados, and Debussy, and above all the very-profound Russians, so mysterious and mournful. I think all these qualities are no more than a transcript of the tragedy of their race, mystical and overshadowed, and that is why my attraction toward them grows. So I imagine that the Scriabin Prelude—owing to the passionate force it holds—could only be created in tears! The same goes for Borodin, Tchaikovsky, and Rachmaninoff."

Sentimental Confessions

"Intense impressions of my career?" and after a short meditation accompanied by a light slap on the forehead, "Well, look here, the most intense impressions in my life I owe to Madrid and London. Nowhere else, until then, had I received such extraordinary proof of admiration. Later—I don't want you to think I am vain—they were repeated in other places, but I was never able to relive the impression of that first moment. Am I growing old?"

We could only laugh lightheartedly at the question. But this confession, it is clear, does not satisfy the chronicler. What is important is to grasp the sentimental aspect, the sleeping passion, the old dream of glory or unrequited love, that can cast a faint shadow of unrest or melancholy on the smiling figure of this young woman. Paquita, however, is very happy—at least, that is what she says and attests to elsewhere, if her pink cheeks and very bright eyes can attest to it.

"Everything is going too well," she tells us. "I am where I am and that is enough. Why have more aspirations?"

But since we think it absurd for Paquita to be satisfied with the present triumphal reality and not dream of something even bigger, she finally tells us, upon our insistence, that her biggest ambition is to conduct an orchestra: "It is my biggest aspiration, because the piano does not dutifully accomplish the idea that always grips me when I perform. I think there is nothing better for interpreting it than a great orchestra, well-tuned and rehearsed, that can be controlled!"

However, the writer is still not satisfied; between the gray light filtering through the balconies of the small apartment, the shadow of "El Caballero Audaz" (The Bold Knight) seems agitated,[13] as if to reproach us for how lacking this picture is that we have been outlining. One last trait remains unexplored, and it is then—oh, a miracle of our will and of the protective shadow that has placed itself on the window—that Paquita, raising her arms to the sky as if begging forgiveness for the sacrilege she is about to commit, tells us: "Now something astounding—I have never had a boyfriend. I would like to have one, just for after a concert, because before it is uncomfortable; but afterward, I always feel like talking with a person I like. And when I do not find someone like that, I feel like crying! What's more, before the concerts I do not want a boyfriend because I would have to divide my soul between him and the piano. On the other hand, this one [the piano] is my best boyfriend, because he is one of those who does not cheat, while the others. . . . I was to have married once, but I never had a true boyfriend—I never really knew my courter. We treated our relationship with such seriousness and did not address each other with the formality of "Your Excellency" only because we were not government officials. Later I came to the Río de la Plata area and he stayed at his bank, because he was a banker in Cuba."

Paquita pauses for a minute to look through the windows at the gray, sullen skies of the humid evening, and quickly observes, "Well, a banker and a pianist. The 'bank' would have enabled me to play the piano. . . ."

The interview ends here—the interview that a reporter, a critic, a secretary, and a photographer did with an extraordinary woman. The report is finished, but the first chords of a piano sound in the small living room.

The day after that first concert in the Teatro Albéniz, the same newspaper published a laudatory review of the pianist and her program:

Paquita Madriguera obtained a broad triumph in her premiere at the Albéniz. The great Spanish concert pianist does not owe her success to a formidable technique. The upper limit of the resources of the *doigté* [fingering] is a matter of time, with the physical robustness of the pianist almost always playing an important role. In the first sense, Paquita Madriguera has already reached incredible heights. It will be difficult to chronicle many cases like hers in the history of the piano. At the age of twenty, there are few pianists who have addressed programs of the highest order, such as the one from last night's event, with the brilliant luster that Paquita produces. It should be presumed that the notable artist's mechanical means will continue to grow in the direction of strength and agility. If that refinement process is not spoiled, Paquita Madriguera will perhaps be the only woman who will rise to the higher level of the great male concert pianists.

Miss Madriguera's outstanding quality is her sense of interpretation and insight. Her artistic flexibility is admirable. Almost all of the piano genres and music styles emerged in her first concert, and she revealed the hallmark of her undeniable talent in all of them. The stress and emphasis in the fugues of Bach and Beethoven, terrible pitfalls for all instrumentalists, arise impeccably from Paquita Madriguera's hands. That would be enough to consecrate her. Following such an admirable classical beginning, she dealt with the exquisitely modern Spaniards, winning deserved acclamation for the excellent versions she offered of pieces by Granados. The enthusiasm was somewhat less for the works of Albéniz. And in the third part of the program, her eclectic approach and talent triumphed noisily for the success with which she interpreted *Soirée dans Granada* [Evening in Granada] by Debussy, the spiritual anointing that she executed in the great composition by Borodin *En el Convento* [In the Convent], and owing to the expressive power that she gave *San Francisco* [Saint Francis] by Liszt. This finale to the program brought Paquita Madriguera continued and roaring ovations. There were so many that the pianist had to play more pieces; among them, some of simple virtuosity, like *Witches' Dance* by Mac Dowell, . . . also provided special demonstrations of approval.

She gives her second concert this afternoon at 3:30.[14]

The repertoire Paquita selected for her second presentation at the Teatro Albéniz on that early Sunday afternoon in September included works by Beethoven (the Sonata Op. 31, No. 3, and the Turkish March from *The Ruins of Athens*), Albéniz, Granados, Chopin, Moszkowsky, Scriabin, Cyril Scott, Rachmaninoff, and Liszt. For encores she had to play *Seguidillas* by Albéniz and a Chopin waltz.

As mentioned earlier, the enthusiastic reception given the pianist by the Montevideo audience led her agent to agree to two more concerts in the same hall. On Thursday, September 22, and Sunday, September 25, Paquita presented repertoires completely different from those of the two previous concerts. She included two of her own works (*Pastoral* and *Serenata*) in the first one, in addition to pieces by Gluck, Mendelssohn, Chopin, and Liszt, as well as the familiar Albéniz and Granados. In the Sunday program, the Chaconne by Bach (piano version by Busoni), *Carnaval* by Schumann, and a set of variations by Handel stand out, as well as other works by Spanish composers that she normally played. The review published in *El País* the day following that fourth concert remarked that one of the encores was Paquita's own *Pastoral*, which had been a success with the attendees of the previous concerts.[15]

Following the fourth performance, the last one her agent had organized, Paquita and her mother returned to Buenos Aires to do some concerts there. If not in June, it was probably during these days that she met Segovia at Teatro Odeón. As if to reaffirm how much the Catalonian artist's visit had impacted the public in Montevideo, *El País* published a portrait of Paquita by the artist J. Brugnini on the front page of the edition of Wednesday, September 28, a few days after the last concert at the Albéniz.

A couple of weeks after her last appearance there, the pianist returned to perform in Montevideo. This time it was a concert organized by a group of society ladies from Montevideo to benefit the Centro de Estudios Ariel (Ariel Studies Center),[16] and it took place in Sala La Lira—the same stage where Segovia had made his Montevideo debut in June of the previous year. Under the title "Paquita Madriguera—Farewell Concert," it was announced in *El País* that the concert would take place on that same Sunday, October 9, and the newspaper published a sketch of the pianist based on the success of her previous four concerts:

> The event, whose high artistic merit we don't need to stress, given the performer's worthiness and the program selections that she will perform, will benefit the Centro de Estudios Ariel, an institution firmly rooted in our intellectual environment and university, where courageous and fruitful action has been developing over the last few years. The event is headed by a commission of distinguished ladies.

It is quite probable that during this second visit to Montevideo, after spending some days in Buenos Aires, Paquita and her mother stayed at the home of the Mathó Puig family, and that during those days of October 1921, prior to the concert in La Lira, the first meeting with Arturo Puig took place. Paquita's daughter María Rosa shares the part of the story that she heard as a child:

> The story of how Mama came to Montevideo is like this: the Mathó Puigs, my dad's cousins, traveled to Barcelona, and there they met my grandmother, Mama, and the rest of the family. When Mama came to Buenos Aires to give concerts, single and with my grandmother, the Mathós crossed the river and went to hear her. There they invited them to come to Montevideo to spend some time at their home. They accepted, and since Papa's house was next to that of the Mathós (on Chucarro Street) and he was a widower and lived alone,[17] he went to have coffee with his cousins every evening after his work as a lawyer. And there Mama and Papa met. There

are novelistic details that should not be wasted and that I will tell you personally, because I have gone further than I had intended.[18]

The following dialogue comes from one of the many interviews of this author with the sisters Sofía and María Rosa Puig Madriguera, and it provides some of those "novelistic details." The passage is unedited so as to make clear the differences that arose as time passed in their respective memories, as well as the different family stories they had been told since childhood.

María Rosa: Mama met Dad at the house of his cousin, Aunt Elvira. After becoming a widower, he would go over and have coffee at their home, which was around the corner, on the same block as his house. Aunt Elvira had gone to Buenos Aires, and after one of Mama's concerts she had invited Mama and Mamá Paqui to visit her in Montevideo. They were at the home of Aunt Elvira when Dad came in, as he did every night, to have coffee, and Mama told me that when she saw him, with those blue eyes of his, she thought, "I am going to marry this man."

He was a lot older than her. At that time Papa talked on the phone every night with some sort of girlfriend he had. Since they were under the same roof, Mama and my cousin [Aunt Elvira's daughter] went up to the roof one night . . . and they cut Papa's telephone cable with a pair of scissors . . . so that he would not be able to talk to her! . . . It was bad luck because Dad was the lawyer for the telephone company, so he made them come and check it out immediately, and they told him that the cable had been cut on purpose. My aunt began questioning them, and they responded that they knew nothing about it. But in the end, my cousin confessed and said it was Paquita's idea. From that moment on, he started noticing her.

Sofía: They met at one of Mama's concerts. Mama told me that she bowed after every piece and she always found his eyes in the audience. At the end, she realized that she was always bowing in his direction.

María Rosa: That could have been later because the other is just how Mama told me.

The memories of Paquita's daughters have failed to uncover a categorical explanation to the questions posed at the beginning of this chapter. Perhaps something can be found at the end of that long interview granted to the journalists of *El País* on September 17 (mentioned earlier), something that anticipated the sudden turnaround in the pianist's feelings and artistic vocation. When it was suggested to María Rosa that Paquita had felt the need to be free of an overzealous mother and to make her own life, Paquita's youngest daughter speculated:

> It is difficult for me to give a concrete answer because I don't know it. I can only speculate through what other people knew and some comments. Mamá Paqui was not a person capable of pushing anyone. As a mother she wanted the best for her children. I heard many times how difficult and painful the tours were and the effort that it took to live dedicated to them. Andrés told me some time ago that in one year he had taken 109 flights.[19] At the beginning of the last century, to come to America by ship to give concerts took many days and even months. The marriage to Papa, who was a lawyer and a renowned politician, meant security and protection for Mama (besides the love). I know this is certain because I saw it; Papa sent a letter to Grandpa Madriguera asking for Mama's hand in marriage, and it was quickly answered. Another thing—a successful life is very tiring. Back then, women married young. Mamá Paqui married at sixteen, so getting married at twenty-one was the logical thing for Mama to do, to settle down and have children. These are my speculations.[20]

What is certain is that after the exchange of letters between Arturo Puig and Don Enrique Madriguera (with letters having to cross the Atlantic by boat, it would be at least a month or two before he could have received a response to his petition), the young pianist remained in Montevideo to make a new life.

The wedding took place on April 27, 1922, at the same time the newspapers in Montevideo were busy with the most relevant musical event of the moment—the premiere of the symphonic poem *Campo* (Countryside) by Eduardo Fabini.[21] Arturo Puig was already forty-seven years old and Paquita was not yet twenty-two. In the family comings and goings, much of the documentation has been lost, but a 1922 photo of Paquita Madriguera has surfaced. She is on horseback, and the background is the landscape of the

Paquita Madriguera shortly after her marriage to Arturo Puig.

home called El Campito (The Little Field), then the property of Arturo Puig and the place where Beatriz Segovia Madriguera would take her first steps seventeen years later.

However, the exact reasons that Paquita Madriguera completely abandoned her life as a concert pianist once she married Puig and settled down in the house on José Martí Street have not been determined.[22] In addition to speculations about how tiring the rigors of her concert career were for Paquita, her daughters relate (from the fragmented family stories they heard) that Puig did not approve of her leading the lifestyle necessary to carry out her role as an internationally known artist. It is also possible that Puig was somewhat jealous of the social activity required of his wife's vocation. Furthermore, in a few years Paquita became the mother of three girls, which brought her a new set of responsibilities. And quite probably, the family environment and her circle of friends mandated that she not be distracted from those responsibilities for a profession—far from the artistic centers to which she was accustomed and in which she had so shone—that she was unable to maintain with the continuity and permanence it demanded. No matter how advanced the social laws were in the Uruguay of the 1920s, Montevideo's patriarchal society—especially its more conservative sectors—did not take well to the intellectual, cultural, or economic independence of women. Sofía Puig Madriguera, Paquita's second daughter, made reference to these issues in the 1993 radio interview cited in chapter 3:

> Before marrying my dad, Mama was a very famous concert pianist. She was a child prodigy. She was one of those geniuses who come along occasionally. She had played the piano since she was very young, and at the age of three she was already composing. . . .
>
> Well, then she married my father. He was not a musician at all. They met in a very special way that had nothing to do with music. He was a lawyer. Since my mother was a very pretty woman, he was a bit jealous. There was quite a bit of an age difference between them, and he did not want Mama to play the piano, go out of the country, or give concerts. . . . He was quite jealous of Mama. Later, we were born, and Mama had to follow the life of a housewife and mother.[23]

Paquita Puig Madriguera, affectionately nicknamed "Pitusa," was born on June 1, 1923.[24] The couple's second daughter, Sofía Eulalia Guadalupe, was born on December 12, 1925, and their third, María Rosa Amelia Áurea, on August 24, 1927. Once the family grew, Arturo and Paquita decided to move to a larger house less than two hundred yards from the one in which they had lived until that time, and barely fifty yards from Pocitos Beach. Andrés Segovia would come to live in that house at 3410 Ramón Massini about twelve years later. During an interview with Sofía and María Rosa in December 2006, they began looking at a photo taken on Pocitos Beach:

> *María Rosa:* Here is when we had that dog named Muchacho [Boy], do you remember? A watchdog that would come with us to the beach. How do I remember that if I was just a little mite? I was three years old there. However, I remember that perfectly, about the dog. We don't look sad there. [Shortly before, while observing another photo of the three girls, taken in 1935 after moving to Spain, María Rosa stated, "What sad faces we always have! Ah, yes, what sadness! Look at the expressions of the three of us! And how could we not be sad, if we were always alone!"]

Sofía: No!

María Rosa: But there we lived well, with Mama and Papa and at home.

Sofía: With nannies.

María Rosa: At the beach with our beautiful dog.

When Segovia visited Uruguay at the beginning of July 1928, Paquita Madriguera was living in the house on Ramón Massini and was the mother of three girls. She recalled that visit in her memoirs, as we have read in the

Pitusa, María Rosa, and Sofía Puig Madriguera, in 1930 at Pocitos Beach.
In the background is the Hotel de los Pocitos, which operated
until 1935 and was later demolished.

previous chapter. In the days when the guitarist gave his six concerts in the Teatro Solís, Montevideo was still enjoying the collective euphoria that resulted from the second Olympics victory by the Uruguayan soccer team in Amsterdam, during the month of June. That triumphant climate, which permeated all levels of national life, would become more heated in 1930 (in spite of the general economic crisis that unfolded in the wake of the international events of 1929) with the centennial festivities for the first Constitution of the Republic, the inauguration of the monumental Estadio Centenario (Centennial Stadium), and with Uruguay winning soccer's first World Cup, held in its own capital. Montevideo society was still unaware of the impending dramatic break in the country's democratic life that would occur in 1933.

In April 1929 Paquita traveled to Spain for the first time since her marriage. She arrived in her native land accompanied by her husband and three girls to introduce them to the rest of the Madriguera family and to attend the festivities of the inauguration of the great International Exposition that was to be held in Barcelona between May 19 and the beginning of 1930. That event had motivated the construction of monumental architectural works in one

Aerial view of Pocitos Beach in 1930 with the Hotel de los Pocitos in front. Ramón Massini is the first street that goes to the Rambla,[25] on the extreme right of the photo. It is possible to see the home of the Puig Madriguera family in the first block, near the corner with the street Benito Blanco (parallel to the Rambla). The second street from the right is José Martí.

Detail of the previous photo showing the house on Massini Street.

sector of the city under the direction of a famous Catalonian architect, also named Puig. The pianist's visit did not go unnoticed by the Barcelona press. *La Vanguardia* published an article on April 16, 1929, that said: "On the 18th of this month, the ex–concert pianist Paquita Madriguera will arrive from Montevideo, accompanied by her husband, the politician and journalist Don Arturo Puig, and their three daughters. She will spend some time here because of the Exposition." About this trip, her first to Europe, María Rosa remembered:

> I recalled family stories that can clear up something about this trip. Mamá Paqui (my grandmother) and Aunt Carmen (my mother's third sister) were in Montevideo when Mama and Dad were married. They were there so long that Aunt Carmen acquired a boyfriend, a Uruguayan dentist with a well-known family name, but it didn't work out. She said that on one of the ship parties on the return voyage to Spain, she dressed me up as a doll. She made me a pink paper dress and put me in a box. It was so successful that it won first prize.[26]

The two Puig Madriguera sisters said that they have few direct memories from that first part of their childhood, when they lived with their father:

> *Sofía:* I loved my father and I was his favorite. Because Pitusa was tremendously mischievous—very naughty and always threw tantrums. I was the second one. And María Rosa was very little. So he always went out with me. He took me everywhere. Then, when Papa died, it was a total loss for me.
>
> *María Rosa:* I remember that he used to go to Las Palmas,[27] on Saturdays and Sundays at noon. He would go have a drink with friends, and sometimes he would take us. And there was a friend—look at the things one remembers—that would hold me and say, "Oh, how pretty!" And he would throw me up in the air and catch me—and that scared me so badly that I remember

María Rosa, Pitusa, Paquita, and Sofía (*left to right*) in September 1930.

it to this day! He probably enjoyed it, but I thought it was frightening!

When asked for more information regarding her father, María Rosa explained in writing:

I regret not being able to give you the information you ask for in a concrete manner. Do not forget that I had turned four just ten days before Papa died.... The only thing I remember having heard is that he was a representative for the Department of Thirty-three, and that he financed the newspaper of his party for many years. Mama once said that he was the most successful and important lawyer at that time and he helped the newspaper of the National Party financially; and on one occasion he went to the Hague Tribunal, I think as a representative of our country. He was also a professor at the University of the Republic, but when we went to look for that information, since he donated his salary (in other words, he was honorary), his name did not come up anywhere. We then left for Spain as students, and when Mama was married to Andrés, the topic of Papa was not discussed in front of him. The few things that I know are due to Aparicio,[28] although when he came to visit the house, since Andrés was there, the topic of Papa was not broached. Forgive me for not being able to be more specific.[29]

On another occasion, María Rosa also wrote:

I have always regretted, and I still do, not having more information about my father's life, especially keeping in mind that he was the person who protected us the most; but family life then was not like now. For example, when Aparicio, who could have told us a lot of things, came to visit, we would greet him and then leave to do our homework or others things, and the adults stayed alone. You also have to understand that the presence of Andrés was not conducive to talking about Papa.[30]

She related that in the course of her father's political trips to the interior of the country during the campaigns of the National Party, he met a young man in the city of Rivera whose intelligence and convictions drew his attention. Since this youth came from a family with modest financial means, Puig hired him to work in his firm so that he would be able to continue studying law at the university in Montevideo. The young man, who aspired to be a lawyer and politician, was named Aparicio Méndez. He did all of his studies at the law school while working for Puig, and he became a lawyer and in a short time a partner of his mentor.

Méndez was barely twenty-five when Puig died suddenly of a heart attack on September 3, 1931. He went on to take over all his affairs and became the executor who guarded the three girls' inheritance while they were under age. Suddenly, after nine years of marriage, Paquita Madriguera had become a widow a few days before her thirty-first birthday. Alone in Montevideo with her three daughters, and in the middle of the family conflicts that usually arise when there is a considerable inheritance with no agreement as to how to manage it, she decided soon afterward to return to Spain with her daughters. The end of 1931 found her still in Uruguay, sharing the Christmas reunion in the country establishment with Mamá Paqui and members of the Puig family.

Christmas Day, 1931, at El Campito. Notice the mourning dress of Paquita (*standing, leaning on the right column*) and of Mamá Paqui, at her side. Also in black is María Rosa, who is barely four years old. Next to Mamá Paqui is Elvira Mathó Puig, owner of the house where Paquita met Arturo Puig and where the story of the severed phone line occurred.

Paquita Madriguera took her three daughters to Spain at some point in 1932, but only in 1935 did they learn that their father had died.

> *Sofía:* When Papa died, I remember that they made us go to give him a kiss, but they didn't tell us that he had died. For a long time they didn't tell us anything. I would ask about my dad, and nothing. . . . They would not tell me anything. Just when we got to Barcelona and Mama told us that she was going to marry Andrés, and I asked about my dad again, then she told me that he had died. And I cried a lot.

> *María Rosa:* You were the one who resisted the most when they told us that they were going to get married. I remember that you took a few steps backward and could not believe it.

> *Sofía:* They never told me that Dad had died! Then I thought, "And my dad?" until they finally told me and I cried a lot.

Chapter 8

Barcelona—Prelude, Marriage, and Fugue

Barcelona, 1933[1]

Joan Manén said,[2] "Segovia, Paquita Madriguera is waiting for me at her home. Do you want to come with me?"

"Paquita Madriguera is in Barcelona?"

"Yes, she became a widow in 1931 and has moved here with her three little daughters."

"Okay, I'll go with you."

Manén announced their visit to me by phone. I hid my uneasiness—I felt uncomfortable facing my traditional "opposite wave" again. They arrived. I coldly observed and analyzed the artist and the man. He was more human. His look did not shoot off those giant lightning bolts that tried to explode when they deigned to look at me. His thicker voice slowly uttered the words, carefully measuring them. He retained his epicurean hands intact. The sideburns had been removed from his face. The cravat was now a discreet velvet ribbon. The vest was the same as before, with the exception that the black buttons had been replaced by engraved silver ones. His hair was less abundant, I don't know if it was because he had lost it or because he had given locks to each of his female admirers. "It has been many years since we last saw each other, right?" he told me. "Along the way, I calculated the years; eleven, because the last year we met was in 1921, in Buenos Aires."

"But you saw me in Buenos Aires?" I asked.

"Naturally! In the hallway of Teatro Odeón, don't you remember? You were with your mother."

It was interesting to see the serene and friendly transformation that fame had brought out in him, and which pleasantly surprised me. He had forced himself to acquire profound knowledge in philosophy, literature, and all the arts, unlike musicians in general. His company resulted in being beautiful, and that affectionate, paternal air unveiled a caring Segovia who I did not have even the slightest idea existed.

He soon awakened my friendship toward him, which, aided by growing admiration, turned into deep affection. Manén, Segovia, and I went to eat at the Hotel del Sol, and we talked till dawn. The next morning Segovia asked to come and practice at my home because the silence there, according to him, made it more suitable than the Hotel Ritz, where he was staying. I set him up in a room and began to leave, to give him freedom, when he called me, pleading that I stay. He took out his guitar from its soft case, with economical gestures that seemed to me like the ritual of a priest toward his deity. He tuned it very softly, and out of it came the Andante of the Sonata in C Major by Mozart. A heavy curtain opened in my mind, and I went back to when I was fifteen. Granados Hall, a bittersweet evocation, admiration, antipathy.

"Oh, Segovia! What an impression I feel when I hear that Andante!"

"I have not played it for many years, but you told me at Granados Hall when you were almost a young lady, 'What impressed me the most was your Mozart, Segovia.' That is why I played it now."

This is the story Paquita Madriguera told about her reunion with Segovia in 1933, the prelude to an almost immediate romance. In fact, it had been twelve years, not eleven (as stated in a short fragment of this passage presented in the last chapter), since that brief encounter in the hallway of a Buenos Aires theater. And recall that Paquita had rejected the offer of her husband, Arturo Puig, to invite Segovia to their house for dinner when the guitarist was in Montevideo in 1928. For this reason, Segovia probably never found out that Paquita was there in a box seat at the Teatro Solís. In the five years that had passed since Paquita last heard him play, the boundaries of Segovia's career had widened immensely. In 1929 he did a second tour of the United States and made recordings in London. At the end of the year he gave concerts in Japan and China and then returned to Geneva by land, crossing the Soviet

Union aboard the famous Trans-Siberian Railway. As Segovia tells Ponce in a letter dated in December of that year, the trip had taken eighteen days, fourteen of which were spent without leaving one of the sleepers of the train, "traveling through the Bolsheviks."[3] It does not seem likely that Segovia would have performed in the Soviet Union on that occasion. He had already done two tours through those lands in 1926 and 1927, and he would do a third one in 1936, accompanied by Paquita. Segovia toured year after year in different parts of the world, and his prestige would also spread via his increasing number of recordings. However, some of the letters he wrote to Manuel Ponce give us an idea of his money problems, created by the new regulations that several European countries had adopted in the financial crisis they were experiencing at the time. On February 12, 1932, from Madrid, he told his friend that he (Segovia) had to leave the proceeds of his concerts in Italy in a bank there because of the new laws in that country. At that same time Germany, Spain, Austria, and other countries didn't allow the exportation of money. He said to Ponce that the result was disastrous, adding that he would have to take his entire family with him, so that they could eat the proceeds of his concerts in each country, traveling on a big truck "like the gypsies."[4]

Although he never had to put this plan into effect, Segovia's family life went on in Geneva, where he lived with his wife, Adelaida, and their two sons, Andresito and Leonardo. But that was not without problems, as he told Ponce in his next letter from Geneva, on March 5 of that year. He had arrived in that city and had to stay away from his home because Adelaida's "reverend mother" filled the small apartment with her hatred. Segovia said that he couldn't even breathe the air at the house and finished the first paragraph of his letter telling his friend that Adelaida preferred that he leave home over not having her mother with them. So, given her stubbornness, he would have to make a painful, yet unavoidable, decision.[5]

In the next line, he asked Ponce, who was in Paris, to look for a hotel for him in the French capital—and also a garage, because he planned to go by car. Financial matters were still a concern, and Segovia asked his friend to get a more acceptable price from the Villa Majestic or the Hotel Balzac, adding that if the Ponces could not get a lower rate they should look for another hotel.[6]

Segovia's worry about his situation is revealed in the same paragraph, when he changed his mind about the hotel and told Ponce to check another one instead of going to the Balzac. He suggested that his friend go to the Hotel des Champs-Elysées, which was situated across the same street, and make them the same proposition, keeping in mind that it was a hotel of a lower rank and for that reason the price should normally be lower, and even more at that time because of the economic crisis.[7]

At the end of June 1932, he wrote to Ponce that he was discussing, by cablegram, his tour of Java, and that things were going slowly. Segovia was anxiously awaiting a reply and he didn't dare leave, for fear that it might be misplaced. He didn't want to put the completion of the project at risk, because if it was confirmed he would have twenty concerts from which he would earn three hundred dollars each, with paid trips, adding, in his gracious Spanish way, that the money would come at just the right time.[8]

His wishes were not fulfilled, and in January 1933 Segovia was still awaiting the longed-for tour of Java. Because it seemed as though a series of performances in Indonesia was going to be confirmed for May of that year, he was able to proceed with a projected tour of Mexico and Cuba. He left at the end of January, accompanied by Manuel Ponce, who was going back to his homeland. Segovia returned to Europe in April, and on May 15 he wrote from Geneva to his friend, who had remained in Mexico, telling him that he had resolved the big conflict regarding his "reverend mother-in-law." He had been in Cuba, where part of Adelaida's family lived, and—as all of them liked him very much—he was able to confirm that his mother-in-law had been defaming him. So he wrote to Adelaida urging her to get her mother out of their life. When Segovia arrived home, he was happy to find "the cage without the parrot." For that reason, he changed his previous plans to live in Paris and notified Clema that she should sell her furniture instead of putting it in the hotel room Segovia had planned to rent.[9]

Segovia's optimism did not last long. Just two weeks later he wrote again, but from a different perspective. This letter was directed to Clema in Paris, and Segovia told her that he had changed his mind and was not going to take an apartment in that city, and he would not need the use of her furniture while she was away from France. He told Clema that his relationship with Adelaida was not going well at all and, despite her mother having left the house, everything was as difficult as before. He accused his wife of being "dry and nervous" and said that their life was a permanent hell. He assured Clema that he was writing with perfect calmness and was judging his and Adelaida's situation accurately, and that his new resolution was based on serious grounds. He said that he would like to live in Paris for an extended period and share his home in Geneva with his wife as little as possible, without getting a legal separation—to circumvent a scandal and for the children's sake. He also told Clema that in case he didn't go to Java, Adelaida would go to Lloret del Mar[10] and he would either stay in Geneva or go to Paris.[11]

Apparently the trip to Java never materialized. When Segovia wrote to Ponce again in December 1933, he began by telling his friend that he had returned to Geneva two days before, after an absence of a whole month, and that he had run to the Societé de Banque Suisse to look for his letter.[12]

Segovia remained in Geneva and was cautious, receiving his private correspondence away from home. The only mention of Adelaida is at the end of the letter, following the signature, telling Ponce that she will write to Clema to ask about her health. There are some references to important facts about the history of the guitar in this letter, and a remark that is particularly important to the development of this chronicle. Among the first, he comments about already playing *Variazioni (attraverso i secoli)* (Variations Across the Centuries), the first work that Mario Castelnuovo-Tedesco composed for the guitar at Segovia's request. He says that he is also practicing the first movement of a piece paying homage to Boccherini, suggested by Segovia when he ran into Castelnuovo-Tedesco at Toscanini's home in May.[13] The reference that has to do with this story is the comment that he had recently been with Joan Manén in Barcelona. It is also known that he was there with Paquita Madriguera, a determining event in their future that was not mentioned in the letter. A few months would pass before Ponce would receive Paquita Madriguera and Andrés Segovia together in Mexico. For now the focus is back on Paquita and her daughters.

When Paquita arrived in Barcelona in 1932, she settled with her three girls in the family home on Casanova Street. María Rosa, the youngest, was about to turn five. She recalls that time in her life:

> I have a vague idea of the [Barcelona] house on Casanova Street. I do remember that we had two floors, one that faced the back, with a fairly large garden with a fountain and flowerbeds. That is where Yayita, our great-grandmother, who had long hair that fell below her waist, sat in the sun one day to dry her hair after washing it. She dozed off, and Pitusa decided that we could cut some of it off without her knowing it. That is what we did, but since we were little it did not go well. I don't remember how long our punishment lasted. To the side of the garden there was a stairway to go up

to the second floor and a sort of enclosed winter garden. There was a piano and then a large dining room and the bedrooms and bathrooms. I remember our bedroom well. It was huge, and the three of us slept together.[14]

Sofía, who was not quite seven at that time, told us that she had always loved to sing, but that she did it quite badly. On the other hand, she said her sisters both had a good ear for music:

> My sisters sang well. Pitusa . . . and María Rosa sang very well, but not me. When we first came to Spain, in 1932, everyone had parties for us, the three Uruguayan sisters who had just arrived. They would tell us, "Sing something!" My sisters did not want to, but I would start singing loudly and happily. They would all laugh because I was a bad singer! I laughed also.[15]

This topic came up in another interview with both Sofía and María Rosa, and the dialogue allowed them to remember more details:

> *María Rosa:* When company came when we lived on Casanova Street, they would say, "Girls, come and sing!" Because that's the way it was. Then we, Pitusa and I, said, "No, no!" and Sofía said, "Me, me!" And they would say "No, not you. No!" [*Laughter*]
>
> *Sofía:* They wouldn't let me!
>
> *María Rosa:* Our aunts and Mamá Paqui would say "No, not you!"
>
> *Sofía:* They wouldn't let me and they would pull me back.
>
> *María Rosa:* "In the home of a blacksmith you find a wooden knife," the visitors would say.[16]
>
> *Sofía:* There was some sort of railing, and I would come out to some type of stage and sing, but terribly; it was obviously bad, and Mama would say, "My child, please! [*Laughter*] Let your sisters do it." And they did not want to. And I would say, "Me, it's my turn. I'll do it, I will," not the least bit shy.

The remainder of the dialogue also brought out other artistic activities and immediately led to their remembering other events that took place a few years later—more difficult years and events that had quite a different tone:

María Rosa: They could have said: "No, but Sofía, show us your drawings," because she drew and painted beautifully.

Sofía: I won a first prize in Barcelona. The first children's award of Barcelona.

María Rosa: If you could see how well she painted. They could have told her, using a bit of psychology, "No, we are going to let the girls sing," which we did not want to do, "but let her show us her drawings."

Sofía: I had a horrible disaster, because I was already painting here in Montevideo. When we went to Barcelona, I did little drawings [of] ranches. They were all ranches and trees and they got me a teacher because I was a very good student.

María Rosa: Very good!

Sofía: [My teacher] liked them because the ranches I sketched were the ones from Montevideo—there was a lot of ambience and everyone loved them. I liked the flowers also. One day I went to class and [learned that] they had murdered him. The Requetés, the UGT[17]—who knows! They had murdered him. I remember that I started to cry and cry there. It was horrible and I never wanted to paint again. Our life was quite fragmented because we kept moving from one place to another.

These "comings and goings" to which Sofía alludes were marked—in all the stories about this period of their lives—by numerous changes of schools and countries of residence. In a space of five years spent outside of Montevideo, the three girls lived in Barcelona, then moved to Geneva, then back to Barcelona, Genoa, New York (at the home of their uncle, Enric), and in a New Jersey school. Each change of schools likewise meant a change of language. In Barcelona, they were pupils in a Catholic boarding school where they spoke Catalan;[18] then, in a school in Geneva, they spoke French; and finally, in the United States, they of course had to speak English. In each of the schools at which they arrived, they had many problems adapting:

I have a vague memory of when we first arrived in Barcelona, after Papa died; they placed us initially (for a short time) in a German school where there was no boarding, and almost immediately we were pupils at a nuns' school. We were in boarding school for a long time and we did not even leave during vacations. I think we finished our courses because I remember the end-of-the-year parties.[19]

María Rosa and Sofía shared memories of themselves and their sister in several interviews done between October 2005 and December 2007:

María Rosa: When we arrived in Barcelona, they put us in a boarding school with nuns in Montserrat. We felt totally out of place there, where they spoke Catalan. The other girls stayed away from us. We could not get used to the food, especially that bread soup.

> The nuns in Barcelona made us bathe with a T-shirt on because it was a sin to touch the body. Once, I was ill and had a fever, and the doctor had asked that they give me a bath to lower it. When the doctor came in where they were bathing me and saw that they had me with the T-shirt on, he was furious. He stood me up in the tub and took my T-shirt off. The nuns made the sign of the cross. . . .

> I remember that I cried so much at school, do you remember? Pitusa would tell me at night, "Don't cry! Don't cry!" Then she would feel bad and tell me, "OK, come and lie down with me," and that consoled me; but I cried so much that I don't think I have cried since. Not even over the worst tragedies have I ever cried. It's not that I don't feel or suffer, it's just that I don't get the urge to cry. My tears dried up when I was a child. . . . Also, the school in Barcelona was very old. It was sort of a convent. There were some galleries and an open courtyard, and the rooms faced the galleries. It was so cold! You would get such bad chilblains in the winter. Do you remember? Everyone would leave at Christmas and New Year's.

Sofía: The three of us stayed behind.

María Rosa: And Margarita Griffin, who was from the United States and older than us. In the summer, it was the same thing.

Sofía: The three of us were left behind alone.

María Rosa: With Margarita Griffin, another unfortunate girl like us. I remember a punishment. One summer it was so hot that the flies were dropping and we had gone to walk through the woods. There was a little creek, and she jumped in the water. There were rocks to cross [on], but she made believe she was slipping and jumped in the water, and then nobody could get her out of the water. Do you remember? The nuns were upset. The nuns would get upset over everything. They were bitter. That really affected me a lot, so much that I was too much the caretaker of the family. It affected me a lot, a lot, a lot.

The return to Barcelona and her roots quite probably meant, for Paquita Madriguera, that she was dreaming of a possible return to her artistic life, which had been interrupted when she settled in Montevideo. A few months after her arrival, on February 3, 1933, the pianist performed in the Palau de la Música. The event merited several announcements in the newspapers in the days prior to the concert. The following note appeared on January 29 in *La Vanguardia*:

Juan Manén, the eminent violinist and great composer, lends his prestige to the concert that pianist Paquita Madriguera will give at the Palau de la Música Catalana, on Friday, February 3, thus showing his admiration and support. Maestro Manén will not only appear in his specialty as a violinist performing with Paquita Madriguera his brilliant Suite for Violin, Piano, and Orchestra, but also as conductor of the orchestra in Saint-Saëns's Piano Concerto No. 2.[20]

The same Barcelona newspaper published a review two days after the concert:

Following an absence of some years, filled with triumphs before the most demanding foreign audiences for the graceful pianist, Paquita Madriguera reappeared the night before last at the Palau, for the Sociedad Filarmónica de Barcelona. Once again it was a success for Paquita Madriguera, whose fully matured art revealed a sensitive pianist, careful, expressive, with a delicate, many-hued technique that showed forcefulness when it was necessary. Her involvement in the Piano Concerto No. 1 in E-flat Major by Liszt; in the Suite No. 1 (for violin, piano and orchestra) by Manén; and in the Piano Concerto No. 2 by Saint-Saëns displayed at the same time an admirable mastery and how much she has studied the works. Presented with flowers and ovations, Paquita Madriguera was obliged to take repeated bows.[21]

Paquita's other performance during this period, according to the information gathered until now, was on April 7, 1934 (shortly before going back to Latin America with Segovia). On this occasion she performed—also at the Palau—as a soloist with the Pablo Casals Orchestra, directed by the famous Catalonian cellist, who had founded it in 1919. *La Vanguardia* again published a review the next day under the headline "Paquita Madriguera and the Casals Orchestra":

> The acceptance by Barcelona's musical public of Paquita Madriguera, the pianist who had already shown astonishing examples of her art at the age of three and who today remains mostly secluded in her home, has not decreased with the passage of time—in numbers or intensity. A good example was the warm welcome that the gentle artist received last night at the Palau. . . . Paquita Madriguera joined the Pablo Casals Orchestra in the performance of Grieg's Concerto in A Minor, a work of extraordinary emotional force, unjustly excluded from programs. . . . Paquita Madriguera, with art, intelligence, and sensitivity, overcame all the pitfalls and was received very warmly.[22]

Probably one of the main reasons Paquita sent her three daughters to boarding schools was to give her time to practice and to reestablish her social and artistic contacts. In Montevideo her daughters were in the care of nannies, which was probably economically impossible while they were living in Barcelona, since she stayed in her parents' home and had no personal income. We know that Paquita received money from Montevideo from the three girls' inheritance, for which she had to account in detail to Aparicio Méndez, the executor of Arturo Puig's will and estate. Perhaps it was easier to document the dispersal of the funds if all the expenses could be charged to the same place—the school, which included education, room, and board. This is only speculation, but the fact is that the three girls spent most of those five years in various boarding schools, and now, as grandmothers and "too much caretaker[s] of [their] own families," they feel that they suffered devastating abandonment during those years. In one of their many interviews, María Rosa Puig stated, "I reached the conclusion long ago that Andrés's only real loves were music and the guitar. Everyone else remained in second place; but isn't that the way it is with all great artists?"

It would not be surprising if she also asked herself that question more than once regarding her mother, who was a great artist as well. The second period of that boarding-school life of the Puig Madriguera sisters was in 1934 in Geneva. They do not have a categorical answer, even today, as to why they were taken to a boarding school in that city, away from the family and where the spoken language was French. They were given some vague explanation relating to Sofía's health problems, but they are not convinced of its veracity. They remember that before moving into the school, they stayed briefly at the home of a friend of their mother's, but they do not recall that Paquita moved to live in that Swiss city. It could be surmised that it was because the romantic relationship between Paquita and Segovia had already begun, he was living alone in Geneva, and they had started traveling together during that year. The author spoke about this with the two Puig sisters and Sofía's daughter, Roxana Delgado, regarding that topic:

> *María Rosa:* The school in Geneva was very distinguished. But very distinguished! They were so distinguished that we could not touch the velour curtains in order to close them. There was an enormous window that faced the lake, across from the bed, and there were some huge blue corduroy curtains with tassels and swags. In the early hours of the morning, the light came through, and then Pitusa would get up, take the ties off, and close the curtains; and every day they would confront us, because we were not to touch the curtains.

> *Sofía:* In the school in Geneva we felt isolated. They all spoke French, and we arrived with the customs of the nuns' school in Barcelona. We spent our time making lace with bobbins. One day the three of us decided to escape. So, early in the morning we went out and down the mountain until we got to Geneva. We had to cross the railroad tracks. Years later, Andrés told us that little Leonardo [Segovia's second son] died in an accident on a railroad track like that one in Geneva.[23]

María Rosa: Leonardo had gone on an excursion with his school; it was a humid and rainy day. He had a long stick that he leaned on to walk, and the stick was wet. When he went to cross the tracks, he wanted to be funny and touched the overhead [electrical] cable with the stick, and he was electrocuted and died. . . .

Sofía: We escaped from there because Pitusa was very ill and was uncomfortable there. When we escaped from the school, I remembered by chance how we got there. So, we went down the mountain, and when we got to Geneva, I started to think, "It was through that street, it was through this other one." We were so nervous! Until finally we found the house—I remember the tree, which is what I recalled well, the house where that friend of mom's lived. And there they welcomed us in; and after that I do not remember. It was so hard to go down that mountain, because in those mountains is where Leonardo was electrocuted.

Alfredo Escande: But that was later when you three had already returned to Montevideo?

Sofía: Yes, but there were electric rails and you had to be careful going down. Well, we were, and we got to Geneva and found the house. And, well, then, I do not know if we stayed a day or two.

María Rosa: No, no, but they sent us back. [*To Sofía*] Go back!

Sofía: We hopped around every year. Good grief! We were always in boarding schools. There were not many boarders. I think we were the only ones. . . . They stole everything we had, the jewelry—the girls, the Swiss classmates. We had left Spain with three pillows with the things to make lace with bobbins, because the nuns forced us. We embroidered our panties, everything. We were smart because I was probably seven, eight, nine years old—not ten or fifteen—but we embroidered, we did everything. But there in Switzerland they stole everything from us, the girls.

María Rosa: Luckily. [*Laughter*]

Sofía: Until one night we decided to flee the school.

As the conversation progressed, their memories about the life in the Swiss school became more detailed, but the sisters were unable to reach a conclusion about the real reasons that motivated their move to Geneva. They ventured a hypothesis:

Left to right: Pitusa, María Rosa, and Sofía in 1935, after returning to Barcelona.

> *Escande:* Now, when you were in Geneva, Paquita was already with Andrés. Is that why you went to Geneva? Because he had a home in Geneva?
>
> *Sofía:* Huh?
>
> *María Rosa:* What? The three of us were alone.
>
> *Escande:* Yes, for sure, but why did you go to Geneva?
>
> *María Rosa:* Ah, because Sofía was very weak.
>
> *Sofía:* Because I was very skinny and they always wanted me to gain weight, and I was always skinny, skinny, skinny.
>
> *Escande:* Perhaps thinking that the fresh air in the mountains would do you well.
>
> *Sofía:* First, I was in a Swiss hospital two or three days. They did all kinds of things to see what was wrong, and I did not have anything wrong.
>
> *Escande:* Maybe you were homesick for Montevideo.
>
> *María Rosa:* More in the mountains than in Montserrat? Impossible. They would take us down to the lake, backwards. In other words, it was all nonsense! I don't know why they sent us there.
>
> *Escande:* My guess was that since Segovia lived in Geneva.
>
> *María Rosa:* At that time?
>
> *Escande:* Of course.
>
> *Sofía:* Andrés? Not with us, he didn't. We were at the boarding school.
>
> *María Rosa:* On Sundays, a couple, friends of Mama's, would come and take us out to walk for a while.
>
> *Escande:* But where was Paquita?

María Rosa: Ah, who knows!

Sofía: I don't know. She was probably in Spain giving concerts, who knows.

Roxana: I ask them that question also, because it makes sense; but they don't know.

María Rosa: I don't know. When we went to Andrés's funeral, do you remember? A lady came to greet us and said, "Ah, I used to take you out for walks in Geneva!"

Escande: And why did that person go to Andrés's funeral?

María Rosa: Because she was a friend.

Escande: Of Andrés's?

María Rosa: Of course.

Escande: And why did she take you out for walks when you were in Geneva? What's the link?

Paquita Madriguera's daughters did not have an answer for these last few questions, but it must be taken into account that they could not include Segovia among the hypotheses that would explain their move to Geneva simply because they did not know of his existence until almost a year later, away from Switzerland. It was in October 1935—while they were back in Barcelona—that Paquita introduced them to the man who was already her life partner, announcing at the same time that they were going to get married in the near future.

María Rosa: What I do remember—but I am seeing it—is when Mama told us she was going to marry Andrés, and that was on Casanova Street.

Escande: At her family's house.

María Rosa: But just the three of us were there, Pitusa, Sofía, and I, and them. . . . Andrés was sitting there in a sort of entrance hall where there were a sofa and some armchairs. And then Mama told us, "Ah, girls, I want to tell you that Andrés and I are going to get married." And Sofía started moving back, back, back— that I cannot forget. Pitusa was undaunted. And I, who probably did not understand a thing, just stayed still, and Andrés grabbed me and sat me on his lap. I agreed to sit on his lap. But I looked, like this, and Pitusa was standing still, and Sofía kept moving back. Sofía didn't like it at all.

Escande: Had you had any contact with him before that?

Sofía: No.

María Rosa: No. This was the first time. I remember he sat me on his lap and told me, ah, I don't know what.

Paquita and Segovia in 1934.

When this took place, probably during the 1935 boreal summer, the girls were already back in Barcelona, at the home of Paquita's parents, and ready to go back as boarding students to the school in Montserrat—the one of lace with bobbins and bread soup. From there they were to leave abruptly a year later, when the Spanish Civil War broke out. What is known about Paquita and Segovia during that period, from the beginning of their relationship at the end of 1933 until their marriage in October of 1935? One of the few sources of information comes from carefully reading the few, but revealing, letters the guitarist sent to Ponce during that time. It can be affirmed that Paquita traveled with Andrés Segovia to North and South America in June of 1934, and that they spent some time at Ponce's home and then went to Lima, Santiago de Chile, Buenos Aires, and—at least the guitarist—also to Montevideo. The letter, dated July 22 of that year and stamped in the Peruvian capital, alludes to the first part of this trip and ends by sending Clemita a brotherly hug "from both of us" and another one for Ponce from Segovia.[24]

If there is any doubt regarding the meaning Segovia assigned to "both of us," his next letter, dated February 1935, shows with certainty that he alluded to the recently formed couple. After complaining about Ponce's lack of response to several letters he had written to him, Don Andrés says that he and Paquita had sent him numerous postcards and long letters along the trip and once they arrived in Europe.[25]

One detail that emerges with crystal clarity at the very beginning of this letter is that Andrés Segovia and Paquita Madriguera traveled from Mexico City to Lima in what appears to have been the guitarist's first airplane trip. According to the first paragraph written on July 22, 1934, at the Gran Hotel Bolívar in Lima, the flight had been wonderful for Segovia and Paquita. He said that its most beautiful part was from Mexico to Panama, and that they could observe very beautiful landscapes, which he described; but they were most impressed with the height (they had climbed up to 13,000 feet), and from that perspective everything seemed surprisingly small. The people, he said, looked like worms.[26]

Following the performances in Lima and Santiago de Chile, Andrés and Paquita traveled to Buenos Aires, and from there they boarded a ship headed to Europe. In the Río de la Plata area, Segovia gave two concerts in Montevideo, this time at the Teatro 18 de Julio.[27] There is no evidence that Paquita traveled with Segovia to the Uruguayan capital, and most likely she did not because her husband's death was too recent (as was the beginning of her relationship with Segovia) for her to accompany him in the city where Arturo Puig's entire family lived. At the same time, it is difficult to imagine that Paquita did not have matters to resolve in Montevideo, since she was owner of several properties there. She could well have taken advantage of the trip to settle more than one such problem. An article appeared in *El País* announcing the presence of the guitarist, but it made no mention of any companion other than the manager in charge of organizing his concerts. The article, with a title in large type running the entire width of page 7 of the August 22 edition, read: "ANDRÉS SEGOVIA REAPPEARS THIS EVENING":

> The eminent Spanish guitarist will give a concert today at the 18th [de Julio Theater]. Anxious to again travel to Montevideo, a city that has been so generous in applause and from which he has been absent for many years, the great Spanish guitarist Andrés Segovia arrived yesterday in our capital, accompanied by Mr. Quesada, one of the members of the "Daniel Society of Concerts," through whom he will be presented to our audience from the stage of 18 de Julio this evening. Segovia excused himself from the interviews and the concert preparations for a few hours to take a tour of Montevideo, whose progress he wanted to check "de visu" [firsthand].
>
> With the positive impression expressed afterward to the representatives of the press, Segovia had to reappear before the public; and to this initial inducement for his premature arrival one must undoubtedly add that of the applause with which our public praises him, as they have not forgotten this greatest of guitarists, who revived interest in the instrument and imparted excellence to concerts featuring it. This evening's concert at the 18 de Julio, almost sold out as of yesterday, has a remarkable program of classical and modern composers.

The program Segovia presented in his first concert of 1934 in Montevideo included works by Sor, Moreno Torroba (*Piezas Características*), Granados, Bach, Haydn, and Albéniz, in addition to the city's premiere of the *Sonatina Meridional* by Ponce. He also played two of the "a la antigua" works composed by his Mexican friend, but which Segovia attributed to Alessandro Scarlatti.[28]

A little more than two weeks later, on Friday, September 7, Andrés Segovia played again in the same Teatro 18 de Julio. This new performance by the guitarist again received wide press coverage during the days prior to the concert and was once more played to a full house.[29] Again, there is no record

Segovia in Montevideo, 1934. Photo taken at his hotel by Juan Caruso
for *El Día* and published in *El País* in 2008.

that Paquita had traveled with him during that second crossing from Buenos
Aires. Perhaps she awaited him in the Argentinean capital, from where they
sailed for Spain in the second week of September, working on their respective
personal situations.

The guitarist's letter to Ponce from New York in February 1935 "has three
pieces of news in particular," as Segovia expressed it. The first of them has
nothing to do with this topic; the second one was that Segovia had left his
house in Geneva and settled in Barcelona; and the third piece of news concerned his divorce from Adelaida and his upcoming marriage. He and Paquita
were waiting for some documents they needed to marry, which were held

up at the Ministry of State, and they
expected to have no more obstacles and
delays once they had returned the next
time to Spain. Segovia asked Ponce to
clarify the issue of their impending marriage for Clema, told him that they were
leaving for Europe on March 15 on the
Olympic and that, while in New York,
they were living in the apartment that
Paquita's brother had given them.[30]

Enric Madriguera, the brother to
whom Segovia is referring, had been living for a few years in New York, where
he had established permanent residence.
He too was considered a child prodigy and had studied violin with Joan
Manén. Enric had stopped playing in

Enric Madriguera.

public following an accident that immobilized a finger of his left hand, and
in 1929 he started his own Latin-pop orchestra to play for parties and dances.
At the time, it rivaled the Xavier Cugat and Siboney Orchestras in prestige,
and the three vied for work in the finest hotels. Enric composed some pieces
in that style, and they became hits in the 1930s and 1940s in New York as well
as Havana, his main centers of activity.

Around that time in February 1935, when Segovia wrote to Ponce from
Enric Madriguera's New York apartment, it is also possible to see some references in Paquita's book, *Visto y oído*:

New York, 1935

My business cards already read Madriguera de Segovia. When we arrived
there, Mischa called me immediately inviting us to eat at his home.[31] He
lived in a large and elegantly furnished apartment, and from its high windows one could observe an endless view of shining lights that gave the
impression of belonging to a new universe, and to contemplate it one had
to lower the head rather than raise it.... Arturo Toscanini's wife invited
Andrés and me to her box to hear a concert directed by her husband in
Carnegie Hall. Jascha Heifetz was the soloist in the beautiful Brahms Violin
Concerto.[32] It is unnecessary to say what this performance was like. I have

no adjectives to describe it. They have been so frequently used for things of minor value that when you reach out to use them, they seem cheap.[33]

A few months earlier, in November 1934, Paquita had been in Barcelona when Mischa Elman performed at the Palau de la Música. As she narrates in *Visto y oído*, she was unable to attend the concert because she was expecting a call from Segovia, who was in London. She was able to share an after-concert dinner in honor of Elman, whom Paquita was going just then to meet personally. During dinner they spoke of Heifetz specifically. And it is interesting to learn about Paquita's aesthetic and musical tastes. It is Mischa Elman who begins asking:

"Have you heard Heifetz?"
"Yes."
"Do you like how he plays?"
"Very much."
"Don't you find him cold?"
"Absolutely not."
"How strange! Almost all the ladies I know think he is, and, keeping in mind that you are Spanish, I was more certain of your agreement with them."
"I do not like artists who overpower."
He laughed heartily and continued, "And what are the reasons that you admire Heifetz so much?"
"Because Heifetz has the qualities that I would want for my dearest and favorite friend—a golden sound, a marvelous technique that is does not call attention to itself, and serious interpretations worthy of admiration."
"Do you know what surprises me about you? The finality of your judgments."
"They are my own—I don't borrow them from others."
He laughed again and continued, "Since we have Heifetz on the table, let's continue with him. What do you think of him as a man? The overriding criterion is that he has too much pride."
"I also think that is his fame, but personally, for me, I assure you he is very nice."
"Hallelujah for Heifetz!" he shouted. "For you, perfection itself!"

"I would be holding back a lot if I said so. I limit myself to answering the topics you bring up. I don't know what dark nooks Jascha's conscience contains, and I wish to continue not knowing them."[34]

Paquita and Segovia would have encounters with Heifetz in the future, but, now it's back to the events linked to those first months of the newly formed couple. A good summary of what took place during 1935 is found in a long letter that Segovia wrote to Ponce from Barcelona, probably at the end of October of that year.[35] Before extracting some phrases of interest in the reconstruction of this story, it is worth knowing about Segovia's recurring economic difficulties as he took inventory of his obligations and the management of his household expenses. In New York, Segovia was "unpleasantly surprised" because Coppicus had scheduled such a small number of concerts for him.[36] He had returned to Europe with no more than two thousand dollars and was "mortally scared" because he would have financial difficulties for the first time in many years. And then he gave Ponce a detailed account of his monthly expenses: two thousand pesetas for Adelaida and the boys; five hundred to his mother and his aunt Gertrudis;[37] and, in addition, all that was needed for his living expenses and travel. He emphasized that Paquita was not a financial burden for him (she received an income from Montevideo) and that she managed their home "with the wisdom and frugality of an ant." Segovia didn't want to hide his mood: he said he was "overwhelmingly pessimistic" and that his life had changed greatly. He felt that his times of glory belonged to the past and that—despite being forty—he didn't know how to resolve the difficulties that the near future held in store for him.[38]

The second piece of news that Segovia related to Ponce in this letter referred to the situation of his previous family. He told his friend about the death of his former mother-in-law and informed him that Adelaida and their two sons had also left Geneva to live in Spain. What draws one's attention is that Segovia's sons were also in a boarding school. He told Ponce that he had gone to spend a week with them and that they were doing fine, though experiencing difficulties in their studies while adapting to the Spanish language—Andresito had passed the exams for the first and second year at the same time, and he wrote about Leonardo's intelligence and friendly character. The director of the boarding school had told Segovia that the children were suffering because their mother could not control her nerves, and that she was alienating their affection. They even looked for excuses to avoid spending Sundays with her. Segovia also told Ponce that several times he urged the boys, almost crying, to love their mother and be patient because of her illness.

After mentioning some important facts about his musical career (the premiere in Paris on June 4, 1935, of his transcription of the Chaconne by Bach as well as the Sonata by Castelnuovo-Tedesco, favorable reviews received, recordings of works by Ponce, and plans to edit various materials), Segovia wrote to his Mexican friend regarding his new family life in Barcelona, in an apartment situated at 530 Muntaner Street. He told him that their home was modest, and that they had furnished it with some things he had kept from his house in Geneva and as well as other contributions from Paquita. They were paying two hundred pesetas monthly for the apartment, and the other living expenses cost them eight hundred. As Segovia had to sell his car (losing money, as he told Ponce), they normally used the trolley and sometimes the taxi, which was quite inexpensive, for going to downtown Barcelona. And then he added that from time to time he and Paquita reminisced about being in Mexico, around their table with the Ponces "while Piedad serves us the tasty fruit that delighted us."[39] He said that in those moments and inspired by the memories, Paquita—who had not forgotten how to play—sat at the piano and performed Ponce's Mexican prelude.

Finally the news came out about the wedding. According to the documentation provided by Paquita's daughters, the ceremony took place at the Barcelona Municipal Court Number 6 on October 26, 1935. The certificate says that Andrés Segovia Torres (born in Linares and forty-two years old, divorced, son of Bonifacio and Rosa) and Francisca de A. Madriguera Rodón (born in Igualada, thirty-five years old, widow, daughter of Enrique and Francisca) appeared before the judge in a civil ceremony. Segovia continued his epistolary narrative, telling his friend that he and Paquita had gotten married, and that the ceremony was a very restrained and discreet event, to which they invited just a group of close friends and some of Paquita's relatives. Their life was sliding quietly along, calmly and peacefully; Paquita gave him care and attention and managed with the small income they had. He regretted that Adelaida was not cordial, calm, and sweet like Paquita, or that he did not find Paquita before he married Adelaida.[40]

Ponce's response to this bit of news was to send a work dedicated to the two artists as a wedding present. The composer transcribed and adapted the Prelude in E, a guitar solo that he had previously composed for Segovia, as a duet for guitar and harpsichord; it was completed on February 27, 1936.[41] In March of that year, having just returned from a tour of the United States, Segovia wrote to Ponce saying that the Prelude was the best wedding present that he and Paquita had received. "It is of service to the both us at the same time, and using it gives us indescribable pleasure."[42] And he added that they would make the effort of saving to buy a harpsichord if Ponce would send them the complete suite. The guitarist said that playing one of the composer's works would be sufficient reason for obtaining that instrument.

When Segovia and Paquita first settled in Barcelona, many things were taking place in Spain in the sociopolitical sphere as well as the cultural. They were times of intense creative and intellectual activity but also of upheaval that foretold the terrible events of 1936. In those days, it is probable that both musicians, less than a month after their wedding, attended a theatrical representation that caused great excitement in the Catalonian capital. The news appeared in a Barcelona newspaper under the headline "Lorca Triumphs with *Bodas de Sangre* [Blood Wedding] in Barcelona," and the subhead "The Public Demanded the Presence of the Author and the Actress Margarita Xirgú":[43]

November 24

It is not the premiere of *Bodas de Sangre* in Barcelona. The collaboration of García Lorca and Rivas Chériff, along with Margarita Xirgú's performance as "the mother," adds more to the quality of this presentation than to the work, which deserves the honors of a premiere.... The audience that filled the Principal repeatedly applauded the beauties of *Bodas de Sangre*, demanding the presence of the author over and over; at the end of the poem, the poet García Lorca and the actress Margarita Xirgú had to address the auditorium.

Could either of the two Catalonian artistic celebrities that were in the Teatro Principal of Barcelona on that autumn night of 1935—the pianist and the actress—ever imagine that a few years later they would both meet in Montevideo, that one day they would share a car to cross the Andes, and that each, in her own time, would pass the last years of her life in Montevideo, the city with the magical name?

In the meantime, the great actress—who in December of the same year would also premiere García Lorca's *Doña Rosita la soltera* (Rosita the Spinster) in Barcelona—had just canceled a tour of Italy already scheduled by her and her company. They did so because that month, October 1935 (the same month Paquita and Segovia married), produced a very serious international incident that boded ill for the near future—Italy, by order of Mussolini, had invaded Abyssinia. This military and diplomatic event had another echo, although in a different tone, in Barcelona. Salvador de Madariaga,[44] who had been the Spanish ambassador in Paris and then, representing the Spanish government, joined a major international commission in Geneva, was urgently called to Madrid on special assignment. Paquita tells about Madariaga's layover in the Catalonian capital:

> My husband and I received a telegram: "On such-and-such a day I will leave for Madrid. I will be in Barcelona for ten hours. I beg you to reserve them for me, to spend time with you. Salvador." The police, aware of the message, showed up following the telegraph messenger. "Mr. Madariaga will be with you?" they asked.
>
> "Yes, sir."
>
> "Do you plan to meet him at the airport?"
>
> "Yes, sir."
>
> "Then you will have to allow us to bring you an official car to take you there because we will put into place a cordon that will not allow access to any vehicle, except those of the government."
>
> "That's fine. Thank you."
>
> "During the hours that he plans to stay in this city, will Mr. Madariaga stay at home with you?"
>
> "We think so."
>
> "In that case we request your permission to place police officers inside your home. There will also be police at the door and in the street. We have strict orders not to let anyone get close to bother him with questions, especially the snooping journalists that slip through all the cracks."
>
> "Do whatever you want; we will not be the ones complicating the life of our friend. We will go to the airport in an official car." . . .
>
> The plane arrived. Salvador peeked through the little door. He was greeted by the authorities, and we immediately got into the car to return home, which we found transformed into a fortress. The policemen at the door were driving the doorman crazy with the limitations imposed on

him; the ones inside had upset the maid. The telephone was tapped and answered by a representative of the authorities. Another one broke an antique flower pot during his search of the house.

We went in and Salvador collapsed into a chaise longue, covered with foxskins. Then we sat down to eat lunch, and after coffee he snuggled down in the same chaise longue as before and said to us, "I have an enormous desire to hear Bach's Italian Concerto, and I ask Paquita if she would be willing to satisfy my request by playing it for me."

I agreed. Later we talked about many topics. The conversation turned to music. Salvador was against Brahms, and Andrés and I against Salvador. The conversation didn't last long. . . .

Close to ten at night, we accompanied our friend to the express for Madrid, leaving him settled in his sleeper compartment. The train departed, taking our guest. Andrés and I remained motionless and pensive on the platform for a few seconds. Each passage by Madariaga through our life was like a shining meteor. We left the same way we came in, and the station looked darker to us than when we entered.[45]

In more than one of the interviews with the Puig Madriguera sisters, one could hear with amazement how Sofia—now in her eighties—still retained in her memory and recited with pleasure (and with some correction by María Rosa) a little poem that Madariaga had composed "on the fly" for them during one of his visits to Paquita and Andrés:

> Paquita had three daughters,
> Precious in their youth;
> Their beauty and their enchantment
> Apparent in the three.
> What is more, the birds say,
> Well informed perhaps,
> That wit and talent
> Are found in them as well.

Segovia had become friends with Salvador de Madariaga many years earlier, when they both lived in Geneva. Segovia's youngest child, Carlos Andrés, elaborated on this and provided information about the sources that had fostered his father's political thought and intellectual stance:

Madariaga, seven years older than my father, had arrived in Geneva in 1921 as a journalist, his profession in London since 1916. And in 1922 he had been named chief of the Disarmament Section of the League of Nations—the precursor of today's United Nations—based in Geneva. . . . My father, who during his youth in Spain and during his trips abroad had met and dealt with many artists and intellectuals, frequented more and more, during those years, the company of Madariaga, who would not only be a great and lifelong friend (with whom he maintained monthly correspondence) but also, in a certain way, his teacher. Lacking a rigorous academic education that, little by little, he would supplement with magnificent discernment and through personal study, my father allowed Madariaga to guide him in his readings, which during those years covered, as the books preserved in his Geneva library show, a broad range of fields—philosophy, history, natural sciences, and a long et cetera.[46]

At the beginning of 1936, Paquita Madriguera and Andrés Segovia were immersed in preparations for a new trip they needed to make in order to meet the guitarist's artistic commitments. The girls, who had spent the New Year's holiday with them, returned to the boarding school run by nuns on the evening of January 2. On Sunday, January 5, Paquita went to visit them in the morning; on Monday, the sixth, she took them to eat lunch at Mamá Paqui's home, as a farewell; and on January 8, at 3:00 P.M., both musicians took the train to Paris. They boarded the ship *Deutschland* in Cherbourg on January 10, bound for New York. Notably, such a crossing took only half the time it had when the young pianist had made the trip twenty years earlier—they arrived at their destination in just ten days.

Paquita's meticulously kept diary allows us to trace the flurry of activity in which the Segovia Madrigueras were involved—plays, dinners with different people (among them, several with Heifetz at his home stand out), and Paquita's meetings with friends from previous visits to the city. All alternate with Segovia's concerts. On January 22 he played at New York's Town Hall and on January 28 in Rochester, New York.[47] On February 1 he had a concert in Middlebury, Connecticut, and on February 3, one in Brooklyn. Next, the couple went to Washington, where Segovia played a concert on February 4. On February 6 he played in Toronto, while Paquita remained in New York, and he again played Town Hall on February 8 before they left for California on February 9 by train.

Crossing the United States took three days this time. After several concerts by the guitarist in Los Angeles and San Francisco, they attended one by Heifetz in the Bay City on February 28, had dinner with him afterward, and left the next evening for Chicago, a two-and-a-half-day trip, where they stayed for several days. Segovia's concert was on March 8, and the next day they left for New York. At noon on March 14, 1936, Paquita and Don Andrés boarded the *Île de France*, which six days later landed them in the French port of Le Havre. Traveling by train, they stopped in Paris and Perpignan before arriving in Barcelona on the evening of March 22. That night, Segovia wrote to Ponce thanking him for the wedding present.

SEÑOR AND SEÑORA ANDRES S

Segovia and Paquita.
Photo published in a Chicago
newspaper, March 3, 1936.

In the days following their return to Barcelona, they prepared for their move to a new apartment on April 3. That day, Paquita's diary reads, "In the afternoon we moved into the apartment on 42 Septimania." With the exception of an annotation stating that they had attended a concert by Fritz Kreisler on the evening of March 24 and made two visits to the girls at their school, there is nothing else in the diary—a sign that the change of address was occupying much of the artists' attention.

Segovia and his wife would not get to enjoy their new apartment for long, because twelve days after moving in they left for Italy, where Segovia gave concerts on April 20 in Naples, April 21 in Catania, April 22 in Palermo, April 24 in Rome, and April 27 in Trieste. During three days in Florence at the Hotel Helvetia they shared lunches and dinners with the Castelnuovo-Tedescos. The guitarist gave a benefit concert on April 30 at the Teatro alla Pergola and before leaving received—as a gift for that visit—the manuscript of *Tarantella*, a new work that the composer had created for Segovia.

They arrived in Barcelona on May 3 by train. On May 4 Paquita went to visit the girls at the school, and at 2:00 P.M. on May 6 they departed again—this time for Moscow, via Paris and Berlin, by train.[48] The information provided by Paquita's diary once again allows us to reconstruct the type of trips musicians like Segovia, who wanted to develop an international career, had to make at that time. At 9:00 A.M. on May 7 they arrived in Paris, stayed at the Hotel Windsor a few hours, and then left for Berlin at 7:15 P.M. They arrived at the German capital the next day at 8:30 A.M., rested at the Hotel Der Fürstenhof, and at ten minutes before midnight boarded the train for Moscow, where they arrived thirty-six hours later, at noon on May 10. On the evening of May 11, Segovia received "the guitar maniacs of Moscow." The photo that appeared over fifty years later in two German publications (see page 139) shows Paquita and Segovia with a group of people who could well be those Muscovite "maniacs" to whom Paquita alludes in her diary.[49]

The Segovias spent their first nine days on Soviet soil in Moscow. Besides the meetings, Paquita's diary mentions three of Segovia's concerts (May 13, 16, and 17),[50] attendance at a play,[50] the guitarist's later informal recital for the entire theater company, and a reunion on May 19 with the Russian composers Grigory and Julian Krein and the violinist Vladimir Voulfmann, whom the guitarist knew from his days in Paris.[51] That afternoon they had tea with composer Sergei Prokofiev, his wife, and the great Cuban chess player José Raúl Capablanca.[52] Our two artists shared one of the other legs of the tour through the Soviet Union with Capablanca, whose second wife, Olga Chagodaev, was Russian. On May 20 they arrived in Leningrad, where Segovia gave three more concerts (the first on the day he arrived and the others on May 22 and 23).

After performing for the city's architects and dining with a group of writers on the night of May 24 in Moscow, Segovia and Paquita departed for Tiflis (Tbilisi), where, following a trip that took three full days, the guitarist played three concerts between May 30 and June 2. On June 3–15 there were concerts in Pyatigorsk, Kislovodsk,[53] Yessentuki, Rostov (two concerts on successive days), and Kharkov, after which they went to Kiev. In the Ukrainian capital they again met Capablanca, with whom they shared several walks; they also attended one of his chess matches. Segovia played in Kiev on June 17, and on June 19 they left for Odessa by plane. Following two concerts in that city, the couple returned to Moscow by train, arriving on June 26.

The trip back home took two flights—from Moscow to Berlin and then Berlin to Barcelona, where Mamá Paqui was waiting for them at the airport on the last day of June. Spain as a whole and the Catalonian capital in particular were now experiencing the first palpitations of the disaster that would

Don Andrés and Paquita with unidentified intellectuals—possibly "guitar maniacs" or writers—in Moscow, May 11 or 24, 1936.

erupt in a little more than two weeks. A long period of accumulated tensions in the heart of a society subjected to intertwining disagreements seemed to be condensed in those summer days into a volatile mixture on the verge of exploding. There were unorganized confrontations between social, economic, and hostile military sectors as well as between fragmented and conflicting unions and political groups, in addition to the Catholic church's active participation as a power in itself. Paquita and Segovia returned to this scenario exhausted after several months of activities and many thousands of miles covered without rest. They ignored several warnings alerting them to what was on the horizon (from Salvador de Madariaga, among others) and held firmly to the illusion that they would finally be able to rest and finish moving into what they thought would be their permanent home on Septimania Street.

During those first days of July 1936, the only things that appear in Paquita's diary are the daily lunches at Mamá Paqui's house, the nightly dinners here and there, and the movies or meetings with friends. The pianist was also under a doctor's care for some type of liver ailment. On Sunday morning, July 12, they went to pick up the girls at school "to have them at home during the vacations."

For the first time in many years, it appeared that the three sisters were going to spend a summer with the family. However, they would still have to wait yet another year for that illusion to become a reality, because July 19 is marked in the diary by a single word with triple underlining—<u>REVOLUTION</u>. Nothing more appears until July 31, when Paquita writes, "Andrés, the girls, and I fled to Italy on the Italian ship *Principessa Maria*."

Segovia clearly summarized his impressions of those days in a very long letter he sent Ponce, who was in Mexico, from New York on January 28, 1937.[54] After a first paragraph in which he told the composer about his happiness of having received a letter from him after a long time, he made an account of their sufferings, emotions and sadness during the initial days of the revolution in Barcelona. He told his friend that they had not paid attention to Madariaga, who had sent them a telegram from Madrid warning them about the imminent events. Segovia said that the military had lost the first round and the "communist hordes struck poor Spain." Barcelona and Madrid had become uninhabitable for all except the "criminal" anarchists, unionists, and communists. Paquita had received death threats, and he was "destined, in scorn, to enter the combat militias." So, they had to flee to Genoa on an Italian ship. He said that Adelaida also had to flee with the two boys, in spite of the fact that she was "from the deep red [communists]," [55] and he also informed Ponce that she and the children were now in Switzerland.

It is very difficult for the Puig Madriguera sisters to recall the few days they spent in the Septimania Street apartment. Sofía vaguely remembers that there was a sense of insecurity and danger in the streets, and "when we went to buy milk we had to go with a fist in the air so that it looked like we were in favor of the revolution." On the other hand, they recall small details of their escape from Spain, which undoubtedly scarred them indelibly. On the same day they told the story about their flight from the Geneva school, they continued:

> *María Rosa:* We were three independent powers. They say that what does not kill you makes you strong.
>
> *Sofía:* Later we also escaped from the school in Spain, when they tried to kill the nuns.
>
> *Mara Rosa:* There they went to pick us up.
>
> *Sofía:* No, no, there we had to go down to the funicular.[56]

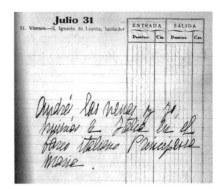

Two pages of Paquita Madriguera's diary of 1936.

Maria Rosa: Yes, we went down but they were waiting for us there. We did not escape, they told us to leave.... When the Civil War began, Mama and Andrés received death threats. Then Mama made arrangements for us so that, as Uruguayans, we could leave Spain. She talked to the consul of Argentina, who said that he would help us get out. But he said that he could not leave two artists like her and Andrés behind to burn in that hell. That is how the three of us left inside a clothes cabinet, in the early hours of the morning, in a truck carrying a Uruguayan flag; nobody knew where it was from, but they respected it. Mama and Andrés were able to flee there also. We were able to get to the port, and there they put us on an Italian ship, the *Principessa Maria*, that carried soldiers from Abyssinia. The three of us were alone, separated from Mama and Andrés, so I began to cry and scream like crazy. Finally, someone located Mama, who was on the other deck, and took me to them. The ship was full of people fleeing, and we had to sleep in bunks the soldiers had used. I got a [scalp] infection. We traveled with nothing, barely two changes of clothes.

Sofia: We were like that for two days until we got to Genoa, and there we had to wait until the consul from each country came to get us in order to leave the ship. Finally, the three of us were alone on the ship, without the sailors or anything, until the Uruguayan consul arrived.

Andrés Segovia and Paquita Madriguera managed to flee to Italy, escaping the hell that Barcelona and the rest of Spain had become. Almost as a premonition of what destiny had in store for them in the coming years, the entire family was able to leave under the protection of the Uruguayan flag—because Paquita's three daughters had been born in Montevideo.

Chapter 9

Intermezzo—From Italy to Montevideo, via Europe and America

The stay of the Spanish-Uruguayan family in Italian territory was to last almost two months, and another nine were to pass before all its members would reunite. This intermission, when the musicians had no permanent home, was marked by almost constant moves using every imaginable mode of transportation and lasted nearly an entire year—until mid-July of 1937, when the Segovia-Madriguera-Puig assemblage was finally brought together again in Montevideo. The flight from Barcelona, with its clamor and violence (not to mention the threat of military duty for Segovia), had been hastily arranged, and the family had no opportunity to take more than the bare essentials.

Soon after arriving in Genoa, and according to what Segovia says in his autobiography and in the long letter to Ponce already cited, they received from one of Paquita's relatives ("veiled," in the words of the guitarist) the news that the apartment on Septimania had been broken into. Although the general tone of the letter to his Mexican friend makes one think that Segovia attributed the break-in to "the Reds," he later says that he and his wife had been victims of "the mob." The truth is that in a situation of confrontations and unleashed hatred like the Catalonian capital was experiencing, all sorts of profiteers and criminals, not linked to either side in the dispute, usually swarm together with the active participants in political and social fights. Segovia is more cautious in his autobiography than in his letter to Ponce when it comes to attributing responsibility. This time he refers only to vandals and ignorant thieves, to whom he assigned the simple purpose of thriving amidst the confusion and lack of authority. He writes that he heard that his home in Barcelona had been sacked and everything destroyed except those items "of commercial value." Segovia says that in addition to manuscripts by famous composers, he lost letters from renowned friends, art works, and books autographed to him by their authors. He was told by neighbors that his valuable objects were sold by the thieves for almost nothing and whatever they could not sell was burned for fuel. The guitarist consoled himself with the fact that since "the spiritual light of those treasures could not illuminate their minds, at least the bonfires they made warmed their bodies." After describing the "treasured souvenirs" from his long trips to the most distant parts of the world and stating that they "wound up in public markets and changed hands in back-street transactions," he states that it was common for the unaware buyer to be visited later by "shady individuals posing as members of some revolutionary group or political committee who, under the guise of legality, would intimidate the poor soul and confiscate his purchase. This type of rabble thrives in any war and demeans any flag."[1]

In a 1973 Spanish magazine interview, Segovia told a story of what, in his opinion, could have triggered the looting of his home. He refers to a certain statement he had made to the Spanish consul in Genoa after the entire family had arrived from Barcelona:

> There I went to the Spanish consul, who was the Count of Bulnes, and I told him, "Look, I am always away from Spain, I have never been affiliated with any political party, but I endorse anything that is not 'the Sovietization of Spain.'" Franco was not the leader of the Movement, it was Sanjurjo.[2] So my statement was used by Queipo de Llano in those picturesque conversations he had on the radio,[3] which caused the break-in of my house in Barcelona.[4]

Whoever the culprits were, Segovia and Paquita were suddenly on Italian soil with only the money they had in their pockets at the time of the hasty flight. To make matters worse, when they received the news that they had lost everything in their new home in Barcelona, they also learned that they had been stripped of whatever savings they had deposited in a bank. The material needs of Paquita's daughters were met by income from the inheritance that was sent to them from Montevideo; but the couple had to think about paying personal expenses and those that Segovia had taken on—the support of his two sons and financial assistance for his mother, aunt, and ex-wife. He wrote to Ponce from New York in a letter dated January 28, 1937, telling him that they had lost everything, and especially he, who only possessed what he had accumulated in Spain. He complained about only having what he would be able to earn to meet all his needs and those of his family, and he told Ponce that, due to conditions and the currency rates, Paquita's income from the inheritance had been reduced by half. For that reason, she was making great efforts in administering the house expenses and supporting her mother and three sisters.[5]

It is not difficult to imagine the state of uncertainty that both Spanish musicians went through in the long hours of exile in Genoa. In the daily notebook of annotations kept by Paquita, always so meticulous in recording her activities, no entries denote any important facts other than occasional visits with friends, a couple of outings to the movies, and dates marked by family birthdays. The arrival of the *Principessa Maria* in the port of Genoa is recorded at 11:00 P.M. on August 1; the family disembarked in the early morning hours of the following day. Paquita writes in her diary on August 3, "The Consulate General of Uruguay and his wife eat with us." She was talking about Julio Bonnet, a physician with whom she and Segovia later maintained a true friendship. During those two and a half months in Genoa they received several visits from Bonnet (sometimes in his capacity as a doctor), and the diplomat and his wife even entertained them with a farewell dinner the night before the whole family left Italy. They spent almost the entire month of August at the health resort of Nervi, staying at the Hotel Pagoda. Paquita's daughters recall it as a month of "vacation" and living at the beach. Several months later from New York, Segovia wrote to Ponce about his concerns and thoughts, telling him that they had spent all their time in Genoa closely watching the news from Spain, the development of events, and the family situation. He couldn't work, write, or do anything more than "devour newspapers" in this period of a "horrible fever."[6]

On August 28 the entire family returned to Genoa, where they settled at the Hotel Astoria until their departure. For the entire month of September Paquita's diary makes no mention of any important activity, and on October 1 Segovia departed for Marseilles, France, by plane. It is likely that both Spanish artists learned some news on that occasion that influenced some of Segovia's later decisions. Barely one week earlier, the de facto Uruguayan government—it had been a dictatorship of right-wing tendencies since 1933—had broken off relations with the Republican government of Spain.

When Segovia arrived in Marseilles to begin a long tour of musical activities that would take him through Europe and America and toward Montevideo, he met Mamá Paqui, who was ready to depart for Genoa with her two youngest daughters—the twins, María (nicknamed Maruja) and Mercedes. The guitarist began his concert season in France, and the three women arrived in Genoa on October 3 to join the family to travel together to the United States. Paquita, her three girls, her mother, and her sisters all left for Paris on October 13. At some time in the weeks previous, for reasons that the daughters cannot recall (or never knew), it was decided that the girls would continue their trip to New York in the company of their grandmother and two aunts. Perhaps the original plan was for Mamá Paqui and her two daughters to leave from Barcelona for the United States, to flee the violence and chaos. Enric Madriguera, Paquita's only brother, had been living in New York for more than a decade, where he had firmly settled in as a successful Latin-pop orchestra leader entertaining at hotels, dances, and parties. Meanwhile, Segovia had to play as many concerts as possible to overcome the economic difficulties already outlined. He was thus obliged to be constantly on the move from one city to another. The only way Paquita could accompany him was for the girls to travel with their grandmother and aunts and settle for some time—in a boarding school, as always—in the city where they were going to live and where Uncle Enric had a home.

The turbulent journey that eventually led the family to Montevideo had begun in a truck protected by the Uruguayan emblem. After that, a train took the four women and three girls to Paris, where their paths would diverge. María Rosa recalled:

> After some time in Genoa, they had to give some concerts in Europe, and so they sent us to the United States. We went by train to Paris and from there to Le Havre. I almost got lost in the Paris train station because I was holding on to someone's hand and all of a sudden, for some reason, she had to let me go, and I grabbed a hand that wasn't the right one. Finally they found me.[7]

Left to right: Sofía, Pitusa, and María Rosa Puig Madriguera in Genoa, Italy on October 8, 1936, five days before leaving for New York.

According to the entry in Paquita's diary, the group of women arrived in Paris at 8:00 A.M. on October 14, where Paquita said farewell to the entire family, who left for the port of Le Havre to board the steamship for New York. Paquita took the train headed to the port of Calais en route to London, where she arrived the same day at 7:30 P.M. Segovia was waiting for her. He had already played some concerts in the British capital and had recorded several pieces for the Gramophone Company (His Master's Voice) the previous day.[8] The couple now resumed the everyday life to which they were accustomed before it was interrupted after their return from the tour of the Soviet Union—trips from one city to another, Segovia's concerts and recordings, gatherings with other musicians and friends, nights at the theater, and attending other artists' concerts. In what seemed like a long-awaited sign marking the end of those hopeless and inactive months in Genoa, on the night Paquita arrived she and Segovia ate at the Restaurant Español with their friend Salvador de Madariaga, the pianist José Iturbi, and Iturbi's wife. The chess player Capablanca, accompanied by his Russian wife, joined the gathering later that night.

The activities were intense during the twelve days that the two artists were in Great Britain. Segovia gave concerts outside the capital on October 16 and 17, while Paquita remained in London. He gave a concert at a private home on October 18, played for the BBC on October 19, had a recording session in the Gramophone studios on October 20, and on the night of October 21 gave a concert at Wigmore Hall. On October 25 they received a visit from Castelnuovo-Tedesco, and together they attended a concert that night by the BBC Symphony Orchestra, conducted by Iturbi. They left for Paris at 2:00 P.M. on October 26, arriving seven hours later. They had several meetings in the French capital with the manager Ernesto Quesada and his son, probably to fine-tune some of the details of Segovia's presentations in the months to follow. At 8:00 P.M. on October 30, Andrés Segovia departed for North Africa on a concert tour. Paquita remained in Paris; her husband's itinerary can be followed from the destinations of the letters she sent him (and that she recorded in her diary)—between November 1 and 3 she wrote to him in Oran (Algeria), on November 5 and 6 in Fez (Morocco), on November 7–10 in Algiers, and finally on November 14 and 15 in Tunisia. On the morning of November 18, Segovia was on his way back to Paris to play two days later at Gaveau Hall.

One point of interest: on November 11 of that year, Paquita's diary entry reads "Andrés's birthday" (as do all of her diary entries for this particular day up through 1948). Both Sofía and María Rosa Puig emphatically confirmed that Segovia's birthday had always been celebrated on November 11 in the family. They have no explanation for the fact that, years later, the guitarist himself would say that his birthday was February 21.

> *María Rosa:* Andrés's birthday was always, for us, November 11. I do not know why he later changed it to February.
>
> *Sofía:* I am steeped in astrology, I even do astrological charts, and for me he was always much more a Scorpio than a Pisces.[9]

Paquita Madriguera and Andrés Segovia left France for Bruges on November 21, 1936. They remained in the beautiful Belgium city until November 26, when they departed for The Hague and another overwhelming number of commitments for the guitarist, this time in the Netherlands. On November 27 Segovia played at Diligentia Hall in The Hague, and in the days that followed the couple traveled by car to the other cities where his concerts were scheduled—Amsterdam on November 29, Rotterdam on November 30, and Hilversum on December 1. After each of these concerts, the couple returned to The Hague, where they had established their temporary residence during the brief but intensive tour of the Netherlands. They returned there for the last time at noon on December 1, and on the afternoon of December 2 they left by train for Prague, where they arrived after a twenty-hour trip. On the night they arrived, Segovia had to play on the radio, and the next day he gave his concert at the Library Hall. The activity was incessant: shortly after noon the next day, the couple left for Vienna. Two months later, in a letter to Ponce written in Chicago, Segovia told his friend that such a hectic life was due to the circumstances, which did not allow him to rest. He had to go on working, tirelessly giving concerts to provide the great amount that his family needed.[10]

The arrival in Vienna, however, represented a kind of haven of tranquility. Both artists had almost a week of welcome rest there in the wake of so much commotion, and they had a chance to relax with people in musical circles. In particular, as seen in Paquita's diary, they attended several gatherings with the guitarist Karl Scheit,[11] who had been teaching at Vienna's Musikhochschule since 1933. Segovia's concert in Austria's capital took place on December 12, and the next day he and his wife left for Geneva, where they would remain for ten days. The couple had a lot of friends in the city where he had once resided, and he took the time to visit his two sons, who were living there again. Since he had to accept every opportunity to play and generate income, Segovia gave a concert in Geneva on December 16 and another in Monte Carlo on December 18. From December 22 to 30 Paquita and her husband remained in the Swiss village of Caux, where they shared several meals and friendly gatherings with the composer Joaquín Nin and his wife. As seen in previous chapters, the ties between Paquita and Nin's children were established while she was visiting New York as a pianist. Finally, on December 30, the couple departed for Genoa. On the night that marked the end of a year that had been so unique, so agitated, and so distinctly trimmed with distress, Andrés Segovia and Paquita Madriguera had dinner with their friend Bonnet, the consul general of Uruguay in Genoa.

Following ten days of rest (taking advantage of the Christmas vacations), the opening of 1937 was marked by the sign of work and trips for the artistic couple. On New Year's Day, both musicians traveled to Rome to begin

Segovia's series of three performances in Italy; meanwhile, they prepared again to cross the Atlantic from Genoa. The guitarist's Italian concerts took place in Rome (Saturday, January 2), Turin (Tuesday, January 5), and Bologna (Sunday, January 10). On January 11 Bonnet visited them to say farewell before their trip to America. Three days afterward Don Andrés and Paquita boarded the *Conte di Savoia* headed to New York, where they arrived exactly a week later. Enric, Maruja, and Mercedes Madriguera awaited them at the port, in addition to people linked to the company that was sponsoring the guitarist's concerts. The next day, January 22, Paquita went to visit her daughters at the boarding school, three months and eight days after having left them at the train station in Paris.

Paquita's three daughters had arrived in New York at the end of October 1936 and had been sent to board at the Holy Angels School, located then in Fort Lee, New Jersey—just across the Hudson River from New York City. Seventy years later at Sofía's home, on December 8, 2006, Sofía and María Rosa recalled that trip and their stay at the American boarding school, run by nuns:

> *Sofía:* After we fled to Italy, because of the war, we went to France and there we took—we took? [*She laughs*] They sent us on a ship, the three of us, in the care of the captain.
>
> *María Rosa:* No, we went there with the family, with Mamá Paqui and with two aunts, the twins, Aunt María and Aunt Mercedes. On arrival, Uncle Enrique [Enric] went to pick us up.
>
> *Sofía:* Do you know what happened that I recall? There was a horrible storm, and everyone on the ship was dizzy. The only one who walked outdoors with a sailor, to fix some little thing, was me, who was also little. And that is why I retain the feeling that we were alone.

Shortly after the girls arrived in the United States, Uncle Enric and Mamá Paqui registered them at the school:

> *Sofía:* During those same days they took us to a school, so that we could begin classes there (we were going to be boarders), and when we got to the place, I said that I did not want to go inside

María Rosa (the taller girl) with a friend at the Holy Angels School.

because someone had died there. Everyone said, "No," that it was a school and they knew that we were coming. When we went in, it turned out that the school gardener had died a little while earlier. At the New Jersey school, where we were boarders, nobody explained the meal system to us. In the morning they gave you a big breakfast, but we had to buy the evening meal, and we did not take money for that. We were so hungry!

María Rosa: We also did not speak English. Pitusa tapped a glass with a fork one night, stood on the table and, babbling in English, she told the nuns, in front of the whole school, that we were starving. What for! We couldn't write.

Sofía: They placed us in an English-speaking school where nobody spoke Spanish and we didn't speak a single word of English.

María Rosa: No, but we wanted to write to Uncle Enrique so that he would send us money, because in the evening they opened a beautiful snack bar where they had milk and those things, but you had to pay extra. And we didn't have any money. I swear we were starving. At night, they would give us some chips and a bit of ham.

Sofía: And a glass of cold milk, if you wanted.

María Rosa: At noon they gave us a "snack" as they say. This "lunch," the breakfast, and dinner were included in the fees. But we didn't have any money to pay when they opened that snack bar where they sold that wonderful milk and other things that I saw. The nuns read our letters, and then Pitusa decided to write in Catalan. Do you remember that? Telling Uncle Enrique that we were starving. The nuns were furious. "What language are you writing in?" they asked. Poor Pitusa was punished! Because she defended us, eh?

In the meantime, Mamá Paqui and her twins had rented an apartment in New York City, where Segovia and Paquita also settled when they arrived in the United States. A week later, the guitarist wrote to Ponce to tell him that everyone was settled in at 171 West Seventy-first Street.[12] The couple would be in North America for two months during the first part of 1937, during which time Segovia gave concerts in several different U.S. and Canadian cities while Paquita remained in New York. She did, however, go to Washington, D.C., in response to an invitation from the city's Segovia Guitar Society to be present when her husband arrived from Minneapolis to give a concert in the nation's capital.

While they lived in New York, the vibrant social life of both artists included gatherings and dinners with other musicians and intellectuals, the most frequent being Salvador de Madariaga, Gaspar Cassadó, Jascha Heifetz, and Sophocles Papas.[13] Sundays were usually reserved for visiting the girls at their school or taking them out to lunch. On March 3–17, Segovia toured California and Canada for what would be his last series of North American concerts for that year.

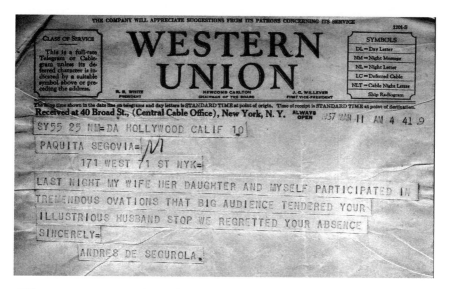

Telegram sent to Paquita by Andrés de Segurola on March 11, 1937, from Hollywood, California.[14] She had met the singer, who was born in 1874 in Valencia, in 1915 during her first tour of North America.

After having Paquita's daughters with them for four days, "on the occasion of Easter vacation" (as the pianist records it in her diary), on March 28 the musician couple boarded a train in New York bound for Miami. They arrived the following day, and on the morning of March 30 they flew to Barranquilla, Colombia. From there, again by plane, they continued the trip on Wednesday, March 31, to Bogotá. Thus began a tour of South America and the Caribbean that would last a month and end with the couple's arrival in Montevideo.

It is quite probable that they were already traveling with the idea of settling in the Uruguayan capital, at least for some time. There does not seem to be a definite answer in the documents read nor in the memories of Paquita's daughters as to why or when they decided to move permanently to Montevideo, since all five of them were settled in New York and the girls had been at the boarding school in New Jersey for several months. Sofía and María Rosa have said only that "Mama had kept in contact with our relatives in Montevideo and with Aparicio Méndez, and that is why she decided to come back here."

The first thing that comes to mind is that Paquita had inherited property that generated some income, which she received in money orders sent to her by Méndez, Arturo Puig's former partner. Also, in Montevideo she had her own place to live. Furthermore, this was her daughters' hometown, and the language spoken here was the entire family's native tongue. But it is also true that the girls had been taken to Catalan-, French-, and English-speaking areas, and both Don Andrés and Paquita were used to living in places where Spanish was not spoken. These reasons carried some weight, but they could not be the only, or the determining, factors. It also seems that the political environment, which could favor or hinder Segovia's own plans in cultivating his concert career, was of great importance.

In that sense, three considerations, which will be presented now and analyzed in detail later, acquire particular relevance: Segovia's opinion of the United States, his ideas about the state of affairs in Mexico, and the news he had heard regarding Uruguay's political climate. A return to Europe was ruled out because it did not seem feasible. These three countries were therefore the only possible options for a base in which the family could establish a home: the United States, because they were already there, because they would have the support of Paquita's brother, and because the country would offer better opportunities for the artist; Mexico, because they had been invited by Ponce and because they would have no problem with the language; and, finally, Uruguay, with its family-related advantages.

Segovia wrote twice to Ponce regarding the seemingly hopeless possibility of settling in the United States. In the first occasion, he told his friend that the situation in the United States was very difficult for those who spoke against the government of Valencia,[15] as they received death threats; and, in case of artists, their careers were affected by the lack of support of the press. Segovia said that he did not pretend to be a communist—"God forbid," he wrote— but he avoided imprudent statements when he was in America. In any case, he added, he helped Franco all he could, though being very discreet while in that country.[16] In a second letter, Segovia said that he was astonished to see the "devastating influence" of Russia in America, and that the communists had succeeded in putting the problem of Spain as an issue of anti-Semitism. He described Franklin D. Roosevelt's government as "the mellifluous and soft U.S. un-government," and he accused it of supporting or at least silently permitting the plans of the international communist movement. He finished by predicting that the U.S. would soon have to deal with the communist movement and be unable to do so.[17]

Obviously, under no circumstances would Segovia consider viable (or at least convenient) the prospect of establishing his home in the United States—not at that time when, according to what he explicitly told Ponce, a good number of the concert managers were Jewish.[18] Through a reply to Ponce it can be inferred that Segovia had been invited to move, at least temporarily, to Mexico. Segovia thanked him emphatically while giving him his own vision of that country's political situation, which, consequently, meant that he could not settle there either. He told his friend that he could not accept his invitation to go to Mexico, even though it was such a beautiful and attractive country. Segovia didn't dare to play in Ponce's land in those days because his position in the Spanish conflict was very well known; in addition, Russia had a very strong influence in Mexico and would attempt to put obstacles against his presence there. He preferred to let the storm pass.[19] In another letter he further wondered whether, "in a country so won over by communism" as Mexico, there was still an independent press.[20]

Segovia's opinions about the United States, President Franklin D. Roosevelt, and Mexico (governed by the democratically elected Lázaro Cárdenas) seem very clear. The only alternative left was Uruguay, which at that time had, in Segovia's eyes, features exactly opposite those he described regarding the two North American nations. Toward the end of 1935, before Uruguay's right-wing dictatorship made clear its position on the Spanish conflict and broke with the Republic of Spain in September 1936, it had broken off relations with the Soviet Union. The Uruguayan government had emerged from a coup supported by the more conservative parts of the country's two oldest political parties, with the sector of the National Party to which Aparicio Méndez belonged forming part of this coalition. And Méndez was, according to Paquita's daughters, one of the biggest influences on the family's decision to settle in Uruguay. Supporting this point of view, Paquita's diary states that on the evening of July 31, 1937—about three weeks after the family moved into an apartment in downtown Montevideo—Méndez took Segovia, Paquita, and the three Puig girls to visit Uruguay's president, Gabriel Terra.

The final stage of the long episode that began after leaving Genoa in October 1936 and was to end in Montevideo was an intensive artistic tour that took Segovia and his wife to Colombia, Venezuela, Trinidad and Tobago, and Brazil for the first time. The activity began with a concert by the guitarist at the

Teatro Colón in Bogotá on April 1, 1937. After two more concerts at the same theater on April 3 and 5, they left for Caracas, where Segovia performed at the Teatro Municipal on April 7 and 8. On April 9 he played at the Empire Theatre in Port of Spain, Trinidad and Tobago, and on April 10 they both flew to Brazil. The first concert on Brazilian territory was on April 12 in Recife, and on April 16 they went on a journey of four days by ship to arrive at Rio de Janeiro on April 19. Awaiting them at the port was the Spanish pianist Tomás Terán,[21] accompanied by his wife and others with ties to the musical circles of the city, which was then the capital of Brazil. During their six-day stay in Rio, Paquita and Segovia had several meetings with the Teráns, who invited them to visit and dine at their home. An entry in Paquita's diary describes her time in Rio: "The beautiful and evocative word *saudades* [nostalgia] is not for the use of the Brazilians, but for those who, after seeing this beautiful country, have to move on."

Segovia also felt the impact of the captivating Brazilian capital of those days. A story by the guitarist Pedro Duval was published in Italy a few months later:

> Segovia had two very pleasant surprises in Rio. The first was the magnificence of the natural beauties that give this city its fabulous façade. Segovia, often recalling the impressions this city left him with, kept repeating, "It's wonderful!" And he expressed his desire to return soon to spend some time at Copacabana Beach. The second surprise was meeting the Brazilian composer Villa-Lobos, the greatest Latin American composer, who showed Segovia a collection of twelve studies for guitar. Villa-Lobos knows this instrument, theoretically and practically, to which he had previously dedicated some works. Those studies awakened the keenest interest in Segovia, so much so that he promised to prepare three of them to introduce in his upcoming concerts.[22]

On April 23, 1937, Andrés Segovia's Rio debut took place at the Teatro Municipal, and the next day he and Paquita were invited by Heitor Villa-Lobos to dinner and then to visit at his apartment. On that occasion, the Brazilian composer gave Segovia a copy of his *Chôros* for guitar, showed him the manuscripts of his other works, and promised to send copies of his Twelve Studies to the guitarist in Montevideo once the composer had made them.[23] On the night of April 25, the couple left by train for São Paulo and Segovia's concert there on April 26 at the Teatro Municipal, and at sundown on April 27 both artists boarded the steamship *Highland Monarch* for Buenos Aires. From the Argentinean capital, they crossed the Río de la Plata on the night of April 29, finally arriving in Montevideo early the next morning—four and a half years after the widowed Paquita had left with her three girls for Barcelona. Once in Montevideo, the couple settled in the Parque Hotel for the entire month of May, because the concert tour had not yet ended. There remained two performances in Montevideo (on May 5 and 11 at Teatro Solís) and four in Argentina (May 7 and 19 at the Teatro Odeón in Buenos Aires, May 20 in Rosario, and May 24 in Santa Fe).

Those days in May—the first that the couple had shared in a city that for each had so many memories—alternated artistic engagements with an endless number of social gatherings, particularly reunions of Paquita with members of the Puig family and friends from when she first lived in the Uruguayan capital. On May 29, 1937, Segovia and his wife put an end to that restless and roaming intermezzo that began brutally with the flight from Barcelona. They left the Parque Hotel to spend two weeks at the country estate that, upon the death of Arturo Puig, Paquita and her daughters had inherited in Piedras de Afilar, about forty-five miles north of Montevideo in the department of Canelones. Following this brief vacation period, which must have been meaningful (in spite of not a single entry in the pianist's diary) during their first weeks in complete privacy and without professional

The Parque Hotel in 1916, viewed from Playa Ramírez (*left*), and as it is seen today from the Rambla (*right*). The building no longer operates as a hotel; it is now the headquarters of MERCOSUR.[24]

or social engagements, they returned to Montevideo on the morning of June 14. Here they prepared their permanent residence and put together what would be, for almost a decade, the stable home of Andrés Segovia, Paquita Madriguera, and the girls—children whose number was to grow to four in the coming year.

Chapter 10

Montevideo—Putting Down Roots in a Hospitable Land

The first month that Paquita Madriguera and Andrés Segovia spent together in Montevideo was one of transition. On one hand, Segovia was still immersed in the maelstrom of concerts of a South American tour that had begun in Colombia at the beginning of April and would now take him to six concerts in twenty days on both sides of the Río de la Plata. On the other hand, the couple took advantage of that time to define the new coordinates of their life. They had to evaluate the opportunities and possibilities of their new territory, get reacquainted with the environment frequented by Paquita during the ten years of her previous stay, and also learn about—especially in Segovia's case—the music, artistic, and intellectual circles with which they were going to share this new period. They had decided to establish their home in this city, and sent for Paquita's daughters from the United States. The Uruguay they found upon their return was substantially different from the one they had each known more than fifteen years earlier. The Great Depression of the 1930s also had had repercussions there, and the currency had started to lose value. In 1937 a Uruguayan peso was worth less than half of a United States dollar—a circumstance that was, at least for the moment, favorable for Segovia, who arrived with income earned in countries with stronger currencies. And in addition to his concert earnings, he had begun to receive royalties for his published editions and recordings.

The country's population was a bit over two million, and a good part of the growth was due to the strong flow of immigration, which had heightened following the European conflicts. Although the stance of the Uruguayan government regarding Spain's problems was expressed by its breaking off relations with the Republican government, the heart of the population (particularly in the artistic and intellectual circles) supported and sympathized with the Republicans' resistance to Franco's Nationalist movement.

> While at the top of the government there were clear sympathies toward Italian fascism and the Spanish Phalange, the world's tension, increasing day by day, imposed caution on those who wanted to copy their models and institutional norms, because we were in an area of the world where the British imperial interests were relevant. In addition, the outbreak of the Spanish Civil War (1936) and the favorable echo that the pro-Republican propaganda had on public opinion—encouraged by intellectuals, artists, politicians, etc., through the Ateneo of Montevideo,[1] for example—demonstrated to what point our society, especially in the capital, could resist totalitarian ideas.[2]

Montevideo was experiencing a relatively intense artistic and cultural period, and the location of a port across the Río de la Plata from Buenos Aires enabled this capital to receive all the people that were attracted to the large neighboring city. Some notable examples are the Nobel Prize–winning novelist and playwright Luigi Pirandello (who came in 1933), Federico García Lorca (whose visit in February 1934 had enormous significance), Ottorino Respighi [who conducted the SODRE Symphony Orchestra in 1934 at Teatro Solís,[3] premiering his opera *La fiamma* (The Flame)]; and Igor Stravinsky, who arrived in May 1936 to conduct the SODRE Symphony in two concerts presenting his works. The pianist Hugo Balzo pinpoints some memories on the Montevideo music scene at that time in an interview published in 1971:[4]

> *Interviewer:* What was musical life like in Montevideo at that time?
>
> *Balzo:* It was quite important. There were concerts, especially at the Verdi Institute and at the [Teatro] Albéniz, which was later transformed into Cine Radio City. Once in a while we would put an orchestra together. The one Sambucetti founded did not

come to the Verdi often.[5] The Orchestral Society, whose groups were conducted by Scarabelli and Vicente Pablo,[6] was presented at the Teatro Solís. The Albéniz was used mainly for the solo concerts; all this before the Studio Auditorium and the SODRE Symphony Orchestra. Important figures visited us. I do not remember well, but I do know that in 1923 Richard Strauss was here with the Vienna Philharmonic. In 1928 Respighi came with his wife, who was a singer, and gave a concert. He returned later in 1934 to conduct the SODRE Symphony. I played piano in that program, in his concerto for five instruments and orchestra. I have the best memories of [Arthur] Rubinstein.

Interviewer: Did Rubinstein come to Montevideo often?

Balzo: Yes, of course, back then. The first concert I heard him was more or less from that period. We became very good friends. We competed with each other on *La Cumparsita*—he insisted that he could play it better than any Uruguayan.[7] The first advice he gave me was in going out on the stage: the soloist had to steal the show. He would make his entrance at fantastic speed, and quite often he would take everything along with him. The system was a double-edged sword—one day I saw him trip over the piano bench, which got him into a fix he didn't know how to get out of. But for these unforeseen problems he used his sense of humor, which he had plenty of, as well as talent. One day at the Solís (or at the Albéniz, I don't recall), after many encores and much applause, he came out to bow for the last time with his overcoat, hat, and suitcase in hand. If he had not done that, he would not have made it to his concerts in Buenos Aires on time. I also remember Robert Casadesus, who played in 1931 and with whom I later studied, and Jan Kubelík, the violinist, and [Sergei] Rachmaninoff. . . .[8]

Above all, Lamberto Baldi should be noted because he was a decisive figure. They brought him from Brazil at the end of 1931, and he remained at the head of the SODRE Symphony as principal conductor for several years. Until then, it had been the position of maestros Scarabelli and Vicente Pablo. But when Baldi took over, he worked tirelessly, premiering a great number of contemporary works. That is in regard to symphonic music. I premiered twelve-tone works between 1932 and 1933, works that I would probably not dare present now. They were very difficult pieces to play, and I think what helped me was the typical eighteen-year-old's lack of self-awareness.

Interviewer: Did you play Schoenberg?

Balzo: Of course. And all the others as well. Even the first works of the Argentinean Juan Carlos Paz. Regarding Ravel, I brought his concerto in 1940. I had met the composer at the beginning of 1937 in Paris at the classes I received as part of a scholarship that was extended for three years. . . . But let's return to Montevideo, to the presenters of new works, as you asked me. I tell you again that Baldi was fundamental. When Stravinsky came . . . he was shocked at the number of his works that had been performed here, and which he thought nobody would know by name. In the music for piano, Rubinstein was decisively important. And another pianist, a great pianist, was Ricardo Viñes.[9]

The guitar activity in Montevideo was equally fruitful. Thanks to a combination of internal and external factors, the tradition that had already developed the instrument's following in various levels of musical life had merged in the field of classical guitar. At the turn of the twentieth century the guitar was an instrument that was widespread in all social strata—from the peasant singers and accompanists of *tangos* and *milongas* through the "society ladies" and on up to the academically trained musicians. The tradition even extended to the musicians of African roots accompanying their *milongones* and *candombes*. When performers from Spain and other parts of the world started arriving here in the early 1900s, they found not only an avid listening public, but also instrumentalists who had developed very personal and often unique playing styles. The Río de la Plata was already an appealing place for guitarists who came from the mother country. The most prominent were Gaspar Sagreras (1838–1901), Carlos García Tolsa (1858–1905) and, more notably, Antonio Giménez Manjón (1866–1919). Blind since childhood, Giménez Manjón came to Montevideo for the first time in 1893 and was, according to Cédar Viglietti, "the greatest Spanish guitarist who had come to these shores up to then."[10] These musicians interacted with the local guitarists, providing—and also receiving—musical and technical pointers. Starting in 1912, the Paraguayan virtuoso Agustín Barrios became a frequent visitor. The guitar environment that had developed in Montevideo encouraged Barrios and, at the same time, helped him polish his technique and cultivate his composing talent. The friendship and support offered him by Martín Borda Pagola in Montevideo, Luis Pasquet in Salto, and Eduardo Fabini in Minas was fundamental in these respects.

Some of the heirs to Francisco Tárrega's school who began to arrive in Montevideo in the middle of World War I include Josefina Robledo, Miguel Llobet, and Emilio Pujol. Pujol, who went on to a long career as a teacher and musicologist, described the state of the Uruguayan guitar in a conference paper read for the first time in Buenos Aires in 1928:

> While Martín Borda Pagola (an intelligent musician), Pedro Vittone, and Julio Otermin espoused the old school of Aguado in Montevideo, the young Uruguayan guitarists have been leaning toward the modern school, the result of frequent contact with the current concert guitarists who periodically visit the city. Josefina Robledo was the first exponent of Tárrega's school in Montevideo. The later concerts by Llobet, Segovia, and other

Program for one of Calleja's concerts in 1939.

guitarists encouraged and channeled the guidance of ... Conrado Koch, Telémaco Morales (a specialist in Uruguayan folk music), Martínez Oyanguren, Mascaró y Reissig (a professor and composer), and Rosendo Barreiro (a famous performer).[11]

Another Spanish artist who was very influential and who contributed greatly to advancing the guitar culture of Montevideo was Francisco Calleja,[12] who immigrated to Uruguay in 1912. He later returned to Spain but came back in 1930 to settle in Uruguay. He gave several concerts at SODRE in 1931 and performed there again in 1939.[13] He also taught for several years at the Municipal Conservatory in Tacuarembó, directed by the Basque composer and organist José Tomás Mujica.

Segovia's previous visits to Montevideo in 1920, 1921, 1928, and 1934 added to this flurry of activity. The presence of the then-emerging Spanish performer gave a special impetus to this part of the music scene in the Uruguayan capital, not only because of his unique artistic magnetism, but also because of his tenacious energy in the development of both the guitar's repertoire and its reputation as a serious instrument. He probably noticed, during his fifth visit to the Uruguayan capital, how much guitar culture had evolved along these lines throughout that period, and, as a result, how well some instrumentalists of serious importance had flourished there. The most notable when Segovia settled in Montevideo, who had already gained considerable fame in the United States that the Andalusian artist had just toured, was Julio Martínez Oyanguren.[14] He was an officer in the Uruguayan Navy and made his debut as a concert guitarist in Montevideo in 1929, at the Teatro Solís. After his presentation in Argentina and Brazil, and enjoying a position as a diplomat in New York (as a naval attaché of the Uruguayan embassy), Martínez Oyanguren made his American debut at New York's Town Hall on October 1, 1935. From that moment on, different doors and opportunities opened—concert tours, a contract with the NBC Radio network to play every Sunday during the noon hour (from 12:15 to 12:30, a broadcast that was even transmitted to Canada), and recordings for RCA Victor and Columbia record companies.

In 1939, when Segovia found the doors to American concert stages closed to him, Martínez Oyanguren was invited to give a concert at the White House before President Roosevelt and his wife. Also that year, in New York, he was the first guitarist to give a complete concert on television, and there were some in the United States who called this Uruguayan artist "The King of the Guitar." In Montevideo, as is usually the case, Oyanguren had his admirers and his critics. But his fame and prestige, based on the news of his successes in North America, had grown considerably by the time Segovia had arrived with Paquita. Once back in Uruguay, his musical activity declined, he was later chosen chief of police in his hometown of Durazno, and he gradually stopped appearing in concert. Needless to say, Segovia did not think much of him, given that there was a period when the Uruguayan guitarist vied with him for a privileged place before the North American audiences.

The growth of guitar activity in Montevideo witnessed the founding of the Centro Guitarrístico del Uruguay on April 10, 1937, just a few weeks before Segovia arrived to settle with his family there. This organization existed, with some brief interruptions, until the beginning of the twenty-first century, and during several periods it played a prominent role in the promotion of the instrument and up-and-coming guitarists. Pedro Mascaró y Reissig was its first president, and its founding members—Américo Castillo, Eugenio Segovia (no relation to Andrés), Pedro Marín Sánchez, Ramon Ayestarán, Olga Pierri, Atilio Rapat, and the Carlevaro brothers Agustín and Abel—performed at the inaugural concert on August 25 of that year. Segovia was unable to attend the concert because it was the Uruguayan Independence Day holiday and, according to Paquita's diary, the entire family went on an excursion to Minas (seventy-five miles northeast of Montevideo), organized by members of the Rotary Club. However, some of the members of the recently founded association had visited Segovia on May 13, and he had signed and made a dedication in the center's record book. During that visit Segovia and Paquita were staying at the Parque Hotel; it would be more than six weeks before they settled into a downtown Montevideo apartment. The directors of the center visited him again after his return from a long tour, in April 1938—this time at his downtown apartment—to request his participation in a planned tribute to Miguel Llobet, who had died in Barcelona just two months earlier.

> In April 1938, the center held an homage for Llobet, presided over by Segovia, who said that Llobet was not only a great guitarist but also a profound musician, as reflected in his excellent harmonization of *El Mestre* (The Master) and many of his other high-level transcriptions. He made reference to the frank and generous character of the musician, with whom he shared a close friendship and great sympathy. Segovia's words touched everyone in the auditorium.[15]

It was in the Parque Hotel, probably on May 14, 1937, that Segovia received the young man who was to become his most prominent student during this period—the young Abel Carlevaro, one of the founding members of the Centro Guitarrístico. He had begun giving concerts in Montevideo and Buenos Aires the previous year, and his uncle, Héctor R. Carlevaro, a proficient guitar aficionado and years later a builder of fine instruments, introduced him to the Spanish maestro.

> Segovia was in Montevideo and I was probably eighteen or nineteen years old when my uncle Héctor told me, "Abel, I want to take you to meet Segovia." . . . Segovia lived at the beginning of his stay in Montevideo at the Parque Hotel. It was there that I played for him the first time, among others, several works that he had arranged, including the Chaconne by Johann Sebastian Bach—the famous Chaconne.[16]

Apparently the young Uruguayan guitarist's playing caught Segovia's attention, because Segovia offered to give him lessons. Those lessons would go on for several years, and Carlevaro became the first student that Segovia publicly presented in concert.[17] Segovia probably began teaching Carlevaro during the month of July, once the Spanish maestro and Paquita had settled in their apartment at Palacio Lapido on Avenida 18 de Julio.

> I had taken the guitar and Segovia asked me what I was going to play. "The Chaconne by Bach," I replied. And I played the Chaconne, which I had fingered entirely by myself. I then played other works and heard Segovia tell my uncle, "Abel has a right hand like I have never seen before."[18]

> He told me, "Look, Abel, I want you to study with me, I want to give you lessons." That is how I began to work with Segovia. For me that was essential as you can imagine. But not even the great Segovia would give me the solution for a series of problems that bothered me. I would constantly ask him and he would always answer me, but I was never satisfied.[19]

An autographed photo of Segovia remains as testimony of those first meetings he had with Carlevaro: "To Abel Carlevaro, who I hope broadens the borders of Uruguay with his guitar."

Abel Carlevaro, shortly before Segovia's arrival in Montevideo.

None of the other musicians who participated in the inaugural concert at the Centro Guitarrístico opted to take lessons with Segovia, probably for different reasons. But all attained different levels of fame and contributed, in one way or another, to raising the standards of the guitar in Montevideo during that time, with far-reaching effects for the future. Atilio Rapat,[20] in particular, was a local legend in his pedagogic work, successfully training students such as Oscar Cáceres and Antonio Pereira Arias, who attained international prominence.

At the time of Segovia's arrival, SODRE—the state radio station devoted entirely to playing classical music—broadcast a series of live guitar concerts in 1937 from its studios, usually transmitted at 8:30 P.M. on Saturdays. Those programs included Pedro Marín Sánchez playing works by Tárrega, Donostia, and Albéniz (May 29); Abel Carlevaro performing music by Donostia, Sor, Bach, Beethoven, and Agustín Barrios (June 19); Marín Sánchez and Carlevaro again (July 10); and the duo of Atilio Rapat and Olga Pierri (September 18).

Atilio Rapat.

Meanwhile, Andrés Segovia and Paquita Madriguera continued in their prep-arations to establish residence in this city, where the sounds of the guitar resonated so strongly. After resting for two weeks at Paquita's country estate of El Campito, the couple returned to Montevideo and settled at the Hotel Las Palmas to decide their future plans. They first rented an apartment in the Palacio Lapido, a modern building with large apartments located in the center of the city at the corner of Avenida 18 de Julio and Rio Branco Street (now called Wilson Ferreira Aldunante). Paquita's detailed accounting of all their expenses shows that the monthly rent was 135 pesos (about US$70 or 17 pounds sterling at that time). In comparison, the total cost for electricity, gas, water, and telephone for the month of August, when Paquita's daughters were now living with them, was nineteen pesos, while taking the girls to the movies cost only two pesos total for Paquita and the three girls. It took the couple ten days to get the new home ready for habitation, and the entry in Paquita's diary for July 2, 1937, reads: "We are moving to live at the apartment." Segovia gave Ponce their "permanent" (his word) address—948 Avenida 18 de Julio, Fourth Floor, Apartment 3—in a letter dated August 10, telling him that they had an apartment there. He also informed his friend that Paquita's "cute little girls" had arrived from New York, and that all of them had finally settled down in that "friendly and welcoming city of Montevideo."[21]

Avenida 18 de Julio, in 1935. The white building, with many long
balconies, is the Palacio Lapido.

Paquita's daughters arrived on July 6, at 9:00 A.M. aboard the *Western World*. While preparing for their return home, they were to live another adventure exactly two months before their arrival in Montevideo. Sofía Puig tells what happened when their uncle Enric invited them to go for a short ride in his car to witness an event that had generated great excitement, an event which would have a tragic and horrible outcome and mark an indelible impression on the girls' final weeks in the United States—the *Hindenburg* disaster:

> I always had—I don't know—something like intuitions. When we were
> with my sisters in New York, we rode in my Uncle Enrique's car, which was
> a convertible. We were in New Jersey and I was looking up, to the sky. And
> suddenly I see flying by, enormous, over us, the zeppelin. We all looked, and
> I said that it was very dangerous and it could crash at any moment. I saw it
> hit against something, an antenna, and it burst into flames.[22]

In exchange for so many setbacks, hardships, and disappointments experienced in the five years they were away from their homeland, the Puig Madriguera sisters happily and enthusiastically recalled those days on the *Western World* with pleasure, a trip they made accompanied only by a German nurse and under the direct responsibility of the captain of the ship:

> Sofía: We also returned from the United States alone, but that was a beautiful trip. Alfonso Ortiz Tirado and Ernesto de Llano,[23] his guitarist, were aboard, and we sang with them.
>
> María Rosa: I had the feeling that everyone treated us with so much affection during that trip. So much so that I always had the impression that they felt sorry for us. And now I am certain they felt sorry for us. Because I recall the affection. You have to remember, Sofía, how they treated us. And the beautiful things they wrote and said to us, and they would hug and kiss us.

María Rosa on the deck of the *Western World*. On the back of the photo, in her handwriting, it reads: "When we were on our way to Montevideo they took this photo of me with my German nurse who took care of me and taught me German."

> Sofía: I remember that Ortiz Tirado sang and Ernesto de Llano was the guitarist. And I loved to sing. I was a terrible singer, out of tune. But I would sit on Ortiz Tirado's lap [*laughter*] and I would make him sing, and I sang along with him. Then, everyone would applaud me and I felt happy. I was terribly out of tune because I did not have an ear. [Pitusa and María Rosa] were embarrassed and would move away from me.

María Rosa: She was never embarrassed to sing, and she was a horrible singer.

Sofía: But I would sit there, and once or twice I would make the guitarist play the guitar so I could sing alone. I would tell Ortiz Tirado, "No," that I would sing alone. [*Laughter*] At home they said I did not have an ear. Actually, I do have an ear, because I can recognize perfectly. What I could not do was reproduce. I always sang badly, but I listened well. Andrés had a lot of confidence in me in that aspect, and he would sit and play and would ask me to listen to him. "My daughter, did I play the same thing as yesterday?" And I was able to tell him exactly where he had made a mistake, when he used a different note.

The weeks following the arrival of Paquita Madriguera's three daughters in Montevideo passed without any special activities for the two artists other than reestablishing the family environment. Through the diary entries we learn that during the months of July and August they dedicated their time to their social life, the visit with Uruguay's President Terra, and some nights at the theater, including the presentation of Pirandello's play *Tutto per bene* (All's Well) at the Teatro Solís by Anton Bragaglia's Italian company.[24] Segovia and Paquita were also present at the reception given for the visiting theater group at the Italian embassy after the show. They also took walks and made a visit to the Estadio Centenario (Centennial Stadium) to watch a soccer game. The fact that Paquita made no mention in her diary about two noted visits from artists who were her countrymen draws attention in a negative way. We can probably find the reason in the clear division of opposing sides that the Spanish Civil War had created in Montevideo. These visitors were none other than Margarita Xirgú and Pablo Casals. The famous Catalonian cellist and conductor performed as soloist with the SODRE Symphony, conducted by Lamberto Baldi, at the Studio Auditorium of SODRE on December 1, 1937, after Casals had already been in Montevideo for several days. Segovia had written to Ponce about him when sharing his impressions of the political climate in Barcelona before the outbreak of the war, stating that those who remained had not fled for three reasons: being held prisoner, being afraid of leaving their families, or having made "bad calculations in the entrepreneurial spirit."[25] He included Casals among them, because he was part of those three reasons, and added that the Catalan cellist was sharing his existence in Barcelona with murderers and thieves.[26]

What is certain is that neither Segovia nor Paquita seemed interested in Casals's presence in Montevideo, just as the pianist's notes do not reflect that they had attended any of Margarita Xirgú's numerous performances at the Teatro 18 de Julio, just a few blocks from their home. This seems logical, since the magnificent Catalonian actress was seen in Montevideo as a symbol of Republican Spain, and she was always surrounded by an atmosphere of excitement and sympathy for her and what she stood for. Also, she had come to premiere *Doña Rosita la soltera* by García Lorca, a Republican supporter who had been murdered less than a year prior by Nationalist militia. Xirgú's performances generated such enthusiasm from audiences that the shows were performed up to three times a day. *Yerma* (Barren), also by García Lorca, was presented fifteen times during the month of August, alternating with seven other works—two others by García Lorca and works by Pirandello, George Bernard Shaw, and Alejandro Casona. As the researcher Cecilia Pérez Mondino stated,[27] "The Spanish Club, having already played its cards in favor of Franco, ignores the presence of Margarita Xirgú in Montevideo."

Times, and with them enmities, would change, little by little, and some years later Paquita and Segovia would establish friendly ties with the Catalonian actress before she settled permanently in Montevideo to become the key figure in the development of the Uruguayan theater. Margarita Xirgú's season ended on August 31, and the following day she was honored by the entire group of theater critics from the different press media, among them the writer Francisco Espínola from the newspaper *El País*. Pablo Casals showed up at the end of the event, having performed at the Studio Auditorium that same day.[28]

Preparations for Segovia's next concert tour of Europe and the United States occupied the first three weeks of September 1937. His only professional activity during those days was participating in a literary-musical event at the SODRE Studio Auditorium on September 7, providing a cameo appearance for a conference given by the Uruguayan jurist and intellectual Eduardo J. Couture. The guitarist had been preparing new transcriptions and adding other original works for guitar to his repertoire.[29] His departure, which had been scheduled for September 8, according to his letter to Ponce of August 10, was postponed to September 21. On Sunday, September 19, the couple was honored by a group of friends with a farewell luncheon at the Golf Club of Montevideo, but the departure suffered a new, yet brief, delay. Paquita states in her diary on that day, "We were to depart at 7 AM on the *Cap Arcona*, but it ran aground as soon as it left B. Aires."

The great German ship, the largest of those arriving in South American ports at that time, finally departed at sundown on September 23 with the two musicians aboard. The girls were at the dock to bid them farewell, accompanied by other family members with whom they would remain during Paquita's long absence. The couple had a four-hour layover in Rio de Janeiro on the morning of September 26, which they took advantage of by lunching at the home of the Teráns. On the night of October 7 they arrived at the British port of Plymouth.

The next morning they traveled overland to London. There, two weeks later, they received news of a horrible accident that resulted in the death of Segovia's youngest son, who was thirteen. The accident occurred on October 21 in Versoix, close to Geneva. Leonardo and two of his classmates from the Monnier Institute in Versoix were walking less than a mile from school in the afternoon, following the tracks of an electric railway system with the idea of building a hut in the woods. Leonardo decided to cross over the tracks running between two hills via an overhead metallic aqueduct, which formed part of the Versoix flood canal and carried about an inch of water at the time. The bridgelike viaduct had gates and warning signs posted at each end to keep people from walking across it, but the boys had crossed this way before and apparently were not afraid. About halfway across, and with his two companions close behind, Leonardo stooped down to go under one of the live cables that supplied current to the trains passing below and touched it with a wet stick. Standing in water on the metal viaduct, the young boy provided an almost perfect conduit to the ground, and he was immediately struck by a flaming bolt of 15,000 volts that enveloped his body in flames. The powerful shock created a noise like a thunderclap that was heard throughout the neighborhood; it also short-circuited the train system. The other two boys were temporarily blinded by the flash but recovered quickly and, seeing the charred and lifeless body of their companion lying in the viaduct channel, ran back to report the tragedy to Institute officials.[30] Don Andrés found out about the mishap shortly before going on stage at Wigmore Hall the next day. María Rosa explained:

I have a vague memory about comments family members made concerning the day Leonardo died; Andrés had a concert, and they notified him about the death just before the concert. Andrés, with that sorrow upon him, still performed. And I understand from family comments that it was a magnificent concert. Perhaps the pain he carried within added something to his playing.[31]

After finishing the programmed activities in London, and probably still suffering under the weight of the tragedy, Segovia and his wife went to Hamburg, and on November 9 it was on to Berlin. The entries in Paquita's diary were interrupted on October 14, and until November 17 the only note is the usual reference to Segovia's birthday on November 11 (probably entered beforehand). On Wednesday, November 17, while the couple was in Berlin, there is an important clarification regarding the prolonged "silence" with this

WIGMORE HALL.			October 22nd, 1937.

SEGOVIA

PROGRAMME.

Chaconne	-	-	-	-	PACHELBEL (1653-1706)
Allemande	-	-	)		
Bourrée	-	-	) -	-	J. S. BACH
Andante et Menuet	-	-	-	-	HAYDN
Canzonetta	-	-	-	-	MENDELSSOHN
Prelude	-				
Allemande	-				
Capriccio	-	-	-	-	S. L. WEISS (1686-1750)
Ballet	-		Written for the lute.		
Sarabande	-				
Gavotte	-				
Gigue	-				
Sonatina Meridional (Dedicated to Segovia)		-	-	M. PONCE
Campo. Copla. Fiesta.				
Tarantella (Dedicated to Segovia)	-	CASTELNUOVO—TEDESCO		
Serenata	-	-	-	-	MALATS
Torre Bermeja	-	-	-	-	ALBENIZ

GUITAR by RAMIREZ   HIS MASTER'S VOICE RECORDS

IBBS & TILLETT, 124, WIGMORE STREET. W.1

Telephone : Welbeck 2525 (5 lines)   Ticket Office : Welbeck 8418
Telegrams : "Organol. Wesdo. London"   Hours, 10—8. Saturdays, 10—12

London, October 22, 1937.

note: "Due to a constant unrest related to my pregnancy, I have not made my daily entries in over a month."

It is quite likely that Paquita perceived the first signs of the pregnancy a few weeks after starting out on the trip, but there are no entries in the diary. The day following that entry, and also from the German capital, she sent her youngest daughter, María Rosa, who had turned ten in August, a typed letter in which she makes no mention at all of her state or the dramatic news that was overwhelming them. However, she shared some other bits of information relevant to our story:

Thank you for your little letter. We are so happy to hear that you are doing well. We see that you are having a lot of fun and going to a lot of places; we really are happy when you tell us that you go to a party or an excursion, etc., etc. Andrés gives his last concert here today,[32] and goes on to Hungary, Austria, Czechoslovakia, Kaunas (Lithuania), and Riga (Latvia); and later to Paris, Switzerland and a return to Germany in January, where he has to play again. I still do not know if I will leave or stay here. But since I will continue to write to you, you will find out. Always send the letters to Geneva. Dr. Méndez gives you a lot of gifts,[33] and I would love to see the Japanese parrot. I also suspect the radio must be on day and night.

Are you behaving? Remember that on vacations you must make your own beds because Basilisa, having to prepare lunch and wash so many dishes, etc., has no time, and you should not overload her with work. Are you taking your supplements? Do you eat a lot? When I return I want to ask, "Who is that big and pretty girl?" And they will tell me, "María Rosa." You do not know how much Andrés has been wondering if you are still studying the guitar, and when you said that you like it a lot in your letter, it made him very happy. Does Mr. Rodríguez get there on time?[34]

We anxiously await your letters and we read them three or four times; so tell me things and do not stop writing. I did not think about arranging solfeggio lessons during vacations for you and Pitusa, and piano for you. It would be desirable, if it is not too expensive, for the same teacher to come from Crandon to continue the lessons two days a week.[35] You could schedule them during the sunniest part of the day, like two to three or three to four in the afternoon; that is when you must make yourself stay indoors. Tell Dr. Méndez this.

With our fondest regards for Dr. Méndez, Uncle Alberto and Aunt Josefina, Marta, Aguiar, and everyone whom you see often, and kisses for everyone's children from me, the three of you receive many kisses from Andrés and your mommy, who loves you always.

Following Segovia's last concert in Berlin, the couple was feted by the city's Uruguayan ambassador on November 20, and on the morning of November 21 Segovia left for Budapest. Paquita remained a few more days in Berlin, and on Thursday, November 25, she left for Vienna, where Andrés was awaiting her. After a few days in the Austrian capital, sharing reunions with friends and colleagues, the two musicians left for Segovia's concerts in Prague and, 115 miles away, in Brno. While in Prague they met several times with Uruguayan and Spanish diplomats. Later they left for Switzerland, making a one-day stopover in Berlin for another reunion with the Uruguayan ambassador. The trip to Switzerland meant facing the details of the tragedy that had occurred a month earlier, although there is no mention of it at all in Paquita's diary. They arrived in Montreux on December 6, and Segovia continued on that day, alone, to Geneva. The next day Paquita traveled there and they stayed, as usual, at the Hotel Victoria. According to the pianist's diary, Andresito went almost every day to eat or spend the day with them, but there is no mention of either Leonardo or the fatal accident. Paquita and Segovia stayed until the end of the year in the Swiss city,[36] and on December 30 she wrote in her notebook, "Andresito leaves in the morning."

Paquita returned to Montevideo in January, probably because of her advanced pregnancy; or perhaps she was having other health problems—in addition to the economic reasons that Segovia invoked in the letter to Ponce below. In the meantime, Don Andrés headed for what would be his last tour in North America for five years. On February 14, 1938, from New York, he wrote Ponce, still weighed down with grief, thanking him and Clema for a letter in which his friends expressed their sympathy to Don Andrés. He also told Ponce that perhaps someday he would be able to openly talk with him about the circumstances of the accident and about Adelaida's resultant responsibility in the tragedy. The loss of Leonardo was so terribly felt by the father that he declined to elaborate on the subject at that occasion. But there was, at the same time, a certain light shining on the horizon, and he communicated the news to his friend: Paquita was expecting a baby, and Segovia felt that

Sofía, María Rosa, and Pitusa Puig Madriguera surround Segovia at his
arrival in Montevideo on April 18, 1938; Aparicio Méndez is on the far left.
This photo was published on April 19, 1938, in *El Diario* (Montevideo).

it would be a kind of repenting of destiny after the harm it had caused him
through his son's death. The baby was expected toward the last days of May,
but Segovia felt that his life had changed immensely and that he was "as old
as the world." Feeling hopeless, his only relief was working.[37]

Andrés Segovia returned to Montevideo on April 18, 1938, to recover at
home from the tragedy he had suffered, to rest from the long and tiring tour,
and to await the arrival of the new baby. Of the almost twelve months that had
passed since he and Paquita had arrived in that city, Segovia had only spent
four of them in Uruguay. Just nine days after arriving, the artist obtained his
Uruguayan identification document (expedited by the police headquarters in
Montevideo) and his driver's license. Both documents bear the date of April
27, 1938.[38] On June 5 Paquita's fourth daughter, Beatriz Isabel Segovia Madriguera, was born in a private clinic in Montevideo, and Don Andrés became
a father for the third time. The godfather was Aparicio Méndez, and the baby
came into the world surrounded by three sisters who awaited her with the
eager expectation of again living in a stable family environment. Montevideo
was assuming a new significance in the life of Andrés Segovia.

Chapter 11

Montevideo—Fruitful Isle of Stability

Various circumstances were to converge in the near future to give Montevideo an increasingly complex significance in the life of Andrés Segovia. It is very probable that, halfway through 1938, the guitarist still believed that this "cute little country" (as he described it more than once) would be a rest station between tours until events, including the stabilization of the economy, allowed him to settle with the entire family in some location closer to the musical and economic centers that he considered important. At the same time, Paquita, who had stayed away from an active music life since her first marriage sixteen years earlier, seemed to now be subjugated to the role of the distinguished, illustrious lady accompanying the relevant artist. Segovia's next trip to Europe, in September 1938, a few months after the birth of their daughter, generated some circumstances that called for sudden and considerable changes in the future perspective of both musicians. He began the tour alone, and Paquita joined him in Italy a month later after recovering from an operation.[1]

The first event of outstanding importance took place following three months of intense concert activity for Segovia in dozens of halls throughout Europe. Around the traditional holidays that mark the end of the year and a brief recess in the northern hemisphere's music season, the Segovia-Madriguera couple went to Florence at the invitation of Mario Castelnuovo-Tedesco. The composer, of Jewish origin and suffering persecution under

Mussolini's regime, was contemplating the possibility of going into exile in the United States. At a time when Castelnuovo-Tedesco had become an outcast in his own country, with most of his colleagues turning their backs on him out of fear or complicity, the fact that his Spanish friends had consented to share his home, celebrations, and family meals could be seen as a sign of solid support. The visit with the composer also had other consequences that would significantly influence the life of the couple during the coming years. Corazón Otero—the Mexican guitarist, writer, and biographer of Castelnuovo-Tedesco—narrates what happened during those weeks linking 1938 and 1939:

> [The Castelnuovo-Tedescos] were indecisive about which goal they should choose, for no European location seemed safe. After thinking about it long and hard, they decided to leave for the United States, a free country— strong and full of resources—where they also had friends waiting who would help them. Castelnuovo-Tedesco decided not to write to them from Italy because the correspondence was censored. He traveled to Switzerland and from there he wrote to Toscanini, Heifetz, and Spalding explaining his situation.[2] He received moving proof of friendship and solidarity. Toscanini immediately sent a telegram assuring Castelnuovo-Tedesco that Heifetz, Spalding, and he would provide him a place to live and find him a job. Castelnuovo-Tedesco returned to Florence more optimistic and comforted. They continued to write to each other, but in code. Later Heifetz wrote saying that he would find him a job in the movie industry, and further procedures were needed for housing. The censor was probably surprised to read the letter in which he said that the editor needed to know the ages of his wife and children in order to publish his music.
>
> Andrés Segovia's gesture was exquisite, and Castelnuovo-Tedesco would never forget it: [Segovia] traveled to Florence to spend Christmas with him and encourage him to hope for a better future. He advised him by telling him not to lose hope—that with his talent he would get ahead in America, starting a new life. Segovia's words and solidarity comforted him enormously. Castelnuovo-Tedesco was moved by this true test of friendship and pledged that the first work he wrote would be the concerto for guitar and orchestra that he had promised him so many times. Andrés Segovia was very happy and continued to encourage him; Castelnuovo-Tedesco wrote the first movement of the concerto in one sitting, and together they

revised it. Segovia, satisfied, left for Uruguay, where he was living at the time. In January 1939 Castelnuovo-Tedesco finished the other two movements of the guitar concerto and sent them to Segovia.[3]

This work was destined to play an important role in both the history of the guitar repertoire and the Segovia-Madrigueras' music practice once they returned to Montevideo. The Concerto in D Major for Guitar and Orchestra was the beginning of an intense joint effort by the couple as Segovia prepared the concerto's premiere in Montevideo, with Paquita playing the orchestra reduction on the piano. It was also this concerto that motivated the pianist's return to the stage, when she and her husband began presenting it in a version for guitar and piano in a number of Latin American cities.

Castelnuovo-Tedesco finally received his immigration permit on April 3, 1939, and was able to board ship with his entire family for North America on July 13, less than two months before the outbreak of World War II. Paquita included in her book some memories of the visit to Florence, while their friend's drama unfolded and bloodshed was brewing in Europe:

The composer Mario Castelnuovo-Tedesco, who, like Mendelssohn, belonged to a family of bankers without the figures having dried up their source of musical inspiration, invited us to spend Christmas Eve with him, his family, and some close friends, who are the family God forgets to give. We had just returned from Siena. My husband had given a concert in the chapel of the Palace of Count Chigi Saracini. This very distinguished and cultured gentleman is a difficult figure to forget and is envisaged only when surrounded by refined grandeur. He offered us a place to stay at his medieval palace, its interior brimming with masterpieces of art. . . .

Commander Alberto Passigli and his wife invited me to a luncheon at their beautiful estate, Il Leccio [The Holly Oak].[4] I saw Riberas hanging on the walls and other paintings just as admirable. The owner's keen artistic taste can be seen in the smallest details. They saved a special surprise for me that day. They introduced me to an old, but still very energetic, lady— the Countess Gravina, daughter of Hans Guido von Bülow and Cosima Liszt,[5] and granddaughter of the great Liszt. She talked to me extensively about her grandfather and her father—about the musical gatherings at their respective homes, about their opinions of pianists of that period. I absorbed everything as the thirsty ground does the rain. I would have liked to carve the conversation in granite. At one point I had the misfortune to mention Wagner and she got furious. The mere name of her mother's seducer made her furious, as if the event had taken place recently.[6] . . .

Mr. and Mrs. Contini-Bonacossi showed us their valuable collection of works by Greco, Velázquez, Murillo, Ribera, Sasseta, Piero della Francesca, Titian, and I do not remember how many more.[7] The galleries that store their treasures are far away from the coldness of a museum, and, on the contrary, live very intelligently arranged between beautiful pink azaleas, which are set in attractive planters that divide the rooms in half. In spite of which I have to confess that it is the only house in Italy that, amidst the accumulation of important works of art, I guessed where the typewriters and registers were hidden.[8]

The marquis of Antinori and his wife invited us to their villa. I hesitate to describe the interior of their palace. It is sufficient to say once and for all that in Italy the wonders are so numerous that they are found in every house whose owners have wealth and refinement.

The park surrounding the villa was astonishing. Its structure and the type of flowers adorning it—it's among the most beautiful I have ever seen in my life.[9]

The concerto that was born during the days of the visit in Florence is not mentioned in Paquita's chronicle, written some years after its premiere. However, a letter to María Rosa from this city on January 3, 1939, includes a phrase referring to this unique piece: "Andrés is very happy because the composer Castelnuovo-Tedesco is writing a concerto for guitar and orchestra for him, having already finished the first movement."

Segovia discussed the work in detail in the course of a long letter he wrote to Ponce on August 26 of that year (several months after returning to Montevideo), while urging the Mexican composer to continue writing the concerto he had begun several years earlier. He told his friend that Castelnuovo-Tedesco had written a "delicious" concerto for him. He was in Florence with Paquita when the Italian composer wrote the first movement, and then Segovia and his wife recalled for him the theme of the concerto that Ponce had begun.[10]

The second relevant event that took place in January 1939 was the suspension of Segovia's tour of the United States, scheduled to begin in February. When he and Paquita were preparing to travel to North America, a telegram

notified him of the reluctance of the impresarios to carry out the organization
of concerts scheduled there. They had departed from Florence on January
15 and arrived in London the next day, when Segovia played on both BBC
Radio and Television. He had a long studio session for His Master's Voice on
the January 17, recording works by Albéniz (*Granada* and *Sevilla*), Granados
(*Spanish Dances Nos. 5* and *10*), de Visée, and Froberger. Segovia played again
on the radio on January 18, and that night he received a notice sent by the
American concert manager F. C. Coppicus, as recorded in Paquita's diary and
by the guitarist to Ponce in the letter just cited. He wrote that "the infamous
Mr. Coppicus" had announced to him by telegram that his American tour had
been canceled, and that it was easy to imagine the reason: "It was the retaliation of the Jewish societies." Segovia said that they had already warned him
that if he did not retract his pro-Franco statements he would not be able to
play in the United States. So, he and Paquita had returned to Montevideo,
where he awaited the musical season of that part of South America to play
in various parts of Argentina.[11]

Coppicus's telegram forced the two musicians to change their plans just
as they were getting ready to leave for the United States. They extended their
stay in the British capital until February 4, probably awaiting the departure
of a ship for the Río de la Plata. Paquita's diary records that those unexpected weeks of vacation were put to use by sharing lunches and dinners with
friends, going to see a collection of old instruments, and attending a concert
by the Uruguayan cellist Oscar Nicastro.[12] They had several meetings with
the consul general of Uruguay in Great Britain, César Montero Bustamante,
and had lunch on January 27 with him, his wife, and Salvador de Madariaga.
On January 30, after the conclusion of Nicastro's concert, they visited the
consul's home.

On February 4, 1939, Don Andrés and Paquita boarded the *Andalucía
Star* at the port of Tilbury. They arrived in Montevideo twenty days later,
after stopovers in Lisbon, Madeira, and Tenerife. For the rest of February
and the entire month of March they remained at the apartment on Avenida
18 de Julio, devoting themselves to family life. Paquita's diary entries mention
occasional outings to the countryside and to Colonia Suiza.[13]

Barcelona fell to Franco's troops on February 10, while the couple was returning from Europe. A few days after they arrived in Montevideo, the triumph
of the rebels over the Spanish Republic was proclaimed. Segovia included an

optimistic and euphoric phrase in a letter dated March 8 written (in English) to his friend Sophocles Papas in Washington, D.C.: "The war in Spain is almost won, with the victory of our ideals! I cannot finish this letter without setting down, in Spanish, our Nationalist cry: ¡*Arriba España!* [Up with Spain!]"[14]

Madrid fell on March 28, 1939, and on April 1 General Francisco Franco officially declared the end of the war. Over the next few days Paquita Madriguera and Andrés Segovia attended several festivities organized by Spanish Nationalists residing in Montevideo. On April 6 they were present at an event organized by the Spanish Phalange at the Teatro Solís,[15] on April 11 there was another celebration at the Cine Azul, and on April 16 they participated in a Te Deum in the cathedral—"for the peace in Spain," as Paquita states in her diary.[16]

Segovia's musical activities were restarting, little by little, following those first few weeks of rest, celebrations, and rebuilding the family's life together. There were several concerts in Buenos Aires and Montevideo during the month of May, and the guitarist started traveling alone to the family's country estate, probably looking for the essential peace and quiet he needed to practice (the family now included three teen-aged girls and a baby who was less than a year old), sometimes accompanied by Paquita. On April 18, they received a visit for tea from the composer Eduardo Fabini and the guitarist Abel Carlevaro at their apartment, as recorded in Paquita's diary. Many years later, recalling that period when the Uruguayan guitarist was his student, Segovia would state in a letter published on December 8, 1976, in the Montevideo newspaper *El País*: "It would be unfair to overlook the affectionate reference to Abel Carlevaro. From those afternoons when my lessons concluded with a family cup of tea, his talent continues to evolve."

Carlevaro referred to his relationship with the Spanish maestro on many occasions. He described his teacher's customs and the environment in which he lived after settling into the home in Pocitos:

> I worked with him for nine years, but I really did not learn these things [referring to guitar technique]. I learned other things. Among the first was the discipline that he had. It was very important because I had always been very undisciplined. . . . When I saw that Segovia was always so exact, methodical, that he got up at a certain time, that he worked seven or eight hours, and he called me by phone to walk with him (to rest his hands)

along the entire length of Pocitos Beach, the Rambla. I do not know how many kilometers we walked. . . . He had a beautiful home that belonged to Paquita Madriguera, his previous wife—Spanish, a very good pianist and very pretty. It was like a little castle, on Massini and Benito Blanco Streets; the palm trees remain because later this house was demolished and they constructed an apartment building there. Well, the location was very pretty and a lot of people went there. In that house I met Ponce, Manuel de Falla—many people that, when Segovia came to Montevideo, were there with him, and I was there also.[17]

Segovia's concerts in Argentina took place from the first days of May to July 9, 1939. The agenda was very intense during those days, alternating trips to the neighboring republic and returns to Montevideo. Sometimes he went alone and other times he was accompanied by Paquita (and even one of her daughters). Some crossings of the Río de la Plata were by ship from the Uruguayan capital, others were made by ferry after driving the car a hundred miles west to Colonia del Sacramento, and some were made by plane. Between May 3 and June 20, Segovia made six trips to Buenos Aires to perform in concert halls and play on the radio. Each of these excursions lasted between three and four days, and on some of those trips he and Paquita also had meetings with the painter Miguel del Pino and his wife,[18] as well as with the Spanish pianist José Iturbi.[19] Alternating with these visits to the Argentinean capital, the guitarist gave two concerts at Teatro Solís, on May 19 and 26.

Segovia's ties with Paquita's daughters were strong. On May 20 he traveled to Buenos Aires accompanied by María Rosa. On June 10, he was joined by Paquita and Sofía in a car the couple had purchased a few weeks earlier, crossing by ferry at Colonia. On the night of their arrival in the Argentinean capital the three attended José Iturbi's concert at the Teatro Colón.

Segovia left on the night of July 6, 1939, for the last of these trips to Argentina for performances on July 8 and 9 at the Teatro Rivera Indarte in Córdoba, 450 miles northwest of Buenos Aires. A curious detail appears on the printed program of the second Córdoba concert, the third part of which opened with the famous *Chôros No. 1* by Heitor Villa-Lobos. Segovia had them add the following comment after the name of the piece: "From a group of works for guitar, twelve of which are dedicated to A. Segovia."[20] The guitarist was obviously trying to hide the fact that this particular work had not been dedicated to him by putting it into a package with the great Brazilian

Segovia in 1939. The dedication to his stepdaughter reads: "To my dear Sofía, in whom affection and knowledge, sensitivity, and intelligence are concentrated. With all love from your Andrés, XXXIX."

composer's Twelve Etudes, of which Segovia had only four at that time. It has become well-known that Segovia's impression of Villa-Lobos's Etudes, written in 1928–29, was fairly poor at that time, and it would be more than another twelve years before the set was finally published.

At the end of June, a few days before Segovia traveled to Córdoba and two years after moving into the apartment on Avenida 18 de Julio, the family decided to move to Paquita's country home in the department of Canelones, just north of Montevideo. This was an intermediate step before moving into the house on Massini Street, which was being vacated and renovated for them. Since the couple's trip to Europe was scheduled to begin in September (though it was later canceled by the outbreak of World War II), Mamá Paqui had arrived to settle in Montevideo and take charge of the four girls while Andrés and Paquita were in the Old World. The three older ones were again placed as boarders in the same school they were already attending, so that they would not have to travel every day from the country to Montevideo for classes. Segovia's August 26 letter to Ponce stated that his plans at that moment included a new tour of Europe, although he feared that it would be interrupted by what seemed like the imminent outbreak of war. His manager, Ernesto de Quesada, also proposed continuing afterward through the Caribbean countries and Central America. The decision on whether to include Mexico in the tour depended, for Segovia, on Ponce's instructions regarding repercussions there over the guitarist's political positions concerning Spain. He feared that his well-known opinions about Franco would provoke demonstrations against him and his friends. Besides, he was not able to afford the impact of the "popular anger of Mexico" or "the attitude of the Spanish refugees" at the box office. So, he told Ponce that he would be happy to go to Mexico if the political situation would calm down and his friend could assure him that none of what he feared would happen.[21]

In the postscript, Segovia told Ponce about his change of address, informing him that they had been in the country for two months, as the house in Montevideo had been packed. He asked his friend to send his letters to Banco Francés, Supervielle and Co., where they were going to pick up their mail twice a week.

Those two months that Don Andrés and Paquita spent in the peaceful and quiet tranquility of the Uruguayan countryside—and the two months that followed, after the war forced a change in their plans—were used by the guitarist to work intensely on the Castelnuovo-Tedesco concerto, with

Two photos of Paquita taken at the country home.

his wife playing the orchestra part on the piano. The Italian composer had finished the last two movements of the work before completing his plans for exile, and the package with the entire work must have arrived in Montevideo shortly after Paquita and her husband returned to the city in February; but it is possible that Segovia's hectic activity in May and June, along with the move from the downtown apartment, delayed work on the concerto until he and Paquita were both settled in at the country estate.

No written evidence has been found regarding the degree of participation by the pianist-composer-wife in the adaptation process of Castelnuovo's originals to the final version of the guitar part by Segovia. Knowing Paquita Madriguera's strong personality and the abundant references to her musical talent, it would not be surprising if she did play a decisive role more than once in Segovia's work with the concerto, through her opinions and suggestions. At the same time, it is easy to imagine the enthusiasm she must have felt by the revival of the vocation that had lay dormant for so many years, or at least reduced in importance by her family responsibilities and social activities. Paquita's home life had been substantially modified in the months spent at the country estate, considering the pace since the return to Barcelona and the beginning of her ties to Segovia. Beatriz was cared for with the help of a nanny, the older daughters were at boarding school Monday through Friday, and Mamá Paqui took command of a good part of the household chores. The favorable conditions and bucolic environment did its work, and Paquita's return to the concert stage was gradual—at first accompanying Segovia on Castelnuovo-Tedesco's Guitar Concerto. Probably feeling confident after passing those "tests," she could later be seen as a soloist in Manuel Ponce's Concerto for Piano and Orchestra, as well as giving concerts with her wealth of important works from the piano repertoire, which she had never totally abandoned in her practice routine. María Rosa confirmed that her mother never lost the habit of daily practice, at least from the time they all settled again in Montevideo:

> Mama never stopped playing the piano for one day. What's more, at the house on Massini Street there were two—the baby grand Steinway and an upright (Bluthner) that she had in her bedroom. She said [the action of] the latter was stiffer and better to practice with. The only time she did not study was when she was ill. I really cannot remember a day I did not hear the piano.[22]

Paquita's daughters also pointed out that the musical coexistence of the two artists was complicated. Except for those moments of collaboration when Segovia worked on the Castelnuovo-Tedesco and Ponce concertos, it was not feasible for them both to practice at the same time, since the sound produced by one would interfere with the work of the other. They were forced to take turns—six hours each, dispersed throughout the day. While Paquita practiced, Don Andrés would go out on his walks or write, and vice versa: when it was the guitarist's turn to practice, she would go shopping or visit her friends. Sofía Puig stated that there was a more subjective aspect to the division as well. According to her, two such strong musical temperaments could not be free of some rivalry, of a certain dose of competition that would at times generate disagreements and illustrate the interesting contrast in background between the well-trained pianist and the self-taught guitarist. A daughter may be forgiven some bias toward her mother. Nevertheless, Sofía did state her opinion: "Mama was more of a musician. She had received a more complete education. Besides, she was a composer and he was not."[23]

What is certain is that at both the country estate and the residence in Pocitos—starting the following year—music was being played nonstop. Piano, guitar, or both at the same time gave a special atmosphere to the Segovia-Madriguera home, and according to María Rosa's recollections, "the maids and cooks all did their work humming classical music."

The decision to premiere Castelnuovo-Tedesco's concerto in Montevideo was made at the beginning of September 1939, after the outbreak of war spoiled Segovia's plans for the European tour scheduled to begin that month. He had planned to play it for the first time during a BBC radio program in London, commenting to Ponce (in the letter of August 26) that in a radio performance it would be easier to balance the sound. Segovia also told Ponce that the concerto was very ingenious and successful, and that José Iturbi hoped to premiere it with him. However, the guitarist expressed some distrust that the conductor would put the orchestra against him, making it sound too loud, and ruin in a moment what he had taken so many years to obtain.

The terrible and tragic sequence of military and political events that were triggered in Europe just a few days after Segovia wrote this long letter created a decisive turn in his plans for the immediate future, including the premiere of the concerto. The doors in the United States had been closed earlier that year for political reasons, and the hope of concerts in Europe was shut down for a foreseeably long time. What remained was the alternative offered by the rich musical atmosphere of the Río de la Plata area. In particular, Segovia could count on Montevideo, with the state institution of SODRE, which had the resources of its excellent Studio Auditorium and a radio station that broadcast classical music all year round.[24] And SODRE had built a highly competent orchestra conducted since 1932 by its Italian music director, Lamberto Baldi. It thus seems natural that Segovia should have decided to give the world premiere there of the work that Castelnuovo-Tedesco had dedicated to him in Florence in January, and on which he and Paquita had ardently worked for the past three or four months in the country house where they lived.

During that time, as recorded in Paquita's diary, the couple traveled to Montevideo just twice a week—on Mondays, to take the girls to the Crandon Institute, and on Fridays, to pick them up and bring them back to the country. That apparent routine of a peaceful life with limited trips to the capital was broken several times due to some dispute, which should not be surprising in this marriage of strongly individual personalities. Occasional entries in the pianist's diary to the effect that "Andrés leaves home" are followed two or three days later by, "Andrés returns."

There is a striking reflection written by Paquita the day after one of Segovia's departures: "The artistic genius is a disease that attacks both the refined spirits and commoners alike; they carry it as the oyster carries the pearl."

On October 23, 1939, Andrés Segovia traveled to Montevideo to rehearse the Castelnuovo-Tedesco concerto with the SODRE Symphony. Paquita, who accompanied him, was assigned to sit some distance from the stage to test the balance between the guitar and the orchestra. The guitarist himself reflected on this in an interview in Havana a few years later, in 1943:

> To a question put to him about the limited sound of the guitar—if it could be heard clearly when accompanied by an entire orchestra—he responded that his wife, Paquita Madariaga [sic]—a great pianist, by the way—had that same doubt when they were rehearsing the work in Montevideo, which is why she sat in the last row and marveled at the effect achieved by the sound of this instrument. Segovia then quoted something Stravinsky told him: "Your guitar cannot be heard a little; it can be heard afar."[25]

Segovia then returned to the country, but on October 26 Paquita took him back to the city by car. The guitarist preferred to stay alone at the Hotel

Hotel Alhambra in Montevideo.

Alhambra, situated in Ciudad Vieja (Old City, in the port area just off the main downtown), about a hundred yards away from the hall where two days later he would premiere the concerto. He needed tranquility even more than usual, since he was taking a very big step: this would be the first time he had ever performed solo with a symphony orchestra, although the orchestration chosen by Castelnuovo-Tedesco was quite reduced. The day of the concert was a Saturday and the country home was going to be hectic, as was common during the weekends with the presence of all the girls, in addition to Mamá Paqui, Paquita, and the servants. The Concerto in D Major for Guitar and Orchestra by Mario Castelnuovo-Tedesco was premiered at the SODRE Studio Auditorium at 6:00 P.M. on October 28, 1939. The SODRE Symphony Orchestra was conducted by Lamberto Baldi, and Andrés Segovia's performance was a resounding success. The recording preserved in the historical archives of the Uruguayan state organization allows us to appreciate—in spite of some deterioration due to the conditions under which it was made and the passage of time—Segovia's interpretative powers at that stage

The Studio Auditorium of SODRE. Photograph taken around 1948.

in his career, as well as the benefits of playing with the orchestra conducted by Maestro Baldi. The trial was successfully overcome, and the guitarist had proof that he could match his instrument with a properly integrated and managed orchestra. After the concert, Don Andrés and Paquita serenely left to see a movie in a Montevideo theater.

The day following the premiere, the Montevideo press—whose front pages were occupied with news of the war in Europe, which had been going on for almost two months—highlighted, in the reduced space designated for cultural and artistic life, the fact that a world premiere of that category had taken place in the Uruguayan capital. Under the title "First Performance of a Concerto for Guitar and Orchestra," one review read:

Next came the Concerto for Guitar and Orchestra by Castelnuovo-Tedesco, a work awaited with great interest by our public because the guitar has been incorporated for the first time with the entire orchestra. And to play that instrument we had to have an artist on the scale of the

Spanish guitarist, Andrés Segovia. Indeed, a plausible task of the illustrious Italian composer, elevating the guitar to the place it occupied in past centuries, putting it back in the category as a noble instrument it had in orchestral history [*sic*]. With this criterion, Castelnuovo-Tedesco has composed a modern, original, and inspired work that gives natural prominence to the guitar and provides a new opportunity for Andrés Segovia to highlight his remarkable qualities as a guitar performer.... It was without doubt a musical performance of great interest, because of the ability of the performers as well as for the cited concertos by Vivaldi and Castelnuovo-Tedesco, the latter offered for the first time in the world.[26]

Lamberto Baldi, conductor of the SODRE Symphony Orchestra.

The remainder of 1939 passed without any other professional activity for the couple other than the daily practice of their respective instruments and, in the case of the guitarist, the preparation of new transcriptions to be printed—by Argentinean publishers because of the war in Europe. Segovia also dedicated the last two months of the year to preparing a tour of Mexico, the Caribbean, and some of the South American countries on the Pacific coast, starting in January. The traditional diary entry on every November 11, "Andrés's birthday," stands out during this stage. On that day, because it was a Saturday, they went to pick up the girls in Montevideo for a celebration with the entire family. Beginning on December 6, the Segovia-Madrigueras hosted a visit at their country home by the Spanish painter Miguel del Pino and his wife, who were living in Buenos Aires and had arrived to spend their summer vacation in the company of friends.

The usual quiet of those days was shattered by the Battle of the River Plate (as the British call the Río de la Plata), fought off the coast of Punta del Este (sixty-five miles east of Montevideo, where the Río de la Plata meets the Atlantic Ocean) between British and New Zealand cruisers and the German battleship *Admiral Graf Spee*. After suffering thirty-nine deaths and damage to the fuel and desalination systems, the German ship took refuge in the neutral port of Montevideo for repairs. Forced by international law to leave within seventy-two hours, the German captain left the bay on December 17, mistakenly believing that he was up against overwhelming odds. Four miles out in the Río and across from the hill that gave the city its name, he blew up and sank the battleship rather than risk the lives of his crew.[27] The spectacular and violent explosion, with flames and smoke rising high into the sky, was observed by the city's inhabitants from the Rambla and excited the entire population. Segovia went to Montevideo the next day, quite probably to see firsthand the consequences of this unique event, as the upper portion of the ship protruded above the water for many years until it gradually sank into the muddy bottom. Paquita and the Pinos followed him a day later, and they all went to the movies to watch the newsreel account of what had taken place in the capital while they were in El Campito.

On January 7, 1940, Andrés Segovia left Montevideo on a tour that would take him to Cuba, Puerto Rico, Mexico, Costa Rica, Peru, and Chile. Paquita remained in the country with her four daughters and Mamá Paqui; but, she was preparing for another important change of residence: the house on Massini Street would soon be vacant, and it was time to get it into condition for the family to live there in what would be, they hoped, their permanent residence. It was thus necessary for them to move to the capital to take charge of all the tasks required to get the house ready. On March 1 (a little before the older girls would have to resume classes and thirteen days before Segovia would return early from his tour) Paquita, her mother, and the four girls moved into the Hotel Cervantes, in downtown Montevideo, where they would all live for the next three months. This hotel still exists. It is located on Soriano Street, near the corner of Andes, and was declared a National Historical Monument in 2002 for its history as well as its architectural value. Its walls hold memories of such famous travelers as Carlos Gardel, Jorge Luis Borges, Atahualpa Yupanqui, and Julio Cortázar,[28] in addition to the two musicians of this story. Perhaps the words that Cortázar used to begin his short story *La puerta condenada* (The Condemned Door) can describe for us—even if just figuratively—the environment and atmosphere that he had perceived in this Montevideo hotel:

> Petrone liked the Hotel Cervantes for reasons others would not have liked. It was a somber hotel, tranquil, almost deserted. An acquaintance of the moment recommended it to him when he crossed the river in the express steamship, telling him that it was in downtown Montevideo....
>
> The elevator left you in front of the reception area, where there was a counter with daily newspapers and the telephone switchboard. He had

only to walk a few yards to get to the room. The water came out boiling, and that compensated for the lack of sun and air. There was a small window in the room that faced the roof of the movie theater next door; at times a pigeon would walk there. The bathroom had a larger window that sadly opened to a post and a far piece of sky, almost pointless. The furniture was good, and there were more than enough drawers and shelves. And lots of hangers—a rarity.[29]

Segovia arrived in Montevideo from Santiago de Chile on the morning of March 14, a few days ahead of schedule because, as he wrote to Manuel Ponce on the following day, his manager had made the mistake of choosing dates when the music season had not yet begun. At the same time, he proudly told him that the family was very happy because of his unexpected return.[30] The tour had started in Cuba and continued on to Puerto Rico before moving for a good part of February to Mexico, where Segovia stayed at the home of Manuel Ponce. There both musicians gave a final push to the decision to compose the guitar concerto that the Mexican had been putting off for several years. Segovia's success with Castelnuovo-Tedesco's work probably provided the momentum, always available from his guitarist friend, needed for Ponce's project. And the Mexican composer conducted the orchestra when Segovia premiered Castelnuovo-Tedesco's Concerto in D in Aztec lands that February. In 1948, shortly after Manuel Ponce's death, Segovia wrote an article that *Guitar Review* published in the composer's memory, one paragraph of which refers to the gestation of the *Concierto del sur*:

> Anyhow, the work waited. It waited until the tranquil confidence and foresight of Mario Castelnuovo-Tedesco—another composer to whom the guitar owes much—who, overcoming fears and hesitations, got ahead of Ponce, creating the delectable Concerto in D. Ponce himself accompanied me in Mexico conducting the orchestra, and that unforgettable experience was the best prodding for the Mexican musician to unearth and revive old themes, and set out to work on them with ardor.[31]

The final realization of the concerto by Ponce was not the only significant result (besides the guitarist's artistic activities) of Segovia's visit to Mexico. The basic idea of promoting an homage to the composer in Montevideo, where they would both premiere the concerto, was born during those days. The guitarist wasted no time and, on the day he arrived at the Hotel

Cervantes, got in touch with SODRE's authorities to organize Ponce's activities while in Montevideo. Segovia wrote to his friend on the following day and told him of the progress that he had made in just twenty-four hours: he had called Curt Lange[32] and talked with him to officially invite the Mexican composer to Montevideo; Lange immediately discussed it with the directors of SODRE; and Segovia would call his friends in Buenos Aires to extend the organization of the homage there. In any case, he did not want to make that call until all of the plans were finalized in Montevideo. He explained to Ponce that he was not being overcautious, "because the Argentineans do not want to be left behind by this small and friendly country," and they would be able to steal the idea and get the priority for the presence of Ponce.[33]

There is a lot of meaning in this last sentence if we keep in mind the enormous size difference between Buenos Aires and Montevideo—in terms of economic power, the size of the prospective audience, and the future impact on other markets that kept their eyes and ears on what was happening in the Argentinean capital while often ignoring the mere existence of the "small and friendly country" of Uruguay. Considering the weight that the guitarist usually attached to the material and tangible aspects of his professional life, his determination to preserve the Uruguayan capital standing in the organization of Ponce's activities is quite remarkable. It is a clear indication of how Don Andrés Segovia was bonding, at that stage in his life, with the city where he had established his home.

Another paragraph in the same letter allows us to infer that Segovia also had other ideas about Ponce's visit to Montevideo—ideas about Paquita and her relevance as a pianist. On the one hand, it seems clear that he wanted to repeat and deepen his earlier experience of preparing Castelnuovo-Tedesco's concerto with his wife. On the other hand, in a reference to Paquita's help, he asked Ponce to send him the orchestral score for his piano concerto. A week following the premiere of the *Concierto del sur*, Paquita Madriguera would reappear before the Montevideo public, after an absence of twenty years, as a soloist in Ponce's Concerto for Piano and Orchestra. Segovia also urged his friend to finish the parts for guitar and orchestra and to make a reduction for piano and guitar so that he could begin working on it immediately with Paquita.[34]

Segovia and Paquita's joint work on Ponce's concerto would still have to wait a few months, though in the *Guitar Review* homage Don Andrés said: "When I returned to my home in Montevideo, weeks later, I found the first results of his work."[35] It was in October 1940 that the first pages of the reduction for guitar and piano arrived in very thin airmail stationery. After initiating the plans for the tribute to Ponce and while waiting to return for the postponed concerts in Chile, Segovia rested at the country home and learned about Uruguayan traditions of the local celebrations of Holy Week,[36] while the family remained at the Hotel Cervantes. Paquita's diary says that on the evening of Tuesday, March 19, the two of them went to see the shows at the horse coliseum, which were the main attraction of Creole Week at the Prado of Montevideo.[37]

After those first days of rest, Segovia began preparations for the remainder of the suspended tour. This time he would go with Paquita, by plane, to Santiago de Chile, with a one-day stopover in Buenos Aires. Five concerts were scheduled in the Chilean capital—one presenting Castelnuovo-Tedesco's work with orchestra—between April 7 and 22. Segovia's reply to Ponce on April 15 from the Hotel Crillon adds details to the story, as in it he said that Paquita had gone for a walk but had returned immediately to the room when she saw the composer's envelope at the hotel's reception desk, anticipating the "fresh news" it would contain and the pleasure it would bring to her husband. Segovia was very emphatic in telling Ponce that he wished him to be much more successful than Castelnuovo-Tedesco with his concerto. This wish, he said, was motivated by the greater affection and admiration he felt for Ponce, with respect to what he felt for the Italian composer. He added that everyone, at his home, considered Ponce as "spiritual kin," and his success would fill all of them with joy.[38]

The "spiritual kin" reference to Ponce with the Segovia-Madrigueras ("all of us at home" must include Mamá Paqui as well), in contrast to the feelings about Castelnuovo, seems to allude to the positions of each one regarding the problems of Europe in general and Spain in particular, if the antifascist position of the Italian composer is kept in mind.[39] It also seems clear, from reading other fragments, that Segovia had not yet received the concerto materials, and that his knowledge of it came only from what he had seen in Mexico during his visit the previous February. It is evident that Paquita's musical opinions were well respected, and they were mentioned by Segovia when he informed Ponce that she suggested he use in the cadenza the formula of repeated notes that the composer had included in one of the variations he wrote for *Las*

Folías. Segovia added that he agreed with his wife's idea, and submitted it for Ponce's opinion. He also suggested that he add "*rasgueados*, fast scales, and chord arpeggios in close position."[40]

At the end of this long letter Segovia insists once more that Ponce send to Montevideo—looking at the homage that the guitarist is arranging for him—the work for piano and orchestra that he had already requested. It seems obvious that behind this order lies the intention that Paquita would take charge of its performance.

On their return from Chile, Don Andrés and Paquita made a stopover in Mendoza, Argentina, for the guitarist to give a concert on April 23 at the Municipal Theater. They left by plane the next day for Buenos Aires, and that night they traveled to Montevideo on the *Vapor de la Carrera.* Upon arriving at the Uruguayan capital, they received news that the house in Pocitos was finally ready, and on April 26 they went to inspect it, accompanied by their artist friend Miguel del Pino.[41]

The first two weeks of May in Montevideo were marked by the presence of Jascha Heifetz, who gave two concerts at Teatro Solís, on May 2 and 13. The violinist was accompanied by his wife, and on several occasions during his visit the Segovia-Madriguera couple shared reunions and meals with them and with Quesada, the manager who also represented Heifetz and had arrived with him. The meetings continued a few days later in Buenos Aires. On May 26, 1940, the couple attended Heifetz's concert at the Teatro Colón, and that night, after Segovia played a radio concert, he and Paquita had dinner with the violinist and his wife. The next day, following Segovia's concert at the Teatro Cervantes, they went to dinner with the Argentinean director Juan José Castro and his wife, the Chilean director Armando Carvajal (also accompanied by his wife), the musicologist Carlos Vega, and del Pino.

Once they returned to Montevideo, on the afternoon of May 28, Paquita Madriguera and Andrés Segovia had the task of moving into the house on Ramón Massini, half a block from Pocitos Beach. On Wednesday, May 29, as stated in the pianist's diary, they went to the country to move the furniture to Montevideo, and on the next day, May 30, Paquita writes: "We are leaving Hotel Cervantes for home (Massini)."

The residence had been purchased by Arturo Puig after his marriage to Paquita and had therefore been inherited by her as well as her three daughters, who were heirs to half of the properties. On September 15, Paquita

Madriguera's fortieth birthday and more than three months after the entire family was settled in what Segovia explicitly considered their final move, the guitarist told his friend Manuel Ponce that they had moved to Montevideo, to the beautiful house owned by Paquita and the Puig girls. The house was next to the beach and had a garden. He also informed Ponce that the property had been rented and for that reason they had been unable to move before. He described the house as bright and spacious, adding that it was as quiet as his friend's own house.[42]

The house where Segovia and Paquita lived with the four girls, in addition to Mamá Paqui during long periods of time, no longer exists. An apartment building has been erected in its place, and all that remains from the family's time there is the palm trees in front. María Rosa provides more details in her description:

> The house on Massini had fifteen hundred [square] meters of garden. As you entered, there was a great open room, all marbled. Then there was another large open room, and to each side there were two parts. In the one on the left, Mama had her baby grand piano, and she practiced there. The one on the right was Andrés's studio. It had furniture that was custom made to store his guitars; his desk was there, his footstools, his stand. They took turns practicing because, although the house was big, if Mama played the piano Andrés could not play the guitar. So they each had six hours. When Andrés was not playing, he sat at his desk and there he would write—"I am transcribing," he would say.

Interior of the house on Massini Street. The view is from Segovia's studio.

Then there were a great dining room and my parents' bedroom, with a private bathroom suite. At the end were the service bedrooms (we had a maid, a cook—well, service people). The second floor was our territory. There were several bedrooms and also one for my grandmother, Mamá Paqui, to use when she came. When Ponce came, I let him have my bedroom.[43]

After four years of constant relocation and travel, with all the ups and downs, the Segovia-Madrigueras and their four girls were finally settled in a large, comfortable home, located in a choice section of Montevideo where they could enjoy the stability that had, for many reasons, been so elusive. Significantly, a year would pass after the move to their Pocitos home before Segovia and his wife would travel abroad, not counting two brief crossings to Buenos Aires by the guitarist during the first days of June 1940 and another brief visit to neighboring Brazil at the end of March 1941. This can be seen as the first extended period in which the entire family shared the same house, united with long hours of a full home life. For Beatriz, who turned two years old five days after the move, it was the first extensive period of enjoying permanent contact with her mother. Although Paquita's older daughters were already adolescents, ranging in age from thirteen to seventeen, this was the period of family life when they formed their strongest bonds with Segovia, aided by a more stable coexistence. The ties that the three girls made with their stepfather were to transcend the unexpected changes in the married life

Exterior view of the house and part of the garden. María Rosa (in the dark dress) is posing with a friend, and Beatriz is going down the steps. Photograph taken in 1941.

of Don Andrés and Paquita and would remain intact for the twenty-one and a half years that the guitarist survived his second wife. In a radio interview, Paquita's second daughter recalled those years spent with Andrés Segovia:

> *Sofía:* It was a very cordial relationship. Andrés was a very friendly person. Very smooth and very much an artist, and all that was reflected in the family life. I would say that the period of his life where I think he had a great family, and the enjoyment of being a family man, was when he lived in Montevideo.... He did not live like a foreigner, because as soon as he got here the Puig family welcomed him and took him in as a member. He was surrounded here by a great family—he who did not have a great family background. Our family was very kind to him and loved him a lot. On the other hand, his life was very normal. We went to the Rambla to walk; the three of us somehow hung on to Andrés's two arms to be able to walk with him.
>
> *Interviewer:* Apparently you had a good relationship as stepdaughters and stepfather.
>
> *Sofía:* Yes, very good. We loved him a lot. Andrés really won each one of us over in different areas and aspects, the three of us.... I got great companionship from Andrés. Andrés and I ended up being partners. He would ask me and I would ask him what I did not know, what I wanted to know. He always answered me. He was very intelligent and the best for me. And he would consult me also: "What do you think about what I played today, how does it sound?" We were buddies. And Mama was a very fine woman, very artistic.... He always insisted that you could not get anything in life without discipline. And we could see it when we lived with him. He practiced rigorously two or three hours in the morning and two or three hours in the afternoon. And there was no way to put it off or not do it. He said that if he did not do it, the guitar resented it because the work was not done....
>
> I would have liked to study piano or guitar. I insisted a lot but, of course, they were excellent. They were geniuses, and they could not stand for anyone to learn or start to learn near them.[44]

María Rosa, the youngest of the three sisters, provides another point of view of the link with Segovia, noting that Don Andrés was never able to fill the paternal absence they had suffered since they were little. This is how she remembered the good times during those years:

The Rambla in Pocitos in 1940. The arrow indicates the approximate location of Paquita Madriguera's house, half a block from the Rambla.

> I never saw Andrés as a real father. It is true that he treated us very well, and if we asked for help with homework he would always do it. And he was always in a good mood when he played with us. When we went out to walk on the Rambla, he would sometimes play jokes. Everyone knew him, with his hat and that pipe and his attire. He would fake being lame to tease us. Then sometimes I would cross to the other side of the Rambla because I was embarrassed, and he would yell, "That is my daughter!" But he never got involved in our education with the authority of a father.[45]

In the first of the many interviews with Sofía Puig, she shared other impressions about Andrés Segovia that she developed during those years on Ramón Massini Street:

> I would ask him, "How did you become an artist?" And he would tell me that he didn't know. He had no formal education; instead, he learned in the streets. But he did something that was very much like him. For example, he had three or four guitars that were his favorites, and he got the same sound from each—that was his very own. I think it was a matter of touch, vibration, or something, I don't know what....
>
> I don't think Andrés had a life—rather, he had several fragments of a life. But the part he lived here marked him in a special way.[46]

The first four months at the new house meant a haven of family life, practice, and quiet work for the musical couple, without a single activity that would force them to leave that often-postponed genial atmosphere. October

1940 saw the beginning of some significant events for the history of the guitar and its repertoire. On the morning of Saturday, October 5, the unexpected arrival of the mailman with a large envelope from Mexico made Segovia change his plans for the day. The long-awaited first pages of the *Concierto del sur* had arrived, as Manuel Ponce had promised to his guitarist friend the month before. This initiated a series of similar shipments of successive fragments of the concerto over the following weeks. The letter that Segovia wrote to confirm receipt of that first part is very eloquent, openly showing his and also Paquita's enthusiasm for the work that would be prepared—from beginning to end—through their joint efforts. He told Ponce that he and his wife immediately sat down to read his very small handwriting, and that they wanted to deeply congratulate him. Segovia also wrote that he and Paquita would be anxiously awaiting the continuation of that first movement, and suggested to his friend that he write a brilliant cadenza similar to those he had written for Beethoven.[47]

In the memorial article for *Guitar Review*, Segovia discussed how he and Paquita worked with the materials that Ponce sent them:

> With that admirable patience equally ennobled in all his occupations, the mechanical as well as the spiritual, he would write the concerto on very fine airmail stationery, sending it to me for its final adaptation to the indomitable guitar. Each time the mailman came to the house with the bulky envelope, it was a holiday for my wife and me. We would suspend our daily practices and would dedicate the day to reading and rereading, with all our soul, what had just been produced by the Maestro's venturous pen.[48]

Abel Carlevaro, who was then visiting Segovia almost daily, described more than once the "very fine airmail stationery" on which Ponce had traced, with a ruler and the utmost care, the staves where he spread out his tiny music notation. On the first page that Ponce sent to Segovia, the composer had written at the bottom of its five systems:

> My dear Andrés,
>
> I beg you to send me the corrections or changes in the guitar part so that the orchestra score can be corrected. You will receive the rest of the concerto in sections. I think this way we will save time and you will be

able to work on it, of course. Mille amitiès pour Paquita et les enfants [a thousand friendly greetings to Paquita and the girls].[49] Clema has the flu.

A big hug from your old,
Manuel

On October 8, three days after receiving the first delivery, Segovia wrote to Ponce again, excited about the concerto on which he and Paquita were progressing, almost always using the first person plural and thus showing Paquita's involvement. At the same time, he was worried about the seriousness of the international situation, and was especially fearful that Spain's entry into the war could mean some sort of retaliation against him in case the Allies dragged the little South American countries into the fight. The guitarist also gave the composer some advice, encouraging him to indulge the audience with some superficial devices rather than focusing solely on "musical purity," to which he alluded here and in other letters. After telling him that he was excited about his work, he asked Ponce not to limit the spontaneity of his pen and to include some "wild ideas" to also please those listeners with "fat ears." Segovia described the audience in Montevideo as "sophisticated and enthusiastic," although rather short on money. He also told Ponce that he would work hard to fill the halls for his performances, even considering that there had been lots of concerts that year, including those by Toscanini, Stokowski, Heifetz, and Rubinstein.[50]

In a new letter written on October 22, Segovia said that the second set of concerto materials had not yet reached his and Paquita's hands. The guitarist expressed, on behalf of them both, the impatience that had overtaken, while at the same time remarking that "everyone" liked this music by Ponce much more than the concerto by Castelnuovo.[51] Segovia's use of the word "everyone" had a very broad meaning; it was not limited to just his family. It was in those October days of 1940 that another important event took place. Heitor Villa-Lobos had been visiting Montevideo since Wednesday, October 9, accompanied by a large delegation of musicians from his country.[52] Three days after his arrival, Segovia and Paquita went to visit him at his hotel, and on Tuesday, October 15, they attended the first chamber concert performed by the Brazilian musicians at the Studio Auditorium, and on Saturday, October 19, they went to the concert by the SODRE Symphony Orchestra conducted by Villa-Lobos. On Sunday afternoon, October 20, the composer visited the house on Massini Street, accompanied by Arminda Neves d'Almeida and one of the musicians who made up the entourage.[53] The nature of the meeting is recorded in Paquita's diary, although there are no details. Yet the facts become quite clear from an analysis of the letter from October 22 and several more that Segovia wrote to Ponce around that time.[54] Mamá Paqui also attended the reunion, with Segovia, Paquita, Villa-Lobos, Arminda, and the other Brazilian musician, Gazzi Galvao de Sá, accompanying the Brazilian composer. It is clear from the letter to Ponce that Villa-Lobos arrived at Segovia's house to show him several of his new Five Preludes for guitar and "tried" (in the words of the guitarist) to play one of them—probably the third, given the description.[55]

If we stick to the story Segovia told Ponce, Don Andrés was so upset with the Brazilian's music that he could not wait to make him listen to "other" music, especially that of his Mexican friend, but he preferred not to rush into it. With that intention, according to the guitarist, he took the guitar and played—accompanied by Paquita—the concerto by Castelnuovo-Tedesco. He also performed, alone, the suite "in baroque style" that Ponce had composed for him, which Segovia usually presented in public as a creation of the lutenist Silvius Leopold Weiss. He later played other works for guitar by the Mexican composer, and finally, again accompanied by Paquita on the piano, he played the fragment that he had received of the *Concierto del sur*. The visitors liked that initial section of the first movement of the concerto so much that they had to repeat it seven or more times, according to what the guitarist told Ponce in the long letter of October 22, in which he also included strong negative comments about the Brazilian composer and his music.[56] At the end of the evening, Segovia wrote a note to Ponce, with his signature accompanied by that of Villa-Lobos, Arminda, Galvao de Sá, and Mamá Paqui, in addition to greetings from Paquita. This is apparently what Segovia meant by "everyone" when referring to the preference for Ponce's music by those around him. All of them had admired his "delectable concerto" and encouraged him to finish it and immediately send it to Montevideo.[57]

Segovia mentioned the October 20 gathering in a letter of introduction to Ponce, also written on October 22, in which he asked that a certain businessman from Buenos Aires be received as a friend of Segovia. Finally, he told Ponce that the beginning of the second theme was charming and that they were awaiting more.[58]

But it would take three more weeks before the next fragment of the new concerto would reach the hands of Segovia and Paquita. In the meantime there is documentation of two other meetings with Villa-Lobos. The first took place on October 25, when the Centro Guitarrístico del Uruguay honored the Brazilian composer at its social headquarters. The focus of the homage was a brief concert given by the twenty-three-year-old Abel Carlevaro, who was Segovia's main student in Montevideo and was seen as the most promising local guitarist. Villa-Lobos and Segovia were invited to sign and write a few words in the Guitar Center's guestbook, resulting in:

> A guitar, a nostalgia
> A Country, a sound,
> An homage, a sufferer,
> A chord, a consolation.
> > The guitar moans
> > it does not talk,
> > if only it could talk . . .
>
> Montevideo 10/25/40
> H. Villa-Lobos

If the guitar could "talk," it would tell Villa-Lobos: ["]Do not leave me forgotten for so long, create a valuable work for my future, utilizing your immense talent."

> The interpreter,
> A. Segovia
> Montevideo XL

At the end of the concert, Villa-Lobos went up to Abel Carlevaro to greet him and to make some comments regarding his interpretation of *Chôros No. 1*, which the Brazilian had composed and the guitarist had included in his program. He also invited Carlevaro to Rio de Janeiro to see other works that he had produced for guitar—the same etudes and preludes for which Segovia had showed so little enthusiasm, if not open rejection. At the end of 1943 Carlevaro's visit to Villa-Lobos in Brazil finally materialized, and the young guitarist could then get into the composer's music with a much more

Page 205 of the guest book of the Centro Guitarrístico containing the signatures of Villa-Lobos and Segovia, as well as those of Arminda, Gazzi de Sá, and Francisco Curt Lange.

open spirit than that of his conservative maestro. This would be their second area of disagreement—although the Uruguayan's reserved character never allowed him to openly confront his mentor—since Segovia had more than once expressed his disagreement with Carlevaro's high esteem for the music of Agustín Barrios. The more profound and lasting difference, which had to do with musical concepts in general, was unfolding regarding the technique and pedagogy of the instrument. This entire story has already been related in depth and only needs a comment here,[59] made by Segovia to Sofía Puig, after one of the lessons the Spanish guitarist gave his Uruguayan student had concluded with a family tea: "I don't know why this young man comes here if he then doesn't do what I tell him."[60]

Two days after the homage to Villa-Lobos at the Centro Guitarrístico, Segovia and Paquita gave a formal reception at their Pocitos home in honor of the Brazilian composer. The next day, the main Montevideo newspapers reported the gathering on the society page:

> Mr. Andrés Segovia and his wife, Paquita Madriguera, gave a reception in honor of the eminent Brazilian maestro Héctor Villa-Lobos yesterday at their elegant residence on Massini Street. It was a fine note of cordiality and included representative figures of our society gracefully and distinctively passing the time and thus contributing to the hospitality extended by the charming couple. The main room of honor, like the parlors and hall of such a welcoming mansion, were brightly enhanced by a number of baskets of seasonal flowers tastefully scattered about. Maestro Villa-Lobos received with this honor evident proof of the prestige that surrounded him. The attendees were served a fine lunch in the dining room on a table set with fine china.[61]

The list of attendees at the reception (which Paquita had probably sent to the press and which she pinned to the corresponding page of her diary) appears complete in both newspapers consulted. At the top of the list was Doña Francisca Rodón de Madriguera (Mamá Paqui), followed by the ambassadors of Argentina, Brazil, and Spain (and their respective wives), the Uruguayan secretary of the exterior, others in the diplomatic and social fields, several members of the Puig family, and a wide array of artists—including the sculptor José Luis Zorrilla de San Martín, the composers Eduardo Fabini and Luis Cluzeau Mortet, the musicologist Francisco Curt Lange, the conductor Lamberto Baldi, and the pianists Hugo Balzo and Nybia Mariño. The young

Fragment of the article that appeared in *La Mañana* on October 28, 1940.
In the upper photo, Segovia and Villa-Lobos are second and fourth in the
row of men, and Paquita is third from the left in the picture of the women.

guitarist who had played before Villa-Lobos two days earlier was not among
the guests in the list published in the papers or that Paquita kept.

On November 9, the next envelope from Mexico finally arrived with the
long-awaited second fragment of the first movement of the concerto, still
without a name at this point. Segovia acknowledged its receipt that afternoon
after he and Paquita had worked feverishly on the new staves that the mailman had delivered that morning ("practiced and learned in a few hours," in his
words). He again expressed their enthusiasm to Ponce, telling him that he and
Paquita had been working on it. Segovia was so emphatic about his impression of the work that he told Ponce he did not want to die before having made

it known, while urging his friend to send the rest of that movement. He said that Paquita joined him in his plea.[62]

Finally, on November 26, Segovia was able to tell his friend that he now had the complete version of the first movement in his hands and that he had already practiced it in its entirety, accompanied by Paquita. He also sent him a series of suggestions for the remaining two movements and certain changes in the first. And, after saying that they both were very pleased with his work, he told Ponce the couple's impressions about that movement: "Nothing fails in it; it is all at the same superior level of art." He finished by telling the composer about his fervent desire to work on the entire piece.[63]

On December 10, Segovia received the first part of the second movement, an Andante, and two days later he sent a letter to Ponce confirming his satisfaction with what the composer had sent him. The guitarist wrote to his Mexican friend shortly before a dazzling party ("with lots of guests," states Paquita's diary) at the Massini Street house to celebrate Sofía's fifteenth birthday. Segovia corresponded with Ponce again on December 17 to inform him that he had received the rest of the second movement and that it did not matter if this part was not easy for the public.[64] He described it as "pure poetry," saying that it could touch the soul of anyone with musical sensitivity. He also said that he and Paquita played that Andante several times a day for their own pleasure. Segovia added at the end that he would like to bring other local musicians and critics to his house to hear the first two movements of the concerto.[65]

The year 1941, during which Manuel Ponce visited Montevideo to premiere the *Concierto del sur*, began for Segovia and Paquita with the arrival of the first pages of the third, and final, movement. The guitarist had written Ponce a letter on January 5, but he felt obliged to add something before putting it in the mail, due to the arrival of the long-awaited envelope from Mexico. So, he opened the letter and added a new sheet to express his and Paquita's profound enthusiasm. Segovia also wrote that they both had just played together the new part of the last movement, and he used seven of his most expressive adjectives in only one phrase to describe their impressions on that piece of music "of superior dignity."[66]

Ponce's last delivery arrived on January 20, 1941. Segovia finally had the entire concerto for guitar and orchestra in hand. The guitarist transmitted his intense happiness in a letter that day, pointing out that he does all his work on the concerto with his wife and saying that he and Paquita never tired working on it or repeating it many times. He told Ponce that he was hoping to learn the fingering well enough to gather some important Montevideo critics and musicians at his home to play it for them and watch their reaction.[67]

A few days later Don Andrés wrote to his Mexican friend again, telling him that he and Paquita were continuing to polish "the playing of that splendid concerto." During the final weeks of 1940 and the entire first month of the following year, Segovia had been concerned about Quesada's delays regarding the finalization of his expected tour of various Central American countries—even aspiring to get to Mexico and, with a certain degree of skepticism, to the United States. A letter from his manager, received in February, was like a bucket of not cold but ice water, as he told Ponce, informing him that Quesada was pessimistic about the possibility of Segovia's return to North America that year. Segovia supposed that there had been a plot between artists and "Jewish businessmen" to keep him out of that country, and said that Heifetz had told Quesada that it was not possible to help him because Segovia had gotten himself involved in politics. So, Segovia had no choice but to resign himself that year to giving the concerts that could be organized in Uruguay, Argentina, and Brazil.[68]

Andrés Segovia's concerts in Brazil took place between March 26 and April 2. The guitarist was still making arrangements in May for Ponce's visit to Montevideo. In the meantime, he and Paquita continued to practice the *Concierto del sur*. The idea that the pianist would return to the stage continued to mature, and Segovia insisted that the Mexican composer send Paquita his works. On May 16, at the end of a very long letter, he told him that they were still polishing the concerto, which was always a pleasure to play, and that he had promised a certain diplomat that he would perform it for him at the first opportunity.[69] Finally, he said that Paquita would be an enthusiastic performer of Ponce's piano works and urged his friend to send the pieces he had promised to her many times.[70]

In April, May, and June 1941, Don Andrés and Paquita spent long stretches of time at their countryside home in Piedras de Afilar, where they could study with more concentration—surrounded by silence and without the chaos that the adolescents and little Beatriz naturally created at the house in Pocitos. For the pianist, the decisive moment when she would again appear before the public was drawing near. Although at first she would simply accompany her husband, as soon as Ponce arrived with the material for the piano concerto she would get to work on a solo piece. At the beginning of July, Segovia wrote to Ponce (whose visit had been confirmed for the end of August) and included a description of the advantages of the country house, saying that the Segovia-Madriguera home would be the composer's shell. He was planning that he and Ponce would immediately move alone to the country house, where there was a piano, so that they could practice the concerto and the composer could rest from the agitation of the trip. Segovia also wrote that afterward they would go back to Montevideo and have a reception full of important people for whom to introduce Ponce. He emphasized that he had not played in Montevideo for one year, so the premiere of Ponce's work would be even more brilliant, and also added that he was making the arrangements for a performance in Buenos Aires.[71]

But there would be more activity before Ponce's arrival in Montevideo. During the previous thirteen months—since his last performance in Buenos Aires on June 9, 1940—Segovia's professional activity as a concert guitarist had consisted of just the two recent April concerts that he gave in Brazil. July of that year broke the long dry spell: the guitarist performed again in the Argentinean capital in a series of concerts. He went there alone on July 17 for the first concert and returned to Montevideo two days later. Then, on July 25, he and Paquita traveled to Buenos Aires and moved into the Hotel Continental, where they would remain until August 17. During that period there were three concerts at the Teatro Odeón in Buenos Aires and one forty miles southwest in the city of La Plata, in addition to some performances on the radio. Several letters written by Paquita to her almost-fourteen-year-old daughter imply that as the activities on the Argentinean stages were concluding, others were still being planned. It is also interesting to observe Paquita's modesty regarding a fact that was probably already integrated into the couple's plans, but which she avoids communicating openly to her daughter. The first letter is dated August 2:

> My dear María Rosa:
>
> We have just received your little letter that has made us very happy for the remembrances it signifies, and for the news of your promotion to "leader," for which we congratulate you wholeheartedly. I wrote to Mamá Paqui today and you will see in that letter that our stay has already been extended by a few more days because it is quite likely that Andrés will give

a third concert this coming week. On Wednesday he will play on Radio El Mundo, and on Sunday, the 10th, at La Plata. . . .

I am ordering Beatriz's "little mom" to give her lots of kisses from us, and we hope that Sofía the "star" and Pitusa write to us.

A kiss for Mamá Paqui and, for you, many more from your

Mamá

A week later, on Saturday, August 9, Paquita wrote to María Rosa again:

In effect, I am very proud of my three super students who honor the name they bear. Andrés and I congratulate you wholeheartedly. . . .

We cannot leave for Montevideo until Saturday the 16th, and we will arrive there early Sunday morning. The owners of the anisette Ocho Hermanos have sent us six bottles of that liqueur. We bought glasses and invited the visitors to taste it. This afternoon Conchita Badía was here with her husband and other people. She sang really well.

Well, a kiss from the both of us to all of you, and a very big and affectionate one for you from your Mommy.

What Paquita did not mention in her letters is that in the third concert given in the Argentinean capital, on August 15, she would accompany Segovia in the guitar and piano version of Castelnuovo-Tedesco's Concerto in D. This is how Paquita Madriguera would return to the concert stage after many years of public inactivity. And as if the hand of fate were determined to make its presence known, this return occurred at the same theater where she and Andrés Segovia had met, for the second time in their lives, twenty years earlier. For the guitarist, the event did not go unnoticed, and he made it known through a significant message that must have been well understood by his wife. A copy of the printed program for August 15, 1941, at Teatro Odeón is not available, but some existing copies of the newspapers that covered the concert show its significance. Segovia opened the concert with Tárrega's transcription of the Andante by Mozart that had so impressed Paquita the first time she had heard it on his guitar, followed by two Haydn minuets and the Canzonetta by Mendelssohn. The second part included the Torroba Sonatina and the *Sevillana* by Turina, and the third was devoted to the Concerto in D. The second section, under the subtitle "Castelnuovo-Tedesco," of one article read:

The third part of the concert was dedicated to the Concerto in D for Guitar and Orchestra by Castelnuovo-Tedesco, a work that was premiered by Andrés Segovia during last year's season of the Wagnerian Society, and which on this occasion was presented in the author's version for guitar and piano, with the assistance of the pianist Paquita Madriguera de Segovia, remarkable instrumentalist and interpreter of rare quality, who on her first visit to our country, about two decades ago, showed us exceptional technical and musical qualities in spite of her youth.

In this new version of the Concerto in D by Castelnuovo-Tedesco, the piano has been treated with such mastery and touch that at no time does it overpower the intimate sound of the guitar, while the pianist bears the responsibility for making the blend perfect and the adjustments precise. Needless to say, Andrés Segovia, the artist of nuances and intangible timbres, could not have had a better collaborator than Paquita Madriguera de Segovia, as she is identified, intimately, with the famous guitarist and is aware of his sensitivity and temperament. Thus, taking the piano part with subtlety and understanding, displaying a lightness of touch and a force that outlined the themes with clarity and alternated the dialog with precise accents, Paquita Madriguera de Segovia at no time drowned out the sound of the guitar, merging both sounds with marvelous flexibility. Having already had the opportunity to admire the Segovia transcription of the work of Castelnuovo-Tedesco, it should be recognized that in this version both performers—it had to be that way—gave the sensation of being one, such was the homogeneity of technical resources and the spiritual unity that prevailed in bringing this concerto to life, through the vivacity of the first movement, the noble elegance and emotion of the Andante, and the euphoric grace of the third and last, at the end of which the public honored the two artists with a long and warm ovation. The concert hall enthusiastically applauded each work in the program and forced Andrés Segovia to add other pieces, listening with the same devotion and giving similar demonstrations of admiration.[72]

Once both musicians had returned to Montevideo, and after Segovia had recovered from an illness that kept him in bed for a few days, they returned to prepare for the arrival of Manuel Ponce and to give the final touches to the concerto, of which they had yet to receive the final copy. In a letter of July 8, the last Segovia wrote to the composer before his arrival in Uruguay, he still alluded to it—in capital letters—as CONCERTO FOR GUITAR AND ORCHESTRA.

Ponce arrived in Montevideo on Wednesday, August 27, crossing from Buenos Aires on one of the seaplanes that regularly made the 140-mile trip between the two ports, and immediately settled in at the home in Pocitos, occupying the bedroom on the top floor that María Rosa had vacated for him. That part of the residence, which in those days had bedrooms for the four daughters and Mamá Paqui, also became home to Manuel Ponce during the almost fifty days that he spent in Uruguay as a member of the Segovia-Madriguera family. Due to the circumstances, the stay that the guitarist offered his Mexican friend at the country house never materialized because events unfolded in such rapid succession. On the day of his arrival, several people appeared at the residence on Massini Street to greet Ponce—the musicologist Francisco Curt Lange and his wife (who had accompanied Segovia to welcome the composer at the port), Aparicio Méndez, and Eduardo Ferreira (president of the board of directors of SODRE), among others. On August 29 Ponce wrote to his wife, Clema:

> I left at 8:30 for this city in a little plane that crosses the Río de la Plata in an hour. What a river! They say that it is 30 miles in the narrowest part. I finally arrived in Montevideo. At the port were Andrés (in spite of his flu), Lange and his wife, and other people. To enter the city they required a deposit of $500. Naturally, Andrés cleared everything up. We went to his house, very pretty, old, in the style of Don Porfirio,[73] good location, waterfront, with a garden. The girls are at school since they get out at 5:00 P.M. . . .
>
> The night after my arrival, Lange gave a reception in my honor. The most outstanding journalists and musicians gathered there. Everyone treated me cordially and with affection.[74]

The final days of August marked several social activities, such as a visit by the ambassador of Mexico and lunches at the Mexican Embassy. During the first two weeks of September Segovia excused himself to do a ten-day tour of Argentina. On September 20, a conference by Ponce took place at the SODRE, and during the last week, the composer and the guitarist had to alternate social gatherings with the final touchups to the work that then received its title of *Concierto del sur*. On more than one occasion during the last two weeks of September, Segovia gathered several people from the music scene at his home to hear these changes, as well as the final version. Almost four decades later, one of the attendees remembered those musical reunions:

> We still recall those events in September of 1941, when we were visited by the Mexican maestro Manuel Ponce, author of the *Concierto del sur* (for guitar and orchestra), which was dedicated to Segovia. Evening after evening, composer and guitarist polished the facets of this dense and at the same time transparent work—a plethora of Latin American melodies and rhythms.... During some of the rehearsal breaks, Segovia made us listen to pieces by old Spanish lutenists, transcriptions by Bach, and recent works by Ponce and Castelnuovo-Tedesco.[75]

At the beginning of October, when the first three or four pages of the Montevideo newspapers were taken up by the terrible news coming from Russia (the main front of the war at the time), there was still ample space in the sections dedicated to cultural and social life to cover the significant musical event created by the presence of Manuel Ponce in the Uruguayan capital, as well as the imminent premiere of his latest work. This was not an isolated event whose inclusion interrupted a passive cultural environment. On the contrary, other artistic activities were abundant in the then-fertile territory of the Uruguayan capital. Two days before the premiere of *Concierto del sur*, the famous husband-and-wife ballet duo of Clotilde von der Planitz and Alexander Sakharoff performed at the Teatro Solís, accompanied by the pianist Hugo Balzo, and the following week Aaron Copland presented several of his works and gave a conference on creating contemporary music. A photo in *La Mañana* of those in attendance at Copland's conference shows Manuel Ponce seated in the front row, with his unmistakable white hair. The presence of the Mexican composer at Copland's conference is mentioned in an article published in the same newspaper by the musicologist Francisco Curt Lange. Nothing is said, however, of attendance by Segovia or his wife, and it is not possible to identify them in the photo. Given the notoriety of the guitarist's confrontation with North American Jews and the fact that Copland was Jewish, it would have been unusual for Segovia and Paquita to attend the symposium.

Reception at the home of Francisco Curt Lange on August 27, 1941. *From left to right, standing*: Eduardo Ferreira, president of SODRE; the critic Roberto Lagarmilla; the pianist and composer Héctor Tosar; Lange; the composer Alberto Soriano; and an unidentified man. *Seated*: Segovia; a woman, probably Mrs. Lange; Ponce; the composer Eduardo Fabini; and the composer Carlos Estrada.

On Saturday October 4, 1941, the new concerto was finally presented in a full and eager Studio Auditorium by the SODRE Symphony Orchestra, conducted by Manuel Ponce, in a program devoted entirely to music by the Mexican composer. The program listed *Pequeña suite en estilo antiguo* (Little Suite in the Old Style), *Concierto del sur for Guitar and Orchestra*,[76] *Poema Elegíaco*, and *Chapultepec: Three Symphonic Sketches*.[77] It included a following description of the *Concierto del sur*:

The title of this work alludes to the folkloric environment of Andalusia, the land of Andrés Segovia and the home of the guitar. Without leaning on any definite theme, its fine musical inspiration develops according to the suggestions of the following epigraphs:

I. *Allegro*: You are the soul that speaks its solitary harmony to the passing souls (*Guitarra*, by Antonio Machado).

II. *Andante*: Return to Granada the eyes and the soul to its Felisarda (*Romance of Abenumeya*).[78]

III. *Final*: Sounds of a distant party.

At almost the last minute, Manuel Ponce opted to hand over the baton to the permanent conductor of the SODRE Symphony Orchestra, Lamberto Baldi, when the program reached the *Concierto del sur*. The composer, anxious to fully appreciate the acoustical result of his much-anticipated work, preferred to listen to Segovia and the orchestra from a box seat in the auditorium. The printed program stated that Maestro Baldi would conduct the premiered concerto, but a press release published three days before the concert—on Wednesday, October 1—mentioned that Ponce would be conducting the orchestra:

The performance of concert guitarist Andrés Segovia with our symphony in the concerto that it will offer on Saturday at the SODRE, with the Mexican composer Manuel Ponce conducting some of his works, is undoubtedly one of the best attractions in the magnificent program announced for this exceptional concert.

Segovia is the one in modern times who has really given a new impetus, a remarkable increase of literature for the instrument he defined so beautifully "as a faraway and mysterious orchestra whose sound would come to us from a smaller and more delicate planet than ours." The great Spanish artist will reappear performing as a soloist in a work for guitar and orchestra dedicated to him and which he performs for the first time in the world, also presented under the direction of its composer.

All factors about the exceptional characteristics of the concert that will be offered on Saturday at the SODRE have drawn the attention of our music fans and created an excitement that is leading to a heavy demand for tickets. The work involving the performance of Segovia, as a soloist in a collaboration for guitar and orchestra, consists of three movements and takes the name *Concierto del sur,* because of its inspiration in the folkloric environment of the region of Andalusia, land of Segovia and home of the guitar, which suggests without incorporating a specific theme of that region.[79]

The day following the premiere, the newspapers in Montevideo highlighted the success attained by the work, its creator, and the guitarist to whom it was dedicated. The critic Roberto E. Lagarmilla wrote a long and elaborate review:

A truly important event within the present music season is, without a doubt, the personal and artistic presence of the great Mexican composer Manuel Ponce, some of whose works were made known yesterday at the SODRE, under the direction of the composer. Within the general importance of this concert is the world premiere of the *Concierto del sur* for guitar and chamber orchestra, which

Program for the concert of
October 4, 1941.

is highlighted by its outstanding features. The soloist part belonged to the Spanish guitarist Andrés Segovia, to whom it is also dedicated. With this concerto being the most important part of yesterday's concert, it is necessary to alter the order of critical examination of the complete program, to give some of its main features in a first hearing of this fresh and attractive *Concierto del sur,* put onstage for the first time since its composition, in Montevideo and at the end of September.

Concerning the *Concierto del sur* it needs to be pointed out, above all, its commendable striving for purity and clarity, shown in the very wise management of the small orchestra, always subordinate to the expressive virtues of the solo instrument. Its three movements (Allegro moderato ed espressivo, Andante, Allegro moderato e festivo) are locked together so firmly that it is difficult to disentangle the uniqueness of each without compromising the judgment of the entire work.

It is interesting to observe that Ponce has constructed his *Concierto* without drawing a definite thematic picture; nonetheless, the sense of unity is omnipresent. This depends more on a strange synthesis of musical ideas than on a proper formal grouping according to harmonic or thematic designs. The entire work is subordinated to the guitar, a solo instrument also treated with great expertise in both its writing and in achieving its natural means of expression. The numerous and delicate harmonic shadings (we cannot speak here of "modulations" in the classical sense of the word) that perhaps respond to distant resonances transmitted by the guitar itself to the soul of the composer. On the other hand, the general movement (alternation of rhythms) is absolutely rational. Despite its astonishing clarity and originality, the shape—seemingly very distant from the classical model—is fully balanced if one looks at the underlying values of the set musical experiences. The developments are normal.

Manuel Ponce does not ignore the classical cadenza of the solo instrument. Incidentally, the placement of the cadenza within the first movement is at a true "strong point" of the composition, a beautiful aesthetic effect not to be ruined by subsequent virtuosic passages. Do not think, therefore, that Ponce's writings for the guitar can be situated on a simplistic level. On the contrary, his numerous effects, sometimes alternating with force, require that the performer have, in addition to a precise understanding of the work, a solid working technique to achieve a truly effective interpretation.

The Andante of the *Concierto del sur* represents a narrow and dark valley between the two sharp emotional peaks represented by the outer movements. The finale functions as a kind of "re-exposition," although this is implied rather than a formal repetition. In one place in this movement the percussion makes an appearance, intelligently used in the form of the tambourine. Manuel Ponce's instrumental equilibrium is here seen with clarity, because in a composition for few instruments the inclusion of such a device would represent a failure for any composer who does not maintain tight control over his expressive material. At all times in this concerto there is a faithful representation of atmospheric clarity, a calm atmosphere and a spiritual joy worthy of a noble and artistic soul, while representing a loud and clear example of the musicality of America (its ideas, in fact, though distantly rooted in Spain, have a marked Latin American accent).

The interpretation Andrés Segovia gave us of this work by Ponce is deserving of the highest praise. This artist's musicality consistently liberated his work from a mere exhibition of instrumental effects, allowing him to penetrate deeply the musical meaning of the warm Mexican message. His legatos, the phrasing, the absolute clarity of his technique, and mastery of the volume of the sound undoubtedly contributed to the veracity of the expression achieved.

Lamberto Baldi, heading the orchestra, had a very accurate understanding of this work of art. We must also note the remarkable cleanness and adjustments made by the SODRE Symphony Orchestra, whose intonation and flexibility were factors in the high artistic level reached.

The audience, very large, gave a well-deserved and resounding ovation to the work of Manuel Ponce and its first performer, Andrés Segovia. Their sustained applause forced the composer to take numerous bows on the stage to acknowledge the warm approval of his newest work. The insistence of the ovation compelled Andrés Segovia to repeat the entire third movement of *Concierto del sur*. And thus the new creation of our visiting Mexican composer was splendidly premiered....

[The other works in the program] were also applauded enthusiastically, although the hearing of the *Concierto* for guitar and orchestra captured for itself almost all the spiritual energy necessary for genuine understanding. That is why this concerto is actually the *clou* [centerpiece] of yesterday's concert.[80]

The critic added at the end that he would need to hear the concerto again to form a more complete and subjective impression of all the work's dimensions. Obviously, in his enthusiasm over the freshness of the work and its local significance, he failed to mention some of the more obvious formal features, such as the solid and fully neoclassical thematic structure of the concerto, whose first movement adopts the sonata form with two clearly exposed themes (the first being halfway between neo-baroque and Latin American in the opening motif, and typically Andalusian in the phrase when the guitar appears). Also, the second movement has a very clear ABA form, and the third, in rondo form, is based on the melodic cell of the first theme of the opening movement.

A week after the celebrated premiere of *Concierto del sur*, and in the same hall, the audience of Montevideo was called to attend another double musical event. It was the second, and final, presentation of Manuel Ponce conducting the SODRE Symphony Orchestra (in a program again made up exclusively of the Mexican composer's works), and the return of Paquita Madriguera to the music scene as soloist performing his Concerto for Piano. On Saturday, October 11, after having practiced the work intensively during the weeks Ponce had been in Montevideo (the composer brought the concerto materials with him), Paquita had an overwhelming success, as can be seen by all the critics' unanimous verdict regarding her performance. The headline of the review published in *El Diario* acclaimed "a resounding triumph" for the soloist:

Last night, the highly regarded Mexican composer Manuel Ponce, who is our welcome guest, gave his second and last symphony concert at the Studio Auditorium leading the SODRE Symphony Orchestra in the performance of three of his new and highly esteemed works. Our music audience has now had, with the performance of the previous Saturday, the opportunity to hear some of the most important and characteristic creations of the celebrated composer, who conducted the orchestra with a skill and expertise that were appreciated by the large audience that has attended these concerts. Yesterday's concert began with the *Estampas Nocturnas* [Night Imprints], quasi-suggestive evocations in which maestro Ponce managed to highlight his mastery of orchestration, its fluid inspiration, and an artistic and personal sense that distinguishes him from other contemporary composers. Especially applauded were the graceful *En tiempos del Rey Sol* [In the Time of the Sun King] and the formally mischievous *Puck's Scherzo*, with its original harmonies. In the second part, Maestro Ponce conducted his Concerto for Piano and Orchestra, in which he had the subtle and invaluable assistance of the Spanish pianist Mrs. Paquita Madriguera de Segovia, who has been away from our concert halls for many years and whose reappearance was anticipated with justifiable interest.

This concerto is one of the compositions that Maestro Ponce wrote in his youth and deserves the highest praise. Imbued with a strong romanticism, its freshness and spontaneity are triumphant at all times. Maestro Ponce has followed, in his strong personality, in the footsteps of the great romantics, letting his melodic pen flow into musical torrents that are surely and easily understood.

The piano part is very important in this concerto and earned its composer, as a young performer, resounding success. And yesterday he could not have had a better person to display it than the fine pianist Paquita Madriguera, who, in a show of appreciation for the maestro and friend, decided to terminate her prolonged absence from the concert halls, practicing the difficult score, full of technical barriers, for barely three weeks, and offered an impeccable and truly artistic version yesterday. The distinguished concert pianist appeared in full command of her skills with an ample mastery of the instrument's resources—beautiful sound, phenomenal fingering, great expressive phrasing and force—all of which garnered the most enthusiastic and prolonged ovations that resounded at the Studio Auditorium yesterday. Paquita Madriguera, whom we had not heard since the distant era of her presentation at the former [Teatro] Albéniz, is undoubtedly a talented performer who has been reinforcing her musical resources, which, if they were remarkable then, are simply perfect today. Her vigorous spirit, cultured and intellectual, has not rested on its laurels. We hope this concert pianist of such bright qualities, who has spent many long years among us without being heard, will offer us a piano concert of the aesthetic emotions that her refined art knows how to transmit with such freshness and excitement. One of the most outstanding artistic notes in recent times was Paquita Madriguera's reappearance, and the audience that admired her brilliant interpretation of Ponce's work never tired of applauding and calling her back to the stage repeatedly, where, along with the distinguished Mexican composer, she continued to be cheered.

Yesterday's concert ended with *Ferial* [Fair], an entertaining symphonic piece offered for the first time, and one of the newest works by Maestro Ponce. It has skillfully used folk elements within a rich and brilliant orchestration, evoking scenes of a Mexican village fair. It is an interesting work that was outstandingly interpreted by the resources of the SODRE Symphony Orchestra and earned its composer new and prolonged ovations.[81]

Music critics of all the Montevideo newspapers referred to Paquita's reappearance in similar terms, with other review titles such as "Paquita Madriguera Was a Revelation in Ponce's New Concerto" (*El Tiempo*), and "Paquita Madriguera Reappeared in the Concert Yesterday with Success" (*El Pueblo*). Another review stated:

The interpretation that Paquita Madriguera gave to this youthful work by Ponce deserves the highest praise. An ample mastery of piano skills binds it to an almost unlimited capacity for dynamic nuance. Also noteworthy is that peculiar degree of spontaneity with which she knows how to shape the phrases—accentuating the contrasts just to the limit (without resorting to mannerisms) and varying the sounds. The phrases pour forth from her hands. The proper pedaling also contributed, so that Paquita Madriguera could get a true meaning from the instrument—characteristic of an intense and admirably temperamental musicianship. The audience extendedly applauded the distinguished pianist, from whom we should hear, for certain, performances of works of different styles. . . .

Manuel Ponce, the soloist Paquita Madriguera, and the SODRE Symphony Orchestra were very justly applauded by the audience, ending the presentation of symphonic works by one of this century's most illustrious composers of the continent.[82]

On Monday, October 13, two days after that second concert at the SODRE, Manuel Ponce left Montevideo and departed with Segovia for Buenos Aires. The Asociación Wagneriana (Wagner Society) of that city had organized an extraordinary performance for the Mexican composer to conduct some of his works there, among them the *Concierto del sur* (with Segovia as soloist) and *Chapultepec*. The presentation took place at the Teatro Nacional de la Comedia (previously the Teatro Cervantes) on October 20. Paquita traveled to Buenos Aires two days earlier to attend the concert and bid farewell to Ponce, who was returning to his country. Meanwhile, Segovia's activities continued with another performance, this time in the city of Santa Fe (250 miles northwest of the Argentinean capital) on October 24. The couple's return to Montevideo, two days later, marked the end of a season that was particularly significant for them both.

And thus came to an end that fruitful period whose germination had begun during the visit with Castelnuovo-Tedesco in Florence, grown strong over nearly three years, and finally blossomed into the stable and supportive environment the couple had constructed on Uruguayan soil. The important achievements of this period, in which they both were now more Montevidean than ever, were integrated into their respective lives as symbolic peaks

ASOCIACIÓN WAGNERIANA
DE BUENOS AIRES
Santa Fe 1145 - U. T. 41 - Plaza 0296

CORREO ARGENTINO
Tarifa Reducida
Concesión 2435

CONCIERTO SINFONICO EXTRAORDINARIO
BAJO LA DIRECCION
DEL MAESTRO

MANUEL PONCE

SOLISTA:

ANDRES SEGOVIA

LUNES 20 de OCTUBRE
a las 21.30
EN EL
TEATRO NACIONAL DE COMEDIA
(Cervantes)
CEDIDO POR LA COMISION NACIONAL DE CULTURA
1941

Córdoba y Libertad   Buenos Aires

Cover of the October 20 program in Buenos Aires.

reached after intense and committed work—Paquita's successful return to the musical stage, Segovia's triumph in the premieres of two major concertos for guitar and orchestra, and the couple's inexpressible experience of working side by side with mutual enthusiasm in the development of those two premieres. This was all protected by the emotional framework of stability provided by a secure home with all the family members living together for the first time after many long and restless years.

As symbols of the steadiness that had merged in their peaceful surroundings, the two most remarkable events that appear in Paquita's diary during the final months of 1941 are parties held at their home. The first was a formal cocktail party held on November 12 to celebrate Segovia's forty-eighth birthday, attended by members of the diplomatic corps, friends from the music scene, and others in the circle of "high society" to which Don Andrés and his wife now belonged. The second was a casual and youthful reception to celebrate Sofía's sixteenth birthday on December 12.

It is quite probable that the two central figures of this story were neither conscious of the achievements and the personal security that their professional careers had brought together nor aware of the traces of future divergent paths that would disrupt, and place in danger, the stability of this period. The origins of the difficulties that would appear on the horizon in a few years must be traced back to the rapid development of the activities of both artists outside of Uruguayan territory, beginning in 1942. But there would be other factors, both subjective and objective, at play as well, making it necessary to scrutinize the delicate compromise of contemplating and placing them in context in order to understand the entire chronicle of the impending upheaval.

Chapter 12

From South to North— The Agitated Journey from Success to Crisis

The three-month vacation that Paquita Madriguera and Andrés Segovia began at the end of October 1941 was, unbeknownst to them, both the coda to one period and the prelude to another in the lives of the two artists. Like the previous episode, this one was to last around three years. Although this stage was precipitated directly by all the seeds both had planted earlier, its characteristics would be strikingly different and end in a powerful crisis—the preamble to a separation that would take some time to finalize. Those Uruguayan summer days that marked the end of 1941 and the beginning of 1942 showed elements of both periods—long stretches of family life (especially in the country) contrasted with entire weeks in which the two musicians traveled different paths, separately preparing and developing their activities for the upcoming season.

Early in January, after Uruguay broke off relations with the Axis powers (Germany, Italy, and Japan), Segovia left for the country with the four girls, while Paquita stayed in Montevideo with her mother. It is possible that she needed the time, as well as the peace and quiet, to concentrate and practice, which was difficult to do with a young daughter and the three adolescents at home for summer vacation. At the same time, it might have been easier for Don Andrés to isolate himself at the country house to practice and prepare his repertoire for the tours that would begin in February, since the girls would be less demanding with him than with their mother—chores, as always, fell to the servants. On Monday, January 12, Paquita also moved to El Campito, and the entire family remained there for nine days.

On February 4 Segovia departed alone for Chile on a three-week tour, and Paquita remained in Montevideo to prepare for a full artistic calendar that would begin in the middle of the year. One of the few entries of interest in Paquita's diary around this time makes a note of her attendance at the Centennial Stadium on the night of Saturday, February 7, to watch the finals of the thirteenth Copa América (American Cup) in soccer.[1] That day the pianist wrote: "Night, Stadium. Soccer game. Uruguay–Argentina. Uruguay is champion."

Segovia's trip to Chile clearly marked the beginning of a new period of great unsettledness, in terms of a permanent home, that would eventually enable him to reach his main goal of overcoming the boycott of American impresarios and performing once again in the United States—a true mecca for culture as well as income, at a time when Europe was bleeding economically. Don Andrés returned from the trans-Andean country on February 24. Three days earlier Uruguay's president, Alfredo Baldomir, with the support of various political parties, had dissolved parliament in order to facilitate a change in the constitution and return the country to a true democracy from his predecessor's semi-dictatorship. The emergency situation lasted until November, when an act passed by public election allowed the installation of a new democratic government on March 1, 1943.

On March 12, 1942, the guitarist started another tour. This time the couple went to Brazil, where Segovia gave concerts in São Paulo and Rio de Janeiro. They arrived in São Paulo by plane on March 16, and Segovia gave a solo concert at the Teatro Municipal two days later. He returned to the same stage as a soloist in a symphony program that included the Castelnuovo-Tedesco and Ponce concertos, under the direction of João de Souza Lima. In an interview more than a half century later, the Brazilian guitarist Ronoel Simões, who attended those concerts, referred to Segovia's presence in São Paulo:

> He gave two concerts at the Teatro Municipal, one as soloist and one with orchestra, with the concertos by Tedesco and Ponce, Souza Lima conducting. There was a violinist playing in that orchestra named Aguiar who was a friend of mine, and he told me about the concert: "Listen, Simões, I played

in those concerts and Souza Lima was the conductor, but Segovia was the boss there, the one who talked to cellists and violinists, telling them that they were playing too loud and the guitar could not be heard. And Souza Lima remained still, not saying a thing." I went to Souza Lima's house several times . . . and he had much respect for Segovia, whom he kept calling Maestro Segovia.[2]

The trip lasted exactly one month. During their stay in Brazil, Don Andrés and Paquita met with the Uruguayan guitarist Isaías Savio on March 21 in São Paulo, the Spanish pianist Tomás Terán and his wife on April 3 and 9 in Rio, and Heitor Villa-Lobos, with whom they had dinner on April 7.[3] They also attended several concerts, including one at Rio's Teatro Municipal, where Henryk Szeryng was a soloist with an orchestra under the direction of the Brazilian composer Camargo Guarnieri.[4] Segovia's opinion about this April 6 concert—and the violinist's talent—is made plain in a letter he wrote to Manuel Ponce from New York more than a year and a half later expressing his satisfaction that the Mexican composer had not dedicated his Concerto for Violin to the young Polish instrumentalist.[5]

The day after the couple arrived in Montevideo from Brazil, Segovia left again for Buenos Aires. Paquita, who had stayed two days in the Uruguayan capital to get caught up with family business, traveled on April 16 to be present when her husband performed as a soloist with the orchestra of Teatro Colón on April 18, and the next night they both crossed the Río de la Plata to return home. From the end of April to early July, according to Paquita's diary, Segovia made at least four trips to Buenos Aires to give concerts in the Argentinean capital. Also around that time, Don Andrés and Paquita attended concerts given in Montevideo by the Uruguayans Hugo Balzo and Nybia Mariño and the foreigners Claudio Arrau, Alexander Uninsky,[6] Henryk Szeryng, and Argentinean conductor Juan José Castro. Each of these artists was received more than once at the Segovia-Madriguera home, whether for lunch, dinner, or tea, or to share a cocktail. Meanwhile, Beatriz had just turned four and was receiving her first piano lessons, and Paquita continued preparing for her own intense artistic activity during the second half of the year.

In July, Paquita departed alone for southern Brazil to give a concert in the city of Pelotas on July 9 and another at Teatro San Pedro, in Porto Alegre, on Tuesday, July 14. The Pelotas performance was reviewed:

The programs normally reflect the value of the artist, her preferences, and her inclination. Paquita Madriguera's told us that, devoted as she is to the highest level of music, her performance would reveal a refined taste and a disregard for any purely acrobatic effects. And that is exactly what the pianist revealed to us the day before yesterday. Besides the wonderful poetry in her interpretations, she has a great respect for the ideas and style of each composer. An appreciable technique, always at the service of expression, stripped of those effects so beloved by the public unfamiliar with true art. And so, she presented the Variations on *The Harmonious Blacksmith* by Handel, somber and with all the grandiosity of that composer's style; a Fantasia in C by Bach, admirable; [and] a Sonata in F by Mozart, where she revealed the finesse and transparent purity of that great composer's style.

In the second part, Paquita made us listen with fascination to the Fugue in E Minor and the *17 Serious Variations* by Mendelssohn, which we had not seen included in concert programs for a long time and which, by reason of its importance, has a prominent place in the piano literature. At the insistence of the applause, she sat down at the piano once again to play, as an encore, *Spinning Song* by the same composer, which she did with extreme subtlety, elegance, and grace, as if she were painting her self-portrait.

The third part was made up of two pieces by Frutuoso Viana extracted from his *Seven Miniatures*, three Mexican dances by Manuel Ponce, and *The Maiden and the Nightingale* and *The Dummy* by Granados. The performer confirmed her admirable qualities in all these works and played two encores—*Córdoba* by Albéniz and *Spanish Dance* by Granados, that great Spanish musician and Paquita's former teacher.[7]

The Brazilian musician Ênio de Freitas Castro reviewed the concert in Porto Alegre:

Paquita Madriguera, I believe, will have for us pianists, from now on, the value of a symbol or a great example. . . . This is quite a serious artist. From the posture she assumes at the piano to the organization of the program to the pedaling and the shading of the sound; from the careful variation of the dynamics to the tone quality; from the perfect observation of the styles to the purity of the music articulation, it is perceived that—in an ideal of pure music, in a classical ideal—everything she does seems to be neither too much nor too little. Her perfect mastery of technique allows her to put it to the exclusive service of expression, so that it feels effortless, a rare thing even in the greatest of her fellow pianists. The expression is never forced, neither toward the sentimental end (so pleasing for the less informed public and the only weapon that less important artists have), nor toward the intellectual end, which could result in a lack of sensitivity. The nature and intelligence of the artist are absolutely musical. And the maturing of such talents since infancy, the absence of the need to commercialize her art, the passionate cultivation of things of the spirit and of the art itself, the purity of the creations that she offers us, turned Paquita Madriguera into a truly sublime artist.

Paquita Madriguera at the time she returned to her career as a concert pianist.

We should not highlight anything from the program she played on Tuesday at the Teatro San Pedro, but I keep recalling the splendid interpretations in the second part (Prelude and Fugue in E Minor by Mendelssohn and *17 Serious Variations* by the same composer), which will remain unforgettable. Concerts like Paquita Madriguera's—without any romantic mannerisms, no wisps of sterile virtuosity, serious concerts, noble, sensitive, and suggestive—are the ones that are truly interesting from the cultural point of view.[8]

Paquita flew back to Pelotas the day after the concert in Porto Alegre and went from there to Uruguay. Her daughters Sofía and María Rosa boarded at the train station in the city of Treinta y Tres so that they could accompany her on the trip to Montevideo, where the three arrived on the night of July 16. The pianist used the rest of that month to practice for new presentations while she and her husband continued their active social life with musicians who visited Montevideo. Expanding on the letter to Ponce in December 1943, Segovia traveled to Buenos Aires on the night of July 28, 1942, on the steamship *Vapor de la Carrera*, along with the pianist Alexander Uninsky and the violinist Henryk Szeryng, who had performed that evening at the Teatro

Solís, accompanied on the piano by Nybia Mariño. According to his letter, Segovia spoke strongly and honestly to the violinist in front of Uninsky, giving his opinion about the concert Szeryng had given hours before, and advising him to concentrate on the study of a more serious repertoire if he wanted to succeed in New York.[9]

Three days later, on July 31, it would be Paquita's turn to cross the Río de la Plata once more. This time she did not go just to join her husband, who was waiting in Buenos Aires, or to accompany him in one of the recently premiered concertos, but to perform again as a soloist in the concert halls of the Argentinean capital. The Asociación Wagneriana, which had sponsored Paquita Madriguera's debut in Buenos Aires in 1920, was now organizing her reappearance on the city's stages. The concert took place on August 3 at the same Teatro Nacional de la Comedia where Segovia and Ponce had presented the *Concierto del sur* the previous year. The reviews that appeared in the Buenos Aires newspapers are eloquent regarding the impression Paquita made. *La Prensa* stated on August 4: "An artist of fine musical sensibility and an instrumentalist for whom the piano has no secrets; her success of last night was much deserved and unanimous." The music critic José María Fontova concurred a few days later:

After a long time away from our concert halls as a solo pianist, having made her debut while still a young girl, the pianist Paquita Madriguera made her reappearance before the Buenos Aires audience from the stage of the Asociación Wagneriana. She ... recently accompanied her husband, the renowned guitarist Andrés Segovia, at a concert given at the Teatro Colón.

Without a doubt, Paquita Madriguera is today a fully matured instrumentalist and performer, in both technique and culture. The girl who created so much real interest has grown into an artist of solid aesthetic knowledge, refined musical sensibility, and a technique that never overbalances the spirit of the works she plays.

Hence, beyond the clear and delicate fingering, the quality of the nice, robust tone, and the judicious use of the pedals, it is the seriousness and reflection, as well as the elegance and emotion, that arouse our interest in the playing of Paquita Madriguera. The sonority of Handel, the uncompromising refinement of Mozart, Mendelssohn's aristocratic cleanliness, Manuel Ponce's character (represented by *Three Mexican Dances* of intense and beautiful American Indian flavor), and the quintessentially Spanish flavor of Granados (whose favorite student she was)—all had a noble and understanding interpreter in Paquita Madriguera. She plumbed the depths in each case to reveal the ideas and concepts presented by the composers. Her remarkable interpretations won warm applause from the audience, and she had to add several works outside of the program to satisfy the insistent demands of the public.[10]

The month of August 1942, which for Paquita had begun so brilliantly in Buenos Aires, saw her give two more important presentations. In the meantime, Segovia, who had no professional activity during those winter weeks in Montevideo, devoted himself to making transcriptions and incorporating new works into his repertoire.[11] The couple also maintained an intense social life, cultivating ties with musicians from the Río de la Plata area and other parts of the world. Entries in the pianist's diary refer to meetings with the Argentinean composer Carlos López Buchardo and his wife, the Russian-French pianist Alexander Brailowsky (who gave two concerts in Montevideo that month), and the Chilean couple Armando Carvajal, a conductor,[12] and Blanca Hauser, a soprano, who visited the Pocitos house several times to have lunch, dinner, or afternoon tea. That month the Segovia-Madrigueras also hosted Uruguayan musicians from Montevideo—such as Carlos Estrada, Tomás Mujica, Guido Santórsola, and the singer Nilda Müller. On Saturday, August 15, Paquita Madriguera appeared again as a soloist at the Studio Auditorium, this time performing Grieg's Piano Concerto in A Minor with the SODRE Symphony Orchestra, conducted by Armando Carvajal. Once more the admiring appreciation of the critics was unanimous, and one newspaper published a glowing review:

It was the second part of yesterday's concert, the Concerto in A Minor for Piano and Orchestra by Edvard Grieg, in which Mrs. Paquita Madriguera de Segovia appeared as soloist. This beautiful concerto, well-known by our public, had a pleasing interpreter in Paquita Madriguera. The performer's clear artistic sense was highlighted throughout the entire concerto with the ease, purity, and freshness of her playing, which made it possible for her other qualities to be seen.

Thoroughly familiar with the work, she was able to offer it fully and accurately, with true meaning and clean use of the pedals as well as the trills, which she played with perfect clarity. In addition to this truly admirable technique, it is worth noting the fineness and delicacy of expression, especially in the beautiful and marvelously played cadenza, in which each chord was felt and shown in all its true musical and structural value, faithfully following the spirit of the composer in this magnificent piece.[13]

Similar impressions can be read in the reviews of other Montevideo press, such as *El País*, *El Bien Público*, and *El Diario*. Take, for instance, this fragment from *La Tribuna Popular*:

> With a full hall and a select audience, a great symphony concert took place yesterday evening at the SODRE, under the direction of the reputable Chilean maestro Armando Carvajal, with the notable Spanish pianist Paquita Madriguera, deeply rooted here among us, performing in one part....
>
> The participation of the great pianist Paquita Madriguera, whom we had not heard since her concert with the Mexican maestro Manuel Ponce, deserves special mention. We recall the extraordinary impression and the joy with which we then celebrated her return to the musical stage. Paquita Madriguera continues to be one of the deepest and most pleasant memories in the life of this writer as a regular listener. And the miracle of her return, of finding once again the lovely art of Paquita Madriguera, was confirmed in a more positive and sure manner, thanks to the individuality imposed in the Concerto in A Minor by Grieg.
>
> Exquisite. Extremely delicate and tender. An always gleaming sound. With an amazing dexterity with which she ends, in a display of extreme ease, the most difficult passages, scales, and arpeggiated phrases. Her full, round tone, with a beautiful color, is sweet in the cantabiles and brilliant in the allegros, becoming deep and mystical in the Adagio.
>
> A long ovation by the audience forced her to play an Aria by Grieg as an encore, with which she garnered renewed and sustained applause.[14]

Between August 28 and September 2, Paquita and Don Andrés were in Buenos Aires once again. The trip had a double motive, the first being to attend the exhibit of painter Miguel del Pino, a dear friend of many years, whom they also accompanied in a series of events in the Argentinean capital. The other objective was for Paquita to give a concert on Radio El Mundo on the evening of August 29. A few days after they returned to Montevideo, on September 10, she gave another concert—this time a charity event at

SODRE's Studio Auditorium. Meanwhile, preparation for Segovia's professional activities was under way, and he departed on September 16 for a tour that would take him to Bolivia and then to northern Argentina. Almost a month later, on October 13, Paquita left for Buenos Aires and from there boarded a train on Thursday, October 15, for Tucumán, Argentina, to meet her husband and give a few concerts herself. Segovia, although ill, was waiting for her at the train station on October 16, accompanied by others from the city's artistic circles. Don Andrés's condition did not improve, so a doctor (one Dr. Berra) visited him the next day at the Hotel Plaza, where he and Paquita were staying. The guitarist's ill health continued throughout their entire stay in Tucumán but did not stop him and his wife from meeting the professional commitments that had brought them there. The first was a concert by the pianist on Saturday, October 17. Under the

Program for Paquita Madriguera's concert of August 15, 1942.

title "P. Madriguera's Concert Was a Resounding Success," the newspaper *El Orden* printed a review the following day:

> Attracted by the fame that justly preceded the magnificent Catalonian concert pianist Paquita Madriguera, a large audience gathered at the hall of the former Teatro Belgrano and left sincerely pleased by the good artistic event offered by the renowned pianist. Paquita Madriguera did not put together a gimmicky program to highlight the marvels of technique. On the contrary, she chose works of emotional depth, that is, those that need to be "felt" to interpret them to perfection. She emerged from the difficult task completely fresh and graceful. . . .

The program was varied, in technique as well as in interpretation, showing in each of her facets a fine musical perception demonstrating her grasp of the intentions of each composer. We heard her majestically in Bach, deliciously delicate in Mozart, grandly eloquent in Mendelssohn, and expressive and loving in the part dedicated to the Catalonian composers Granados and Albéniz and the Andalusian Falla. With unanimous enthusiasm, the public gave her warm ovations, forcing her to play an encore at the end of the second part and at the end of the concert. The first encore was *Spinning Song* by Mendelssohn, and the second was the *Danza Valenciana* [Spanish Dance No. 7] by Granados, her childhood teacher, whom she seemed to remember with deep feeling in the interpretations of the late composer of *Goyescas*. In all, lovers of good music will remember a very pleasant evening.

Another newspaper referred to the concert in similar terms and included a reference to certain remarks by Paquita that clearly conveyed her deepest artistic conceptions. According to the article, the pianist had stated that "virtuosic interpretation was not in her aesthetic creed, adding that art is not subject to purely technical exhibitionism and that the best technique is one that is not seen, as the means of expression belong to the artist."[15]

Although Segovia's illness continued to bother him, they performed together at this same theater on Monday, October 19. The first two parts of the concert were devoted to solo guitar, and in the third part they performed Castelnuovo-Tedesco's Concerto in D. The same newspaper reviewed the event under the headline "Paquita Madriguera and Andrés Segovia Were Acclaimed at the Philharmonic":

> The presence of Andrés Segovia on any stage of the most important city in the world has always meant a true artistic event. Not surprisingly, so it was also in his performance last night at the former Teatro Belgrano in a concert sponsored by the Philharmonic, a local institution that develops its artistic activities with constant concern to meet the aspirations of its members. . . .
>
> The novelty of the night was the third part of the program, where the eminent Spanish guitarist—with the very intelligent collaboration on piano of Paquita Madriguera—presented the Concerto in D that the Italian composer Mario Castelnuovo-Tedesco wrote and dedicated to Segovia, playing

this time a version for guitar and piano, with the object of facilitating its performance in places where a good orchestra is lacking or there is no time to rehearse it. . . .

Segovia could not have found a better partner than the exquisite pianist Paquita Madriguera, who is so understanding, so delicate and artistic. The three movements of the concerto are beautiful, especially the second—Andantino alla Romanza—where the guitar and piano converse with great nobility and emotion. At the end, both artists were acclaimed by the large audience, who were pleased to hear the second movement repeated.

Paquita Madriguera and Andrés Segovia offered two high-quality concerts to the Philharmonic's subscribers of a kind that will always be remembered with emotion and enthusiasm. . . . And Segovia, in spite of being ill since he arrived from La Paz, has been able to meet his commitments made with the Philharmonic. The public therefore has reason to be grateful to him.[16]

Once the couple returned to Montevideo, Andrés Segovia spent a few days just resting and recovering from the ailments that had plagued him during the latter part of his tour. He then immediately set about preparing for an event that would mark a relevant moment in his own career as well as the official beginning of that of his first prominent student. Almost immediately after Segovia established himself as a distinguished citizen in Montevideo, he became Abel Carlevaro's pedagogic guide. In the five years since then, Carlevaro had made significant strides toward developing a career as a professional musician and on Segovia's advice had set aside his university studies in agronomy to dedicate himself to practicing the guitar and deepening his musical knowledge. He studied harmony and counterpoint intensively and regularly with the maestro Tomás Mujica and was increasingly active as a concert guitarist, with various presentations in Montevideo halls, in the interior of the country, and on radio programs.

All this turned Abel Carlevaro into the student that every teacher aspires to have, and Segovia felt that it was time to present him officially at a very important concert to be held on the renowned stage of SODRE. To present Carlevaro, the Spanish maestro drafted and signed a public declaration on October 25, 1942, for circulation in the media and to be included, verbatim and accompanied by the facsimile reproduction of his own signature and date, in the concert program:

Here Carlevaro premieres his art. Since 1937 I have been watching the development of his musical qualities with growing interest and addressing, though with some discontinuity owing to my numerous trips, his guidance and direction.

Carlevaro is a serious and honest worker. He knows that he who has not first been a patient craftsman of his trade can never become a great artist; he cannot become a maestro if he has not been a good student. This austere young man, whose soul has heard the unmistakable cry of the Vocation—of *vocare, vocatum*, call!—loves the holy discipline of Study, and through it, he will rise to the full mastery of the instrument and comprehend the superior beauties of Music.

The guitar requires natural and very diverse gifts of those who devote themselves to it; very fine sensitivity, so fine that it can feel the disturbance of the shadow of a hair; a subtle ear to perceive, in the inner hearing, the faint resonances that form like the halo of its delicate sound; [and] flexible, sturdy hands to shape the music's body of sound with affection and energy, momentum and accuracy. But for these gifts to be fruitful, they must receive heat from the sun of Culture. Carlevaro does not ignore this, which is why he tries to extract one more lesson from each day, to nourish his qualities and season his spirit.

Today begins his first high-altitude flight. He has strong wings to advance through distant skies, and he merits support from those less compassionate and indulgent than his countrymen. I predict a good journey and a happy arrival at legitimate success, especially if his character is firm in rejecting easy applause—the inappropriate gift to impatient vanity—and provides, instead, obedient attention to spare and restrained praise, the stimulus to future perfection.

In addition to drafting that text, which was published in Montevideo's newspapers as a way to advertise the concert and explicitly point out Segovia's support of the important step that Carlevaro was taking, the Spanish maestro also promoted his young student through the extensive interviews he gave to the Uruguayan press in the days preceding the concert.

As if to emphasize the importance of the event, Segovia kept pointing out that it was the first time in his life that he had sponsored one of his students in this manner. Just three days before Carlevaro's concert, *La Mañana* published a long article about the Spanish guitarist:

Standing before Andrés Segovia, though without the instrument that in his prodigious hands becomes all poetry and all music, it is easy to understand how the artist has been able to achieve so many triumphs through the years. Articulate, relaxed, happy in appearance and rigorous in judgment, the guitarist, when he speaks, reveals a broad and profound level of culture and a gifted memory, exceptional spiritual elements without which no one could climb the peaks in the powerful way Segovia has done.

We are in his family environment, surrounded by his things and his loved ones. There the guitarist gives way to the man of the house, who, without excluding him, tempers him, mutes him, and makes him forget his noble-artist personality to become the happy father of a Uruguayan daughter who attaches him most tenderly to this land of ours. But we touched on the topic that has taken us to him, and in an instant he becomes the maestro whom the world admires.[17]

Inside page of Carlevaro's program for the concert of November 12, 1942.

Later, the reporter transcribes the words of the artist and maestro. In the most important paragraphs, interspersed with explanations of the historical development of the guitar, Segovia states:

Regarding the program Abel Julio Carlevaro is going to perform, with skill, feeling, and artistic integrity that motivate me to present him—I will say that it comprises three groups of works sufficient to demonstrate the status of this young artist, musically and instrumentally. . . .

Now, a few words to summarize my opinion of the young Uruguayan artist who occasioned this interview. I am not a person who changes his views, but one of fixed beliefs. I am saying this so that my words are taken as the exact expression of how I feel. Abel Julio Carlevaro is a work in progress. He has his entire future to develop and confirm his talents. The guitar, more than any other instrument, needs honest artists who love her and who, like a chosen woman, live for her and not from her. It is an instrument that has been excluded from the official classes of the conservatory in almost the entire world. He who devotes his energies to it needs to redouble his efforts toward dedication and toward music and general culture so that no one can reproach him because he is not at the level of a great pianist, a great violinist, or a great cellist. Carlevaro does not ignore this and nobly prepares to achieve a legitimate triumph. Like all young, happy people, he does not yet have a history; but after the next concert he will begin collecting material for one.

Let me just say that I am very happy that the first young man I support is Uruguayan, is a countryman of my daughter Beatriz and the noble people that have welcomed me.

When, on Thursday, November 12, 1942, in his front-row box seat at the SODRE Studio Auditorium, Andrés Segovia gave Abel Carlevaro a standing ovation, he was doing something that went beyond the noteworthy approval of his young student. Segovia consolidated in that moment something like a plateau at the top of what had to do with the cherished expectations of his life and career. During those five years in Montevideo he had managed to establish a home and a stable family under the same roof and had seen his only daughter born in the Uruguayan capital. He had inspired, prepared, and premiered, with the excellent local orchestra, two masterpieces for the guitar repertoire of those days. He had encouraged and sponsored the brilliant artistic reappearance of the great pianist who was his wife. And now he closed the circle by devoting himself for the first time as a teacher and promoter of a new and more-than-promising artist of his instrument. It is easy to imagine all these ideas going quickly through the guitarist's mind while he publicly approved his disciple's diligent efforts. It is also significant that, just a day before that moment of consecration, Segovia had celebrated his forty-ninth birthday with a family gathering in the intimacy of his home. In addition to Paquita and the four girls, Aparicio Méndez and a few members of the Puig family were present.

The subsequent evolution of events, both professional and belonging to the most private aspects of the married couple's life, was to determine that this would be the last birthday party Segovia would celebrate in Montevideo in that climate of family harmony. The sequence of events that ensued in

1943 would mark a sharp turning point in the lives of both artists, and from then on nothing would be the same.

Except for a concert in late November by the guitarist in Mar del Plata, Argentina,[18] 1942 ended without any other relevant events in the professional lives of the Segovia-Madrigueras. Around that time Paquita visited with the composer Guido Santórsola and his wife, Sarah Bourdillon, who had been Beatriz's piano teacher since

Guido Santórsola and Sarah Bourdillon in 1943.

the previous June. From then on, several entries in Paquita's diary indicate that the Santórsolas visited the residence on Massini Street, or that she went to the house where her youngest daughter had piano lessons. Both couples developed a certain friendship during that time, their relationship based primarily on musical activities. They visited each other at their respective homes and sometimes walked together on the Rambla of Pocitos (the Santórsolas lived just a few blocks away). Paquita also prepared a performance with another student of Sarah Bourdillon, the young pianist Fanny Ingold, in October 1943.

There is little information regarding the development of the relationship between Segovia and Santórsola that could explain the unexpectedly harsh message (mentioned in chapter 3) that the composer recorded in 1979 on the occasion of Don Andrés's final concert in Montevideo. It is surprising that during their friendship Santórsola composed his Concertino for Guitar and Orchestra (the winner of a competition sponsored by SODRE), yet Segovia was not involved in either the dedication or the premiere. Perhaps it was because the guitarist was away from Montevideo for long periods that year and Santórsola had to go to Abel Carlevaro, to whom he finally dedicated the work, for advice on the requirements of the instrument. It was also this Uruguayan guitarist who premiered the piece on September 4, 1943, at the SODRE Studio Auditorium. Segovia left again for a long concert tour two days before the premiere, at which time Carlevaro visited him at his Massini Street home, probably to say farewell. Surely they also talked—the teacher and the student whose career was increasingly taking wing on flights of its own—regarding the details of this work; but it is still not known for certain.[19]

Knowing Don Andrés's strong personality, is it unreasonable to think that he would have been indifferent to the fact that while he was living in Montevideo a work for guitar and orchestra would be dedicated to and premiered by another guitarist? It could have been that Segovia turned down an offer in this regard and recommended his devoted student to replace him in the responsibility of the premiere and the honor of the dedication. If not, it is probable that the event marked the first seed of muted discord between the Uruguayan composer and the Spanish guitarist, mitigated in part by Segovia's increasing absence from Montevideo, which finally burst forth in the aggressive message of August 1979. It is also worth mentioning that Santórsola was a prolific composer for the guitar, yet Andrés Segovia never played a single one of his works in concerts or recordings. It was too much for Don Guido's self-esteem. In any event, it is also important to bear in mind that Paquita Madriguera did attend the premiere of the concertino, conducted by the composer. Despite these differences, which would worsen over time, the situation appeared to be one more of closeness than of rupture.[20]

The year 1943 saw Segovia returning to his old practice of traveling for long periods away from the small area of the Río de la Plata, to which he had been constrained since mid-1940. These renewed journeys—at first accompanied by Paquita, but later alone—would increasingly take him to countries located farther north and culminate with the long-awaited return to the United States in November 1943.[21] The consequences of Segovia's reentry into the powerful North American concert scene would be felt in both the professional and, with decisive repercussions, the most intimate aspects of his personal life.

The first important activity of the year was a trip to Chile the couple made by land in a way that five or six years earlier would have been difficult to imagine. The Segovia-Madrigueras departed by train from Buenos Aires for Mendoza on April 21, arriving late at night. They left by car early the next morning to cross the Andes Mountains with the Catalonian actress Margarita Xirgú, an emblem of the Spanish Republican cause in South American lands, and her husband, Miguel Ortin. The passage of time had gradually dissolved the antagonism that caused Paquita to ignore the triumphant presence of the actress in Montevideo in 1937, and a new relationship had now been established. In fact, the actress and her second husband had visited Segovia and Paquita at their Massini Street home on April 2, when the idea for this trip probably surfaced.

Margarita Xirgú had been established for some time in the Chilean capital of Santiago, where she founded the Escuela de Arte Dramático (School of Dramatic Art), and she came to Montevideo under contract by SODRE to do some theater activities in collaboration with Justino Zavala Muniz.[22] The Catalonian actress and her husband would be in Mendoza with their car on the date that Segovia and Paquita were scheduled to arrive in Chile for a long tour, in which both were booked to give concerts. They arranged to meet in Mendoza and have the picturesque experience of

Margarita Xirgú.

traveling to Santiago over the Andes through the Cristo Redentor (Christ the Redeemer) mountain pass. Paquita's diary states that they departed on April 23 at 5:30 A.M., ate lunch at 1:00 P.M. in Portillo (on the Chilean side), and had tea at 6:00 P.M. at Los Andes. They arrived in the Chilean capital at 8:30 P.M., and while the Catalonian theater couple went to their home, Don Andrés and Paquita stayed at the Hotel Crillon.

Segovia and Paquita's concert activity in Chile had been arranged through the Inter-American Institute of Musicology, directed by Francisco Curt Lange. A letter from him dated May 7 relates the negotiations he was carrying on to extend the tour to Lima and from there to some northern provinces of Argentina:

> Dear Andrés and Paquita,
>
> I had been asking at your home for news and found out about the wonderful arrival and the small, unavoidable accidents that resulted from the trip. I am going to be precise since the post office will close in a few minutes:
>
> LIMA: Alfonso Vargas y Vargas has written to you about that one so you will have to deal with it from there, directly, as he suggests. Buchwald has not written one word to me.[23] This is his habit, and I think that it may even be a technique. He does not commit to anyone, and he only deals with the artists once they are in Lima. I would suggest a trip if everything is settled with Vargas for two concerts at the Teatro Municipal, and the rest will come on its own. In respect to Paquita, other pianists who may have performed a few weeks earlier do not scare me. They have great memories of her everywhere. The rest comes from her personal charm, which we all admire.

MENDOZA: They have not responded to date. I do expect something concrete, however. Couture is going one of these days, and I will ask him to address the matter personally to achieve something concrete.

TUCUMÁN: Mrs. Sarah has written and set a date for July and has booked four dates so far. She said that she has written to Rosario and Santa Fe. I believe it, because she is active and has connections. She went straight to Grewel. He, who seems to be spineless, should answer at any moment.

Today is your first concert, Paquita. I wish you from here, even if this letter arrives late, the best success. I guess there are no difficulties regarding Viña.

Since a concert in Concepción is difficult to arrange from here at the last moment, it would be preferable to request that Carvajal send a telegram to Concepción, proposing to Arturo Medina, the director of the symphony (?) and the choir of Concepción (a very good choral group), proposals for one or two concerts (without an earthquake,[24] that is). Since Chilean musical life has reconcentrated in Santiago in recent times, I would not know of other places to suggest at this time given that everything has been difficult, at least to begin with.

I would appreciate a response to P.O. Box 540 about the arrangements in Lima. That way I will be able to respond to the Carreras and schedule the performance in Argentina. I wish you a good stay and ask you to remember me whenever you eat a lobster or similar creatures. They all represent something like my "weakness," to which I must add wine. Hugs to Domingo and his followers,[25] without making any age or gender distinction. With nothing more for today, accept María Luisa's and my constant affection.

On the day Lange wrote this letter, Paquita made an appearance at the Teatro Municipal in Santiago de Chile as a soloist with the symphony orchestra, conducted by Armando Carvajal. She played the Grieg Piano Concerto, which she had performed the previous year in Montevideo with the Chilean maestro. Segovia, in the meantime, had already performed twice in the same theater—playing the *Concierto del sur* on April 30, with the orchestra conducted by Carvajal, and then on May 3 appearing in a solo presentation. After Paquita's concert with the orchestra, the Segovia-Madrigueras had dinner with the conductor and his wife, the composer Domingo Santa Cruz, and the musicologist Filomena Salas. They all signed a short note addressed to

Ponce that Segovia alludes to in the letter he sent his Mexican friend on May 9.[26] In that same letter, Segovia tells Ponce that arrangements are being made for his reappearance in the United States at the beginning of next winter (the end of that year, 1943). As for Paquita's presentation, the newspaper *La Nación* wrote the next day:

> Paquita Madriguera . . . was in charge of the soloist part of the Concerto in A Minor for Piano and Orchestra by Edvard Grieg. The pianist retains all those artistic qualities as a virtuoso that we have been able to hear on other occasions. The exhibited slow pace, this time, of the three movements that make up the famous work of the Norwegian composer allowed Paquita Madriguera to concentrate on relating everything with clarity of phrasing, correct use of the pedal, and feeling. Her cantabile took on a warm and communicative sound in the Adagio and in the episodes of greater lyricism contained in the Allegro moderato, the final movement of the concerto. Her performance met with an enthusiastic reception from the audience present.

Another review was unfavorable for Paquita:

> It is unfortunate to have again included in a symphonic program the Grieg Concerto, a well-known work, especially considering the vast existing repertoire in this genre. Ignoring the relevant powers of the pianist, she has been forced to play a concerto unsuited to her temperament. This is an artist of undeniable talent, but whose sound lacks the required volume in a work like the Grieg. Paquita Madriguera, conscious of this feature and, at the same time, the innate difficulty of performing it, came up throughout her performance with a hard and dry sound and consequently lacked the necessary rhythmic fluency. This absence was felt especially in the last movement, in which the graceful and brilliant Norwegian dance that inspired the composer was transformed into a heavy and solid Allegro. However, we cannot be unaware of her great talent for melodic clarity, which would be felt in a more obvious form in a Mozart or Beethoven concerto.[27]

On Saturday, May 8, the day following Paquita's Teatro Municipal performance, Margarita Xirgú had a tea at her house in honor of her pianist compatriot. Paquita wrote a letter to her daughter María Rosa telling her about this reception and other news but, strikingly, alludes to the actress who honored her without giving a clue as to her identity:

> In spite of the handwriting, I have been able to read your letter very well, which we appreciate a lot.
>
> It's a shame that I was not able to be there for the mother's party at school, as I have done every year, but things are not always the same, unfortunately; they change, and with the changes they take something from our spirit—that is why nostalgia for things exists, because of the forced changes in our lives. When a few years pass, you will feel the pain of this or that time, whose nuances you have not been able to retain.
>
> I was not able to go to the biggest dinner of the season, which was the one given by the minister of foreign affairs, because I was having liver problems. Now I am feeling good, thank God, but I was very angry when I saw Andrés go out in tails and I had to stay in bed.
>
> A lady gave me a tea the other day where there were a lot of the best ladies from here. So, if we were to listen to everyone, there would be two very fat people giving concerts (a result of eating too much) and playing horribly because they would not leave us the time to practice, if it were up to them.
>
> Will you be able to attend the mandatory [Protestant religious] service—you and Sofía—in addition to the class schedule and homework, and also the freezing short walks along the Rambla?
>
> It is time to go to the dining room, so I am leaving you, but not before sending you a big kiss from Andrés and another very affectionate one from your mother, who loves you.[28]

The series of concerts that Segovia and Paquita gave during their long stay in Chilean territory was very intense. Additional concerts by the guitarist include one at Teatro Cervantes in Santiago (May 10) and a second concert with orchestra four days later at the Teatro Municipal. On May 16 Don Andrés left for Concepción, and on May 17 Paquita went to Viña del Mar. She performed on the evening of May 19 at the Quinta Vergara in a concert organized by the Pro Arte Society of the so-called Garden City. Segovia arrived that night and played the next day at the Viña del Mar's Teatro Municipal. We have his program for this event (structured in his customary three parts):

Part I
Pavane and Galliard (Gaspar Sanz)
Theme and Variations (Fernando Sor)
Sonata (Mario Castelnuovo-Tedesco)
Madroños (Federico Moreno Torroba)

Part II
Sarabande (George Frideric Handel)
Sonata (Domenico Scarlatti)
Prelude, Fugue, and Gavotte (J. S. Bach)
Andante and Minuet (Franz Joseph Haydn)

Part III
Mazurka (Alexander Tansman)
Fandanguillo (Joaquín Turina)
Spanish Dance in G (Enrique Granados)
Sevilla (Isaac Albéniz)

On May 22, both musicians returned to Santiago de Chile, where they performed again at Teatro Cervantes (Segovia on May 24 and Paquita on May 27). On May 29, Paquita played again in Viña del Mar, and two days later Segovia played a special concert for schoolchildren in Santiago. On June 1, having both finished their artistic activities, they attended a concert by the violinist Ricardo Odnoposoff,[29] who was going to play in Montevideo after performing in Chile. They traveled to Mendoza on June 3 by plane, continued on to Buenos Aires by train, and on the night of June 7 took the *Vapor de la Carrera* to Montevideo. This trip had lasted forty-seven days and was the longest since February 1939—a long time ago, considering the number of important events that had taken place in the interim. In a sign of things to come, the couple lived together at home for just a three short weeks, until Don Andrés left for Bolivia on June 30. Among the few activities recorded in Paquita's diary during this brief period are two concerts that the couple attended in the traditional Saturday series of the SODRE Symphony Orchestra: on June 12, Odnoposoff performed as a soloist, and on Saturday, June 26, the violinist Yehudi Menuhin played. Odnoposoff and his wife visited the Massini Street home the day before his concert at the Studio Auditorium.

Segovia remained in Bolivia for July 1943 and arrived back in Montevideo on August 9. Paquita wrote five letters to La Paz between July 5 and July 27, but Segovia's responses are not preserved in the family archives. On August 1, the pianist received a visit at her home from Margarita Xirgú and her husband, Miguel Ortin, who were again passing through Montevideo. Not until the beginning of 1949 did the Catalonian actress accept the directorship of the National Comedy, whereupon she created the Escuela de Arte Dramático and settled permanently in the Uruguayan capital. Segovia's stay in his Montevideo home was once again limited to three weeks before he embarked on a much longer tour that was to keep him away from Montevideo from September 2, 1943 until the end of the following May. He received Abel Carlevaro at his home several times during those days prior to the premiere of Guido Santórsola's Concertino.

During Segovia's long absence, another important event in Carlevaro's progressive independence from his maestro's influence took place. It constitutes another story in itself and concerns the link between Segovia and the inauguration, finally, of the famous Twelve Etudes for Guitar by Heitor Villa-Lobos—an important part of the twentieth-century history of the guitar that has not been properly evaluated. Between November 1943 and May 1944, Carlevaro visited Villa-Lobos in Rio de Janeiro and, in the presence of the composer, gave the first public performances of two of the Five Preludes for Guitar. More important, he studied with the composer those works for which Segovia had shown so little enthusiasm. Villa-Lobos gave Carlevaro manuscript copies of his Prelude No. 1 and Etudes Nos. 1, 2, 3, 4, 5, and 10; the musicologist Francisco Curt Lange had previously given him copies of the Preludes Nos. 3 and 4, which had been published as a music supplement in the Brazilian magazine *Música Viva*. The Uruguayan guitarist studied all of these pieces under the Brazilian maestro's supervision, in some cases with indications added by the composer to the copies during the lessons. Carlevaro brought these manuscripts back to Montevideo, treasuring them with special devotion for the rest of his life.

It is interesting to note that Segovia had received only Etudes Nos. 1, 5, 7, and 8, and, perhaps (provided by Lange), the published copies of Preludes Nos. 3 and 4. Segovia must have found upon returning to Uruguay that Carlevaro had not only premiered Santórsola's Concertino in Montevideo, but had also performed it with great success at the Teatro Municipal in Rio de Janeiro, had studied with Villa-Lobos, and had returned to Uruguay with several of the Brazilian's works that were going to be dedicated to the Spanish maestro but had been given to his student first in appreciation of his enthusiastic receptiveness. Probably perceiving some sign of discomfort in Segovia, Carlevaro was careful to explicitly reaffirm his respect and gratitude toward the maestro the first time he was interviewed by a newspaper following his return to Montevideo. The day after the publication of this piece—August 10, 1944—Segovia was back in the Uruguayan capital, and Carlevaro was going to perform at the SODRE and give the Montevideo premiere of several works that Segovia had never played—Prelude No. 3 and Study No. 1 by Villa-Lobos, *Ponteio* by Camargo Guarnieri (dedicated to Carlevaro), *Preludio* by Santórsola, and *Sonata Clásica* by Ponce (dedicated to Segovia, but which he still had not performed in Uruguay). The interview with Carlevaro, published a day before his concert at SODRE, said in part:

Abel Carlevaro ... talked to us enthusiastically about his recent trip to Brazilian soil. The references to his tour make allusions of gratitude and admiration for all Brazilian people and artists, translated into respect for the maestros he visited and with whom he had the opportunity to collaborate—such as Villa-Lobos, Camargo Guarnieri, Lorenzo Fernández, Mignone, etc.

"There is in Brazil," our fellow guitarist told us, "a notable interest in the guitar.... I should point out in the first place that one of my most successful presentations in Brazil was my performance in the festival at the Teatro Municipal of Rio de Janeiro, where the Concerto for Guitar and Orchestra by Maestro Santórsola, which won last year's competition organized by SODRE, was performed.... I was also the subject of many flattering distinctions, such as the one by Maestro Camargo Guarnieri in promising to write a concerto for guitar and orchestra especially for me. I was asked to do several recordings, which I did in the Brazilian capital and which will be released throughout our sister country."

Gratitude to Segovia

One of the most eloquent traits of Carlevaro's personality is his devout admiration for his teacher, Andrés Segovia....

"During my visits to his house," he told us, "where there is an atmosphere of refined culture, I have seen the greatness of his spirit, the vastness of his knowledge, the goodness of his generous soul. Uruguay shelters an artist who Kreisler said occupies the heights of musical art along with Pablo Casals.

"I have learned much with Segovia; I owe him what one would owe superior men who give generously of their knowledge."[30]

The record that Paquita kept of the letters she sent, month after month, following Segovia's departure from Montevideo in September 1943 allows us to reconstruct the guitarist's journey during the first part of his long tour. She wrote to Lima (September 5 and 6), to Bogotá (September 9 and 11), and to Caracas (four letters between September 15 and 29). In the beginning of October he visited different Central American cities, and on October 21 he gave a concert at the Auditorium theater of Havana. Then, during the entire month of October, Paquita sent her letters to Mexico, and after November 17 she began to send them to the cultural capital that Don Andrés longed so much to reconquer (without realizing what fate awaited him there)—New York. By then Paquita was also doing her own artistic tour, which began on November 12. Mamá Paqui, Sofía, and María Rosa accompanied her to the port to bid her farewell on a trip that would take her to Buenos Aires to board a plane for Lima two days later. The pianist gave two concerts at the Teatro Municipal in the Peruvian capital, with the first, on November 19, containing works by Handel, Bach, Mozart, Mendelssohn, Castelnuovo-Tedesco, Falla, and Granados. Under the heading "Paquita Madriguera Performed Yesterday with Brilliant Success," the review published in Lima's *El Comercio* began by evoking the first appearance of the pianist in the "City of the Viceroys" twenty-two years earlier:

A uniquely gratifying experience to attend the comeback of an artist like Paquita Madriguera, who visited us on her first tour of South America and is back today to our premier theater with the prestige given by time and maturity, with that peculiar tone, so calm and persuasive, typical of a temperament that life filters and distills, leaving the precise balance of the essential, of the fair and accurate, required for a mission of beauty and spiritual gift. Those of us who admired the brilliant student of Granados years ago—the female pianist had just been released from the rigid constraints of the conservatory, impetuous and brilliant, unstoppable in her momentum and her urgency to show off the spectacular elegance of a bright and sparkling technique—have just verified her logical evolution to an almost ritualistic attitude toward the music. Paquita is the quintessential pianist today, fully aware of her aesthetic responsibility, leaving behind, as a subjective remembrance, the colored lights of descriptive and inconsequential virtuosity.

From the initial exposure to the Theme and Variations by Handel ... we are aware of the determination of a musical standard of unalterable serenity that, after also shining through in Bach's Fantasy in C Minor, was convincingly confirmed with the Sonata in F Major by Mozart. Paquita Madriguera gives us a genuine Mozart of constant dynamic balance, sweet tone, fresh, relaxed, which acquires a delicious tranquility in the Adagio, sung with true musical dedication.

We turn then to a part dedicated to Mendelssohn, hearing his Prelude and Fugue in E Minor, developed with musicality and vigorously displaying in the magnificent fugue a quality that could also be appreciated through the *Serious Variations*, of which the pianist offered a rich instrumental version. *Spinning Song* was a true gift, acknowledging the deserved applause with which the audience rewarded her.

Finally, and after giving us the interesting *Nocturne in Hollywood* by Castelnuovo-Tedesco ... Paquita played a beautiful version of the *Andalusia* by Falla, rich in pianistic effects revealing exquisite sensitivity, then achieved a refined poetic sense in *The Maiden and the Nightingale* by Granados. The artist surrenders to the purpose with an undeniable fervor, her goal brilliantly accomplished, bringing out the expressive essence of her teacher's enchanting music, which creates an atmosphere of exceptionally affective devotion. And the concert ended with the sparkling virtuosity of *The Dummy*, which excited the audience and required the artist to add a number to the program amid the warmest reception.

Paquita Madriguera fully justified her return to the musical scene. She has retained priceless technical skills, highlighted with the authority of a cultured discernment and exalted with the refinement of a spirit filled with finesse. Her fine and elegant figure, her manners governed by aristocratic discretion, provided a personality certainly worthy of the accolades given to her yesterday by a public won over by her merits and warmth.

Following this review the paper noted, "As is known, Paquita Madriguera generously gave this concert for the benefit of the Catholic Missions in Peru," and it pointed out that the highest authorities of the church were present.

On Sunday, November 21, Paquita performed at the Teatro Municipal, this time as soloist in Grieg's Concerto in A Minor with the Orquesta Sinfónica Nacional conducted by Theo Buchwald. The reviews that appeared in the Lima press were again enthusiastically favorable. The next day, the newspaper *La Noche* stated in the middle of its review:

> The greatest interest of the evening, naturally, was focused on the performer of whom we had the greatest memories and news. Not only did Paquita Madriguera confirm the expectations of her audience by performing the beautiful Concerto for Piano and Orchestra by Grieg, but the admiration and enthusiasm of the audience was such that she was forced to play a solo piece outside of the program. This performer is so personal in her manner of performing and interpreting, with such power of sound, with such excellent piano playing and unique delicacy that captivates the listener....
>
> Once the concert ended we had the pleasure of greeting the distinguished artist and reminding her of other days and of some of Segovia's remarks. She had intelligent and friendly words for us and for her innumerable fans and signed an enormous number of autographs. Many people are asking to hear her again, and we make that our request because "all of Lima" that admires and loves Paquita Madriguera has not had a chance to hear her.

On November 26, 1943—while Andrés Segovia was taking the first steps in reconquering his audience in New York and, at the same time, probably entering a slippery romantic terrain from which it would take him almost twenty years to escape—Paquita Madriguera left Lima for the Ecuadorian city of Guayaquil. There she remained for a few days, although there is no record of any concerts. It is known that she stayed at the home of a local society lady who made a piano available to her so she could practice. It is probable that she also dedicated the time to managing the details of a series of concerts that she and Segovia were going to give in Ecuador the following April, upon his return to Montevideo from North America. On December 3, Paquita left for Havana on a trip that would take six days, with several stopovers in Colombia (Cali and Barranquilla), Jamaica (where a mechanical problem with the airplane forced her to remain an extra day), and finally in the Cuban city of Cienfuegos. As soon as she arrived in Havana on December 9, she settled at the Hotel Nacional. She met several times with Rosa Culmell and Joaquín Nin Culmell, whom she had known since her girlhood and had not seen in a long time. On Thursday, December 19, Paquita flew to Santiago de Cuba, and that night she gave a concert for the city's Sociedad Filarmónica. The next morning she returned to the Cuban capital, and after a couple of days (during which she got together again with Nin Culmell) she traveled to Mexico. Segovia had already written to Ponce on December 13 from New York informing him that Paquita was due to arrive from Havana, which she finally did on December 24. He was worried that she would be lonely in Mexico until he arrived from the United States, so he asked Ponce to receive her at his home, provided that he would be allowed to share the house expenses. He said that he wanted to be considered as a member of the family, helping as any of them, and that Paquita would work with Clema in sharing the chores and preparing the food for everyone. He also said that he would be arriving on January 20.[31]

Paquita Madriguera spent Christmas of 1943 at the home of Manuel Ponce and the next day accepted his invitation to remain there while she awaited Segovia's return to the Aztec capital. The pianist's stay at the Ponce home was extended for exactly a month, because Don Andrés kept delaying his trip to Mexico. She had to continue practicing during that time for an important series of concerts scheduled to begin in March, but she also managed to do some sightseeing in Mexican territory. Something strange, however, had been disturbing Paquita's mood during those first weeks of 1944, which were extending the already long separation from her husband. It is difficult to know whether Paquita's intuition sensed trouble through the letters of Don Andrés, or whether the daily entries in her diary relate to problems she was having in her host country. She wrote a sequence of reflections during those January days that were strikingly uncharacteristic of her. On January 10, and without any clarification, she wrote: "Are we in the ill-fated planet? As the plants dry in arid lands, here dry the beautiful feelings, which are losing their leaves on our path toward death."

Five days later Paquita wrote:

They say that to know how God despises money, all you have to do is look at those to whom he gives it. I add that God must also despise art. Have you not noticed the rudeness, petulance, and lack of education of most of the messengers of art? Many of whom rarely bathe because they even think their bodies are better than those of everyone else? When humanity improves, the artist will get "wisdom," "kindness," "nobility," "education," "fineness of feelings," [and] "benevolence" and *will know* that despite how much he is worth, he is worth very little in comparison to many other beings.

A tourist excursion undertaken by Paquita the following week, accompanied by Ponce's wife, Clema, and another woman, suggests that not all was harmonious in the residence of the pianist at the home of her friends. On Saturday, January 22, she wrote:

Laurita Estrada, Clema, and I went on an excursion to Paricutín.[32]
10:00 A.M.—Left Mexico City by bus.
4:00 P.M.—We arrived at Morelia. Hotel Alameda. Dissonant note: Clema.

And on Sunday:

At 4:00 P.M. we left by car for Paricutín. At 8:00 P.M. we arrived at San Juan de las Colchas. We got on horseback and rode about a kilometer to the slope of the volcano. Wonderful view. We arrived in Morelia at 3:00 A.M. on the 24th. Dissonant note: Clema.

In a change perhaps signaling that all was not well, Paquita moved to an apartment at 174 Liverpool on January 26, just two days after returning to Mexico City from the excursion. The apartment was probably rented because Segovia had announced his arrival for January 28, a date that would again be postponed. The relationship with the Ponces, at least on the surface, did not appear to be affected. On Thursday, January 27, Paquita had lunch with them at their home, and on January 29 she received a visit from her two excursion companions at her new apartment. On February 2 the piano that Paquita had rented was delivered to her apartment, since she was preparing for her approaching concert tour.

On the afternoon of February 11, 1944, Don Andrés finally arrived from New York, five months and nine days after he and Paquita last said farewell in Montevideo. The lunch at the apartment following his arrival was shared with the Ponces. That night Segovia and Paquita visited their friends for dinner. The guitarist returned elated, for he had fulfilled the plan that had largely driven his desires for the past four years—the resumption of his concerts in the United States. He achieved it with resounding success, and the doors to the largest music market of those years were open for him from that time forward. The clamors of the war that destroyed the European countries and a part of Asia did not affect the splendor of the cultural life developing in the large cities of North America. In the middle of January, Segovia had written from Boston to his sixteen-year-old stepdaughter:

My dear María Rosa,

Thank you for your kind letter. I am responding to you during a break from my work. I am playing at 3:00 P.M. at Jordan Hall—a concert hall in Boston—and I am preparing.

You forget in your lines to mention your boyfriend's name. I would have loved to hear from you what I know through Pitusa and Sofía, that is, that you two still love each other and really look like—as your older sister says facetiously—a single word with two meanings.

I thank you for including little Beatriz in your letter.

I am working hard and well. I have played six concerts in New York, to full halls. I am the musical figure of the day. Last night I attended a concert by a different artist, and both the public and the artist were friendly and affectionate with me.

I am going to record, starting this next Monday, thirty pieces on discs. They give me 6,000—six thousand—dollars for them plus 10 percent of the sales. I have also received offers from Metro Goldwin Mayer [*sic*] to make a film in which, according to the letter issued by them through the person in charge of this project, they will invest more than half a million dollars (these figures are only heard in this wonderful country). However, I will not let them tempt me, and I demand, above all, that they submit the plot of the film and all the scenes it has for my approval. That is where we are.

Mama is in Mexico. I will go meet her on the 28th. She is not coming to New York because the trip would be too slow and complicated due to the priorities of the plane, and even more unpleasant by train.

I have a strong desire to stay home for a few months, quiet, with no trips or concerts.

Regards to your boyfriend and hugs for Mamá Paqui and your sisters, to whom I will write later if I still have time.

And a kiss for you from
Andrés

P.S. I love you very much, little Beatriz.

Segovia had remained in the United States for three months on that first visit after the ban that had been established following his stance in support of Franco during the Spanish Civil War. Those three months were enough for him to regain favor with the public and critics and to significantly increase his production of recordings. Success was smiling down on him once more. But that very success generated the conditions that would force his personal life into a crisis. It was during Segovia's months of solitary residence in New York, while Paquita slowly moved closer to the moment of reunion, that he again found himself part of the elite world of international art, feted by public personalities and given personal attention in hotels and restaurants, while he spent his days free from the concerns of an orderly home and a family consisting of a wife, mother-in-law, three teenage daughters, and a young girl—even if he longed for it in some ways, as he confessed to his stepdaughter. It should not surprise anyone that the cosmopolitan shine of the New York City lifestyle, where he was being spoiled and flattered as the "musical figure of the day," greatly contrasted with the provincial and carefree tranquility of Montevideo. Regardless of how pleasant Don Andrés considered the little Uruguayan capital, the Big Apple had dazzled his mind and exacerbated those characteristics that had led Paquita to write of him: "Segovia's fame extends over the entire Universe. There is much talk about him as a musician and as a conqueror of hearts. A list of females takes a good deal of space in his gallant memories."[33]

It is also not surprising that Andrés Segovia, fifty years old and feeling at the brightest summit of his artistic career, would establish a romantic relationship with the famous Brazilian singer Olga Praguer Coelho, who was married to a poet of the same nationality, Gaspar Coelho. Although it is not known when or where the soprano and guitarist met, it was most likely during one of the many social gatherings in the great city that brought together artists of Hispanic origin. According to a story she told an interviewer in 2001, seven years before her death, events fell out almost immediately following Segovia's first compliment:

> I had been fascinated by him since I was fifteen. I followed his career through the Spanish newspapers that Lorenzo Fernández gave me. He greeted me by saying: "At your service." Irresistible. First I received him at

my apartment. I served him a Bahian meal and introduced him to a Cuban lady friend of mine.[34] Segovia invited me to his hotel room to show me the secrets of his new guitar technique . . . The hotel was close to my house. It was just a room with only a bed, and not a suite. We had the lesson right there. He caressed my hand and I resisted, and I even confessed with a French priest in St. Patrick's Cathedral.[35]

Olga Praguer was born in the Amazon River city of Manaus in 1909 and took up music at an early age, performing popular Brazilian songs and accompanying herself on the guitar. She had learned the instrument with Patricio Teixeira and studied theory and composition with the composer Lorenzo Fernández after settling in Rio de Janeiro with her family in 1923. She received her diploma at the National Institute of Music and later studied voice with the Russian teacher Riva Pasternak and the famous Italian contralto Gabriella Besanzoni. She married Gaspar Coelho in 1931 and developed an international career giving concerts and recording numerous discs. When Segovia met her, she was already famous in the artistic circles of a good part of the world and enjoyed friendships with Heitor Villa-Lobos and many other notable artists. That 2001 interview, when the singer-guitarist was ninety-two, began:

> The soprano Olga Praguer Coelho continues to sing, and well, at the age of ninety-two, even if she has been forgotten by the musical world. She is one of those folk-song goddesses of the 1920s and '30s. Her recordings number two hundred in titles, between 78 r.p.m. and LP, recorded in Brazil, Argentina, the United States, Europe, and even Australia, where she did a tour in the 1940s. At the end of this year a double album with some of her most important hits should be released in New York by BMG. In 1998 Olga participated in the program "Ensaio" (Essay), on Culture TV of São Paulo, and still wants to record a second part, only with songs, for a future edition on CD. She answers the phone in her apartment, located on the eighth floor of a building in Laranjeiras,[36] built on the land of her childhood home.

After recounting her first years as a singer, Olga tells the interviewer that in 1936 she was named Representative of Brazilian Music in Europe by President Getulio Vargas,[37] and she traveled to Berlin for the closing ceremonies of the Olympic Games on the last flight that the *Graf Zeppelin* made between America and the European continent.[38] In her own words: "I was invited to sit in the Brazilian box, which was next to Hitler's. I met the man, who seemed insolent to me, and I refused to say 'Heil, Hitler.'"

During the trip, and on the advice of Villa-Lobos, Olga demanded that the radio transmit her performances on long wave so that the European public could be introduced to Brazilian folklore. When she went to Budapest, she found out that Béla Bartók was seated in the front row, relating in the same 2001 interview:

> "I was speechless, but he later came to the dressing room to congratulate me. He liked the Brazilian folklore, especially the rhythms."
>
> Now famous, on her return to Brazil Olga arranged more trips. Following the suggestions of Villa-Lobos and the writer Erico Verissimo, she was invited by the United States government to perform in Washington, D.C., and New York. In 1938 she sang at the White House for Eleanor Roosevelt and signed a contract with RCA Victor. She and Gaspar settled in an apartment on Seventh Avenue, across from Central Park. Her concert at Town Hall was a success. . . . Camargo Guarnieri called her to premiere his arias, to the envy of Elsie Houston (1902–1943), a soprano friend of Mario de Andrade, who, until Olga's arrival, had had a monopoly on Brazilian folk music in New York. . . .
>
> Everything went well for Olga and Gaspar. He worked for CBS as an announcer. Then Andrés Segovia appeared—gray-haired and a Don Juan. . . . [Olga] recalled, "He had a concert set in Washington, D.C., and wanted to go in the same train coach, but Gaspar did not like the idea. Didn't he stay in the same hotel we did?"
>
> In Washington the romance was irresistible, and Olga separated from Gaspar to follow the guitarist on his endless tours. From then on, the soprano's career picked up, and she toured the world, seeking audiences for Brazilian music in such locales as Bali and New Zealand. She had two children with Segovia, Miguel and Gloria,[39] whom Gaspar adopted as his own, since the virtuoso did not have time for a family.
>
> "My life with Segovia lasted two decades. It was international, from hotel to hotel, until, at the age of seventy, he became infatuated with a twenty-year-old student, the 'innocent' Emilia. He had one child with her. Gaspar was still alive when the separation took place. He devoted himself to my children. He was an announcer until his death. As a poet, he translated

into Portuguese, in verse, the subtitles of the film *Hamlet*, with Laurence Olivier. He never stopped loving me."

Through the many recordings that are preserved today, it is possible to appreciate the level of excellence of Olga Coelho's abilities, both as a singer and as a guitarist. Musicians who knew her well say that she played a 1937 Hauser, obtained through Segovia and purported to be the twin of his famous and beloved instrument. The guitarist composed and dedicated some works to her,[40] improved her playing, and made sophisticated arrangements for Olga to accompany the songs she performed. In an obituary, Fábio Zanon quoted her as saying, "Andrés often forgot that on top of his arrangements, I also had to sing."[41]

She served as the intermediary when Villa-Lobos sent Segovia the remaining Twelve Etudes,[42] and the Brazilian composer arranged and published the famous Aria from his *Bachianas Brasilieras No. 5* for voice and guitar—dedicated to Olga and fingered by Segovia. Olga Praguer Coelho died on February 25, 2008, at the age of ninety-eight.

Paquita Madriguera did not find out about her husband's affair until a few months later, once they were both settled again in Montevideo. Back in Mexico City, when Segovia arrived from New York in February 1944, the professional activity for both artists was very intense at the beginning of this phase of the tour, especially with the emotional tension—which was certainly difficult to hide—that the recent events were probably causing the guitarist. One cannot rule out the possibility that the relentless concert schedule might have been a way for Don Andrés to mask his most intimate feelings, while giving him the ability to slowly assimilate to the new situation and evaluate his real romantic inclinations.

The first musical activity for Segovia on Mexican territory was the premiere of the *Concierto del sur* with the orchestra conducted by Erich Kleiber,[43] a significant event in Ponce's homeland. According to Paquita's diary, on the night of February 15 the Segovia-Madrigueras went to the Ponces' home for dinner and to deliver the concerto manuscripts that Kleiber was to use. The entry in the pianist's diary is not very explicit (it only states "to pass along conc. for Kleiber"), but it could very well refer to the copy of the score bound in blue with gold letters, which the guitarist had ordered for his personal use. It bore

Segovia and Olga Coelho in their New York apartment, 1951.

the initials "A. S.," and he had kept it with him ever since the premiere of the work in Montevideo. The Mexican premiere of *Concierto del sur* took place on February 21, 1944, at the Palacio de Bellas Artes. That was the beginning of an intensive new series of concerts that would keep the two artists busy almost nonstop for the next three months. Between February 21 and March 16, Segovia gave four concerts in Mexico City, and Paquita played at Bellas Artes and a few days later gave a private concert at the home of a family. Finally, to bring an end to their visit to the Aztec capital, they played a concert together on the same stage where Ponce's work had premiered.

The Mexican press covered Paquita Madriguera's presence extensively during the days prior to her debut on March 9 at Bellas Artes. The most interesting, from the point of view of this story, are the two interviews of the spouses that appeared in two different newspapers on successive days. In one of them Paquita talks about her life and her artistic convictions, and in the other Don Andrés outlines a portrait of his wife in which he expresses the admiration he feels for her as an artist—maintaining an objective and professional tone while not revealing the dramatic collision of feelings that was probably going through his mind in those days. In the first, on March 5, an interview with the pianist was published in the newspaper *El Redondel* under the headline "Paquita Madriguera Speaks to Us Enthusiastically About Spanish Music," followed by the subhead "The Russians Do Not Interpret It Well." The interview begins with a reference to her previous visit, when she accompanied Segovia in a non-performing capacity on his concert tour of 1934:

This distinguished artist, a beautiful woman of great intelligence, passed like a meteor through the capital, without giving us the chance to know her as a pianist of outstanding ability. At that time her desire to come to know this "wonderful country"—as she calls it—obeyed the need to take a break, but she looked forward to returning as a concert pianist.

"I met my goal," she tells us with a lovely smile, "to visit it. If I could, I would stay here indefinitely." She immediately begins to talk about her concerts. She tells us about her life, starting more or less with her childhood, when at the age of nine she was already an acclaimed concert pianist in Spain and other countries. She was first the wife of a prominent lawyer from Madrid [*sic*] and after a number of years joined her destiny with the celebrated guitarist Segovia. She was distinguished as a child prodigy, and what happens to most of these supreme intelligences—that they are admired for their early abnormal development—did not happen to her; on the contrary, this pianist's talent, which was admired by the great musician Granados, was developed in an extraordinary way, using the best method and technique to allow her to reach maturity in the art. And that is how the Spanish musician and composer of *Goyescas* imparted his wisdom. She inherited the secret of interpreting his works in the way he wanted, so that when she traveled the world she would be the one who expressed the meaning of his works in the most suitable manner.

"My great successes," Paquita told us, "have come since I was eleven years old. First in Madrid and then in London, when I played at the Albert Hall before thousands of people. After a tour, the war of 1914 prevented me from continuing, and I went with my family to Central America. I then visited all of South [America] and the United States. I played especially in

San Francisco during that great World Fair and later in New York. From there I went to Cuba, where I gave a lot of concerts."

The beautiful artist continues to point out her artistic life. She speaks with immense fervor about the great cellist Casals, about Manén the violinist, and about other eminent musicians with whom she toured. Paquita also tells us that many years ago they proposed to her in Madrid that she come to Mexico to give concerts at El Toreo [Mexico City's bullring]; but on top of the fact that she did not like the idea, the "revolutions" scared her, and she decided not to come in spite of the fact that Casals had talked to her about concerts in this arena that had found great audience success.

"Would you like to talk to us about other types of artistic appreciation?" we interrupted.

"Besides my great admiration for Granados and Casals, the works of all the great Hispanic composers, from Albéniz to Falla, fascinate me. I think that the musical panorama is quite vast. I like all music as long as it is good. Everything is admirable in any style. I do not devote myself to a single composer. The classics fascinate me in an extraordinary way, like the romantics and contemporary music. My music panorama is broad, but it is true," Paquita emphasizes, "that I cannot stand bad music or music that simply confuses, when there is no talent. It seems like a trade and a dishonorable art."

"What can you tell us about Johann Sebastian Bach?"

"Bach is very great; he is the foundation of music. Bach is who we really need to cite, not that I believe that Beethoven and Mozart are not great. The same could be said about the romantics, because a Chopin and a Schubert are not unequal in their worth. I respect them all. When I play a work on the piano, I believe at that moment that it is the best and the most beautiful. I live with all my soul in that artistic moment, and I transcend; I feel elevated above the rest at that so happy moment."

"What repertoire will you play for us in your concerts?"

"I will try to please this cultured and demanding audience. I will play a complete repertoire, as I have done everywhere, and, above all, I will play Spanish music as it should be interpreted, because most of the pianists do not know its meters, its rhythms, and the character that it should possess. This occurs especially among the Russian pianists. I don't try to hide it. For example, with Granados, I acquired his tradition; I possess his

Headline of the *El Redondel* article with Paquita's handwritten
notation of "March 5, 1944."

corrections that only I, and no one else, have. I think Spanish music is not
at all easy to play in the sense of true interpretation. For us, the Spaniards,
it is familiar because it is ours and we feel it."

El Universal Gráfico, also from the Mexican capital, published Segovia's
interview the following day in its daily column titled "Contrapuntal Things."
The article was titled "Segovia Talks about His Wife, the Pianist Paquita
Madriguera."

On March 9 the excellent Spanish pianist Paquita Madriguera, wife of the
exceptional guitarist Andrés Segovia, will make her presentation. It seemed
an odd experience for the reporter to ask the husband what he thinks about
his wife, given that they are both artists. And he got right to work. Andrés
Segovia did not quail before the unexpected and almost hostile nature of
the question.

"What I think about my wife as a pianist?" he replied. "I can tell you
bluntly and without my opinion being influenced by our marital affection.
I think she is a great concert pianist. I could not stand being by the side of
someone who did not play well."

Since the argument is forceful, the reporter insisted that Mr. Segovia
state his opinion plainly and with all objectivity.

"My wife is one of the most extraordinary musical cases that I know; that
is how the great musicians who have heard her play see it as well. Look here,
the study of piano has turned into a technical preoccupation, and that is not
enough to make good pianists. The technique is a sort of dictionary, where
all the possibilities of expression are accumulated, but if he who uses it does
not have ideas, feelings, style, and talent, those means lie inert on paper. The

same thing happens with technique when it is superimposed on expression; the result is coldness and dryness. For Paquita Madriguera, technique is simply a means of transmitting the profound poetry that one feels in the music."

"Who are your wife's favorite composers?"

Andrés Segovia replies without hesitation, "Among the composers to whom she pays lasting devotion are Bach, Handel, and Mozart. Her way of interpreting them is as far from the rhythmic dryness whereby the current German school has converted these creators into its own image as it is from the softness and excessive romantic warmth with which many Italian interpreters turn them into superficialities. We must agree with the Spanish artists, because the inherent gravity of their nature is well placed for understanding and interpreting these great classics without leaning to one side or the other. A vivid example of this is Pablo Casals."

"And what about the romantics?"

"Among the romantics, she has chosen the least likely to lend to local specialization, as is happening with Chopin. The romantics chosen by Paquita Madriguera are Schumann, Brahms, and Mendelssohn. The last one unjustly banned from the programs of almost all pianists today, with honorable exceptions, and deserves to be reinstated. The Prelude and Fugue in E Minor and his *Serious Variations* are undying works that, for reasons that can be explained only by the guilty submission of many pianists to fads, have remained relegated to pedagogical use or to brief appearances in concerts."

"I suppose your wife has preferences in Spanish music?"

"As for Spanish music, I refer to what Enrique Granados, who was Paquita Madriguera's teacher, said of her interpretations, and which was printed in the newspapers of that period," Andrés Segovia says, referring to a remark written and published by Granados in the main New York newspaper: "Paquita Madriguera interprets my works better than I do."

And [Segovia] adds, "I am sure that if Albéniz had heard her, his judgment would be much the same as that of Granados."

Don Andrés and Paquita left Mexico by plane on March 17, 1944—almost three months after the pianist arrived in Manuel Ponce's homeland—at 2:30 p.m., landing about four hours later in Guatemala City. That evening the guitarist played his concert in the Guatemalan capital, and at 5:30 a.m. the next day Paquita departed for Costa Rica. Segovia stayed behind to play another concert, traveled to El Salvador,[44] and then reunited with his wife in

San José, Costa Rica. Paquita arrived there in the morning, where a couple of old acquaintances, Spain's commerce manager and his wife, were waiting for her. At noon, immediately after she had settled in the hotel, they took her to a country estate to participate in a luncheon at which members of the diplomatic corps were paying tribute to Nelson Rockefeller, who at that time was director of the Office of Inter-American Affairs for the United States government. Two days later, on March 20, Paquita gave a concert at the Teatro Nacional. She performed the first two parts alone and was joined in the third by the Orquesta Sinfónica Nacional of Costa Rica for a performance of Grieg's Piano Concerto in A Minor. The press took note of Paquita Madriguera's first performance in this Central American country:

> The audience received coldly the Schumann pieces that were included in the first part of the program. The coldness was not justified, because the performer actually played these miniatures with heartfelt emotion, affection, and tenderness, with the feminine charm that seem to inspire these compositions by the great romantic.
>
> The public "warmed up" in the second part of the program, with Spanish music, and enthusiastically applauded the pieces by Albéniz and Granados. This is natural for our public, which always feels the vibrations of their racial fiber when they are presented with music from Spain. At the same time it is true that Paquita Madriguera interprets this music with absolute severity, in a manner stripped of cheap histrionics, and with an absolute understanding of the strict artistic heritage that guides the musical creations of an Albéniz or a Manuel de Falla, not adulterating it with false impressions of excessive zealousness.
>
> However, where Paquita Madriguera gave us a greater sense of her extraordinary ability as a pianist was in the Grieg Concerto, which she mastered with grace and the honesty of a profound artist. Throughout the three movements of the great Norwegian's Concerto, Paquita displayed an admirable and weighty technique—clear, sober, and convincing. That high standard was also met by the orchestra, which Mariani conducted in a discreet and commendable performance. Paquita Madriguera's concert tomorrow will provide a better opportunity to appreciate her exquisite qualities as a pianist.[45]

That concert took place on March 22 at the Teatro Municipal in San José. Segovia arrived two days later from El Salvador, and played that evening and again two days later at the Teatro Nacional. Paquita did not stay for Segovia's third concert in Costa Rica, leaving on the morning of Tuesday, March 28, for Panama. It is possible, though no proof exists, that Segovia took advantage of those differences in his and his wife's schedules to communicate—by telegram or mail—with the Brazilian singer, who had remained in New York. He did, however, write a letter to María Rosa on the day Paquita left for Panama, praising the girl's mother. Over time, the red ink that Segovia used on this occasion has caused the paper to deteriorate somewhat:

I am using for the first time a magnificent "Parker 51" pen with ink of the same brand to write these lines. It is one of two that I own. The other one has blue ink; this one has red ink. The reason is the music that I am pre-paring for publication requires both colors—while the notes are written in dark, the corresponding little numbers for the fingerings, strings, etc., etc., have to be marked in more vivid colors so the typesetter can see them and does not pass them over.

I received your little letter, which I appreciate. Mommy left today for Panama, where she will be giving two concerts before I arrive. I have already received a telegram from her telling me that she had a good trip and inform-ing me of the hotel in which she is staying.

The concerts here in Costa Rica have been magnificent. Mama [there is a piece missing that probably had four or five words] a concert. They continue to talk about both of us with great praise for the artist who has won the admiration of all for her elegance, beauty, and distinction as well. I have also played two concerts, and the day after tomorrow, on the 30th, I will play Castelnuovo's Concerto with orchestra. I will join Mama in Panama on the 31st, and after I play two concerts there—one to benefit the construction of the city's cathedral—we will both leave for Ecuador, where we will be for approximately twenty days. During that time I will play three concerts in Quito and three in Guayaquil, while Mama will give two in each one of those cities. From Ecuador, without any delays other than those needed to get seats on the plane, we will head for that lovely Montevideo—through Peru, Chile, and Argentina. We will get there in mid-May.

Give everyone at home a hug for me and also one for you.

Andrés

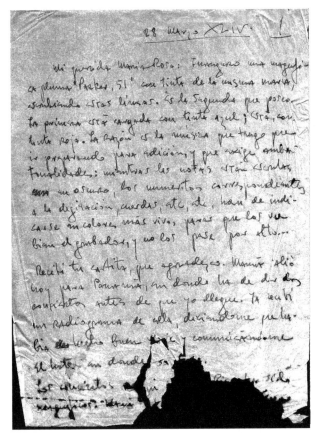

First page of Segovia's letter to María Rosa.

P.S. I forgot to tell you that we have spent all the time with Manolo and Lolita Moralejo. They are Spain's Commerce Managers in this city. They have not allowed us to eat at the hotel one single day—neither your mom, before I arrived from Guatemala and El Salvador, nor me, now that your mommy has left. After my first concert they gave a reception in our honor with more than a hundred people, including diplomats and society people. They are always telling me to send their regards to all of you at home.

Paquita's two concerts in Panama, to which Segovia alludes in his letter, are not in the pianist's diary and should have taken place between March

28 and 31, the date the guitarist arrived in that country. What does show up in the diary during their one-week stay in the Central American country is a whirl of social activity with members of the Spanish diplomatic corps in Panama as well as with members of the Spanish Nationalist party. They got together every day—first Paquita, and then both spouses after Segovia's arrival—with Manuel Oñós de Plandolit, secretary of the Spanish Embassy in Panama and an active Phalange propagandist since his recent assignment to the Spanish diplomatic corps in that part of Latin America. Segovia's concerts took place on April 1 and 2, 1944. The day following the second concert (for the cathedral), Paquita wrote in her diary: "Lunch at the Golf Club with Oñós de Plandolit, the bishop of Colón, and other priests."

On April 4 Segovia and Paquita flew to Guayaquil, Ecuador. They arrived in the afternoon and were received by Víctor Manuel Janer and his wife, Lucía Porres, who invited them to stay at their home. Segovia left the next day for Quito, and Paquita left on April 8, in time to attend the guitarist's first concert in the Ecuadorian capital, at the Teatro Sucre. Segovia played the same theater twice more, on April 15 and 18, and then on Friday, April 21, Paquita Madriguera performed there. An Ecuadorian critic and essayist wrote a review two days later, on the same day the musical couple was scheduled to perform a shared concert:

> In her piano concert the night before last at the Teatro Sucre, Paquita Madriguera told us musically the secret—which we had already sensed and announced previously—of the affinity that brought these artists together. Andrés Segovia and she are embedded in a common aesthetic service and consequently hold the keys to a mystery of two lives that, under the spell of art, sound like the harmonic of a fundamental tone.
>
> I will not do a mechanical criticism. The severe analysis and cold academic glossary disgust my temperament in the sphere of art, although they push it toward pure ideas. But I also flee conventional praise. If some emphasis overloads a comment and makes its expression ornate, that emphasis must come from the passion with which it highlights legitimate values and from sincere spontaneity, which conventionalism does not gag.
>
> For that reason I will say, in plain language, that Paquita Madriguera is an authentic pianist, whose school, style, and interpretation satisfy completely. Whether interpreting the Theme and Variations by Handel, the Fantasia in C Major by Bach, or the Sonata in F by the indescribable

Mozart, Paquita is fully aware of the polyphonic plot. She confirms this awareness in the Prelude and Fugue in G Minor by Mendelssohn, the smiling and happy composer who displays with an almost naive delight that bubbling flow of notes that never obscures the theme, but gives it a brightness that presages and supplements the transcendent virtuosity of Liszt. Perhaps the melancholy temperament of Mendelssohn, the composer who "had his soul tuned to a minor key," finds its home in the excellent Catalonian pianist—she makes it sound that way.

But her rapport is much more decisive and profound with the soul of "her" Peninsula, which is her own soul. She reveals the themes and emphasizes the rhythms of that music with such delicacy! She recreates a Debussyesque atmosphere for the *Evocation* by Albéniz, puts a unique poetic accent in *Andalusia* by Falla, and confirms its origin in the spiritual realm where the brilliant creations of the unforgettable Enrique Granados flourished.

The last concert by our two visiting performers has been announced. For the last time, the chill of pure art will blow from the soundboards of the two wonderful instruments—guitar and piano—and blend their polyphony to reach the absolute limits in the purity and timbre of their sounds.[46]

The Segovia-Madrigueras' joint concert in Quito was made up of four parts. In the first, Paquita played works by Bach, Schumann, and Albéniz, while Segovia performed Haydn, Albéniz, and Tárrega in the third. They joined forces to play the Concerto in D by Castelnuovo-Tedesco in the second part and the *Concierto del sur* in the fourth. This performance by both artists was alluded to in a letter that the guitarist wrote to Manuel Ponce on May 2 from Guayaquil.[47] Segovia enclosed a clipping of the concert given in Quito with a review of both artists' joint recital. He told his friend that the orchestra for Ponce's concerto had been Paquita, more loving and tender than any conductor. Segovia also emphasized the fact that the reviewer stated that Ponce's work was the best received and the one most applauded. Trying to give his friend an impulse for going on with a new work, Segovia told him that Paquita occasionally dreamed that she was playing Ponce's concerto for piano and chamber orchestra, but then awoke and realized that she only had one page of the work. And he reminded the composer of a promise he had made to Paquita about that concerto.[48]

Paquita actually had two pages of the first movement (Allegro scherzoso) of the Chamber Concerto for Piano and Orchestra, which the composer had given her during the recent stay in Mexico City.

The seeds of crisis were slowly germinating during this long tour that the two artists made. Except for those initial and fruitful shared projects, each artist was now moved by separate dreams and motivations. The trip had, without a doubt, very different characteristics for each of the spouses; the spirit in which they faced the gradual return to the home that they had left behind many months ago, on that long journey north, could not be the same in both cases. Paquita was returning to her daughters—three of them almost adults, and a little girl about to turn six years old—with the sensation that this prolonged trip meant her definite return as a successful and active concert pianist. Montevideo, again awaiting her in the faraway south, was already entrenched in her as a port of arrival, though in her view the desire to leave from time to time would remain.

Segovia, however, made this trip carrying the weight of a secret that he well knew could trigger explosive storms, putting at risk much of what he had gained over the past ten years. At the same time, those conflicts would tend to place the gravitational center of his world once again in that environment from which he had been banned for a short period and to which he had finally managed to return—the spectacular world of New York.

The two musicians' last artistic stopover on the route that would lead them to the old house on Massini Street was in Lima between May 13 and May 20. Paquita performed at the Teatro Municipal on May 17 as a soloist in Mozart's Concerto No. 20 in D Minor. The National Symphony Orchestra was conducted by Theo Buchwald, and the rest of the program consisted of the Symphony No. 85 by Haydn, *An Outdoor Overture* by Aaron Copland, *Janitzio* by the Mexican composer Silvestre Revueltas, and *Batuque* by the Brazilian Lorenzo Fernández—who, coincidentally, had given Olga Coelho the Spanish newspapers informing her of Andrés Segovia's existence. Several Lima newspapers published laudatory reviews of Paquita's performance:

> The second part was devoted to the Concerto in D Minor (K. 466) by Mozart, a work no less charming and quite familiar to our public, but this time with the pleasant prospect of being played by a fine artist with such a cultured music background as Paquita Madriguera. This Hispanic pianist—so tied to the musical life of Lima during the unforgettable days of

the inauguration of this same theater because she was its first concert pianist,[49] admired and applauded in Liszt's Piano Concerto in E-flat Major—reappeared yesterday to offer us precisely the antithesis of that spectacular demonstration, performing one of the most beautiful and poetic of the Mozart concertos. In that score of such noble and balanced inspiration, Paquita Madriguera found an element suitable to her instrumental finesse and to the exquisite sensitivity of her temperament, to which we owe a fair interpretation of character—transparent and with all the shades of grace typical of such a demanding work of genius. The public applauded with the most eloquent demonstration of admiration and affection, especially praising the Romanza.[50]

Following a stopover in Salta, in northwestern Argentina, and another in Buenos Aires, Paquita Madriguera and Andrés Segovia finally arrived in Montevideo on May 23, 1944. The guitarist's absence had lasted eight months and twenty days, while Paquita had been gone for six months and ten days. This was not to be the last trip of the year, though. Segovia would travel to Argentina quite frequently during the month of June and the first two weeks of July, and the two of them still had joint artistic commitments there during the last two weeks in July. Although there is no information regarding this travel, the diversity of movements suggests that there were already some signs of distance between the spouses. During the entire month of June, Paquita took vacations at the recently opened Hotel Nirvana, in Colonia Suiza, about sixty-five miles west of Montevideo. The hotel had been in operation since the previous November and had quickly become one of the most attractive resort and rest centers in Uruguay. It seems normal that Paquita would want to see it and opt to spend there the time she needed to recuperate from the long trip (instead of going, as in other times, to the country estate) and would dedicate herself to reconstructing ties with her youngest daughter in that fresh environment. In the years that followed these events, Segovia visited the hotel many times after he stopped living in Uruguay, and he would meet Paquita and his daughter there on more than one occasion.

The pianist moved into the Hotel Nirvana on June 3 with Beatriz and María Rosa and stayed there until June 27. Meanwhile, Don Andrés remained in Montevideo for a few days, visited his family at the hotel three times—for a couple of days each—and traveled to Buenos Aires during the last week in June. He was not present on June 5, when Beatriz turned six.

It is possible that after eight and a half months away from Montevideo, the guitarist had a great many chores piled up and, after dedicating the first few days of his return to the resumption of family life, again needed time for his professional activity. He surely had a lot of publications and transcriptions to prepare,[51] and he needed to practice new repertoire for the coming season in the United States as well as to look over the new music from various composers that kept arriving in the mail. Segovia also devoted time to composing brief works for guitar, many of which were created in Montevideo during this time. Some were dedicated to Paquita and others to Beatriz's godfather, Aparicio Méndez, who was a fan of the instrument and with whom the guitarist maintained a friendly relationship until the early 1960s.

Segovia may have opted to immerse himself in his work, rather than accompanying Paquita and their six-year-old daughter on vacation, as a way of maintaining a certain distance and concealing any mood that might betray his romantic feelings over the affair in New York. He was not very successful, for something was soon to trigger the conflict that had been brewing.

During July, Andrés Segovia traveled repeatedly to Argentina. He was in Buenos Aires from Saturday, July 1, to Wednesday, July 5, and flew back again on July 7, taking Beatriz and Pitusa, Paquita's oldest daughter, who had turned twenty-one a few days earlier. The three of them returned to Montevideo on Wednesday, July 12, but two days later the guitarist flew again to Buenos Aires, this time accompanied by his wife. From the Argentinean capital they both went to Rosario by train, where they gave two concerts together—on Saturday and Sunday, July 15 and 16, at the Opera Theater. The two concerts had the same structure—each player took one part and on the third they played one of the two concertos, in the version for guitar and piano, recently composed for Segovia. On Saturday they played the Tedesco concerto, and on Sunday it was the *Concierto del sur*. The newspaper published a write-up of the first presentation:

> Andrés Segovia, well-known in our musical sphere for his previous performances, which left us with enduring memories, was in charge of the first part. A program made up of works by Handel, Rameau, Weiss, Bach, and Albéniz allowed the virtuoso concert guitarist to highlight the remarkable attributes that made him one of the most illustrious figures of contemporary guitar performance. His marvelous technique, his ample and generous sound with its beautiful timbre, and his fiery and communicative

temperament allow his interpretations immediately to be admired and to seduce. That is how the audience understood it, and they applauded him warmly. In the second part of the program, the pianist Paquita Madriguera, who was performing for the second time at the theater, made her appearance. In the fullness of her interpretive medium, the pianist showed a secure technique, a generous sound, and a fine and elegant musical sense. These qualities were elaborated in significant works—beginning with Prelude and *Serious Variations*, by Mendelssohn, animated with force and sincere emotion; continuing with *Andalusia* by Falla, in a colorful version; and ending with *The Maiden and the Nightingale* and *The Dummy* from *Goyescas* by Granados, in an interpretation of adjusted style and beautiful sound. It was widely applauded.

In the third part of the program we heard the Concerto in D (dedicated to Segovia) for piano and guitar [*sic*] by the Italian composer Castelnuovo-Tedesco, Andrés Segovia and Paquita Madriguera performing together. Both artists gave a sensitive and strong interpretation of this compelling work, realizing its meaning, and their work was rewarded with expressive demonstrations of approval by the audience.[52]

After Segovia gave a concert on Monday, July 17, at the Teatro Odeón in Buenos Aires, the couple went to Montevideo for a few days, then returned immediately to the Argentinean capital. On July 24 the guitarist concluded a long series of concerts in that city, performing with Paquita in a new program:

Andrés Segovia, with the collaboration of Paquita Madriguera, gave a farewell concert at the Odeón, where he was warmly applauded, a success that he shared with his wife, a pianist of outstanding merit. The celebrated guitarist delighted the audience with his very expressive versions and technically perfect works by Bach, Haydn, Paganini, and Sor, discharged with that sound, so beautiful and captivating, for which he alone seems to have the infallible formula. Paquita Madriguera, meanwhile, performed Beethoven's Sonata Op. 86 and short pieces by Castelnuovo-Tedesco and Albéniz with her attractive artistic personality and the efficiency of her resources. One of those pieces, *Nocturne in Hollywood*, by the second composer cited, was a novelty; though not one of the composer's best achievements, the construction is solid and its contents interesting. Both performers perfectly brought out the spirit of the works and later gave impeccable versions of the

Concerto in D Major by Castelnuovo-Tedesco, a work of particular merit, and the notable *Concierto del sur*, by M. Ponce, in versions for guitar and piano written for the two musicians. One could not fail to note how well these two pieces suit the two instruments and the persuasive expression of their musical ideas.[53]

Although this would not be the last joint performance for Andrés Segovia and Paquita Madriguera, it would signal the end of a period of remarkable richness in the lives of both artists. Once they were back in Montevideo, and probably due to stripping away the cover that the intense activities had provided Don Andrés during the two months since their return from the long tour, the suppressed conflict eventually surfaced and exploded. On August 25, 1944, while they were celebrating Independence Day in Uruguay, Paquita allowed a natural and understandable anger to bring forth her prejudices and stereotyping while she wrote her daily entry: "Andrés's infidelity with the Brazilian woman Olga Praguer de Coelho is discovered. Song stylist and of an inferior genre of music who accompanies herself on the guitar. A woman with Jewish features, a very pointed nose, and mediocre social experiences."

The following months were of comings and goings, of reunions and intrigues, of meetings in Buenos Aires and also at the Hotel Nirvana. When Paquita celebrated her forty-fourth birthday on September 15, Segovia was in the Argentinean capital. Paquita traveled there at night, in the *Vapor de la Carrera*, and the next day they had lunch together in that city. They returned on Sunday, September 17, to attend a recital by the students of Sarah Bourdillon de Santórsola, among them little Beatriz. Don Andrés remained on the other side of the Río de la Plata throughout October, with the exception of a couple of brief crossings to Montevideo to see his daughter. Meanwhile, Paquita went once to meet with him in Buenos Aires. Segovia returned to the Massini Street home on November 4 for a few days, and on Saturday, November 11, as was customary, they celebrated his birthday, as Paquita states in her diary. At noon they had lunch together at a restaurant in Pocitos, close to home, and in the evening they received several family members and friends, although it is hard to believe that the climate would have been similar to that of reunions in previous years.

On Monday, November 13, Andrés Segovia left for the mountains of Córdoba, in north-central Argentina, accompanied only by Beatriz. It was their first long trip alone, father and daughter, the motivation for which must have been to strengthen a bond that had had little opportunity to cement, and that he knew would be threatened by the clouds of an impending long estrangement. They shared two weeks there, and the letters that Paquita sent them between November 17 and 22 (three to Segovia and one to Beatriz) are all addressed to the town of La Falda; but it is probable that Don Andrés and his young daughter traveled to many places in this beautiful mountain region. It is also possible that they went to nearby Alta Gracia to visit Manuel de Falla, who had lived in that area since the end of the Spanish Civil War.

On the morning of November 29, Don Andrés and his daughter returned from the mountains of Argentina to the home on Massini Street. That evening Paquita went up Bulevar España from Pocitos to El Centro, Montevideo's downtown district, and then to the movies, alone. The stage for the crisis was set.

Chapter 13

Montevideo and Buenos Aires—Poles of a Shifting Crisis

At the end of November 1944, after Don Andrés and Beatriz had returned from the trip to Córdoba, the guitarist continued to live at the Massini Street house for a few days, although the entries in Paquita's diary indicate that she went on walks alone or accompanied by a friend. Sometimes she would go to the movies, other times to a concert at the SODRE Studio Auditorium. Segovia, in the meantime, got ready for a trip to New York to begin a new concert season in North America. The prospect of Olga awaiting him there most certainly aggravated the situation between the couple. The day before leaving, Segovia went to lunch with Aparicio Méndez, who took care of the guitarist's financial and legal matters while he was out of the country. On December 12 (Sofía's nineteenth birthday), Segovia again had lunch away from home. He left that evening by boat for Buenos Aires, to spend the night there and fly to the United States the next day. A letter mailed to Paquita by the eminent Argentinean musicologist Carlos Vega (1898–1966) on December 14 talks about the guitarist's quick passage through the Argentinean capital:

> My distinguished friend and artist Paquita Madriguera de Segovia,
>
> I wrote a note about Andrés a long time ago. He saw a draft of it and asked me to finish it. Always fearful of not doing him justice, I insisted [that he do it himself], with no results. I saw him yesterday by chance. He was

running to make a flight. I got up very early this morning and managed to finish the note (badly). When I tried to look for him, I could not find him. He must have left. I do not have his address in New York. So let me send you the note (which perhaps he wants to use in programs, as he said) so that you can send it to him immediately by airmail. Keep a copy; I have another one in case it gets lost. And write telling me that you have received it and sent it; that way I am satisfied, although the note is not worth much (I will still see if I can find him in another hotel). Thanks for everything. I hope you are doing well with your girls, especially with little Beatriz, and accept my best regards.

A few days after Segovia's departure, Paquita attended a concert by the guitarist Abel Carlevaro at the SODRE on Saturday, December 16. The printed program read:

Concert sponsored by the National Committee for:

- Democratic Reaffirmation
- American Solidarity
- Support for the United Nations

Proceeds for aid to the countries fighting Nazi-Fascism, with the generous collaboration of the guitarist ABEL CARLEVARO.

The program developed by Carlevaro for this concert, structured in the three-part style he had adopted from Segovia, had two striking elements. The last section included, for the second time, two works by Villa-Lobos that the Spanish maestro had still never played in public (Prelude No. 3 and Etude No. 1), and, more interestingly, two recent works by Segovia—Prelude and Study.

Shortly after Don Andrés's departure, Paquita was composing with relative intensity. In the files of the Catalonian singer Conchita Badía are manuscripts of three pieces for voice and piano composed by Paquita Madriguera in Montevideo in December 1944: a religious song, *Alleluia!*, and two Spanish songs, *Se fue el día de mi corazón* (The Day of My Heart Has Gone) and *Romancillo* (Little Romance: An Homage to Conchita Badía). Both the music and the lyrics belong to Paquita and can be considered a venue for her to sublimate her energies during the grave crisis through which she was passing. An entry in her diary for December 31 is an eloquent sign of the surprising course that the pianist's life had taken in the latter part of a year that had begun with intense and successful professional activity: "We ended the year accompanying Sofía, who is in the hospital (appendicitis)—Pitusa, María Rosa, Cholo, Abo, and me. I hope the coming year is better."

Perhaps the long vacations she took in Punta del Este, beginning on January 8, 1945, were also a means of purging her spirit of the many problems that piled up during the second half of the year, taking her from the peak of glory to the shattered bits of her personal world. Paquita spent the three months of the Uruguayan summer in an apartment at this Atlantic coast health spa on the peninsula. It was far from being the international resort that it is today; still, it was already the vacation spot of the Uruguayan upper crust. She wrote Segovia four letters during the month of January, all addressed to New York. By March the destination of the letters changed, and the two she sent to Lima during the last two weeks of the month indicate that Don Andrés was headed south again.

Paquita went to Buenos Aires on April 17, and Segovia arrived on April 19. They stayed in the big city for a week, and on April 26 they returned to Montevideo together. During this time Andrés Segovia completed another work that he had been composing and whose manuscript he gave to Paquita. Whether it was anything special cannot be confirmed, as it bears no dedication. The *Fandango de la madrugada* (Dawn Fandango) is dated April 29, 1945, in Montevideo, and to date it has not been catalogued among the guitarist's compositions, nor has it been published. The original manuscript, which has suffered severe deterioration from humidity and mold, remains in the hands of Paquita's daughters. For some reason, probably motivated by events that occurred later, the pianist did not take steps to protect those papers, nor did she release them. Apparently an outline of the *Fandango*, in draft form, formed part of a package with many papers that Segovia left at the family home of Aparicio Méndez for safekeeping after he removed his personal belongings from the Massini Street house. Many of those manuscripts became known to the guitar world only after they were sold at auction in 2002.

Cover sheet of the
Fandango de la madrugada.

It appears that the conflicts in the couple's thorny relationship had calmed down somewhat and that they were headed toward a reconciliation. However, the apparent peace did not last long, and on May 4 Paquita wrote in her diary, "Andrés is leaving home."

There is no record of Segovia's activities during the coming weeks, but it is known that he stayed for a while at the Hotel Nirvana, in Colonia Suiza, and that Paquita sent him a letter on May 9 at that address. During May 1945, as the world was going through decisive events, Paquita was busy preparing a concert that would take place in early June. She was surely also preoccupied with emotional conflicts, as well as the general expectations regarding the outcome of the war in Europe. On Tuesday, May 8, the day following Germany's unconditional surrender, she wrote in her diary, "Peace in Europe!" The absence of other relevant entries confirm that those last weeks of May were dedicated to the preparation of her new performance at SODRE's Studio Auditorium, a hall in which she had not played for three years. Paquita's concert in honor of the Critic's Circle, a group that brought together the theater and music critics of Montevideo, took place on June 7. All of Montevideo's newspapers highlighted the pianist's performance on the following day, including this review:[1]

> Paquita Madriguera is one of those pianists who imprint a personal stamp on everything they do. Because it is evident that in the simple task of interpretation, when the performer sticks to a bland and literal kind of correctness, the listener misses the subtle but essential personal inflection that the interpreter must provide. It is the enabling interpretation of the journey that leads us to the composer's original thought.
>
> In Paquita Madriguera, the response to that aesthetic premise is a spontaneous need. Her technical resources empower her to carry it out comfortably. In her version of Bach's Fantasy in C Minor, she neatly took care of the sound; in the Sonata Op. 81 by Beethoven, she showed a good appreciation of style within a tempered smoothing out of mild histrionics (not lacking in this work), in which the intelligent phrasing and the deliberate nuance of tone color fit nicely.
>
> Four of the *Fantastic Pieces* and two of the *Songs Without Words* by Mendelssohn, performed with soft finesse, were included in the second part. In the last part, Paquita Madriguera presented for the first time

the *Nocturne in Hollywood* by Castelnuovo-Tedesco. A witty melody touched with occasional Ravellike harmonies, elaborated in the usual intelligent manner of this composer, completely free of sensationalism.

In the Spanish works, Paquita Madriguera is not satisfied with anything less than perfection, in the intimate and accessible meaning of that awful word. This could be seen in her version of *Two Dances* by Granados and in *Seguidilla*, *Evocación*, and *Navarra* by Albéniz. Finesse and noble sobriety are the two main interpretive characteristics of Paquita Madriguera.

PAQUITA MADRIGUERA * La exquisita concertista de piano, sorprendida en momentos que hace un aparte durante la recepción que en su honor realizara el Círculo de la Crítica en la sede de la calle Duvimioso Terra. La simpática Paquita Madriguera se vió rodeada de destacadas figuras de nuestro mundo artístico y social, alcanzando la recepción excepcionales perfiles

Paquita (*right*) at the Critic's Circle tribute. Published in the newspaper *La Razón*, August 19, 1945.

Some of the concert's reviews state that the public received the artist's performance with such enthusiasm that she had to play several encores. Two days after the recital at SODRE, Paquita wrote letters to Castelnuovo-Tedesco (probably informing him of the premiere of his work in Montevideo), Curt Lange (who was in Rio de Janeiro), and Segovia (who was in Colonia Suiza). The guitarist later left for Buenos Aires, where he had several activities scheduled,[2] and Paquita went to visit him there in early July, on a trip lasting barely twenty-four hours. In August, Segovia returned across the Río de la Plata and stayed at the Hotel Nirvana. A few days after receiving a tribute from the Critic's Circle, Paquita traveled with Beatriz to Colonia Suiza on August 22 so that the girl could spend two days with her father. Paquita went again, this time alone, on August 25 (Uruguayan Independence Day) and stayed at the Hotel Nirvana until August 28, when she returned to Montevideo; Segovia stayed behind in Colonia Suiza. On September 10 Paquita attended a new concert by Abel Carlevaro at the Teatro 18 de Julio.

Don Andrés, in the meantime, traveled again to Buenos Aires and returned to the Uruguayan capital on September 13, accompanied by his stepdaughter Sofía. After ten days in Montevideo, he and Paquita went back to

Buenos Aires to begin a tour together of northern Argentina. The couple left by train on September 25 for Tucumán, where they arrived following a journey of more than twenty-four hours. Segovia gave his concert on September 29 and the next day he traveled by plane to Salta while Paquita Madriguera played a concert in Tucumán at La Filarmónica (the former Teatro Belgrano), which produced the following review:

> Paquita Madriguera's undeniable talent, her exquisite temperament, and her substantial personal attraction are qualities that ensure that success will always be her faithful companion.
>
> With her magnificent training, technique, and musicianship, she interprets composers by putting the stamp of her elegant and prominent artistic personality on all of her interpretations.
>
> With these extraordinary qualities and without flaunting exaggerated virtuosity, she gave us the three movements of Sonata in D by Haydn, as well as the three of [the] Sonata Op. 81 by Beethoven, a work we had not heard and which represented the first signs of approval by the audience for the intelligent concert pianist—once again before a full hall at the former Teatro Belgrano, where the echo of the Segovia's wonderful guitar still resounded.
>
> With a restrained romanticism, she masterfully poured forth . . . four brief, delicate, and beautiful pieces that Schumann wrote under the title of *Fantasy Pieces*, along with the Andante Tranquillo and *Spinning Song* by Mendelssohn—played with pristine clarity.
>
> In the third part, after offering us the premiere of an interesting piece by the Italian composer Castelnuovo-Tedesco entitled *Nocturne in Hollywood*, she interpreted with passion *Two Dances*, by her teacher, the late Enrique Granados, and three beautiful pages by that musician-painter named Isaac Albéniz. They were *Seguidillas*, *Rondeña*, and *Navarra*—all with vivid color, which the pianist was able to highlight with her spontaneous and justified Spanish temperament.
>
> As a show of appreciation for the warm applause, she added as an encore Debussy's *Claire de lune*, which she interpreted attractively and with great elegance.
>
> Andrés Segovia left for Salta yesterday, where he will give a concert, and today Paquita Madriguera will depart for Buenos Aires. Both artists leave us an unforgettable memory of their weighty performances at La Filarmónica.[3]

Andrés Segovia arrived in Buenos Aires, where Paquita awaited him, on the afternoon of October 2. They boarded the *Vapor de la Carrera* together on the night of Thursday, October 5, for the crossing and the next morning were again at the Massini Street house. Segovia remained there for the entire month of October, and at the beginning of November they both went to Punta del Este for three days. There are no entries to show what the emotional climate was during the nearly five weeks that the couple spent together. On November 6, 1945, the guitarist departed once more for the northern land that was pressing on him with the force of economic prospects, powerful appreciation for his art, and the romantic sentiments that continued growing there.

The highs and lows of this time show that the world Don Andrés left in Montevideo continued to have an attraction for him—another kind, perhaps, but also powerful—that made difficult any decision to leave the Uruguayan capital permanently. Paquita's letters to him in those final two months of 1945 reveal that Segovia was first in Mexico, then Caracas, and finally Havana, before settling in New York in December and most of January. On January 13, he premiered for the North American audience his two new concertos for guitar and orchestra at Carnegie Hall, with the Symphonette Orchestra conducted by Ignace Strasfogel. Segovia wrote to María Rosa from New York on January 5 to tell her that he would try to be present in Montevideo for her wedding: "I hope to attend this most important ceremony, that of your wedding, since only your mom was present at the [engagement party]."

Paquita spent the entire austral summer, until the end of March 1946, in Punta del Este, and Don Andrés arrived home on April 24 after giving concerts in various South American countries. He spent a few days in Colonia Suiza, perhaps alone, but then Paquita joined him at the Hotel Nirvana, and from there they returned to the house in Pocitos. On May 18 Segovia wrote a letter to Sophocles Papas, ending with a recommendation for his New York friends: "I ask you also to tell Bobri,[4] if you see him or write to him, not to send my letters to the Hotel Nirvana, not to speak to me about arrangements for guitar and voice, and to remember that I am at home."[5]

Don Andrés and Paquita attended a couple of concerts by the French cellist Bernard Michelin (1915–2003) at the Teatro 18 de Julio, and on May 25 they both attended the wedding of María Rosa—Paquita's first daughter to be married. During the last week of May and almost the entire month of June, both artists spent considerable time in Buenos Aires for fundamental reasons: Segovia was developing his usual concert season in the Argentinean capital, and Paquita was preparing a concert—along with her friend Conchita Badía, who was now living there—in honor of Enrique Granados. This event was announced to take place in Montevideo a few days later. One critic made mention of Paquita's youth:

> The European music world attended, with amazement, Paquita Madriguera's precocious appearance, which bordered on that of a miracle (a rarely exceptional case). She continues to maintain the same mysterious virtues over time, intact, and with added years of wise experience remains an artist of universal recognition and renown....
>
> Granados's declaration—"Paquita Madriguera interprets my works better than I"—would suffice to consecrate her as the only interpreter of her maestro, if a piece of information so suggestive and revealing did not exist in the musician's biography that it was she to whom he entrusted the premiere performance of the splendid *Intermezzo* (from *Goyescas*), which in reality was written feverishly on the day before and had not even been performed by its creator.[6]

The tribute took place at the Studio Auditorium of SODRE on July 10, 1946. A review by the musicologist Lauro Ayestarán provides a description of the program presented by the two artists:

> As a tribute in honor of Granados, a concert of his beautiful music was performed by the pianist Paquita Madriguera and the singer Conchita Badía yesterday at the SODRE hall....
>
> Paquita Madriguera first played six of the *Spanish Dances* with extraordinary grace, in the rhythm especially, and in the second part Concepción Badía, in a notable demonstration of musicianship, sang several *tonadillas* accompanied by piano. The great Spanish singer rose above the composer's intentions by bringing out the fragrant elegance of these short, light pieces and ended her part with three works from the cycle *Love Songs*. She sang all of her pieces with clear diction....
>
> In the final part, Paquita Madriguera again showed off her strong piano playing by emphasizing her personal and firm temperament in a completed version of *The Maiden and the Nightingale*.[7]

The two Spanish artists repeated this concert at the Teatro Cervantes in Buenos Aires on October 14. During the month of August, Paquita traveled several times to Buenos Aires to be with Segovia, and later, throughout September, she devoted herself to preparing the Montevideo premiere of Castelnuovo-Tedesco's Concerto No. 2 for Piano and Orchestra, which had had its world premiere in New York shortly before, with the orchestra conducted by the composer. Andrés Segovia was present at the Studio Auditorium on September 21 when his wife presented it as a soloist with the SODRE Symphony Orchestra. The reviews that appeared in different Montevideo newspapers again praised the pianist without exception, though some critics objected to the quality of the music itself:

> The Concerto in F by Castelnuovo-Tedesco is a poor work, musically, where an abominable mixture of styles reveals the gross caricatures of the music of Albéniz, Strauss and even César Franck.... In compensation, it possesses an undeniable brilliance in brief moments, but that served only to demonstrate the point to which an outstanding pianist is able to redeem the defects in some works. Paquita Madriguera has, to a great degree, those qualities—of honesty, clarity, and a beautiful tone—which come from a balanced musical spirit, and they are controlled at every moment by an irreproachable technique.[8]

Paquita Madriguera and Andrés Segovia made their last appearance together on a concert stage on October 11, 1946, in a three-part program at the SODRE Studio Auditorium. In the first part they performed the Concerto in D by Castelnuovo-Tedesco, the second was Segovia playing works from his regular soloist repertoire, and in the third they played Ponce's *Concierto del sur*. One review read:

> After a long absence, the great guitarist Andrés Segovia reappeared yesterday at the Studio Auditorium. This event, awaited with particular interest, filled the seats of the large hall of the SODRE. The presence of his wife, the exceptional pianist Paquita Madriguera, added interest to Segovia's appearance. The two great artists gave the best of themselves to blend two instruments of such diverse character ... Paquita softening the lush eloquence of the piano and Segovia expanding the privacy of his heavenly guitar. The

concerto by Castelnuovo, more cerebral than poetic, was poorly suited to that combination and was pulled off thanks only to the good fortune of having the incomparable art of yesterday's performers.

Andrés Segovia was exclusively in charge of the second part, and it was the highlight of the concert because the admirable artist, in a steady progression, has continued to better himself musically, culminating in the works of Bach—truly magnificent—as well as those by Turina and Albéniz.

In the *Concierto del sur* by Ponce, the interpenetration by both performers and the musical quality of each managed the marvel of making this work something with a real sense of unity, deserving of the applause with which it was received by the public. The festival was great, and there is little we could say that would not add the most justified praise for this couple, who yesterday gave us one of the highest musical notes of the season.[9]

Don Andrés and Paquita, following another trip to Buenos Aires during which the pianist and Conchita Badía repeated their tribute to Granados, packed up the house on Massini Street and moved the family, on October 26, 1946, into an apartment in Pocitos about a mile up the nearby Avenida Brasil. Segovia lived there for only two weeks, until November 12, when something happened that started another crisis, and the couple separated for good. María Rosa gave an example of the problems caused by Segovia's indecisiveness—while trying to rebuild the relationship with his wife, he would not completely sever ties with the Brazilian singer:

> One time Mama went into Andrés's studio when he was writing a letter to Olga. "What are you writing?" she asked him, because he had immediately torn the paper [from the pad] and rolled it into a little ball in his fist.
> "Nothing," he replied.
> "So, nothing? Let's see. Show me!"
> When he refused to show her, she got mad and kept insisting, until he put the wad of thin airmail stationery in his mouth and ate it![10]

Whether or not that was the last straw, Paquita decided to file for divorce, and Don Andrés left the apartment. He went to Buenos Aires and left a few days later for the United States. His next trip to Montevideo, in July of the following year, was to see his daughter and remove his personal belongings

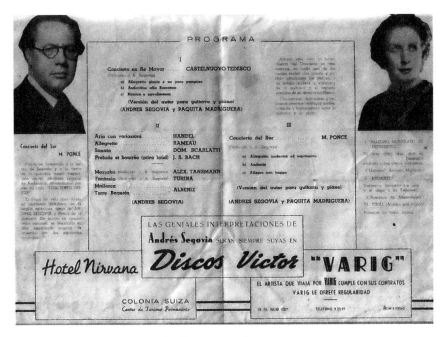

Program for the concert of October 11, 1946.

from the family home. There is little information regarding Paquita's activities during 1947, and it is quite probable that she devoted a great part of her time to drafting her memoirs, *Visto y oído*, fragments of which have been quoted throughout these pages. The book, which included a novelette entitled *La estrella del alba* (The Morning Star), was printed in Buenos Aires in September 1947 and earned several reviews in the press of the Argentinean capital in November of that year. The short novel, a love story, has a passage that could well be interpreted as a reference to these incidents that were now disrupting both the private and the professional lives of the pianist, now also a writer. The fragment is called "Intermezzo" and has to do with an evil couple that interferes in the personal lives of, up to that point, happy but naive people. The attentive reader can easily find clues implying the identities of the characters:

> Dr. Gerard had recently arrived in Switzerland, where he extended his shady activities with the complicity of his wife, Olga Kramer. Her origins were obscure—a mixture of black, Jewish, and Saxon blood ran through her

veins. Because of a bad trait in the mood of the Creator, who had separated the virtues of each of these races, all of their defects remained in her blood cells. Excessive selfishness, unscrupulousness, and lust.

This couple had dealings ranging from drug smuggling to the most disgusting "blackmail." They traveled widely. The collaboration of the woman in the "business" was to deceive the alleged victims, chosen by the same Dr. Gerard. They appeared to be decent people in a comfortable economic position, so as to not raise suspicion from the "big fish" they were trying to hook. They pretended to love each other passionately in order to make their conquest more lucrative in the eyes of the victim, who was persuaded that it was his fault that the woman sinned.[11]

The short novel was quite probably written during the first half of 1947, when the marriage crisis was at its worst and Paquita had decided to reject any reconciliation Don Andrés initiated. At the end of that July, Segovia again traveled to the Río de la Plata and visited the apartment on Avenida Brasil, where Paquita lived with Beatriz and one of her older daughters. On July 27 he wrote to Ponce from a hotel, perhaps in Buenos Aires, after having been to Montevideo, where he spent some hours with Beatriz. It was very sad for him, he said, to separate from his daughter and to abandon his refined house for the "anonymous room" of the hotel. Paquita had left for El Campito with María Rosa and her boy when she knew that he was going to take some clothes and books from the house.[12] Segovia also told Ponce that he had not seen Paquita at all, but he knew that the divorce proceedings were under way. Some friends of the pianist had told him that she regretted having initiated the divorce but, from Don Andrés's point of view, "pride [was] getting in our way," and he could not make any new gestures toward her, for fear of being interpreted "maliciously," as had happened before.

Sofía Puig confirmed in an interview at her home that Segovia made several attempts, in vain, to rebuild the marriage:

Andrés wanted to return with Mama many times, but she always refused. "Because of dignity," she would say. Once, when I was the only one still living with her, she even consulted me over what to do. And I would tell her to let him return, because I was going to get married and she was going to be all alone. But she did not want to. She felt that something had broken, that he had dirtied the relationship, and she wanted to maintain her dignity.[13]

At the beginning of July 1947, Segovia had been in México, where he played the *Concierto del sur* twice under the direction of Carlos Chávez at the Palacio de Bellas Artes. During that visit to the Aztec country, the guitarist was accompanied by Olga Coelho. In the same letter alluded to before, he told Ponce that a certain Shavitch[14] was courting Paquita, and Segovia supposed that this man had told her that he had seen him and Olga together in Cuernavaca and Mexico City. He said that he was sure that Paquita would not return his attentions, because of the "deep antipathy" she had for the Jewish race (not including Castelnuovo-Tedesco and many others, he stated). He also told Ponce that in case he met that man, he would have to constrain himself from giving him a punch, fearing that Shavitch would take revenge by turning "the entire race" against him.[15]

Vladimir Shavitch, his wife, Tina Lerner, and Eduardo Fabini at the hall of Teatro Albéniz in April 1922, before the premiere of Fabini's *Campo*.

Segovia then made another reference to the singer and the status of his relationship with her at that moment, telling Ponce that they had almost stopped communicating. He had written her a pair of letters, quite bitter and violent, with no reply, and hoped that the silence would be a sign of calm in her life. He longed for the first days of their relationship, when they had no serious differences and she was nice and attractive, without the "touch of madness" that had transformed her character.[16]

Actually, the true dramas in Segovia's life were not those related directly to his relations with women, but rather the most horrible events in his life linked to his role as father. The unsettled existence of Andrés Segovia—the effect, triply, of his traveling as a concert guitarist, his exile prompted by the war, and the ups and downs of his emotional life—always had painful consequences in his relationships with his children. Andresito and Leonardo, the progeny of his first marriage, had remained in Europe with their mother when he fled from Spain and eventually landed in Montevideo. When he had the first opportunity to visit them again, at the end of 1937, he was met with the horrible news of the accident that had just cost Leonardo his life at the age of thirteen. At that time, Paquita was pregnant with Beatriz, who, even before she was born, brought the difficult task of opening for Andrés Segovia a new opportunity to cultivate a paternal side that he had not been able to exercise fully and had not enjoyed during his own childhood. The marriage crisis that was now risking the rich world created by more than ten years of love with Paquita was also affecting the relationship that he was trying laboriously, between trips, to build with his young daughter. Up to this crisis, Montevideo had been for Andrés Segovia the brightest symbol of a peaceful and creative life in a harmonious and affectionate environment, and it held for him many, many good memories. But from then on, beyond the repeated attempts to salvage the irreconcilable differences in his marriage, the growing city on the Río de la Plata became, more and more, the pole that tenaciously claimed the filial affection of Beatriz.

This girl has only been seen sporadically in these pages, and they have not left the reader a clear image of her development. This must also have been true of her parents, whose activities and trips prevented them from seeing her grow up with the continuity a child requires. The focal setting on the life and artistic evolution of Don Andrés and Paquita must now be widened to a panoramic view encompassing the spiritual journey of Beatriz Segovia Madriguera—a voyage that leads to the tragic completion of this story.

Chapter 14

Beatriz

The arrival of Beatriz Segovia Madriguera into the world on June 5, 1938, six and a half months following the death of Segovia's son Leonardo, had given a degree of comfort to the father crushed by the recent tragedy. However, the Segovia-Madrigueras were not able to enjoy an uneventful life for long. Barely a month after the delivery, Paquita had to undergo gallbladder surgery related to the birth. There are no specifics regarding either her illness or how long the recovery took, because the pianist stopped writing entries in her diary for some time due to the ailments caused by the pregnancy. Also, Beatriz was a little over a year old when Segovia resumed writing to Ponce. Several months after returning from the long trip to Europe, on August 26, 1939, the guitarist sent his friend the news from El Campito, where the family was living until the house on Massini Street was vacated by its renters and to eliminate the expense of a centrally located apartment. He informed Ponce that Paquita had given him a baby girl named Beatriz, who was born on June 5 of the previous year. The girl had a strong resemblance to Segovia, softened—he said—by some features from the "physical heritage" of Paquita. He described the baby's eyes, ears, nose, and lips, and said that she looked healthy and very intelligent, showing a strong attraction for getting close to the piano. Both parents had tested her ear, with lots of tricks, and were able to predict that she would become a refined musician. When the baby was one month old, Segovia continued, Paquita had to have an emergency surgery. But she was now feeling quite well.[1]

With respect to the bond Beatriz was able to develop with her mother, the first nine months of her life can be classified as constant instability. When she was barely four weeks old, mother and baby were separated for several weeks on account of Paquita's surgery and recovery. Following a brief period of tranquility, a long separation of five months began in the middle of September when the musical couple again went to Europe for Segovia's final concert tour there before the outbreak of World War II. Don Andrés and Paquita did not return to Montevideo until the end of February 1939. In other words, just a little more than two out of Beatriz's first nine months were spent in her mother's company. Two days after Beatriz was seven months old, the pianist sent eleven-year-old María Rosa a typed letter, in the form of a lesson in the art and history of Florence, from the home of Castelnuovo-Tedesco:

> How is everyone? We received your last letter seven days ago, and today or tomorrow I expect the next one. We are always thinking about you and I hope you are having a good time with the swimming and excursions. And little Beatriz? Does the heat bother her?
>
> We are doing well; I was in bed for two days with a cold, but I'm up and about now. The weather is very bad. Cold and rainy. It gets dark early, preventing us from seeing the paintings in the churches and palaces because we must take advantage of the few hours of light, and even that is dim. You and your sisters would love seeing the works of art, of which Italy is full—especially Florence. You would be impressed seeing Saint Mark's Abbey, where in each of the monks' cells (they no longer live there and they are vacant, so they can show them) there is a fresco (a painting on the wall) made by Fra Angelico. This fifteenth-century painter has made such marvels that in his frescoes it does not seem like there are saints or the Virgin, but rather the idea of them. The colors are very soft, and when you go outside, the one who feels like a saint is the one who has contemplated his frescoes. Here are the cells of Savonarola, the friar who was burned at the stake for being too stormy with the lords and the customs of that time (of the same century as Fra Angelico), and they burned him in the Piazza della Signoria in Florence.[2] Now, in the place where they built the fire there is a stone plaque on the ground commemorating this barbaric act. In the cells you can see the furniture he used, the books he studied, with his notes in the margins, the Christ that Fra Angelico had painted for his devotions, the clothes [Savonarola] wore when they took him prisoner and which they

removed as a sign of degradation, in short, everything belonging to the poor wise man, good, but too intense for those times. Walking through this city you can see the palaces of the great lords of the fifteenth and sixteenth centuries, the house of Michelangelo, the spot where Dante sat and reflected, etc., etc. If a war does not destroy these marvels, when you grow up you have to come see this country and spend a good amount of time here; but first you have to get up to date on the events, characters, and artists of the Renaissance so that you can enjoy your entire visit.

Andrés is very happy because the composer Castelnuovo-Tedesco is writing a concerto for guitar and orchestra for him and has already finished the first movement. I am anxiously awaiting your letter, and with lots of kisses for all of you and a hug for Nena and Fernando, receive the affection of your

Paquita[3]

That first impression of Beatriz's innate music abilities that the optimistic and excited Segovia transmitted to Ponce is shared by one of her sisters.

Beatriz in Segovia's studio in the apartment in the Palacio Lapido building, downtown Montevideo, 1939.

Once, while talking about the fact that none of Paquita's older daughters had studied an instrument, and about her own musical abilities, Sofía remarked:

> [Andrés and Paquita] did not want us to study an instrument. It was like they were the artists. But I wanted to study piano. There were pianos at home, and I wanted to play them. At that time, they gave us some money every week that we were to give to the church, to put in the basket. Then one day, on the way back from classes (we were studying at Crandon Institute), I saw a sign advertising piano classes. I thought I could use the money they gave us for the church. So I went and said, "I want to learn to play piano," and arranged it so the teacher would come to the house on a day Mama was not going to be there. But [Mama] arrived! And she asked, "What is that woman doing here?"
>
> And when I told her that I wanted to study piano and that I had paid her with the priest's money, she got angry and told me that I could not study the piano: "You do not have an ear for music!"
>
> But little Beatriz, yes. It came easy to her, and she played piano and guitar. They never taught her, but she learned by watching and trying. Little Beatriz inherited the music talents from both of them, because I always say that Andrés knew more about musical expression and Mama had the gift for composition. And little Beatriz, from the time she was very young, would compose her own songs. There is a lullaby that I have continued singing to all the children in the family and even to the dogs [*laughs*]. She composed it! And she sang it to herself to fall asleep. It went like this: [*and she sings it herself, in tune, at eighty years of age*] "Barabún, bam, bum. . . ."

In her diary, her mother writes that Beatriz began piano lessons on June 2, 1942, but she does not name the teacher. At that time, Paquita's own musical career was picking up with intensity in the concert halls, and Beatriz was sent a few blocks away to study at the home of the composer Guido Santórsola with his wife, Sarah Bourdillon. According to María Rosa's recollections, Beatriz's music studies did not go beyond the first lessons:

> Beatriz would have been about seven, and I think she only attended one or two years. I think she quit the classes before she moved with Mama to Buenos Aires. You already know that it was very difficult to study music at home—she was not very enthused about it. I remember that Pitusa

Two-year-old Beatriz in her father's studio at the home on Massini Street, 1940.

would force her to study because otherwise she wouldn't do it, she would let it slide. Besides solfeggio and scales, I never heard her play anything, not even *Für Elise*.

The teenage sister probably did not pay attention to that aspect of the little one's development, since the postscript of a January 1943 letter that Segovia wrote to Ponce appears to contradict her recollections. He said that Beatriz was "a prodigy of grace, intelligence, and memory." He told his friend that the girl played several things by Schumann on the piano and that—being just four and a half—she created her own compositions.[4]

After she had been studying piano for two years, Beatriz participated, along with other students of Sarah Bourdillon, in a recital that took place on September 17, 1944, at the hall of the Christian Youth Association. She had started preschool at the Liceo Francés (French School) in March 1943, and in 1944 she began primary school at the same Crandon Institute where her older sisters were studying.

Her first years at school were marked by her mother's increasingly frequent artistic engagements, which called for long hours of practice, trips, and prolonged absences. During that time Mamá Paqui lived in Montevideo for extended periods, taking care of the home and supervising the girls. At the end of August 1944, when Beatriz was recovering from measles, the conflict

Beatriz at the door of the Massini Street home around the time she started preschool.

that would lead to the breakup of the Segovia-Madriguera marriage broke out. From then on, there were years of comings and goings in the relationship, with several attempts at reconciliation. Don Andrés was increasingly absent from the family home until he abandoned it altogether. Once the couple's separation seemed inevitable, Paquita decided to sell the Massini Street house—large, costly to maintain, and probably full of memories—and she and Segovia agreed to rent a second-floor apartment in the same neighborhood, Pocitos, at 2645 Avenida Brasil. Paquita lived at that apartment for two years, from October 26, 1946, with two of her older daughters and Beatriz (María Rosa had gotten married a few months earlier), while Don Andrés went to live at a hotel two weeks after the move.

Paquita finished the draft of *Visto y oído* in 1947, at which time the idea of leaving Montevideo was maturing within her. In the last quarter of 1948, and definitively separated from Don Andrés,[5] the pianist finalized her intention to move to Buenos Aires, taking Beatriz with her. Pitusa and Sofía had also married by then, and life in Montevideo, probably with its many attached memories, had become more difficult for Paquita. On November 8, mother and daughter left the apartment on Avenida Brasil and went to live in two rooms at the Hotel Rambla, facing Pocitos Beach, and a few days later the

A photograph of Beatriz in 1945 sent to her father. The inscription on the back reads, "For my dearest friend, hugs and kisses, Beatris."

sale of the house on Massini Street was finalized—after two years of trying to sell it, they finally had to put it up for auction.

December 1948 brought more troubles. Beatriz underwent an operation to have her tonsils and adenoids removed and suffered complications with a series of hemorrhages. After the operation, Paquita went with her youngest daughter to spend a few days at the home of Sofía while she got ready to move to Buenos Aires. She had already been in touch with a school in that city to enroll Beatriz as a boarder, and in March 1949 Paquita and Beatriz were settled in the Argentinean capital. The pianist rented a room at the Hotel Lafayette, while Beatriz—in what seemed like a repetition of her older sisters' story—remained in boarding school at the Ward School, located in the Ramos Mejía area of Buenos Aires. Extant school bills are addressed to Andrés Segovia, while a letter that the school authorities sent Paquita to inform her that they had received Beatriz's application was addressed, in a striking and humorous coincidence, to "Mrs. Madariaga de Segovia."

For ten-year-old Beatriz, the process of adapting to the new school and change of country was more than problematic. This is how her sister María Rosa tells it:

When Mama decided to leave with Beatriz to live in Buenos Aires, she told us it was for economic reasons given that the Argentinean peso was lower and you could live much better there than here with the same amount of money. It turned out that Beatriz could not get used to the change. Don't

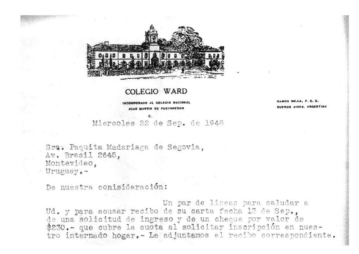

COLEGIO WARD

INCORPORADO AL COLEGIO NACIONAL
JUAN MARTIN DE PUEYRREDON

RAMOS MEJIA, F. C. O.
BUENOS AIRES, ARGENTINA

Miercoles 22 de Sep. de 1948

Sra. Paquita Madariaga de Segovia,
Av. Brasil 2645,
Montevideo,
Uruguay.-

De nuestra conisideración:

Un par de lineas para saludar a
Ud. y para acusar recibo de su carta fecha 13 de Sep.,
de una solicitud de ingreso y de un cheque por valor de
$230.- que cubre la cuota al solicitar inscripción en nues-
tro internado hogar.- Le adjuntamos el recibo correspondiente.

Fragment of the letter from the Ward School to Paquita.

forget that she left a big family in Montevideo, along with all her classmates and friends. She was always sad and cried all the time.[6]

A letter from Paquita to María Rosa (now the mother of a boy almost two years old) just over a month after settling in Argentinean territory confirms this story:

I have just spoken with Beatriz; she is very sad. I have encouraged her a little. Yesterday I went to visit her and take her some books and things to color. Her lack of acclimation to the school is a big problem for me, because I will have to look for a larger apartment and we will need a maid; and the air here is not as healthy as in Ramos Mejía.

As I had to pay a large sum for the quarter, on top of the huge expense for furnishings, luggage transfer, etc. etc., I do not want to take her out now, because in addition to losing that money I would have to pay the hotel, that is, we would duplicate our spending. I also told her that I would take her out, to relieve her spirits, and not to look at that place as somewhere she is forced to be, but as a temporary place; but she is so stubborn that not even this thought is a relief.

During Holy Week, she will have Thursday, Friday, Saturday, and Sunday to be with me, and then come the languid eyes and tears. I swear I'm suffering as much as or more than she is, because at night the anxiety of knowing that she is restless keeps me awake.[7]

Another letter from Paquita to María Rosa, written on August 15, 1949, when mother and daughter had moved to an apartment at 1557 Posadas Street in Buenos Aires, gives some details about how Beatriz was feeling:

We are captivated by what you tell us about Carlitos.[8] How we would love to have him close to play with him! Beatriz continues with her homesickness and talks about him constantly. It is understandable that she would need children to play with, without which her future is at risk. Anyway, it will not be long before we can all see each other.

Thank you very much for the offer of a room in your house, which I accept with great joy. . . .

Beatriz has been in bed with a high fever since yesterday. I suppose it must be the flu, and I'm waiting for the doctor. Just as I was feeling so happy because she was better, stronger, and even happier! You can tell that this girl will never let me rest more than ten days without her having some ailment. It is a nuisance!

Exactly two weeks later, just before the visit to Montevideo, Paquita writes again to her youngest Puig daughter with information of another sort about Beatriz:

As soon as I have Beatriz's documents all set, we will begin to make preparations to go there. I estimate that we will be there about two weeks. We definitely accept the invitation to stay at your house or Sofía's.

I found your in-laws very elegant and doing splendidly. It is a shame that I was not able to entertain them as I should, since their arrival coincided with my flu. . . . My illness has been very bad, and I got it from Beatriz. She has behaved admirably during my sickness, becoming a caring nurse, loving and not a bit lazy, getting up in the middle of the night to give me medicine or make me fruit juice, etc. etc. She is a charming creature, each day more and more grown-up and intelligent. She is on extended vacation, as the schools here are closed due to an epidemic of scarlet fever and flu that plagues the city . . .

Well, it will not be long before we see each other again and have long chats. You cannot imagine how I long to see you.

Lots of kisses from me and tell Carlitos that we will dance a *zamba* when I get there.[9]

Paquita and Beatriz remained in Montevideo from the end of September to the beginning of December 1949, and Segovia sent two telegrams to his ex-wife at the home of Sofía. In the first, from Stockholm, he stated that he was sending a letter accompanied by a check. In the second one, from Helsinki on October 5, Segovia asked Paquita to forgive him for the delay of the check, with hopes that Aparicio would not resent it. He ended by sending kisses to Beatriz and hugs to Paquita.

A few days earlier Paquita had received a letter from Segovia's aunt, Sister Gertrudis,[10] telling her:

> After four long years without receiving a letter from Andrés, I had the consolation of seeing his long-desired handwriting on August 26, including in his letter from New York a check for 500 pesetas that I have already cashed. Thanks to the money I have been able to get out of debt.[11] . . .
>
> Concerning this matter he has said absolutely nothing, only that he sends little Beatriz $150 a month, complaining about the many expenses he has, paying two alimonies and helping his son Andrés, who is becoming a famous painter, is married to a Swedish woman, and has a little one named Rafael. I am anxious to see my little girl's handwriting, that she knows I am her aunt, that since I found out that she is so good with her mama I love her twice as much.

In Segovia's third telegram to Montevideo, sent on December 6 from Marseilles, he confirms having received several letters and says that he will send a certain "authorization," probably having to do with the required paternal permit allowing Beatriz to leave the country. Mother and daughter made a lot of trips to Montevideo in 1950, and the destinations of the telegrams from Don Andrés and the letters from his aunt alternated between the two capitals of the Río de la Plata. One of the letters that Sister Gertrudis wrote to the woman whom she still considered her niece supplies a striking piece of information regarding the pianist's situation. Dated May 5, 1950, it is addressed to Buenos Aires, and she says in one of its main paragraphs, "It hurt me deeply to hear that due to economic tightness you have found it necessary to give piano lessons to provide for your needs, and from what I can see they are greater every day; it breaks my heart that at your age and in your position you are in this state."

In June 1950 Beatriz spent her twelfth birthday in Montevideo, and in July she was again in Buenos Aires with Paquita in their new apartment at 1565 Evaristo Uriburu. Segovia, arriving from Santiago de Chile via Mendoza, visited them at their new home between July 25 and August 8. Paquita had written to Sister Gertrudis on August 2 telling her about the visit, and the guitarist's aunt responded on September 8, while recuperating from a serious illness:

> You do not know how happy I am that Andrés was so loving and caring with you and the girl, and I enjoyed reading this immensely. At the same time my heart weeps because that woman who looks like a firebrand from Hell has taken your peace and happiness. Who knows if things will go back to what they were. It is a shame that he has fallen under the spell of one who does not know how to preserve the dignity of a woman or be a good mother, who after suckling it is suffocating it to death. May God forgive her and open his eyes.

When Beatriz continued to have difficulties adjusting to Buenos Aires, Paquita finally decided to send her back to Montevideo, while she herself remained in the Argentinean capital. According to María Rosa:

> Beatriz was always distraught at the school in Buenos Aires (Ward). She missed her classmates from here and the large family to which she was accustomed. It was so bad that Mama decided to send her back to Montevideo. Both Sofía and I had many children by then. Mama decided to put her in boarding school at Crandon, and we went to get her on weekends and holidays, which she spent at Sofía's house or at mine, in Montevideo or in Punta del Este. In the summer, she would usually go to Punta del Este with Mama and also to Sofía's house.
>
> Mama came often, but it was not ideal for [Beatriz] or for Mama to be alone in Buenos Aires.[12]

In April 1951, Beatriz was already living in Uruguay, while Paquita had a new address in Buenos Aires, on the third floor of 758 Pozos Street. From there on April 5 she wrote to María Rosa, now the mother of three:

Pitusa, who wrote to me, is delighted with your children; about Carlitos, she tells me that he is a little man and is talking; Guillermito, a delightful little one; but the prettiest of all is little María Rosita. She drools over her! She is hoping to celebrate her birthday and Beatriz's together with a barbecue in the countryside. She is anxious for you and me . . . to go.

For me, that's not a problem, and if you want to combine them, I would like that very much, because, as I told Beatriz in a letter, I wish to be reunited with everyone, taking advantage of both dates. Of course, I did not mean to go to the countryside, but I still would like to go.

Beatriz says many thanks for the offer made to celebrate it at home, if you are already in Malvín.[13]

Speaking of whom, it looks like the school provides an amount of distraction that neither she nor I expected. And, I had just written to her father, who is annoyed by her silence, defending her and telling him that she had changed a lot, for she had become sad, melancholy, and even distant from the family. A heartbreaking picture! How I enjoy her letters, which seem like rockets of joy and delight. She made up a story in verse about that picnic for me. . . .

Thank you very much for the work you do with Beatriz. You do not know how my heart thanks you.

Beatriz turned fourteen in June 1952, and Don Andrés went to Montevideo especially for this occasion; there is no evidence that he played a concert while there. Paquita wrote to María Rosa from Buenos Aires on May 16 telling her about his imminent arrival:

I appreciate it wholeheartedly that you have taken Beatriz out. Her father will arrive shortly. I suggested to him (but do not know if he will agree) that he go spend a week at Sofía's house (according to what Beatriz told me, she had suggested it) in Punta del Este, with Beatriz. In addition, the air there would do him good. He could peacefully enjoy his daughter's company, and at the same time he could practice in peace, as there is nothing to do there now.

Of course, for Beatriz's birthday we will be there together because she said that at some point she wanted to see both of us, and not one and then the other. I would be delighted if by that date we could all be together, the entire family, even the little ones. Who knows if we will have another similar

Beatriz, Segovia, and Paquita. Undated photo, probably taken in Montevideo in 1952.

occasion later in life! At least on this birthday, this child would be overjoyed with happiness, being surrounded by the family she loves so much.

Another witness to Segovia's presence in Montevideo in 1952 was the guitarist Raúl Sánchez Clagett, who said that during that time he attended a reunion in a downtown restaurant where Don Andrés was present with Beatriz. Also present was the orchestra conductor, composer, and pedagogue Enrique Casal Chapí,[14] with whom Sánchez was studying at the time and who invited him to participate in this gathering, as well as another Spanish musician. It was on this occasion that Segovia urged the young guitarist from Montevideo to travel to Siena, Italy, for the classes he had started to give there. It was in fact from Siena, three months after returning to Europe from this visit to Montevideo, that Segovia wrote a long letter to Beatriz that contained several passages of interest.[15] After relating his happiness for her letter and its spontaneity, he said that he was in Siena at that moment, where they were celebrating the Palio festival,[16] and the city was full of people from different parts of Italy and abroad. He added:

My daughter, I also wish to have not a rented apartment but a home.... If my optimism does not fool me, I think it will happen shortly, and the three of us will be together again. When I return to North America . . . I will observe, I will press to see how the managers have taken my visit to Spain.[17] . . . I am also looking forward to having you with me and hope that you will come with me every once in a while to Europe, the United States, etc. . . . Lots of kisses from your dad.

Another letter from Paquita to María Rosa, written from Buenos Aires exactly two months after this one, shares some interesting news regarding Segovia's presence in Barcelona for the first time since that hasty flight in 1936:

Mamá Paqui writes to me often. She saw Andrés a lot, the same with Uncle Ramón and my sisters. Mama says that when Uncle Ramón gave him a few things salvaged from the communist burning, saved for him over all these years, he was thrilled and immediately gave him a check for $200 as a present for his daughter's wedding.[18]

Mama says that he was quite satisfied because Olga had been quiet for three months. Mama warned him, however, that the silence was perhaps not a good sign, and in effect it seems like he received a letter from del Pino in front of her announcing that the woman of yore had written to him and she wanted to take revenge,[19] and that she was so crazy that it would not surprise [del Pino] if she shot [Andrés]. She has treated him like an idiot and added that in the last few years instead of the guitar, he has been playing the bass.[20] . . .

Mama says that the moment he read the letter [Andrés] was crushed and terribly worried. It seems that between the two of them [Segovia and Mamá Paqui], they were going to purchase an apartment for him in Barcelona, so that Beatriz and I could go there also; and when the letter appeared everything fell apart, and now he has to wait to see what she is going to do. What a role this poor unfortunate man has![21]

Segovia traveled again to Montevideo the following year of 1953. This time he came to give a concert at the Teatro Solís, which took place on April 28, and he remained a few more days for an early family celebration of Beatriz's fifteenth birthday. Don Andrés sent a telegram to María Rosa from Lima on April 24 to announce his coming to the Uruguayan capital, saying that he would arrive on Sunday, April 26, at 11 A.M. He asked his stepdaughter to tell Beatriz about his arrival and to confirm his reservation at the Victoria Plaza Hotel.

Signature of Segovia in the letter from Siena of August 1952.

Paquita, who remained in Buenos Aires, composed a work entitled *Evocación Mediterránea* (Mediterranean Recollection) for the occasion and sent it to Montevideo. Although it is written on the grand staff, as if for piano, it seems evident that the work was composed for guitar, for she explicitly wrote in the dedication on the first page, "So that the sublime guitar of Andrés Segovia can represent me at the family reunion. Paquita."

Two letters from Sister Gertrudis to Paquita confirm Segovia's presence at the family celebration as well as a special invitation extended by the guitarist to his daughter. All this took place between the end of April and the first week of May 1953. When Beatriz actually turned fifteen on June 5, her father had already left Montevideo. María Rosa remembers:

> Andrés was not here for Beatriz's fifteenth birthday. I remember because he sent me money so that I could buy her a gift. I thought about a ring with a rhinestone so that she could always use it as a remembrance of her father,

Program for the concert at Teatro Solís, April 28, 1953.

Fragments of the manuscript of *Evocación Mediterránea* by
Paquita Madriguera, May 1953.

and since the rhinestone is a hard stone it would not break or scratch; it was
the safest for the activities of a young girl and she could preserve it forever.
She agreed, and we bought it at Strauch's jewelry store.[22]

This is what Segovia's aunt says in the first letter to Paquita on this occasion, written in June 1953:

It seems like I have been given new life on the receipt of your dear letter,
and a ceaseless song of hallelujah comes from my heart because of the great
news you give me; your daughter will enjoy her father's affection so much, a
new stage of happiness in the enjoyment of paternal love now begins. I am
so happy that as the crown to so many displays of affection for everyone,

he has offered little Beatriz that trip to Europe and the United States with him, but it would make me happy if you accompanied him. . . . Wish Beatriz a happy birthday for me on her fifteen Aprils [springtimes] and tell her how happy I am with her joy.

Sister Gertrudis's second letter to Paquita is on July 15, and she tells her that she had received a visit from her nephew, anxiously awaited for many years:

Beloved Paquita of my soul,

My ardent desire to see my Andrés of my heart has finally culminated, but since there be no perfection in this life, his visit was very brief. It was not even forty-five minutes long, as he was on his way to Jerez with some men. . . . Your letter is a true reflection of what you said about him. I have found him very good in appearance, heavy, very affectionate, and extremely refined. We've all been pleasantly impressed to hear from his lips how satisfied he is with his daughter Beatriz, and he also told us that he went to introduce her into society,[23] and about you he said with conviction that you are good and noble. . . . You cannot imagine the joy that it has given our entire community to see him, for the older sisters evoked the memory of when he was little and came by our convent, always attentive and affectionate, and the younger ones, having heard of him, have pleasant memories.

Shortly after Segovia's visit to his aunt, an unfortunate event altered (on its own and owing to some unexpected circumstances) his travel plans with his daughter. A detached retina forced him to undergo what in those days was a very delicate operation in Madrid, at a time that coincided with Paquita's plans to return to Spain for a series of concerts in Barcelona. Don Andrés had been helping her to get a new Spanish passport and notified her by telegram from Madrid to Montevideo on July 14 that the document had been issued and she needed to send the required photos.[24] Then the accident occurred, and the surgery triggered a series of misunderstandings when it became unclear as to who had the right to be with Segovia in the hospital—his ex-wife, who happened to be traveling to Spain and could move up her trip to be with him, or the Brazilian singer with whom he had an unstable and turbulent relationship. He attempted, by various means and with fear and uncertainty, to settle

Beatriz with her parents dressed in party attire. The date and occasion are uncertain, but it is probably at Teatro Solís for Segovia's concert of April 28, 1953.

this sticky situation. In an effort to explain the entire story, Segovia first sent a handwritten letter to María Rosa from Madrid on August 24, 1953, with these words: "The letter I wrote to Mama, which I include in this envelope, and this one for you[25] are the first that I write since I suffered the detached retina. I am doing well now, and if you read what I say to your Mama you will see that my vision will be back to normal by the end of August."

Then, Segovia sent María Rosa congratulations for her next birthday and promised her that he would write to Aparicio Méndez begging him to buy her "a belated present—but pretty." He also told her that he would reply to Sofía and Pitusa personally for the interest they had shown in him, as well as to his "cute little Beatriz." And he finished: "Receive a big kiss from your always paternal, Andrés." Segovia then told María Rosa in the postscript that there was an address for her to write him, contained in the letter to Paquita.

On August 30 (before the letter could reach her), Paquita also wrote to María Rosa, from Buenos Aires:

Today, Sunday, the day I usually devote to answering letters, I comply with several and also to yours dated on the 17th. . . .

My plan is to go there on September 14 and stay a few days with you, less than what I had planned because at the end of October I will probably have to leave for Spain, and since I have to play concerts there, I have to practice every day, which is quite difficult for me to do in Montevideo; but, on the other hand, the ongoing work is essential. I have planned, if nothing comes up, to leave on the 26th by plane, so my next visit will also be a farewell, since from there I will take the plane, and I will see you at the stop in Carrasco [Montevideo's airport]. I do not know how long I will be gone, but I calculate that I will be here for part of our summer, and perhaps I can spend some time at Punta del Este upon my return. Tell Sofía and Jorge about this, and if you see Pitusa, do the same, because I do not have enough time to write. Between my practice and house chores, social obligations—increasingly shunned, but there are always obligations—the days pass rapidly. . . .

You did the right thing by writing to Dr. Rubio to make him understand the situation. Mamá [Paqui] in her last letter said that Andrés soon ceased to give signs of life and added, "I am sure that the woman is with him and she has sealed his mouth." Now none of us know his whereabouts. It is a real shame what is happening between him and that tarantula, and on my part, I also wrote to Dr. Rubio asking for news about the development of his convalescence, and I made some extremely discreet, but well-targeted, clarifications in order to not look like a big egomaniac and pass as a bad person while that one looks like the "Good Samaritan." The appearance is, at least from there, that his wife did not even move, did not even show up, while that other one has moved in by his side to nurse him. I told him, in case he is suspicious of the reason why I am going to him rather than going directly to Andrés, that I fear that my letter will be intercepted. In the end I told him that I would like to have been with him, but Andrés's irregular lifestyle prevented me from doing so. That I am always begging God to heal him completely and illuminate his understanding. If Dr. Rubio is sharp, he will understand. He has yet not responded to me.

On September 7, still not knowing that Paquita's letter had been delivered to his doctor, Segovia wrote to Beatriz, by hand, from the Hotel Felipe II in El Escorial, outside of Madrid, telling her that he was resting in a hotel recommended "by Godfather,"[26] and that the following day he would leave for Madrid. "It has all been like a nightmare," he said, but now he was doing well and in two days the doctors would remove the dark glasses he was obliged to wear. He added: "I hope Mama is already by your side. I love the idea of giving joy to you and her."[27] And then, he refers to a subject that will be developed later: "Get ready for next year. I want you to travel with me. This will be very interesting for you, and it will resolve a lot of things for me."[28] Finally, Segovia said goodbye with, "Kisses to your sisters, to their kids . . . and you already know how much your father loves you."

Next came a telegram from Segovia to María Rosa, sent from Madrid on September 13, 1953, in which he begged her to keep her mother in Montevideo until the arrival of a letter from him.

Three days later Segovia wrote a letter, this time to María Rosa, and included one for Paquita that was not saved. He expressed gratitude to his stepdaughter for helping him in spite of her numerous responsibilities. "You are an angel, and your generosity increases the affection that I have always felt for you," he wrote, and asked her to support the message he was sending to Paquita through the letter that María Rosa was going to give her. In any case, he assured María Rosa that he had been discreet: "I have not told Mama that you told me about her trip, in case you have slipped and she did not find it prudent—that way I am sparing you from any discomfort."

Finally, he told her that he was leaving for Switzerland soon, and sent hugs "to Cholo and to his mother,"[29] as well as kisses for María Rosa's children and "a big and affectionate one for you from your Andrés."

Paquita wrote to María Rosa from Buenos Aires on October 1 telling her she had received Segovia's letter:

> Thank you for your letter and the ones you included from Andrés and Hurok.[30] I expect that you read the first one, and you can see what an outrageous impression it has caused me. In short, he does not want me to interfere. What nerve and unfairness, and I said to him what I will copy to you here so that you can see my *truly* heartfelt reaction. I cannot stand this anymore!!! . . .

My departure is set, unless something comes up, for the 19th of this month. The plane will arrive in Carrasco at 4 P.M., stopping there for an hour, which will allow me to give you a few kisses, even when I would prefer not to see anyone, as the farewells do me no good. However, if the weather is good, I hope you can also bring some of the little ones to the airport....

I am uneasy about Beatriz's prolonged silence. I wonder if she is ill. God forbid.

On the return I think everything will be set and we will enjoy free crossings;[31] but if not, I am sure that I can get a permit, which they have already promised me. This will clear my lungs.

Lots of kisses for everyone, everyone, everyone.

Another letter, this time from Sister Gertrudis to Paquita, addressed to Barcelona and dated October 30, 1953,[32] reads:

Dearest Paquita of my soul,

I hope you are feeling good and have made the trip happily. I can imagine the unlimited great happiness your very good mother must have felt hugging you again after a long absence. In this aspect your mother has been happier than me, and she well deserves it. I am really surprised by the sudden change between you two, each going his or her separate way without even showing a little sample of what Andrés told me—that by the end of the year you would come back to Spain for good; and now it looks like the record has changed. No matter how much I think about it, I cannot figure it out since my Andrés told me he loved you very much, and that you are very noble and he would never leave you. Do not think that I am exaggerating. I have such a lump in my throat that I cannot even talk, and I beg you to tell me what has happened in this respect, and in the meantime my soul still longs for a bit of news.

If the reason for your returning to give concerts is to make more money to pay for the move to Spain, I think it is great, but if the reasons have nothing to do with this, I regret it in my soul, because I suffer equally your lack of the affection that you so rightly deserve....

Forgive me for asking again for Andresito's address in Switzerland as I have misplaced it.

Don Andrés wrote Beatriz a very long typed letter on November 23 from Rome, with passages that are very important for understanding the development of this story. After complaining because Beatriz had not answered his last three letters to her, Segovia said that he had returned to his normal activities and had given eighteen concerts in Switzerland, the Netherlands, England, and Italy. He still had several concerts scheduled in different Italian cities, and after that he would go to the United States to continue playing from the first of the year until mid-May. Then he told his daughter: "Everywhere I go, I tell people about your visit next year. I am excited that the two of us will go alone from one country to another,[33] and that you will see for the first time this continent, so full of history, beautiful monuments, and interesting people." He also explained to Beatriz that this trip would be more exciting than the one they both had taken to the interior of her "cute little country," where there were few things to see and whose people were "simple and provincial." But, he emphasized by underlining his words, he needed a confirmation from her without delay, because he had to make his arrangements within a certain time, and the tours would have different itineraries depending on whether or not he was going with his daughter. He assured her that few girls would have such a chance in their life, and told her that they would go to France, England, Switzerland, Germany, the Netherlands, and Italy. And if she enjoyed the trip, the following year he could invite her to Japan, Australia, and South Africa.

After writing those paragraphs, Segovia told his daughter that he was tired because he had given a concert that evening, in which he had played the Chaconne and other important works. From the theater he had gone to have a drink at the Academia de Francia, and "not wanting to accept any other invitation, I came back alone to have dinner at the hotel and to write to you."[34] He finished his letter by saying that he was falling asleep, but the following day he would send her any reviews that were published. Finally, he sent greetings for the whole family "and both a hug and a kiss for you from your father, Andrés."[35]

Segovia included this letter with one to María Rosa, where we find the first signs of discontent between Don Andrés and Aparicio Méndez. Initially he complained once more of the lack of replies from Beatriz, and begged María Rosa to suggest to her sister that she should write her father. Later he asked María Rosa to give Beatriz the enclosed letter, and sent greetings to the whole family. It is in the postscript of the letter where we find the mention of the problems with Aparicio. Segovia had sent an earlier message to María Rosa's husband, asking that he send him the communications from National City Bank. Don Andrés supposed that Méndez was upset because he had asked Cholo, in Aparicio's absence, to verify at his bank in Montevideo whether some money had been deposited in Segovia's account:

> [Méndez] wrote to me bitterly and I, after answering that letter, have not bothered him again. You know how much I like and trust him. But to resent the fact that, while he was away, I sent someone as close as Cholo to find out whether, after ten months of waiting for the fruit of my concerts in England, they finally have received the money at Banco Comercial, and to get angry about such a thing is being too sensitive.

Other letters from Sister Gertrudis to Paquita attribute Segovia's change in plans to the intervention of the woman with whom he had been having an affair for a number of years. According to some of Segovia's letters, he wanted to end the relationship but had received threats that promised to affect (so he thought) his future possibilities for concerts in the United States, his main financial center. In the meantime, Paquita had decided to forbid Beatriz to travel with her father if she did not accompany her, which created a bitter divide in the ex-spouses' relationship. María Rosa subtly tried to smooth things over and prevent more problems for Beatriz:

> Due to this situation and the differences of opinion between Mama and Andrés, with respect to his invitation for Beatriz to make that trip to Europe, it occurred to me that since he was going to spend money, and the Brazilian woman took everything from him that she could, Andrés could buy Beatriz an apartment here in Montevideo, which would mean security for Beatriz and allow Mama and her to be together. You will see through letters that Andrés thought about buying an apartment for her in Barcelona,[36] but I figured that the same thing that happened in Buenos Aires [i.e., Beatriz's unhappiness] would also happen in Barcelona. I wrote to Andrés with that suggestion, and he liked it.[37]

Some years passed before that idea became a reality. In the meantime, the waters were calming, and Beatriz traveled with her father more than once before the apartment in Montevideo was finally purchased.

During the final months of 1953, Paquita Madriguera did make her first, and only, trip back to Spain since that hasty flight in 1936. On October 30, she gave the Barcelona premiere of Castelnuovo-Tedesco's Piano Concerto No. 2 at the Music Palace with the Orquesta Municipal, conducted by Eduardo Toldrá. It was reviewed in a Barcelona newspaper:

> The time—an absence of almost twenty years—has not faded the memories of Paquita Madriguera nor taken a toll on the technique of the famous Catalonian pianist, who was born here to admiration that soon expanded to all latitudes. This was well illustrated in the second of the evening concerts of the Orquesta Municipal, with whom Paquita Madriguera collaborated brilliantly.
>
> Paquita Madriguera, greeted with fervent applause when she appeared on the stage, was soloist in the Concerto No. 2 in F Major by the Italian Mario Castelnuovo-Tedesco, a work that had not yet been performed in Barcelona. As in the past, the pianist performed a task that accurately reflected an exquisitely spiritual temperament and thoughtfully approached the demands of the musical form, while respecting the composer's language. Happily, because of the expression—there is nothing to say about the technique, which remains clear and precise—Paquita Madriguera was given prolonged ovations afterwards and called back to the stage repeatedly between the offerings of bouquets of flowers.[38]

The press of Igualada, the town where Paquita was born fifty-three years earlier, announced her return in mid-November and honored her with a festival at which she was to give a concert. A long article was published on November 21 in the weekly paper *Igualada* under the title: "December 3, 1953: Homage to the Great Pianist from Igualada, Paquita Madriguera, at the National Center, in Collaboration with all the Organizations of Igualada."

Paquita performed again in Barcelona in December, playing several times on the radio as well as giving a concert on the 13th at the law school auditorium, with works by Bach, Beethoven, Mendelssohn, Ponce, Albéniz, Falla, and Granados. The public again rewarded her enthusiastically, as the press reported from the city where she grew up as a pianist. In mid-January 1954, Paquita returned to the Río de la Plata and again alternated living between the Pozos Street apartment in Buenos Aires and the home of one of her daughters in Montevideo. Her relationship with Segovia continued hostile

Sala de Actos del Iltre. Colegio de Abogados

MALLORCA, 283 (chaflán Lauria)

ÚNICO RECITAL

DE LA PIANISTA

PAQUITA MADRIGUERA

Domingo 13 de diciembre de 1953   A las 6 y ½ de la tarde

Program cover for the Barcelona concert of December 13, 1953.

and tense, while her older daughters continued to build bridges to improve the environment in which Beatriz was going through adolescence. In particular, María Rosa, the youngest of the three girls whom Don Andrés always considered his stepdaughters, had his respect and trust, and he accepted her efforts and relied on her communications regarding decisions that could ensure Beatriz's protection.

The enlightening and almost transparent typed letter that Segovia wrote her the following spring from Canada is very long and more than eloquent in this regard. While Segovia was in Chicago he had received a letter from Paquita that he considered very offensive and violent, and he had decided to let some days pass before answering it, for fear of falling into the temptation of answering her with words that were too strong. Almost at the same time, Segovia had received a friendly letter from María Rosa (the one he was now answering), offering her stepfather some ideas for the situation's solution, which he considered as the best option for Beatriz. But he needed to express his actual feelings, wounded as he was by Paquita's words: "Only she . . . dares to commit the intolerable injustice of rating my life as depraved."[39] Segovia told her that the rest of the people knew the perpetual sacrifice that was his life, and the profit that Adelaida, Andresito and his family, Aunt Gertrudis, and Beatriz took from what money was left to the guitarist after deductions for the managers, the income taxes, the travel, and hotels. He said that he was tirelessly risking his life on trips by air, without fear of accidents and without worrying about over-fatigue, in spite of being sixty-one. He also emphasized that he rarely went to the movies or the theater, and never wasted money in dance clubs or places like that. He told María Rosa that every person who knew him was aware of the reasons that had prevented him "from getting out of the situation that I have gotten myself into;"[40] adding that everyone knew that the situation did not provide him any satisfaction, rather only bad times.

Then Segovia elaborated on his tours, his successful concerts, and the fact that for the first time in many years he could hope that he would be able to support himself within two years in case the managers should react against him. Segovia said that the public was entirely on his side, and that three "sold-out" concerts in New York and a few others in Boston, Philadelphia, Chicago, Pittsburgh, San Francisco, Los Angeles, and other cities offered him such great possibilities that the managers would not want to lose him, "in spite of the resentment any person would want to impute to them."[41] Now, he said, he would be able to get some savings for his old age, in case he got there, or for Beatriz, if he disappeared first. He had explained these things to Paquita, but her response left him astonished due to its violent nature and sense of injustice. He then explained to María Rosa that Paquita should have known that there were two important reasons behind his idea of taking Beatriz with him. The first one was to put an end to his present situation, by doing his part with his daughter and taking on the responsibility of carrying it out.[42] The other was to offer Beatriz a marvelous trip through Europe, America, and Asia. He said that he had examined both things in detail with Paquita in Buenos Aires and in Montevideo, and she did not talk about going to juvenile court then. He wondered about the reasons for her change of mind, and supposed that it was motivated by a letter he had sent Paquita from Madrid, saying that she could have traveled to Spain when she got the news about Segovia's illness, and taken her place at his side, where nobody would have dared challenge her: "I was alone at the hospital . . . for more than nineteen days, and, in spite of the negative gesture I made in another direction . . . I stopped being alone."[43]

Segovia told María Rosa that it was then (after Olga appeared) that he wrote to Paquita telling her to wait and not to come to Madrid to meet him. He regretted that she didn't come spontaneously, at the beginning, because, despite their divorce, that was her natural place. Then Segovia explained to María Rosa that he had not called Paquita because he did not want her to think that, under the threat of blindness, he wanted "to lean on her as a seeing-eye dog, forcing her to share a kind of existence in which the rewards would be much less than the sacrifices." Immediately, he referred to the solution that his stepdaughter had suggested, based on the need Beatriz had for her mother's care. He said he had about nine thousand dollars in National City Bank in Montevideo, and that a good part of it could be used for buying an apartment for Beatriz and Paquita. His only conditions were that the property be in Beatriz's name and that the apartment have a third bedroom, "just in case."

Finally, Segovia asked María Rosa to advise her mother to put aside her offensive attitude and communicate with him as before so they could work with more coordination and effectiveness for Beatriz's well-being. After sending his regards to the whole family and affectionate kisses for María Rosa, Segovia signed his letter in Vancouver, B.C., on April 2, 1954.

María Rosa's mediation gradually worked, to judge from the tone of the subsequent writings available. However, it was still possible to feel Paquita's fury in a reply that came from Aunt Gertrudis, written on May 30 of that same year and sent to Montevideo, where the pianist had come, as she normally did at that time, around Beatriz's birthday.

> I received your awaited letter and see that you are well, thank God. It only makes me suffer to know that you are profoundly affected with respect to the black clouds in the future of our Andrés for not having the energy to shake the smut from hell that has conquered him. My health has deteriorated since that short visit Andrés made last year, and I would never believe

such conduct if it had not been confirmed by you. Regarding the long trip to Europe and the United States on which he promised to take our little Beatriz, I am pleased with your gallant attitude in not allowing her to go without being accompanied by you. . . .

Our most cordial congratulations for the excellent grades on the exams by our cute little Beatriz.

Beatriz finished high school at Montevideo's Crandon Institute in 1954. Two of her sisters—having raised three (Sofía) and five (María Rosa) children of their own, having both completed college, and now enjoying retirement after a number of years as professionals—reflected back years later upon Beatriz as a student:[44]

> *Sofía:* Beatriz was a brilliant student, very intelligent.
>
> *María Rosa:* Beatriz studied at the Crandon Institute, here in Montevideo—primary and secondary—and then she went to Junior College (not counting the time she was in Buenos Aires). She later started working at ALALC.[45] She did not pursue a university education.

During the interview it was brought up that Segovia had stated on one occasion that Beatriz had graduated from a school in New York. They both insisted that the information was erroneous, so the journalist probably misunderstood or misinterpreted Segovia's words when she quoted him:

> I gave Beatriz a party when she graduated from the Grandow [*sic*] Institute, in New York. Look, she was an exceptional woman—do not think it is the father talking, it is an observer. . . . She was very calm, not a dumb and crazy girl, no—very intelligent; she read a lot, she spoke magnificent English; she was a very exceptional girl.[46]

María Rosa confirmed the error about both the graduation and the party in New York and provided evidence that Segovia could not have been at the party, which took place in Montevideo:

> Beatriz studied the entire cycle at Crandon, and the party to which Andrés referred is a ceremony in the style of the United States that they do at that

institute when the students finish everything and graduate. They wear a party dress, long, etc. ... Beatriz's graduation party at Crandon was on December 10, 1954. Andrés was not present, and I remember that he sent my husband a letter justifying his absence.[47]

Segovia wrote another long letter, this time from Denver, Colorado, on November 22, 1954, and addressed it to María Rosa's husband. He began by telling Cholo that he did not dare trust some enclosed documents to Beatriz's youth, nor want to burden María Rosa, so busy with her responsibilities as housewife, homemaker, and mother of the family. Segovia wanted Cholo to show Beatriz all the contracts, contained in the letter, and explain to her that because of them it was impossible for him to be present at her graduation party, which made him very sad. He argued that coming to her party would represent a loss of $8,000, plus the travel expenses and lodging, and that he could not afford to lose such earnings. He then described his tours for that year, his income, and all the deductions (20 percent for the managers, 5 percent for publicity expenses, and around 30 percent for income taxes). He calculated that after the huge travel expenses around the United States and Canada, and the hotel and restaurant bills, he would still be able to retain almost 20 percent of his concert earnings, which would represent, at the end of the tour, a savings of eight or nine thousand dollars. He also told Cholo that his performances in Europe were not as well paid, and that with those earnings he had to support his first wife, help his son Andrés and his family, and pay his personal lodging expenses. After his account of earnings and expenses, Segovia asked Cholo to tell Beatriz that for her graduation he would send her a $100 check so that, "as a gift from her faraway dad," she could buy whatever she liked. He also said that he would not send a check at that time, nor another one designated for some gifts for all the children, because he had run out of checks and was waiting for replacements from Chase National Bank.

Segovia was also worried because he had not received enough information from Beatriz "about the withdrawal of funds at National City Bank and about her investment." So he begged Cholo to ask Paquita to send him a detailed statement of what she had done; otherwise he would not send any money and would personally deposit whatever amount he decided in his daughter's name. He clarified that he didn't have "the slightest concern" about how Paquita used that sum, but he was bothered by the "lack of courtesy" of not informing him. "Neither emotionally nor from a business standpoint" did he share the idea of buying an apartment in Buenos Aires. He said that the destiny of Argentina depended on a dictatorship that he considered "more communist than conservative."[48] He rounded out his opinion by saying, "Buenos Aires has for Paquita the same irrational attraction as the aimless trips had for Mamá Paqui."

Tempers finally calmed down, the relationship between Segovia and Paquita returned to friendly terms—even affection, as in previous years—and in mid-1955 Beatriz finally took her long-delayed trip to Europe. During April and May of that year, there were several telegrams from Don Andrés to his ex-wife (who now lived at 1451 Evaristo Uriburu, in Buenos Aires) with news about the arrangements for documentation and money to meet their daughter's travel requirements. A telegram sent from Milan on April 6 said that the permit was sent that day. He advised Beatriz to use KLM Airlines and informed her that the money would be deposited at Commercial Bank at the beginning of May. Another telegram sent from The Hague on April 16 said that Segovia would await Beatriz at the Zurich airport on Tuesday, May 10. And on May 12, Paquita received a telegram from Segovia, sent from Zurich, notifying her that Beatriz had arrived in Europe happy and healthy and was sending kisses to Paquita.

Not all the letters Beatriz sent from Europe on this first trip have survived. Two that made it give an idea of what she did and felt at almost seventeen. On May 21 she wrote from the Hotel Bedford, in Paris:

> My very, very, very dear mommy!!!
>
> How are you doing? How is everyone there? . . .
>
> Well, here I am, in Paris, with more eyes than hair on my head, looking at everything and stumbling in French! No, in respect to the language, I will say that I understand a lot, I comprehend it, but I do not dare to speak it—do you understand what I mean? If I made a mistake in front of Dad or a friend of his, I would die of embarrassment. But sooner or later it is going to come out.
>
> The city, of course, is marvelous. I went to the Louvre once, but I hope to go again, as once is not enough. I also went to Sainte-Chapelle, to Notre Dame, to the Eiffel Tower, and yesterday we took a trip to Versailles, but

without being able to see the inside. For that we will go on Tuesday; but from what I have seen so far, I am very impressed. It is a shame that people growl and are permanently in a bad mood!!

I will give you my next two addresses: from May 25 to 29 I will be at the Hotel Splendid de Bordeaux; and from May 30 to I do not know when, I will be at the Fenix in Madrid. From that city I will send you a letter with the itinerary to follow, and so on!

Thank you for sending me the letters—for a moment I felt like I was in the apartment reading them; and as for missing me, I will tell you that the feeling is very mutual, regardless of how many Eiffel Towers and Notre Dames I see! Do you use the hot-water bottle when you get home at night? I miss it here because it is so cold that it hardens the rocks. Gaspar Cassadó told us that in Spain, especially in Madrid, it is nice and warm. We had lunch with him four days ago, and yesterday he invited us to dinner. He is very nice and refined and sends you many regards.

Last Monday I went to Dad's concert and he was magnificent, and the people applauded wildly. Then Nadia (what a name, eh?)[49] Boulanger gave him a dinner, where I met a Chilean and an Argentinean. We talked a lot and, of course, the constant Río de la Plata rivalry came up! The case ended when the Argentinean said that Punta del Este (look who he comes to tell) was an Argentinean beach! Well, everything went from one joke to another while Dad and the older people talked about other things. . . .

So we have had several dinners and luncheons, but that one was a lot of fun, with the two of them fighting to the end, and the Chilean buttering us up and laughing hard! Actually it was the only dinner where there were young people with whom I could speak Spanish and laugh like I was at home! I asked Dad if we are ever going to go to a dance (or give a dance), and he laughed and said, "Yes." It turns out that in Spain, rather in Madrid, there is a family with whom (if I think they are nice) he is going to leave me while he goes to play in Coppet, Switzerland, because it is a "trivial" trip and it is not worth it for me to go.

WHEN WE GET TO ITALY HE IS GOING TO BUY ME A LAMBRETTA,[50] OR HE IS GOING TO SEND ME THE MONEY TO BUY IT IN BUENOS AIRES. He will probably write to you, not only because of that, but to tell you how I did, etc. See if you can get him to buy it for me; or if not, just do not say anything against it—please.

Well, precious one, I say goodbye, hoping to receive a letter from you soon. . . .

Lots of kisses for Julia and for you, from your daughter who loves you,

Beatriz

The second surviving letter was written by Beatriz in Madrid on June 3, two days before her birthday (which she failed to mention):

My dearest Mama:

Today I had the welcomed joy of receiving your letter from May 28, along with two from Pitusa. . . . It made me very happy because it had been a while since I had received correspondence, and I got three letters from the family (all of you) and one from Mario Berembau asking to go to Dad's concert in Coppet, Switzerland, on June 8.

Now, regarding that concert: Dad leaves on June 6, he plays on the 8th and returns immediately to Madrid, so I have preferred not to go but to

Segovia and Beatriz in Paris, 1955.

stay at the home of the Quintanas (I don't know if you know them). They have five children (two boys and three girls), and they are all very nice. One of the daughters is twenty and one of the boys is around the same age, so we have already planned to have a good time. They are refined people—and very wealthy—and nice.

I love Spain. The people—acquaintances as well as public employees, at the hotel, etc.—are very good and always full of that characteristic and contagious good mood. Yesterday they took me to El Escorial—Mrs. Quintana, the son, and the daughter—and we visited the monastery of Phillip II. It is pretty and impressive! I have become a fan of John of Austria (How handsome he was!). . . .

We went to a dinner last night and there was a painter there who is pretty famous now, in spite of his youth. He is going to paint me, and we have been talking all night. They sat us—the son, the daughter, the painter, and me—at a separate table because we did not all fit at the same table; that helped us become friends, and we laughed a lot more than we ate! They were laughing especially about the way I talk. I never figured that saying *papas* would cause such an eruption of laughter.[51]

We spent a very pleasant evening, between jokes, while those at the large table were engaged in serious conversations. More than once they would all quiet down, and then you could only hear our continuous laughter. One man told us later that he would have preferred to be with us. Well, the painter was "studying" me, and the more he "studied," the more difficult I made it for him to do so. They told jokes about people from Andalusia and Uruguay! And they did not leave me alone! Then, as I was leaving, my three new friends told me that they had feared that I would be very serious, but they were pleasantly surprised that I was very friendly, etc. How interesting! But I was so at ease that I was natural and not formal. At first I remembered what you told me one day, and when the painter started asking me questions about painting, I said, "Ah, well, sorry, but I do not know anything about painting!" And that ended the topic. It is better that way, right? At least I did not put my foot in my mouth. . . .

Well, Mama, I'll say goodbye. I am going to eat; it is 2:30 (this eating schedule in Madrid is killing me), and I am starving.[52]

With lots of love from your daughter who adores you,

Beatriz

Andrés and Beatriz Segovia in the Alhambra Palace in Granada.

There are also traces of Beatriz's first trip to Europe in a letter that Sego-via sent from Milan, on July 14, 1955, to Castelnuovo-Tedesco, who was now living in Los Angeles, California:

> Know that each day I also designate a bit of time to your second con-certo, to the *Fantasía* [*para un gentilhombre* (Fantasia for a Gentleman)] of Rodrigo (as well as his three pieces for guitar), to Villa-Lobos's concerto (in which I need to retouch the cadenza), and to new works by Tansman. Add to this, maintaining the repertoire that I am playing in my concerts, the trips, the people, my daughter's presence, etc. (get "women" out of your mind), and you will understand that my life is quite full.[53]

Once Beatriz returned from the trip, she moved back to Buenos Aires to live with her mother in the apartment on Evaristo Uriburu Street. From then on the relationship between Don Andrés and Paquita took on a cordial tone, and there are frequent telegrams from him about the sending of checks

Father and daughter in Granada.

for different purposes. For example, a telegram addressed to Paquita from New York on April 13, 1956, said that Segovia was sending a letter with the "monthly supplement" for her, and he told her to write whether it seemed sufficient or not. And on November 27 of that year, Segovia sent a telegram from Zurich to thank Paquita for the birthday letter she had sent him and to inform her that he had sent an authorization needed for Beatriz, signing it with "Kisses, hugs."

Another telegram, dated June 1, 1957 (four days before Beatriz's nineteenth birthday), is a perfect example of the change that had taken place in their relationship. Mother and daughter were in Buenos Aires, and it appeared that, for the first time, Beatriz's birthday was going to be celebrated in the Argentinean capital, far from the rest of the family (Beatriz was in Spain for her previous birthday). The novelty was that on this occasion, Segovia was going to spend a long period of time with his daughter and ex-wife, and he wrote that he would like for them to delay the birthday celebration for "Little Beatriz" until his arrival, of which he would inform them.

Andrés Segovia arrived in Buenos Aires on June 13, gave some concerts in Argentina, played at the Teatro Solís in Montevideo on July 4, traveled at the end of the month to play in Chile, and returned to Buenos Aires on August 1. He stayed in the Argentinean capital with Beatriz and Paquita most of that month until he traveled on August 25 to Rio de Janeiro. From there he sent a telegram addressed to them both on August 26, telling them that everything was fine, that he would continue his trip the following day, and that he was sorry to leave them. And he sent kisses for both.

During Segovia's stay in Buenos Aires, Paquita made a public appearance in memory of her teacher, Enrique Granados. An article described the event:

> Beloved student of the late Spanish composer Enrique Granados, the pianist Paquita Madriguera recalled the figure of the maestro and illustrated her talk by playing some of his most characteristic pieces. Episodes from the life of the composer of *Goyescas*, performed with finesse and poetic emotion, made the remembrance of the man and the artist even more valuable to us. Paquita Madriguera had the right opinion in the sense that if the music of Albéniz is music with regional dress, Granados's music profoundly springs up from the native Spanish land with all of the fantastic spirit of former times. The piano performance of some of the *Spanish Dances* was a listening enjoyment because of the expression and authenticity of the performer's playing. The message of a great musician transmitted by someone who is an authentic stockpile of his thought.[54]

At the beginning of 1958, Beatriz traveled again to meet her dad, this time in "problematic" New York—the city where Olga Coelho lived. There is no documented reference to the Brazilian singer during this stay, although family stories indicate that Beatriz did meet her and one of her children at some time.[55] María Rosa says of this trip, which was planned as a continuation of the European one, "On January 2, 1958, Beatriz went to New York to be with Andrés. She was there until the beginning of May of that year and then returned to Montevideo."[56]

During this excursion the young woman shared time not only with her father, but also with another part of her mother's family in New York, headed by her Uncle Enrique (Enric)—the violinist, composer, and orchestra leader. A postcard that Beatriz sent Paquita a few days after her arrival, on January

Two photos of the time Segovia shared with Beatriz and Paquita in Buenos Aires, taken by the renowned photographer Annemarie Heinrich in 1957.[57]

7, shows the squeezed-in handwriting of several members of the Madriguera family (including Paquita's sister Mercedes, who was returning to Spain at that time). Paquita's brother wrote a few lines: "Paquita: I congratulate you, Beatriz is precious. We are celebrating her arrival and the departure of Mercedes and her giant Frankie. Andrés was with us [only] for a cocktail, but we continued [after he left]. He always remembers you, and forgive my silence—my very confidential reservations."[58]

Beatriz wrote a letter to María Rosa on April 10, 1958, from Washington, D.C.:

> I received a letter from Mama, which is how I find out about all of you. The poor thing is pretty worried about the crisis there in Buenos Aires and no wonder ... but I hope someone helps her to invest the money WELL ... because most are advising (and advising her in particular) BADLY. Apart from this, she is very happy and says that despite the twelve grandchildren, she has a lot of energy. And well, it is in our blood ... phooey! If I continue with this reasoning, it is likely that I will be convinced of what you all used to tell me, that I was found in a cabbage patch, because I do not have an abundance of that blood....

By the way, you do not even know where I am or what I am doing. I arrived in Washington yesterday afternoon and will only stay until tomorrow morning, when I will take a train back to New York. I wanted to come, even if it was for a day, to see it (it is nothing spectacular but since I am here!) and then I will stay in N. York until the end of the month. . . .

Kay talked to me, to invite me to eat today, but I could not go because I had a lunch with Dad and other people.[59] . . .

I am sure you know that as it turns out I am not going to Europe this year. I am delaying it until next year and hurray to the desire to travel! Grrr. No, it is much better, in every aspect, to leave it for '59, depending on how things go—not only will I go to Europe, but I will come back here, and, if Dad accepts the concerts they have offered him, I will hop over to no less than Japan! In any event what I have planned is to return to South America at the end of April—I do not know if I will do so, as I am always delaying the date of the trip—and accept Pitusa's invitation to stay a few days with her in Rio before continuing to Buenos Aires. (OK, cutie, now you are going to say: "After all, you are invited, blah, blah, blah.") . . .

Hey, if I do not go to Europe, my second choice is Montevideo!!! Of course! The only bad thing about this is that I am headed for another winter . . . and I tell you, María Rosa, I am shiv-er-ing with cold. As much as I love summer, swimming, the sun, etc., I have to have a third winter in a row, and I hate that terribly. But next year I am not moving until I have taken some good swims in the ocean, eh! Even if I have to go to China, I am not doing it until March or April, which is when spring starts in the northern hemisphere.

Many regards from Dad to all of you and lots of hugs from me. A big kiss for you from your

Bea

Another letter from Beatriz to María Rosa written four days later confirms the cancellation of the trip to Europe: "I am not going to Europe, definitely not. I will do it next year, and I think it is a lot better that way. I just hope it takes place and it does not stay 'in the hat' as has happened other times . . . but I will make it happen."

That same day Paquita wrote to María Rosa from Buenos Aires:

I received a letter from Beatriz. She always thinks about coming but she does not tell me the day. It is because of Dado!!![60] What a shame! She is not going to Europe because of that young man! Her father had promised to buy her an apartment in Madrid and put it in her name, but now he will not do it, it is clear. I am pretty annoyed by this girl's shortsightedness and somewhat for her unwillingness to break affectionate ties with a person with whom she will finally waste years, ending in a failure. It seems like she has had magnificent candidates there. Oh, well, I expect another period of suffering, given that from the time the children are born until one dies, one never stops having problems with them; when they are little, it is because there are illnesses, and when they grow up, it is because things are more important and parents cannot stay out of their business. You will see yourself from your own experiences.

Finally, a telegram from Segovia to Paquita, sent from New York on May 9, announced Beatriz's departure for Rio de Janeiro, informing her that their daughter would arrive the following day and that he had contacted Pitusa.

The idea of Paquita's returning to Montevideo to live close to her youngest daughter was taking shape during the second half of 1958. At the same time, they were finalizing those old plans stemming from María Rosa's idea of buying an apartment in Montevideo in Beatriz's name. More than ten years had passed since Paquita had moved to Buenos Aires, during which time Beatriz alternated between schools and long visits at the home of one or another of her sisters, punctuated by occasional stays with her mother in one of her various apartments in the Argentinean capital. Barely twenty-one, Beatriz would again have a stable place of her own in which to live. In the words of María Rosa:

That is how on October 1, 1958, Mama signed the agreement to buy the apartment at 3304 Gabriel Pereira on the corner of Benito Blanco in Beatriz's name. On December 3, 1958, the two came to live in Montevideo in an apartment at 1161 Coronel Alegre Street, until the one on Pereira would be ready. On October 15, 1959, they moved to the apartment on Pereira, and that was Mama's address until her death.[61]

Andrés Segovia traveled again to the Río de la Plata in May 1960, a few months after Beatriz and Paquita moved to Apartment 502 of the Zeus building on Pereira Street. He announced his travel plans to them in a telegram sent from New York on March 31 of that year and said that he would be playing in Buenos Aires and Montevideo from May 10 to 22, and that he was happy to be seeing them.

On Sunday, May 22— a day before leaving for Peru, Mexico, Colombia, and Puerto Rico—Segovia performed at the Studio Auditorium of SODRE with one of his customary three-part programs. The second section was devoted to his famous transcription of Bach's Chaconne. Two days before, Segovia had played a concert on television that was also broadcast on the radio. He had arrived in Montevideo that same day accompanied by Beatriz and Paquita, who had gone to Buenos Aires to meet him and attend his concerts in the Argentinean capital—on May 13 at Teatro Colón and on May 16 and 17 at Sala Broadway. During this visit, another trip to Europe for Beatriz was planned, and she left on June 28. The day Paquita turned sixty, on September 15, 1960, she received a telegram from Madrid from both Segovia and Beatriz affectionately wishing her a happy birthday with heaven's protection and kisses, and telling her that a gift would arrive soon.

Beatriz's second trip to Europe, when she was twenty-two, lasted more than six months, until January 1961. On January 5 she wrote to her mother from Barcelona, where she had gone for the first time to visit the Madriguera family:

Dearest Mama,

Here I am! Living with Aunt Mercedes, Aunt Maruja, Mamá Paqui, Carmencita, and Frankie! I arrived last night from Madrid, and I am already thrilled with everyone, because they are the best, kindest, and friendliest people there are. What Mamá Paqui says is a lot of nonsense because I am right at home with them and they are taking great care of me.

It occurs to me that while I am away from Madrid I will get a letter from you, because I do not think that I ever received an answer to the one I sent you on my return from Paris. Do not write to me here, because I will be leaving on the 14th, and on the 16th the plane leaves for Rio. The time is getting close, and the farewells are beginning. Last night, as a rehearsal, twenty-three boys and girls went to the airport—and what a rehearsal! These things always leave an impression on me. It looked like some government official was going to Mongolia, and not a girl who, after a flight of an hour and twenty-five minutes, was landing again on Spanish soil! In short, they are a delight. Tito Bertrán de Lis wants to come see me in Barcelona and spent Saturday, Sunday, and Monday trying to convince me not to go.... I have already told him that he will not be able to, but he insists.

How were Christmas and New Year's? We ate with the Quintanas [on Christmas Eve], then went for a little while to the Russells' home, and then the grownups went to bed and the young ones stayed at Primitivo's home (not only the Quintanas but about 800 more) until 6:30 A.M., an hour we thought was decent enough to go have some hot chocolate with *churros*.[62] Then we went to bed at 8:00 A.M. On New Year's Eve we went to the home of one of the kids of the group, named César Foxá, and all records were broken there, because we got home at 9:45 A.M. On January 1, I inaugurated Dad's apartment by giving a big party (we had to rent chairs, glasses, plates, and silverware), and I have continued from party to party—going to bed very late until yesterday, when I started a more normal life.

Before I forget: I want to tell you that I have already sent two suitcases by ship. They will leave on the 12th, I think, and I will probably be there by the time they arrive; but just in case I will send you the information. More news: I have changed my Iberia ticket—with all my respect for the worthy Spanish airline—for one with BOAC that will take me in a powerful Boeing 707 and save me an endless number of flight hours.[63]

How are the girls? Have they already gone to Punta del Este? I imagine this summer you will miss a little of all that; but maybe you can make a getaway.

Well, Mutter, I think this is enough for today. Until the next one. Many regards for everyone and a big kiss from your

Bea

P.S. I have already given Mamá Paqui the 500 pesetas, and she was thrilled. I also brought her 1,000 from dad, as well as 500 for each aunt.

Andrés Segovia recalled those months Beatriz spent in Madrid:

You cannot imagine how high society welcomed her when she was here in Madrid, at the home of Primitivo de Quintana, with whom we bonded in great friendship. And the same thing happened with Castroviejo, before he separated from his wife in New York. They all wanted to be with her because everyone took a liking to her right away. You do not know how much they liked her.... We went everywhere together, and all my friends in Paris, London, America, vied to be with her. Poor girl, I really suffered with her death.[64]

When Beatriz left for Montevideo on January 16, 1961, via Rio de Janeiro, Segovia was already in New York. Not having heard from his daughter, he sent a telegram on January 20 addressed to "Madriguera Segovia" at the apartment on Pereira Street, saying that he was restless and irritated because of the lack of news from Beatriz, who had traveled from Madrid to Rio. He begged Paquita to send a telegram to Hurok's bureau at Fifth Avenue, and he finished by saying that he would be sending a letter with a check.

Beatriz was about to turn twenty-four at the end of May 1962, when Segovia came back to Montevideo. His concert at SODRE (the first guitar concert ever for this author) took place on May 31. During that time Segovia gave an interview to the press at Paquita and Beatriz's apartment on Pereira Street and even received guitarists who wanted to play for him. The interview mentioned in chapter 3, which appeared in the June 6 edition of the weekly *Mundo Uruguayo* accompanied by several photos showing Don Andrés in the living room of the apartment, dates from that occasion.

Andrés Segovia in the Montevideo home of Paquita and Beatriz, 1962.

When he left the Uruguayan capital in early June 1962, Andrés Segovia could never have imagined that in his remaining twenty-five years he would return only two more times—in August 1967 and again in August 1979. He returned to Europe after his 1962 South American tour and married one of his students, Emilia Corral Sancho, on August 23 in Gibraltar.[65]

The last part of 1962 and the first half of the next year marked a radical change in the life of Beatriz Segovia. Sometime after her father's last visit she suffered a romantic disillusionment that led to an attempted suicide, an act that consequently provoked the final break of Beatriz's godfather, Aparicio Méndez, with Don Andrés. According to Sofía and María Rosa, Méndez had strongly urged Segovia to come and be at his daughter's side during that critical time while she was recovering in the hospital. When the guitarist declined on the grounds that he was in the middle of a concert tour, Méndez ended their friendship.

Some months later, Beatriz appeared to have recovered. While working at the Latin American Free Commerce Association, she became engaged to a young Swedish diplomat. On August 21, 1963, Beatriz married Lars Fagerström, the business manager of the Swedish embassy in Montevideo. The

Paquita flanked by Beatriz and Lars Fagerström on their wedding day.

society page in one newspaper announced the character of the rather intimate celebration:

> The wedding of Beatriz Segovia Madriguera and Lars Helge Fagerström, connected with the Embassy of Sweden, has taken place. This wedding brought together a group of family members and close friends. In the civil ceremony that took place at the residence of Paquita Madriguera, Dr. Aparicio Méndez—the Secretary of Public Health—and Walter Pérez Achard signed for the bride, while the Ambassador of Sweden, Gosta Hedengren Mc Indosh, signed for the groom. . . .
>
> To celebrate this event, a small reception was held at the home of Walter Pérez Achard and his wife, María Rosa Puig Madriguera.[66]

During a short period of time, the young couple lived in an apartment on the Republic of Peru Rambla (the section of the Rambla in Pocitos), and Beatriz started living the typical social life of diplomats. An article from the society page of the Montevideo newspaper *La Mañana* describes a reception given at her home to entertain Sweden's new ambassador to Uruguay. The photograph accompanying the article shows Beatriz with her husband, the Swedish ambassador, and the ambassador's wife; the caption reads: "Guest of honor, the Swedish ambassador, Dr. Ake Jonsson; the hostess, Beatriz Segovia de Fagerström; the ambassador's wife, Gunnel Sahlin de Jonsson; and the diplomatic host, Lars Helge Fagerström, business manager of Sweden, during the cocktail party given recently at the Fagerström apartment in Pocitos."

The reporter in charge of the society page refers to Beatriz and Paquita in the usual description of the attendees' dress:

> The very young and attractive hostess (daughter of the famous guitarist Andrés Segovia and the no less renowned pianist Paquita Madriguera) wore a natural silk lavender chiffon sprinkled with tiny polka dots draped in front with a triangle-shaped piece from waist to hem, with a loose flower of the same fabric here and there along the hem and a very low back. Paquita Madriguera, with her unique Spanish beauty, wore a white dress with large brown polka dots with a jabot of white organza and modern jewelry of diamonds and emeralds.

The Fagerströms did not live in Montevideo for long; Lars was assigned to Guatemala at the end of 1963. After settling in Central America, the young couple traveled to Spain on April 2, 1964, to visit Don Andrés in his new family environment, returning from Europe in mid-May to Guatemala. There is no documentation that would shed light on what Beatriz's life was like in that country beyond the normal routines of the diplomatic environment.

Paquita in April 1965.

Beatriz was not present in Montevideo on November 1, 1965, when Paquita died of heart failure. The pianist had an obstruction in one of her arteries and had undergone an operation in hopes of solving the problem, which had caused her constant fatigue. Sofía took her mother to her own home so that she herself could care for her after the operation, and she talked about the pianist's final days: "Mama did not feel well, she was not well, and I took her to my apartment, to my room, so that she would get better. She was there twenty days or a month, but she died—suddenly. It made a horrible impression on me, because she was with me, at my side, in bed. Everything stayed at her apartment. I never went in again."[67]

The press in Montevideo made reference to Paquita's death, and several newspapers published obituaries. One ran in *El País* on Wednesday, November 3:

Madrid, April 1964. *Left to right:* Unidentified woman, Segovia's third wife (Emilia Corral Sancho Segovia), Segovia, Beatriz, and Lars.

Paquita Madriguera: Her Death

We were surprised yesterday by the passing of the very fine lady and great artist that was Paquita Madriguera. She had beauty, elegance, and sympathy. It was impossible to know her and not be attracted by her combination of charms—all sweetness, goodness, and grace. Born to succeed, with triumphs all across the world's most famous stages and concert halls, she was considered one of the best interpreters of Granados. At home she offered her friends delightful and unforgettable hospitality. In recent times, she was surrounded by the love and care of her daughters. Her health was seriously threatened by a circulatory problem that caused her death in a few hours. A group of family, friends, and people from the artistic and press circles bade a very emotional farewell at the Central Cemetery yesterday to this superior woman, endowed so generously with musical aptitude and beautiful human gifts.

Murió Paquita Madriguera

PAQUITA MADRIGUERA

El Diario, November 3, 1965.

Beatriz Segovia Madriguera's father and sisters were far away when, on August 9, 1967, she ended her life in Guatemala. Some of the newspaper articles in Spain and in the Central American country reported the cause as "pneumonia with serious complications," others "heart attack." It bothered her sisters that the truth was never known. Beatriz had come to Montevideo a few months earlier and organized a series of gatherings of all the people with whom, for various reasons, she had been connected.[68] Nobody realized that she was saying goodbye. She had attempted suicide a few years earlier, and probably nobody in her immediate circle understood her cry of loneliness. On this second occasion, there was no warning—she planned it carefully and accomplished it efficiently. Two days later, Lars accompanied the embalmed body to Montevideo and, on August 12, complied with his wife's explicit wishes—to be buried alongside her mother in Montevideo's Central Cemetery.

Sofía: What is certain is that Beatriz committed suicide. And the people who know about it—who knows what stories they make up. I am going to explain how it happened. She had fallen in love with a young Uruguayan man who lived upstairs from where they lived, and he would not court her. And there she attempted suicide in Uruguay and survived. She seemed hopeless [in a coma], but she came out of it. One day I was doing all sorts of things so that she would come to, and suddenly she opened her eyes, "Why are you doing this to me, Sofi? Why did you save me?"

And I was so happy—and she cried and cried. And I knew it was because of that young man. Well, then some time passed, I do not remember how much—a year, a year and a half—she met Lars and married. But she had the same problem. There she relived everything. It is obvious that they did not get along very well, or she remembered [the Uruguayan]—who knows—and she committed suicide.

María Rosa: Beatriz's problem came from before that. That could have been what set her off. Whatever happened in Guatemala, we were never able to find out. After that first suicide attempt here in Montevideo, they put her in treatment. And the treatments back then were, well, they did electroshock. I accompanied her to the first electroshock treatment, and when they brought her out she said, "María Rosa, I don't know what they did to me and I don't want to know. But I beg you, please, don't ever let them do it again."

Sofía: Aparicio Méndez got very angry with Andrés and broke off his friendship with him after little Beatriz's first suicide attempt. She was in the hospital for about ten days, and Aparicio called him on the phone to tell him to come and be with his daughter; and [Andrés] told him that he could not come because he was in the middle of a concert tour. And Aparicio—who did not have any children—got angry, telling him, "But a daughter is a daughter."

María Rosa: When Andrés came in 1979 to give a charity concert in memory of little Beatriz and to get Mama's death certificate (because he had asked us to send it to him, and for several reasons we did not), Aparicio did not go to the concert, even though Andrés expected him to. He sent Dr. Artucio [in his place].[69] Aparicio was little Beatriz's godfather. He had been

Dad's partner in his law firm, and when Dad died he was the family lawyer. He was always very good to us.

Sofía: And in Guatemala she had it all figured out. Because before that, she came to Uruguay and was at the apartment with me. We had parties, farewells, who knows, who knows how much. We had fun, she was very happy in Uruguay. She called four groups of people—different for each of the four days—to celebrate. Then we would have gatherings with this group from school, that other group. But I did not realize it. It turns out that she bought the pills here in Uruguay, but we did not know anything. I found out later when she died, when Lars—the husband—told us. She had it all planned.

María Rosa: Andrés later got very angry with Lars,[70] but Beatriz's problem had deeper roots than that young man she had fallen in love with earlier, or whatever difficulties she might have had with Lars. It went back to her childhood, when Andrés left. It had much deeper roots. Andrés was, for Beatriz, an absent father.

The American guitarist Michael Lorimer was present when Segovia received the terrible news:

In the summer of 1967, I studied with Maestro Segovia at his home, Los Olivos, which was west of Almuñécar and overlooked La Herradura on the Mediterranean coast of the province of Granada. When Maestro Segovia received the news about Beatriz's death, he left immediately for South America. When he returned shortly thereafter, he was extremely sad. He told me that he had not touched the guitar—he couldn't. He asked me to sit with him in an area that looked onto the Mediterranean. He did not want to talk much, just stare out at the sea.

Later, in the early days of his wife's pregnancy, Maestro Segovia referred to the child she was carrying as "she"—and my sense was that the Maestro hoped that somehow the child to be born might be Beatriz returning. Of course, that child was not Beatriz, but his son Carlos Andrés, whom Maestro Segovia loved very much. Beatriz remained in the Maestro's thoughts, and her loss was a blow that I don't think Maestro Segovia ever got over; he carried that pain for the rest of his life.[71]

Portrait of Beatriz Segovia Madriguera made in Guatemala
in 1966 by the Catalonian painter Ramón Ávila.

On the morning of Tuesday, August 15, 1967, seventy-four-year-old
Andrés Segovia arrived in Montevideo. This time it was the father and not
the guitarist who returned. Despite the haste with which he had traveled from
his new home of Los Olivos, forty-five miles south of Granada, he was unable
to arrive in time for the funeral of his Uruguayan daughter.

Chapter 15

Epilogue—The Compass Continues Pointing South

A ndrés Segovia would not return to Montevideo after those tragic days of 1967 for twelve years, when he arrived for the last time to play a concert at the Teatro Solís in honor of his daughter Beatriz.[1] However, the city where she was born and is now buried continued to be for Don Andrés, until his final days, a place that attracted him with particular magnetism. We cannot know how his heart resonated during those hours in 1967 when, at some time during his brief stay in the Uruguayan capital, he went to the Central Cemetery and made his first visit to the place where Paquita was buried and, next to her, just hours earlier, Beatriz.[2] It is not improbable that during those moments he understood that the definite end of a long stage of his life, more than three decades, had come. Probably the happiest and most productive part of his life had vanished, mainly because of his own mistakes, and left in him strong and lasting traces. Perhaps he also felt that during this phase he had established other emotional bonds that were deeply rooted within him and would continue to have a profound meaning throughout his remaining years. It is also quite probable that Andrés Segovia had perceived just how much of that emotional life based in Montevideo had slipped through his fingers, almost without his fully enjoying it, absorbed as he had been by issues that at the moment he considered more important. What is certain is that in the last phase of his life, after establishing a new home in Spain and having become a father again at the age of seventy-seven, a part of him continued to look toward the city where the remains of Beatriz and Paquita lay, and where the pianist's other daughters—the stepdaughters that he met when they were children and whom he saw grow up, study, and become women—had their own children and grandchildren.

In a 1993 radio interview, Sofía Puig Madriguera responded to the interviewer's question about the permanence of those ties that she and her sisters had maintained with Segovia after he married for the third time:

> *Interviewer:* In the case of Don Andrés and his very affectionate relationship with you—did it terminate with [the end of] that marriage?
>
> *Sofía:* No. . . . He always wrote to us. He was always attentive when we traveled. We always went to Spain. He would meet us, look for us, he wanted to be with us. I tell you, even up to a little before his death—two or three months—he wrote to us saying that he wanted to return to that country, for us to go pick him up.[3]

During one of the many conversations this author had with the Puig Madriguera sisters, María Rosa commented:

> When we visited him in Madrid, he would talk about Montevideo. He loved to recall his life in Montevideo, and his young son begged him to tell more stories. Then he would talk about his horse Bicarbonato, who was a dapple. Each one of us had a horse, and we would go out in the countryside with him and Mama. Once I was in his Madrid studio, and in one of his desk drawers, quite visible when you opened it, there was an old photo. His wife said, "I do not know who that Russian family is."
>
> It was us—Mamá Paqui, [our great-grandmother] Yayita, my aunts, and the three of us. It is true that we looked like a Russian family. But it was us, and he had that picture there![4]

Segovia's visit to Montevideo in August 1967 was also an opportunity to repair many years of estrangement with Abel Carlevaro, when the Uruguayan guitarist went to the hotel of his former maestro to offer his condolences on the death of Beatriz. The story of this rupture has already been told,[5] but, most important, that sorrowful meeting began a relatively fluid exchange of letters between the two guitarists. In several of the letters sent to his former student, Don Andrés devoted some paragraphs to asking that Carlevaro act as a link with his stepdaughters from Montevideo when the irregular Uruguayan mail system hampered his contact with them. Reading those letters, it is clear that the communication problems with his loved ones in Montevideo caused Segovia anxiety. Some excerpts confirm Segovia's efforts to maintain the ties with those whom he still considered his stepdaughters:

Los Olivos, Province of Granada, September 3, 1968

If you read these lines, I beg you to call María Rosa Puig de Pérez Achard, telling her that I sent her a long letter at the beginning of the month with an important check to fulfill some orders of mine. I will try to write to her again through some friend who might be going from Buenos Aires to Montevideo.

Los Olivos, May 20, 1969

I have written to my stepdaughters several times and the only thing I have received is a telegram from one of them asking me why I was no longer writing, if I was ill; and one of my letters included a check in dollars as a gift for all their children. I ask therefore that you would be kind enough to call María Rosa ... telling her simply that ... I am restless, thinking of what might be wrong.

Los Olivos, May 27, 1969

I asked you in my previous one ... to do me the favor of calling María Rosa ... telling her that I have a handful of receipts of certified letters addressed to her, some with checks as gifts for her children and those of Sofía, and that I have not heard if she has received them.... Please tell her to write to this address.[6]

Los Olivos, June 15, 1969

Just in case that letter, like the others, is delayed, I ask you to call [María Rosa] one more time.

Reading the letters that Segovia sent his stepdaughters in Montevideo allows us to appreciate his concern for them, their children, and their grandchildren. They also show the retention of a certain complicity, the establishment of certain codes, that allowed them to maintain aspects of the relationship safe from interference and within the limits of trust and intimacy that were very much their own. These ties had been formed three decades earlier, following the upheaval in Barcelona that attended the outbreak of the Spanish Civil War, and perhaps from the time spent in Nervi, Italy, during the summer of 1936 in Europe. They continued during the years Segovia and the girls spent together in Montevideo and in the bringing to light of the events following the breakup of Don Andrés's marriage to Paquita. Segovia corresponded with María Rosa the most; a few of the most significant sections of his letters to her are given below.

A little less than a year after the death of Beatriz, on July 21, 1968, he said in a handwritten letter:

[This paragraph is underlined in red.] I am sending you a random amount—because I do not know if some thief will intercept this letter and cash or destroy the check—of $200 to help with your trip. But be careful. I will not be here until the beginning of September. . . .

[This paragraph is written in the margins of the first page.] Reassure me by telling me that you have received this letter, but make no explicit mention of the paragraph that I marked in red. In that way, you will let me know the check is in your hands.

Goodbye. Many big kisses from your
Andrés

The next letter from Segovia to María Rosa, also handwritten, is dated September 6, 1969 (some of the letters before this were typed from his dictation because of his vision problems): "I venture to send these lines so that I do not have to dictate them. Here is my little gift. To reassure me of its receipt, use the normal key—tell me how Sofía is doing. . . . Emilita or her Aunt Milagros reads my correspondence. You can answer this one, but . . . Kisses from Andrés."

María Rosa traveled to Spain in 1975 and visited Segovia at his home in Madrid. At that time he was finishing the first and only volume of memoirs he ever completed and published. She commented that something kept him from writing about the stage of his life that had to do with Montevideo:

> When I was in Madrid I would go to Andrés's penthouse study and help him a little with the end of the first volume of his biography and the beginning of the second one, which he never finished. When he got to the period where he had to write about Mama and Montevideo, something happened to him, and it was difficult for him to continue. In fact, I don't think he ever wrote it. My help was minimal because his secretary, Maribel Caldevilla, was very efficient. Andrés did not write all the time. . . . He had other activities, and the impression I got was that the biography had gotten to a difficult point and he needed time and consideration in order to write about it. I even thought that I was an obstacle, since I was part of it; but no, when I left he did not do it.[7]

The last chapter brought out the level of confidence that Don Andrés placed in the advice and suggestions of his youngest stepdaughter. The following information is from a letter that Segovia sent María Rosa shortly after her return to Montevideo from that 1975 visit, and dated January 15, 1976, from the Westbury Hotel in New York. Segovia recalled a conversation they had in his study, in which she had assured him that it would be possible to buy excellent properties in Uruguay, and even more in Argentina, with a rather small amount of European or American money. He said that he had no more friends to trust in the second country, but that in Uruguay he had one in her, and so he asked her to get specific information "regarding one of those bargains." In that case, he could risk a sum to purchase it, although not too high because of the "tremendous supplemental living expenses" which "Satan had sent" him in the form of "astronomical taxes" on Los Olivos because, not being used for several months of the year, it was considered to be a luxury residence: "I would make this purchase without any participation at all from Emilita, so that she would find herself, upon my death, with a surprise—land for Carlos Andrés in that country. . . . Are you coming back to Madrid or not? You know that, like the last time, our arms are open to you."

The letter that followed this, handwritten from Madrid, is dated April 20, 1976, and explains that the plan to buy land in Uruguay failed because a letter from María Rosa to Segovia had got to New York with delay. In the meantime, Segovia invested the sum he had in U.S. Savings Bonds and kept them in his New York bank, in the name of his younger son, "so that he has them when he grows up." In any case, he told María Rosa, it didn't mean that he was no longer thinking of investing in Uruguay, but that he would have to wait until the following year, "when the North American tour throws some fresh money into my pocket." And finally, he added his special codes to María Rosa:

> I would like to know if you have finally cashed the check from Geneva. Respond to the last mentioned if the weather is good in Montevideo or if it is raining and windy. In the first case I will understand that everything is going well. In the second I will take immediate measures to find out the reason for the delay. . . .
>
> Nothing more than a big kiss for you and one for each one of your daughters, Andrés

On January 12, 1977, again from the Westbury Hotel in New York, Segovia wrote to María Rosa by hand, and, after a few comments about the recent publishing of the first part of his autobiography and the promise of sending her a copy, he mentioned the enclosure of some checks and said: "I am sending a little gift for you and the girls and another one for Sofía and hers—the ones that are still single. . . . I am sending Pitusa another one directly. Let me know if you receive them. All this is confidential, as you know."

In September of that year from Madrid, Segovia sent his stepdaughter another handwritten letter, in which he proposed a new code to acknowledge the receipt of the gifts to those whom he still considered his family in Montevideo. On this occasion he was sending a check as a present for the wedding of María Rosa's daughter, Soledad. After complaining as usual about the postal service and the government taxes on his different properties—Los Olivos, the two cars, the Concha Espina apartment, "and even the garage and the houses and apartments in Navacerrada"[8]—he finished with, "Well, when you write, do not mention the check. Simply say that you have received my letter sealed, since the Spanish or Uruguayan postal service usually opens it. Goodbye. Kisses from Andrés."

In August 1979, Andrés Segovia went to Montevideo for the last time, accompanied by his third wife and his youngest son, Carlos Andrés, who was close to nine years old. For this event, the government de facto, headed by Beatriz's godfather Aparicio Méndez, declared Segovia the official guest of Uruguay. The beginning of chapter 3 referred to his concert, sponsored by the Department of Education and Culture at Montevideo's main stage of the Teatro Solís, and described how discomforted the guitarist was by the absence of Méndez from the president's box. In a letter to María Rosa, after he and his family had returned to Spain, Segovia specifically mentioned his feelings about that snub. Also, several passages show that Segovia had been with his stepdaughters in Buenos Aires and that Sofía had accompanied him to Chile. After thanking María Rosa for the kind news she had sent about Segovia's brief stay in Montevideo, he wrote:

Segovia's last trip to Montevideo. Photo taken on August 13, 1979, shortly before he left for Buenos Aires, and published the next day in *Mundocolor*.

> It is a shame you could not come along with Sofía to accompany us to Chile, thus extending our reunion in Buenos Aires, since we were unable to do it in Montevideo.... In regards to His Excellency, the president, it is best that I hold back my thoughts, in their graphic expression. It was a disappointment—if expected, felt.

In May 1983, having just turned ninety, Don Andrés was still showing Paquita's daughters his affection—in his special way of sending small sums of money, for which he continued to recommend special and discreet codes—and was also using indirect mentions of his anxiety to see them and hear any news about them. The letter he wrote from Madrid to María Rosa on May 24, on letterhead stationery with his title, the Marquis of Salobreña,[9] is illustrative in that respect. A few days earlier the king and queen of Spain had visited Montevideo, and Spanish television had been showing news filmed in the Uruguayan capital, which stirred with new winds of hope that the dictatorial clouds would be scattered. Don Andrés was unable to deny his magnetic attraction for the city's images, as he admits in the message. Those brief television reports, showing the streets that he had once traveled so widely, captured his attention and sharpened his eyes in search of familiar faces in the crowd. After informing her that he had received his eleventh honorary doctorate, this one from the University of Cádiz, he told María Rosa that he was enclosing some checks, which he asked her to distribute to her sisters and keep the one that was for her. He recommended that she not mention those gifts in her answer but let him know they had arrived by putting a red dot on the margins of her letter, "so that this can be the confirmation that the modest gift has not been lost." Then comes the suggestive paragraph:

> I kept looking for the face of one of you three among the multitude... during the short time Spanish television showed the scene, and, if, instead of the short story, they had shown footage shot over several days, I would have repeated the actions of that Portuguese guy who was surprised to see the balcony of his house in a movie filmed in his town and went to watch it every day, just to see if his wife would appear on the balcony.

In ending, Segovia told María Rosa not to be surprised if the person who sent his letter was not he but his personal secretary. He explained to her that he did it that way because a lot of letters got returned.

One of the last letters Don Andrés sent to Montevideo, a year before his death, inspires some final thoughts. In just two paragraphs of the first page, someone familiar with the life of Segovia can easily perceive a surprising contrast that links the reader to the reason for this book. On June 26, 1986, Andrés Segovia wrote to María Rosa, and at the beginning of the letter he said, "Your letter has moved me because of the accumulation of memories that began in Nervi and concluded in Los Olivos. You also write very well. You go straight to the narrative, and the short [digressions][10] complete the main idea without distracting from it." But in the next paragraph, and after referring to his statue in Linares, he spoke about "the very vast 'curriculum'" of his life, written by one of his "old friends and fellow countrymen." He told María Rosa about Alberto López Poveda and his huge task of accumulating reviews, articles, programs, photographs, and all kinds of things related to his artistic career. Segovia said that his life had been "catalogued by him with truly extraordinary effectiveness."

López Poveda's "very vast curriculum" of Segovia's life, which the guitarist sent to his stepdaughter with so many commendations about the exhaustiveness of the work, is a brief volume entitled *Andrés Segovia: Síntesis biográfica* (Biographical Synthesis) that contains almost no references to Don Andrés's period in Montevideo. This author was aware of the work on this biography of Segovia since at least 1971, because on February 4 of that year the maestro wrote to Abel Carlevaro, telling him that a man from Linares would write to him searching for information about Segovia's concerts in Montevideo, "going back to the earliest date possible." He told his former student that this man was writing a voluminous biography of him, an "enormous work," and for that reason was gathering information from all the countries in which Segovia had performed.

López Poveda had actually written to Carlevaro two days earlier, and the Uruguayan guitarist established a correspondence with him that supposedly resulted in the shipment of some of both Segovia's and Paquita Madriguera's concert programs. The dramatic contrast is more than striking between María Rosa's moving "accumulation of memories" (encompassing the couple's escape from Barcelona through Italy, the year in the United States, and the decade they shared in Montevideo) and the Linares biographical synthesis's reduction of the Uruguayan capital to a mere "provisional residence" from 1940 to 1943, with a brief reference to the premieres of the Castelnuovo-Tedesco and Ponce concertos.[11] Segovia's stay in Montevideo was minimized to the point that it never even mentioned his vast artistic activity with Paquita Madriguera during that long and richly productive period.[12]

It is hard to believe that Segovia even read his friend's work. And it is difficult to imagine that, even if the guitarist was familiar with its contents, he was satisfied with the treatment given in that brief sketch of his years in Montevideo. How could Don Andrés be moved by the memories of María Rosa (in his letter of June 26, 1986) and at the same time recommend the reading of a biographical review that systematically and almost completely ignored all those facts? To understand that flagrant contradiction, it must be kept in mind that the letter was written ten years after the publication of the only volume of Segovia's autobiography, as well as his failed attempt to undertake the task of writing about his life in Montevideo—which was associated with Paquita's relationship, Beatriz's existence, and the strong and long-lasting ties with his Uruguayan stepdaughters.

If it was so difficult for Segovia to recount that part of his life that it impeded the progress of his autobiography beyond 1921, it is not unreasonable to suppose that neither did he want someone else to take charge of recounting a story so deeply marked with happy times as well as the most dramatic events, which continued to have a deep impact upon him emotionally.

Sofía Puig once provided another important factor behind the shadow cones that appear in all biographical reviews of Segovia written to date. In his 1993 radio interview, Ramón Mérica questioned her about how much was known in Spain about Segovia and Paquita's life in Montevideo:

Mérica: In Spain, do they know about these eleven years in Uruguay,[13] whether it was a fruitful stage or not?

Sofía: No. For reasons that go beyond reality and desire, in Spain there is a sort of block, a shield of silence about what Andrés lived, did, and had here. When I was in Spain I saw that nobody knew he had been married to Paquita Madriguera, for whom, on the other hand, they were at the same time preparing a museum in Barcelona.

Mérica: For Paquita?

Sofía: Yes. Back then all those things were somewhat directed so that nobody knew about them or would not be told, for family reasons.

Mérica: Jealousy, right? From his last wife [Emilita]?

Sofía: Yes. That hurt me, but, of course, I understand that there would be jealousy. But well, Mama was a very different person.

Mérica: Yes, I have seen your photo albums, your folder. She was a very pretty woman and also, let's say, with an impressive career. Not everyone can say that they have rooms in the museums.

Sofía: And they also named a street after her in Igualada.[14]

It is not the purpose here to unravel the reasons for these silences, omissions, or concealments, but rather to spell out for the twentieth-century history of the guitar the information provided in this work. For that reason, a very important part of the artistic career and personal life of one of the most relevant musical figures of that epoch is now available to the public that held Don Andrés Segovia in such esteem and to the many followers around the world of the instrument that he helped develop and disseminate, and for which he gained deserved admiration and respect.

In light of this information, one can well imagine the burden of memories awakened in the old maestro by just hearing the word emerging from the crowd of admirers on the London afternoon that opened these accounts— *Montevideo,* the magical key that dissipated the fatigue and boredom and drove him to fulfill the request of a young tourist from Uruguay. It can now be understood why, in contrast to the aforementioned gaps in the official Segovia historiography, the heart of Don Andrés was still facing, with so much affection, south toward Montevideo, where, in many respects, he had grown both artistically and as a person in the context of his emotional and professional relationship with the great artist who was Paquita Madriguera. The sentimental link that enriched him spiritually, produced valuable fruits, and left in him and the environment clear traces of its existence is the central key in understanding those Montevideo years of the man and the guitarist.

Andrés Segovia Torres died at his home in Madrid on Tuesday, June 2, 1987, at the age of ninety-four. The funeral was held nine days later, and the three Puig Madriguera women traveled to Madrid to be present and say farewell to Don Andrés. He had returned home five weeks earlier from an extensive tour in the United States that he had had to cut short in April due to a serious deterioration in his health.[15] He was admitted to Cabrini Hospital in New York City on April 8 and remained hospitalized for twelve days, some of which he spent in the cardiac care unit. Upon his release, he almost immediately began to look to the south. From the Westbury Hotel, he wrote what would be his last letter to Montevideo, to Paquita's three daughters—the sisters and "little mothers" of Beatriz, and the stepdaughters that had been part of his life for more than a half century. Addressing them as "My very dear Pitusa, Sofía and María Rosa," he told them that he had been ill in that "immense city," but had improved quite a bit. He had to cancel four important concerts, and he and his family would leave the following day for Madrid. He would not move from there for several months, and for that reason the Puig sisters could write to him at his house. And he ended his last message to them with, "Hugs and kisses from me for the three of you from your Andrés. April 27, 1987, New York."

Chronology

1917: September—Paquita and her mother leave for Paquita's third tour of the United States.

1918: March: Paquita and Mamá Paqui return to Spain.

1919: January 26—Segovia gives a concert at Granados Hall in Barcelona, where he meets Paquita for the first time.

February–August—Paquita's fourth tour of America.

December 24—Paquita leaves for her fifth tour of America.

1920: May—Segovia leaves for South America and his first concert tour outside of Spain. His Buenos Aires debut is on June 4, and a week later he debuts in Montevideo.

December 23—Andrés Segovia marries Adelaida Portillo.

1921: May—Segovia returns to the Río de la Plata area, accompanied by Adelaida, who is expecting their first child.

June—Paquita is in Argentina, giving concerts in Buenos Aires and the provinces.

September 25—Andrés Segovia Portillo is born in Buenos Aires.

September–October—Paquita travels to Montevideo to play concerts. She is invited by members of the Puig family to stay at their home, where she meets Arturo Puig.

October, Buenos Aires—First meeting between Segovia and Barrios and the second meeting between Segovia and Paquita, who cross paths by chance in a hallway at Teatro Odeón.

1922: April 27—Paquita Madriguera marries Arturo Puig in Montevideo.

1923: Segovia gives concerts in Cuba and Mexico and has his first meeting with Manuel Ponce.

June 1—Paquita's first daughter, Paquita Puig Madriguera (nicknamed Pitusa), is born in Montevideo.

1924: April 7—Segovia's first concert in Paris, considered his debut before "the great musical world" of the time.

November 14—Leonardo Segovia Portillo, Segovia's second child with Adelaida, is born in Geneva, Switzerland.

1925: December 12—Sofía Puig Madriguera, Paquita's second daughter, is born in Montevideo.

1926: March—Segovia's first tour of the Soviet Union.

1927: Segovia's first recordings for the Gramophone Company (His Master's Voice), London.

August 24—Paquita's third daughter, María Rosa Puig Madriguera, is born in Montevideo.

1928: January 8—Segovia's New York debut at Town Hall.

March—Segovia, Adelaida, and their two children settle in Geneva, Switzerland.

July–August—Segovia's third tour of the Río de la Plata. Paquita attends his concerts at the Teatro Solís in Montevideo.

1931: September 3—Arturo Puig dies in Montevideo.

1932: Paquita returns to Barcelona with her three daughters near the end of the year.

1933: Paquita performs with the Philharmonic Society of Barcelona, her first formal concert since her marriage.

November—Segovia's third meeting with Paquita Madriguera, in Barcelona, quickly sparks a romantic relationship between them.

1934: April: Paquita performs with the Pablo Casals Orchestra in Barcelona.

June—Segovia's concert tour of Latin America, from Mexico to the Río de la Plata area, accompanied by Paquita, with Montevideo concerts on August 22 and September 7.

1935: October 20—Salvador de Madariaga visits Paquita and Segovia in Barcelona.

October 26—Andrés Segovia and Paquita Madriguera marry in Barcelona.

1936: February–June—Segovia's tours of the United States, Italy, and the Soviet Union, accompanied by Paquita.

July 18—The Spanish Civil War begins.

July 31—Segovia, Paquita, and her three daughters flee to Genoa, Italy, under the protection of the girls' Uruguayan nationality.

August–October—Segovia, Paquita and the three girls stay in Genoa and Nervi, Italy.

October 14—Paquita's daughters are sent to the United States, and Segovia begins a tour of Europe accompanied by his wife.

1937: January—Segovia and Paquita arrive in New York and depart from Miami for Colombia on March 31.

April—Segovia's concerts in Brazil.

April 23—Segovia meets with Villa-Lobos.

April 30—Segovia and Paquita arrive in Montevideo and settle at the Parque Hotel.

July 2—The Segovia-Madriguera couple settles in an apartment in the Lapido Building in downtown Montevideo.

July 6—The three Puig Madriguera girls arrive from the United States.

September 23—Segovia and Paquita leave by ship for Europe.

October 21—Leonardo Segovia Portillo dies in an accident in Geneva.

1938: January 21—Paquita, pregnant with Beatriz, returns to Montevideo from Europe while Segovia leaves for the United States to begin a tour there.

April 18—Segovia returns to Montevideo.

June 5—Beatriz Segovia Madriguera is born in Montevideo.

September—Segovia leaves for a tour of Europe while Paquita recovers from an operation.

October—Paquita joins Segovia on tour in Europe.

1939: February—After receiving notice that his American tour has been canceled, Segovia and Paquita return from London to Montevideo.

April 1—The Spanish Civil War ends.

September 1—World War II begins.

Enrique Madriguera Haase (Paquita's father) dies in Barcelona at age seventy.

October 28—Segovia premieres Castelnuovo-Tedesco's Concerto in D in Montevideo with the SODRE Symphony Orchestra, conducted by Lamberto Baldi.

1940: January 7–March 14—Segovia's tour, alone, through Central America, the Caribbean, and Peru.

May 31—The Segovia-Madriguera family settles in the house on Ramón Massini Street.

October—Villa-Lobos meets several times with Segovia in Montevideo.

1941: August 15—Segovia and Paquita play the Castelnuovo-Tedesco Concerto in D in Buenos Aires.

August 27—Manuel Ponce arrives in Montevideo, staying at the Massini Street home.

October 4—Premiere of the *Concierto del sur* in the Studio Auditorium of SODRE.

October 11—Paquita plays the Ponce Piano Concerto with the SODRE Symphony Orchestra, conducted by the composer.

1942: February–April—Segovia plays concerts in Chile, Brazil, and Argentina.

July—Paquita tours southern Brazil.

October—Segovia and Paquita give concerts in Tucumán, Argentina.

1943: April–May—Segovia and Paquita give concerts in Chile.

September 3—Segovia leaves alone for a tour of America, his first since 1938.

November—Segovia has his first contact with Olga Praguer Coelho. Paquita gives solo recitals and concerts with orchestra in Peru and Ecuador.

December—Paquita gives concerts in Cuba.

December 24—Paquita arrives in Mexico and stays at the home of Manuel Ponce.

1944: February 11—Segovia arrives in Mexico to meet Paquita.

February 21—Segovia plays the Mexican premiere of Ponce's *Concierto del sur* in the Palacio de Bellas Artes in Mexico City, with the orchestra conducted by Erich Kleiber.

March–May—Paquita and Segovia give concerts in several Central and South American countries, at times performing together onstage.

May 23—Segovia and Paquita return to Montevideo.

July 24—Segovia and Paquita give a concert together at the Teatro Odeón, Buenos Aires.

August 25—The marriage crisis begins when Paquita discovers her husband's infidelity with Olga Coelho.

December 12—Segovia leaves alone for a concert tour of North America.

1945: April 26—Segovia returns to Montevideo after spending a week with Paquita in Buenos Aires. The remainder of the year is one of meetings and disagreements.

1946: October 11—Paquita Madriguera and Andrés Segovia give their last concert together, at the Studio Auditorium of SODRE.

November 12—Paquita files for divorce in a Montevideo court.

1947: Paquita writes and publishes her book *Visto y oído* in Buenos Aires.

1948: The divorce becomes final, and Segovia removes his belongings from the Massini Street home.

1949: Paquita Madriguera sells the house on Massini Street and moves to Buenos Aires with Beatriz.

1950: July 25–August 8—Segovia visits Beatriz and Paquita in Buenos Aires.

1952: June—Segovia comes to Montevideo for Beatriz's fourteenth birthday.

1953: April 28—Segovia returns to play a concert in Montevideo.

October 26—Paquita Madriguera travels to Barcelona to give concerts and visit her family.

1954: January 15—Paquita returns to Montevideo.

1955:   May–July—Beatriz travels to Europe at the invitation of her father.

1957:   June–July—Segovia gives concerts in Argentina and in Montevideo. He shares several weeks in Buenos Aires with Beatriz and Paquita.

1958:   January–May—Beatriz travels to the United States to be with her father.

1960:   May—Segovia visits the Río de la Plata region and sets up another trip to Europe for Beatriz.

      June–mid-January 1961—Beatriz travels to Europe at the invitation of her father.

1962:   May–June—Segovia is in the Río de la Plata area for concerts in Buenos Aires and Montevideo.

      August 23—Andrés Segovia marries Emilia Corral Sancho in Gibraltar.

      Beatriz attempts suicide after a romantic disillusionment.

1963:   August 21—Beatriz Segovia Madriguera marries the Swedish diplomat Lars Fagerström in Montevideo.

1964:   Beatriz and Lars settle in Guatemala after his assignment there.

1965:   November 1—Paquita Madriguera dies in Montevideo at age sixty-five.

1967:   August 9—Beatriz Segovia takes her own life in Guatemala at age twenty-nine.

      August 12—Beatriz is buried in Montevideo, next to her mother in the Central Cemetery.

1970:   May 22—Carlos Andrés Segovia Corral is born in London.

      July 19—Francisca Rodón Canudas (Mamá Paqui) dies in Barcelona at age ninety-one.

1973:   Enric Madriguera, Paquita's brother, dies in Danbury, Connecticut, at age seventy-one.

1979:   August 12—Segovia's final concert in Montevideo.

1980:   October 6—Adelaida Portillo dies in Paris at age eighty-six.

1981:   June 24—Andrés Segovia is ennobled as the marquis of Salobreña by the king of Spain.

1987:   June 2—Andrés Segovia dies in Madrid at age ninety-four.

1996:   June 30—Andrés Segovia Portillo dies in Paris at age seventy-four.

2001:   July 10—Pitusa Puig Madriguera dies in Punta del Este, Uruguay at age seventy-eight.

2008:   February 25—Olga Praguer Coelho dies in Rio de Janeiro at age ninety-eight.

Notes

Chapter 1. Prelude in London

1. On January 3, 2007, in his home in Montevideo, the intended recipient of the autograph, the Uruguayan guitarist Carlos Álvarez, personally related to the author the details of this anecdote, which features his friend and countryman, the architect Fernando Fabiano.

Chapter 2. Information, Slightly Out of Tune

1. For an exception see Pinnell, "Segovia in Exile." His effort is plausible, and his work contains a blend of facts and errors that will be corrected later.
2. Usillos, 30.
3. Ibid. SODRE stands for Servicio Oficial de Difusión Radio-Electrica (Official Service for the Transmission of Electric Radio) and is the Uruguayan state broadcasting service. Its purview has been updated to include television and special shows, and the same acronym now stands for Servicio Oficial de Difusión Radiotelevisión y Espectáculos (Official Service for the Transmission of Radio, Television, and Special Shows).

Chapter 3. Resonances of a Past in Montevideo

1. Segovia's last previous performance in Montevideo was on May 31, 1962, at SODRE's Estudio Auditorio (Studio Auditorium). It was the first guitar concert ever attended by this author and, perhaps, his first strong inclination toward a serious study of the instrument.
2. "Dinámico Andrés Segovia dialoga con *Mundo Color* antes de partir" [Dynamic Andrés Segovia Talks with *Mundo Color* Before Departing], *Mundo Color* (Montevideo), August 14, 1979.
3. I am referring here to Aparicio Méndez (1904–1988), whose relationship with Segovia will be brought out later.

4. This story is from the Argentinean guitarist Néstor Ausqui, who at that time lived in Montevideo on a student scholarship.

5. The author has listened to the recorded version of the first part of the recital that the Spanish artist had performed a week earlier at Teatro Colón in Buenos Aires. The unevenness that seemed to be so evident in Montevideo cannot be perceived on this recording.

6. Santórsola was born in Italy in 1904, became a Uruguayan citizen in 1936, and died in Montevideo in 1994. A copy of the recording (which, according to those close to Santórsola, he had sent to Segovia at the hotel where he was staying) was found among the composer's personal papers.

7. Roberto Lagarmilla, "Andrés Segovia, grato e ilustre huésped" [Andrés Segovia, a Grateful and Distinguished Guest], *El Día* (Montevideo), August 12, 1979, 31.

8. Eduardo J. Couture (1904–1956), a well-known Uruguayan lawyer, was born the same year as Aparicio Méndez, who was also a lawyer and probably Couture's classmate.

9. There is a prelude composed by Segovia, No. 8 in a collection of the guitarist's preludes and studies published in 1997 by Bèrben of Italy. This composition has the title *Prelude on a Theme of Aparicio Méndez*. Segovia's dedication says, "To Aparicio (on one of his themes)" and is dated Montevideo, 1962.

10. Napoleón Cabrera, "Segovia no inventó la guitarra, pero . . ." [Segovia Didn't Invent the Guitar, But . . .], Espectáculo, *Clarín* (Buenos Aires), August 2, 1979, 1.

11. This was the apartment where Paquita Madriguera and her daughter Beatriz Segovia lived on 3304 Gabriel Pereira Street in the Pocitos neighborhood. It was bought by Segovia for his daughter and is where the Spanish pianist spent the last six years of her life.

12. Daniel M. Soto, "Con Segovia" [With Segovia], *Mundo Uruguayo*, June 6, 1962, n.p.

13. Daniel Stéfani, "Caballero quijotesco a lomos de su guitarra" [Quixotic Knight Riding on His Guitar], Supplement, *El Día* (Montevideo), August 23, 1981, 4.

14. In reality, the property legally belonged to Paquita (and her daughters), who had inherited it when her first husband died. Segovia was probably referring to the fact that he was the man of the house. It would have been more correct for him to say, "I had at my disposition a great property . . ." or "We had a great property. . . ."—*Trans.*

15. Julia Rodríguez Larreta, "Cuerdas para rato: Entrevista a Andrés Segovia." [Strings Here to Stay: Interview with Andrés Segovia], Sunday ed., *El País* (Montevideo), July 25, 1976, 4.

16. "Ecos de un reportaje: Nos escribe desde España, Andrés Segovia" [Echos of a Report: Andrés Segovia Writes to Us from Spain], letter published in *El País* (Montevideo), September 8, 1976, 5.

17. Viglietti, 277. The visit to Segovia took place on May 13, 1937. Viglietti was mistaken as to the location of Segovia's apartment, surely owing to the passage of time.

18. The author has already analyzed the relationship between Segovia and this Uruguayan guitarist in *Abel Carlevaro: Un nuevo mundo en la guitarra*.

19. Viglietti, 257–58.

20. His father was Antonio Pereira Velazco, a well-known Uruguayan luthier.

21. Viglietti, 259.

22. A neighborhood on the east side of Montevideo and north of the beachside Malvín neighborhood.—*Trans.*

23. Florencio Vázquez, "El viejo pasaporte de Andrés Segovia apareció en un suburbio Montevideano" [Andrés Segovia's Old Passport Found in a Suburb of Montevideo], *El Día* (Montevideo), August 14, 1987, n.p.

24. The transcription of the interview comes from an unpublished compilation of media articles about Segovia, collected in December 1993 by José L. López Blanco.

Chapter 4. First Exposition of the Theme

1. Some elements included in the first part of chapter 3 of the author's *Abel Carlevaro: Un nuevo mundo en la guitarra* reflect the state of what had been investigated up to 2003, when the editing of that work was completed.

2. Pinnell, 2.

3. Alcázar, *The Segovia–Ponce Letters*, 164. A letter from New York in January or February 1937 will be analyzed later in detail.

4. Carlos Andrés Segovia, "Algunos datos y reflexiones."

5. Alcázar, *The Segovia–Ponce Letters*, 165.

6. Ibid., 186.

Chapter 5. Paquita

1. Francisca Rodón Canudas (known as Mamá Paqui), Paquita Madriguera's mother, was born in 1879 and died in 1970.

2. María Rosa Puig Madriguera, interview by the author at her home, November 23, 2007. In reality, the marriage of Enrique Madriguera and Francisca Rodón took place on October 4, 1899, when she was twenty years old.

3. He usually went by his Catalonian name, Enric Madriguera (b. Barcelona on February 17, 1902; d. Danbury, Connecticut, in 1973). A violinist and bandleader, he too, like his sister, began his career in childhood. He studied violin under Joan Manén in Barcelona and was already doing concert tours in the United States at the age of fourteen.

4. Sofía Puig Madriguera, interview by the author at the home of María Rosa Puig Madriguera, November 23, 2007.

5. María Rosa Puig Madriguera, interview by the author at her home, November 23, 2007.

6. Frank Marshall King (1883–1959) was born in Mataró, in the province of Barcelona. He came from a British family established in Catalonia that was linked to the textile industry. He was a student of Enrique Granados and in 1907 became the assistant director of piano studies at the Academia Granados; he was named director in 1916 following the death of his teacher. The institution changed its name to Academia Marshall in 1920, and from it emerged personalities of the caliber of the soprano Conchita Badía (1897–1975) and the pianist Alicia de Larrocha (1923–2009).

7. Enrique Granados Campiña, born in Lérida, Catalonia, Spain, in 1867, was a pianist, a composer, and one of the most representative exponents of Spanish musical nationalism. He founded the Academia Granados in Barcelona in 1901.

8. Paquita's first concert in the Palau de la Música took place on March 18, 1912, according to the notice published by the Barcelona magazine *Feminal* on March 31 of that year.

9. Torrellas, 703.

10. Madriguera, 10.

11. Ibid., 11–12.

12. Ibid., 87.

13. Ibid., 41–42.

14. Isabel Francisca de Asís de Borbón y Borbón (1851–1931) was the aunt of King Alfonso XIII (grandfather of the present King Juan Carlos de Borbón). Popularly known as "pug-nose" for her flat nose, she was in those days the most popular personality of the Spanish royal family. She was a good pianist and a fan of the popular fiestas, bullfights, and fairs.

15. Madriguera, 45–46. The second visit to Princess Isabel took place on June 8, 1914, as recorded in a note in the *Diario de Gerona*.

16. Ibid., 47–48. María Teresa de Borbón, sister of King Alfonso XIII, was born in 1882 and died on September 23, 1912. The private recital by Paquita took place on the morning of May 14, 1912. According to the Barcelona newspaper *La Vanguardia*: "This morning Juan and Clotilde Godó presented the notable pianist from Igualada, Francisca Madriguera, an eleven-year-old girl, to Princess María Teresa to perform her publicized concert in the presence of her highness and a gathering of distinguished aristocracy. The Madriguera girl played on the piano, with notable mastery, Rondo by Weber and the three compositions *Canción de cuna* (Cradle Song), *Boda India* (Indian Wedding), and *Un Walz* (A Waltz), whose composer is the precocious artist." *La Vanguardia* also stated, "That night Paquita gave a remarkable concert in the Sala Navas, after which she had to repeat numerous works due to thunderous applause." The program on that occasion included music by Chopin, Beethoven, Mendelssohn, and Albéniz.

17. Madriguera, 47.

18. Ibid., 77–78. Abd al-Hafid (1873–1937), also known as Muley Hafid, was the sultan of Morocco between 1908 and 1912. This description is evidence of the pianist's early racial prejudice (surely typical of the period), the social surroundings, and the type of education she received.

19. June 10, 1914, p. 6.

20. Carles Vidiella (1856–1915) was—along with Granados, Ricardo Viñes, and Joaquín Malats—among Catalonia's top pianists at the turn of the twentieth century.—*Trans.*

21. T. de Dafnis, "Paquita Madriguera," *Mediterrania* (Barcelona), February 15, 1915, 26–28.

22. Venezuelan pianist and composer, who was born in Caracas in 1856 and died in New York City on June 12, 1917.

23. On May 27 she also played a duo with her brother Enric at a fund-raiser. *La Vanguardia* relates all these facts in the corresponding editions.

24. By then she was already fifteen. Did Mama Paqui introduce her as being somewhat younger than she really was?

25. Madriguera, 91–93.

26. The report of this vicissitude makes up the chapter titled "El maestro Lambert" (Lambert the Teacher) in *Visto y oído*, 91–98.

27. "Programs of the Week," *New York Times*, January 30, 1916, n.p.

28. Madriguera, 19–20. In reality, Granados signed a contract with the Paris Opéra in June 1914 for the world premiere of *Goyescas*, but the outbreak of World War II a month later caused these plans to be postponed indefinitely. Granados then received an offer from New York, and in June 1915 Paris released him from the contract, with Granados promising them the eventual European premiere of his opera. For a full accounting of these negotiations, see Clark, chapter 9.—*Trans.*

29. Her name was Clotilde Godó Pelegrí (1885–1988), and Paquita describes the scene in *Visto y oído*, pp. 17–19. See the article by Milton, 2006. Paquita also mentioned Clotilde's name in an interview published on April 18, 1961, in *La Mañana* (Montevideo).

30. Madriguera, 20–21.

31. *Nana* in Catalan means "midget" or "dwarf." The affectionate nickname was probably bestowed on Paquita when Granados first met her as a little girl.

32. Ibid., 31.

33. Sagrada Familia (Holy Family) is the landmark, and unfinished, Barcelona cathedral designed by the Catalonian architect Antoni Gaudí (1852–1926). It is considered his masterpiece.—*Trans.*

34. Madriguera, 32, 36.

35. Clark, 163.

36. For a thorough account of this incident see *Papers Relating to the Torpedoing of the SS Sussex*, published and distributed by the U.S. Department of State on May 15, 1916.

A Cornell University copy is available online at http://www.archive.org/stream /cu31924032194031#page/n28/mode/1up.—*Trans.*

37. Concepción Badía Millás (born in Barcelona in 1897; died in the same city in 1975) was an outstanding Spanish soprano who had been a student of Granados during the years Paquita studied with him, meaning that their friendship went back to Paquita's childhood. She was also a pianist and had completed her education with Frank Marshall. Conchita Badía (her stage name) and her entire family fled to Argentina during the Spanish Civil War, but she returned to her country in 1947. She later dedicated herself to teaching; the soprano Montserrat Caballé was her most notable student.

38. Also on some occasions with Paquita's brother, Enric. There are some notes of a "Madriguera Concert" where all three performed—the pianist, the singer, and the violinist.

39. Anaïs Nin Culmell was born in 1903 in Neuilly, France, and died in 1977 in Los Angeles, California.

40. Joaquín Nin Culmell was born in Berlin in 1908 and died in Berkeley, California, in 2004.

41. Spanish writer, journalist, movie actor, and director (1883–1941) who was born in Madrid but lived for many years in the United States, where he died in Hollywood, California.

42. Zárraga, 14.

43. *The Great Female Pianists*, Masters of the Piano Roll Series, vol. 5 (Dal Segno, DSPRCD015, 1992). In the accompanying booklet, the pianist is called Paquita Madriguera Segovia, and her compositions are attributed to "Mme. Segovia." Those recordings were made almost twenty years before Paquita's marriage to Segovia, and when the digital version was produced it was more than thirty years after "Mme. Segovia" referred to a completely different person who had nothing to do with the pianist and composer. To locate and hear some of these recordings, search the internet under "Paquita Segovia."

44. Paquita refers to a "bottle-green jacket."

45. Madriguera, 26.

46. Mexican composer, born December 8, 1882; died April 24, 1948.

47. Madriguera, 29.

48. Ibid., 23.

49. Ibid., 23–24. According to Torrellas, the concert took place on February 9, 1917. Teresa Carreño actually died four months later, on June 17, at the age of sixty-three.

50. For example, on March 9, 1917, a program from New York's Aeolian Hall had a cover photo of both teenagers and announced: "Recital by Paquita Madriguera, pianist, assisted by Enrique Madriguera, violinist."

51. Madriguera, 63–64.

52. See also the guitarist's autobiography, *Segovia: An Autobiography of the Years 1893–1920*, 101.

53. This is the concert (and program illustration) referred to earlier in this chapter.—*Trans.*

54. Madriguera, 64–66.

55. The Granados-Marshall Association in Barcelona provided copies of these programs. It is also possible to find announcements of these concerts in the corresponding editions of *La Vanguardia*.

Chapter 6. Segovia

1. See chapter 20 of Segovia's autobiography. Llobet, about fifteen years older than Segovia, was then an important representative of the guitar and had already earned prestige as a concert artist and transcriber of works for the instrument.

2. The father of cellist Gaspar Cassadó (1897–1966), who would later become a good friend of both Segovia and Paquita for many years.

3. See the collection of Barcelona's *La Vanguardia* during those months, and also Mangado. Segovia has several inaccuracies in his autobiography that in some instances alter the order of the concerts.

4. Madriguera, 61–63.

5. Ibid., 67–68.

6. Though never specifically identified in any program, it is probably K. 330, transcribed by Francisco Tárrega in D major.—*Trans.*

7. Madriguera, 68–69.

8. *Segovia: An Autobiography*, 118–19.

9. María Antonia Iglesias, "Andrés Segovia," *Los Españoles* (Madrid) 23, March 8, 1973, n.p.

10. Ernesto de Quesada was born in 1886 in Cuba, still a Spanish colony, and in 1908, ten years before this encounter, he founded his concert agency in Madrid.

11. *Segovia: An Autobiography*, 130–31.

12. Ibid., 156. Quesada brought Arthur Rubinstein to Montevideo and Buenos Aires in 1917 for the pianist's first South American experience.

13. Ibid., 157.

14. Ibid., 198.

15. Located on a street today called Héctor Gutiérrez Ruiz, a few meters from the Plaza de Cagancha, and which later became the Radio City Movie Theater. The "inauguration" that took place in June 1921 was really only a name change: the hall had been called Teatro Catalunya up to then.

16. *El País* (Montevideo), June 26, 1921, 4.

17. Andrés Segovia Portillo (1921–1996) dedicated his life to painting and lived in Paris after 1951.

18. Madriguera, 70. This last note by Paquita implies that the encounter "in the hallway of Teatro Odeón" is on the occasion of a concert not by Segovia or the pianist, but by another artist also brought to Buenos Aires by Quesada. Perhaps Rubinstein, Cassadó, Ninon Vallin—or someone else?

19. The phrase "eleven years" might lead us to believe that this dialogue took place at the beginning of 1933 (given that the previous encounter was at the end of 1921). But other clues indicate that this new encounter took place around November 1933, and that twelve years had passed from the fleeting crossing of their paths at the Teatro Odeón in Buenos Aires. If that is so, one has to accept that Segovia was often wrong when doing arithmetic on the fly. In a 1940 letter to Ponce, for example, he also makes a notorious error in the number of works that Villa-Lobos had taken to him.

20. Madriguera, 74.

21. Barrios's letter comes from the archives of Borda y Pagola; and it was published in its entirety in Amaro, *Agustín Barrios: Patrimonio de América*, 90–92.

22. López Poveda, *Andrés Segovia: Vida y obra*, 1:167–68.

23. John Williams was actually eighteen at the time: he was born in Australia on April 24, 1941, and the Santiago de Compostela classes were held in the summer of 1959.

24. Godoy and Szarán, 44–47.

25. There are authors who speak of a second meeting in 1944 in El Salvador, a few months before the death of Barrios on August 7. We know that Segovia gave a concert in the Salvadoran capital, where Barrios lived, around March 20 of that year (discussed in chapter 12), but this author does not have the documentation to verify the alleged encounter. It is striking to note that when Segovia talked about Barrios in Santiago de Compostela in 1959, he mentioned the meeting in 1921, but not a later one.

26. The father of guitarist María Luisa Anido (1907–1996). She made her debut in 1918, at the age of eleven, with a full concert in La Argentina, where Segovia would give a concert two years later.

27. Guarnido, 160–63.

28. Persia, 49.

29. Leonardo Segovia Portillo (1924–1937) was born when Segovia was about to perform in Munich. He was given the news by the Spanish consulate there upon his arrival at the train station.

30. German luthier (1882–1952). Andrés Segovia played guitars built by him for many years.

31. Horn, 17–19.

32. Alcázar, *The Segovia–Ponce Letters*, 21.

33. Ibíd., 27.

34. It is not identified by number in the program, but its three movements are named: "Allegro," "Canción," and "Rondo."

35. Madriguera, 72–73.

Chapter 7. Paquita in Montevideo

1. The political figure who marked that period and provided its name was José Batlle y Ordóñez (1856–1929), who served two separate terms as president of the republic, 1903–7 and 1911–15.

2. Nahum, 105. The historian adds on the same page: "Slowly, the habits and ideas of the middle-class Uruguayans came to be integrated with the democratic process. . . . A tradition of democracy and political tolerance grew and blended with the people's idiosyncrasies until it became a major source of national pride."

3. Caetano and Rilla, 140.

4. Ibid.

5. The central Colorado (Red) Party was founded in 1836—uniting conservative, moderate, and social democratic groups—and over the years it has been the dominant party in Uruguay. Its political rival is the right-wing conservative National (White) Party, founded in the same year.—*Trans.*

6. Caetano and Rilla, 138.

7. This is how it is stated in the documentation that his daughter María Rosa found in the Cathedral of Montevideo, although his and Paquita's marriage license gives the year of his birth as 1882.

8. Uruguay is divided into nineteen departments (like states, counties, or provinces in other countries). This department is named in honor of the thirty-three nineteenth-century patriots who initiated the Uruguayan War of Independence from the Portuguese Empire, which controlled it in 1825.—*Trans.*

9. Caetano and Rilla, 138.

10. A residential neighborhood of Montevideo located along the Playa de los Pocitos (Beach of the Little Wells), so named for the holes that were dug in the sand by the washerwomen who gathered there to perform their work.—*Trans.*

11. Letter from María Rosa Puig to the author, December 15, 2005.

12. A new joke of destiny? Andrés Segovia also participated in the inaugural season of the Teatro Albéniz, on June 26, 1921, as stated in the previous chapter.

13. A reference to José María Carretero Novillo (1890–1951), a Spanish writer and journalist who published creative and elaborate interviews of the most important personalities of the time under the pseudonym of "El Caballero Audaz."

14. *El País* (Montevideo), September 18, 1921, 4.

15. *El País* (Montevideo), September 26, 1921, 4.

16. An institution inspired by the ideals of Uruguayan essayist José Enrique Rodó (1871–1917), the center was founded in 1917 by Carlos Quijano (1900–1984), who, years later, was a figure of great political importance and a highly revered journalist.

17. Both houses were on the same square block in Pocitos. Dr. Puig's house was on José Martí Street, while his cousin's fronted on Alejandro Chucarro Street.

18. E-mail from María Rosa Puig to the author, December 13, 2005.

19. Referring to Andrés Segovia.

20. E-mail from María Rosa Puig to the author, December 13, 2007.

21. This concert took place on April 29, in the same Teatro Albéniz where Paquita had debuted seven months earlier.

22. The only information I have been able to find regarding a public performance by Paquita after her marriage says that on April 27, 1928, she participated in a cultural event for charity organized by a group of ladies headed by the wife of the president of Uruguay. On that occasion Paquita—slightly past twenty-seven years old and the mother of three girls—performed a piano duo with another society lady of Montevideo. *El País* reported the following day that Paquita Madriguera de Puig and Mary Bemporat de Hartig used their powerful technical resources in an excellent performance of the *Variations on a Theme of Chopin* by Mario Tarenghi, earning them a formidable ovation.

23. Sofía Puig Madriguera, interview by Ramón Mérica aired on November 23, 1993, on the program *En vivo y en directo*, Radio Sarandí (Montevideo).

24. Her full name was Paquita Josefa Monserrat Puig Madriguera, and she died on July 10, 2001 in Uruguay.

25. The Rambla (a Spanish term for a promenade street) is the boulevard that runs along the entire Montevideo waterfront.

26. E-mail message from María Rosa Puig to the author, November 14, 2008.

27. A famous bakery, located about three blocks from the Puig Madriguera's family home in Pocitos.

28. Referring to Aparicio Méndez, previously mentioned in chapter 3.

29. E-mail from María Rosa Puig to the author, December 12, 2007.

30. E-mail from María Rosa Puig to the author, June 20, 2006.

Chapter 8. Barcelona—Prelude, Fugue, and Marriage

1. The following passage comes from Madriguera, 73–75.

2. Manén, a violinist, conductor, and composer, was born in Barcelona in 1883 and died in that city in 1971. Like Paquita, he was a child prodigy, and in 1893 (the year Segovia was born), at the age of ten, he played in Montevideo's Teatro Solís. In 1930 he published his *Fantasía-Sonata* for guitar, dedicated "Para y por [Because of and for] Andrés Segovia." On November 24, 1933, Segovia presented this work to the

Barcelona public during his concert in the Palau de la Música. It is probable that this meeting with Paquita told took place around that date (perhaps a day or two before the concert).

3. Alcázar, *The Segovia–Ponce Letters*, 46.

4. Ibid., 111.

5. Ibid., 112.

6. Ibid.

7. Ibid.

8. Ibid., 116.

9. Ibid., 140. Clema de Ponce was the composer's wife, who had remained in Paris.

10. A popular Spanish tourist city about forty-five miles south of Barcelona on the Mediterranean coast.—*Trans.*

11. Alcázar, *The Segovia–Ponce Letters*, 143–44.

12. Ibid., 145.

13. Ibid., 146. The work would be called *Sonata (Omaggio a Boccherini)*, also at Segovia's suggestion.

14. E-mail from María Rosa Puig to the author, December 2, 2006.

15. Interview with the author, October 2005.

16. A popular Spanish saying meaning something is out of place—in this case, in a musician's home there is a girl who cannot sing.—*Trans.*

17. The Requetés were the militia of the Carlist movement in Spain seeking a separate line of the Bourbon family for succession to the throne; UGT stands for Unión General de Trabajadores (General Workers Union).—*Trans.*

18. The rules for the students who lived at the school were that they could go out on Sundays (if a relative picked them up). They could also live at the school during vacation periods.

19. E-mail from María Rosa Puig to the author, December 13, 2006.

20. "Música y Teatros" [Music and Theaters], *La Vanguardia* (Barcelona), January 29, 1933, 21.

21. "Paquita Madriguera–Manen," *La Vanguardia* (Barcelona), February 5, 1933, 21.

22. *La Vanguardia* (Barcelona), April 8, 1934, 22.

23. The sisters had already returned to Montevideo when they learned of his death.

24. Alcázar, *The Segovia–Ponce Letters*, 150.

25. Ibid., 151.

26. Ibid., 150.

27. Named after the Uruguayan First Constitution Day and the main avenue of central Montevideo.—*Trans.*

28. Italian baroque composer (1660–1725). This little mini-suite of two dances, Gavotta and Sarabanda, and an entire five-movement baroque Suite in A Minor, attributed for many years to the German baroque lutenist and composer Silvius Leopold Weiss (1687–1750), were composed by Ponce ("a la antigua" meaning "in the old style") for Segovia either as a musical joke or to expand Segovia's repertoire of older music. Segovia passed them off for many years as "authentic" baroque compositions by these two composers until the truth was finally revealed (or discovered) around 1970.—*Trans.*

29. In the first part he played works by Sor (identified on the program as *Variations on an Italian Theme*), Torroba (Sonatina), and Granados. In the second part he played Handel, Bach, Schubert, and Mendelssohn, and in the third, Turina (*Fandanguillo*) and Albéniz.

30. Alcázar, *The Segovia–Ponce Letters*, 152. It is interesting to note the recommendation that Ponce inform Clema about the "formal" aspects of Segovia's relationship with Paquita, of which it is quite probable that the composer's very Catholic wife did not approve.

31. Paquita is talking about Mischa Elman, the renowned violinist who was born in Kiev, Ukraine, in 1891. He became a naturalized citizen of the United States in 1923 and died in New York in 1967. In two chapters of her book, Paquita relates anecdotes about this musician, with whom she shared a lasting friendship.

32. This concert took place on February 24, 1935. The soloist, Jascha Heifetz, was born in Vilna, Lithuania (then part of Russia), in February 1901; he too had been a child prodigy. He became an American citizen in 1925 and died in Los Angeles in 1987.

33. Madriguera, 104.

34. Ibid., 101–2.

35. This letter, which begins on page 153 of Alcázar's book of letters and is numbered letter 86, is not dated accurately by the author (who puts it in February 1936). Paquita's diary states that she and Segovia left Barcelona on January 8, 1936, to travel to the United States, where they stayed until March 14. The letter had to have been written before the end of 1935, but after October 26 (their wedding date), although Segovia seems to indicate that it is still summer. Letter 90 is also incorrectly dated and not placed in chronological order with respect to the three letters that immediately precede it in the book: it was actually written on January 26, 1936, before letters 87 (dated March 22, 1936), 88 (dated May 19), and number 89 (dated the beginning of 1937).

36. F. C. Coppicus, an important New York performing artists' manager of the time.—*Trans.*

37. Segovia's mother's sister, who was a nun secluded in a convent. More will be told about her later.

38. When Segovia wrote this letter, he was already past forty-two and a half.

39. He is referring to the visit that the couple made to Ponce in June 1934.

40. Alcázar, *The Segovia–Ponce Letters*, 153–56.

41. Alcázar, *Obra completa para guitarra de Manuel M. Ponce*, 182.

42. Alcázar, *The Segovia–Ponce Letters*, 161.

43. A famous actress of Catalonian origin. She was born near Barcelona in 1888 and died in Montevideo in 1969. A naturalized Uruguayan, she played a major role in the development of the Comedia Nacional (National Comedy) and the Escuela Municipal de Arte Dramático (Municipal School of Dramatic Art) of Montevideo, which today bears her name. Paquita, Segovia, and Margarita Xirgú had several encounters in the Uruguayan capital, some of which will be discussed in this book.

44. Essayist, historian, and diplomat born in 1886 in La Coruña, Spain; he died in 1978 in Locarno, Switzerland. He was considered one of his country's most brilliant writers and intellectuals of the twentieth century.

45. Madriguera, 111–16. Madariaga's visit occurred on Sunday, October 20, 1935 (as reported by *La Vanguardia*), six days before Segovia and Paquita's wedding.

46. Carlos Andrés Segovia, "Algunos datos y reflexiones."

47. This information allows us to accurately date the letter to Ponce, numbered 90 in Miguel Alcázar's compilation.

48. Journalistic chronicles of the time reported that one reason Segovia and Paquita made the brief trip to Barcelona was so they could leave their jewelry and other valuables at their home (having been alerted that it would not be wise to take them to the Soviet Union). Ironically, the apartment on Septimania Street was broken into on May 24, as reported in *La Vanguardia* (Barcelona) and *Diario de Las Palmas* (Grand Canary Island), May 25, 1936.

49. One of the magazines is the German periodical *Gitarre & Laute* (Guitar & Lute). The articles allude to Segovia's tours in the Soviet Union, but its authors are not able to identify those accompanying the guitarist, who is surrounded by "intellectuals from Moscow," as one of the captions explains. The author of the article also speculates that the photo may have been taken in the 1930s. It is reproduced here to show that it was taken in 1936, with Paquita next to Segovia. If those who are behind Segovia and Paquita are guitarists from Moscow, the photo could have been taken on May 11; if they are writers, then the exact date could be May 24.

50. On May 15, Paquita writes in her diary that the play was *Los Aristócratas* (The Aristocrats).

51. Segovia, Paquita, both Russian composers (father and son), the violinist, and his Mexican wife (Luz Segura) sent a group postcard to Manuel Ponce; Julian (Yulian) Krein and Ponce had attended classes together with Paul Dukás in París. See more in Alcázar, *The Segovia–Ponce Letters*, 162.

52. Havana-born José Raúl Capablanca (1888–1942) was also considered a child prodigy, having begun to play chess by the age of four. Many experts consider him to have been the greatest chess player in history.

53. The city where the writer Aleksandr Solzhenitsyn was born.

54. In Alcázar's collection of correspondence this undated letter is number 89 (page 163 and following). It is possible to date it with certainty by keeping in mind a phrase Segovia uses ("I have just returned this morning from Boston") and Paquita's diary from 1937, which says on January 28, "7 AM, Andrés returns from Boston."

55. In an interview, Paquita's daughter Sofía spoke about one of the disagreements that led to Segovia's divorce: "Andrés had distanced himself from Adelaida because she had become interested in communism. She had even befriended that woman they called 'La Pasionaria' [The Passionflower]"—the nickname for Isidora Dolores Ibárruri Gómez (1895–1989), a communist politician and Republican leader of the Spanish Civil War who was famed for her fiery radio speeches in favor of communism and the Spanish Republic. After Franco's party took control of and finally won the Spanish Civil War, she went into exile to Russia, where she continued her broadcasts to Spain by short-wave radio. She was unable to return to Spain until 1977, two years after Franco's death.—*Trans.*

56. The funicular is a cable-operated railway used to go up and down the steep mountain to Montserrat, where the school was located, about thirty miles inland from Barcelona.—*Trans.*

Chapter 9. Intermezzo—From Italy to Montevideo, via Europe and America

1. *Segovia, An Autobiography*, 143–44.

2. Actually, José Sanjurjo y Sacanell (b. 1872) had died on July 20, 1936. He was one of the main leaders of the Nationalist movement and died in a plane crash while returning to Spain from exile in Portugal at the beginning of the Civil War.

3. Gonzalo Queipo de Llano y Sierra (1875–1951) was a longtime military officer in the Spanish Army and a general in the Civil War's victorious Nationalist Army under Franco. He also did propaganda broadcasts for the Nationalists during the war.—*Trans.*

4. María Antonia Iglesias, "Andrés Segovia," *Los Españoles* (Madrid) 23, March 8, 1973, n.p.

5. Alcázar, *The Segovia–Ponce Letters*, 165.

6. Ibid., 178.

7. Interview by the author of María Rosa Puig Madriguera in the home of Sofía Puig Madriguera, October 18, 2005.

8. Segovia recorded pieces by various composers for around a dozen disks in London that October, including *Canzonetta* by Mendelssohn, the first movement of the *Sonata: Omaggio a Boccherini* by Castelnuovo-Tedesco, *Valse* by Ponce, *Torre Bermeja* by Albéniz, and a prelude by Bach. He used a Ramírez guitar for these sessions,

according to an article by guitarist Pedro Duval in the Italian magazine *La Chitarra*, no. 10, published in October 1937.

9. Interview by the author with María Rosa and Sofía Puig Madriguera, November 24, 2005.

10. Alcázar, *The Segovia–Ponce Letters*, 171.

11. One of the most renowned Austrian guitarists, Scheit also played the lute. He was born in 1909 and died in 1993.

12. Alcázar, *The Segovia–Ponce Letters*, 166.

13. Sophocles Papas was a highly respected Greek-born guitarist (1893–1986) who came to the United States around 1913 and settled in Washington, D.C. He founded Columbia Publishing Company, the largest American publisher of guitar music of its time and which published many Segovia editions in the United States. He was a close friend of Segovia's from their first meeting at the Spanish virtuoso's Town Hall American debut in 1928. Papas founded the Washington Guitar Society, whose name was changed to the Segovia Guitar Society in the 1930s in honor of the Spanish maestro. When Segovia, shying away from honorary associations, asked that his name be dropped from the Society, the designation reverted back to its original form, according to Papas's daughter, Elisabeth Papas Smith.—*Trans.*

14. Andrés Perelló de Segurola (1874–1953) was an operatic bass in the Metropolitan Opera Company (from 1901 to 1920) who later began acting in movies and taught singing.—*Trans.*

15. The ruling Republican government was forced to move from Madrid, under siege by Franco's Nationalist Army, to Valencia in November of 1936.—*Trans.*

16. Alcázar, *The Segovia–Ponce Letters*, 165, letter of January 28, 1937.

17. Ibid., 171, letter written from Chicago, mid-February 1937.

18. Some of his fears were justified, and more than five and a half years would pass before he could return to the United States.

19. Alcázar, *The Segovia–Ponce Letters*, 171.

20. Ibid., 164, letter of January 28, 1937.

21. Tomás Gutiérrez de Terán (Valencia, 1895–Rio de Janeiro, 1964) settled in Brazil in 1930. He had been a friend of Segovia's since the mid-1920s, when they were in Paris at the same time as Heitor Villa-Lobos, with whom Terán also had a close friendship.

22. Duval, "Andrés Segovia nell' America del Sud," n.p. This article was complemented by another published in the following issue of the same magazine, in October 1937, under the title "L'attivitá di Andrea Segovia" (The Activities of Segovia). Pedro Duval, a frequent contributor to the magazine, must have interviewed Segovia at the end of August 1937 in Montevideo, to judge from his article, which contains very precise information regarding Segovia's moves in the Uruguayan capital and where he was going on the European tour that was to begin in October. Later issues of

the same magazine mention the participation of Duval as a guitarist in Montevideo chamber concerts in September and October 1938, and the issue of April 1940 reports that Duval will return to live in the Brazilian city of Pelotas.

23. Segovia—who still did not know what his address would be in Montevideo—told Villa-Lobos to send the correspondence to the French bank Supervielle and Co., which managed the properties of Paquita and her daughters in Montevideo. The corresponding note appears in Segovia's handwriting on a draft of the manuscript of the *Schottisch-Chôro* by the Brazilian composer, which is preserved in the Villa-Lobos Museum in Rio de Janeiro. When Segovia received the first series of the Twelve Etudes (numbers 5, 7, and 8) in Montevideo, a copy of the *Schottisch-Chôro* was included in the envelope (a letter that the guitarist sent to Villa-Lobos from Montevideo, shortly after settling there in July, alludes to this work as "Schottish tropical"). Shortly after this, the guitarist received, also in Montevideo, a copy of the Etude no. 1. For about ten years, these four would be the only Villa-Lobos studies in Segovia's possession. He would receive copies of the remaining studies at the beginning of 1948, through the Brazilian singer Olga Praguer Coelho.

24. The Spanish acronym for Mercado Común del Sur (Common Market of the South), the South American regional economic organization.—*Trans.*

Chapter 10. Montevideo—Putting Down Roots in a Hospitable Land

1. Ateneo de Montevideo, located in the Plaza de Cagancha, is a cultural institution that has continued in existence since its founding in 1886.

2. Nahum, 29.

3. The orchestra was founded in 1931. Its conductor when Segovia arrived was Lamberto Baldi, who was born in Orvieto, Italy, in 1895 and died in Montevideo in 1979. He was the main conductor of the SODRE Symphony Orchestra from 1932 to 1942 and again from 1951 to 1953.

4. Pianist and teacher; he was born in Montevideo in 1912 and died in the same city in 1982.

5. Luis Sambucetti, who was born in Montevideo in 1860 and died there in 1926, was a composer, violinist, orchestra conductor, and founder of the Instituto Verdi in 1890.

6. Virgilio Scarabelli, who was born in Montevideo in 1868 and died there in 1959, was a violinist and orchestra conductor who directed the SODRE Symphony Orchestra for several years.

7. *La Cumparsita* (The Little Parade [of Endless Miseries]) was written in 1917 by the Uruguayan composer Gerardo Matos Rodríguez (1897–1948) and has been called the most famous tango of all time.—*Trans.*

8. Balzo tells a story about the renowned composer-pianist: "I would not say I got a bad impression [of Rachmaninoff] but let's just say, strange. I was amazed because

he was such an imposing figure, and I was very young. At the end, I went to ask him for an autograph. . . . Rachmaninoff responded, 'You paid for your ticket. I gave that concert. I do not owe you anything more.' And he did not sign. Later I thought, 'It must have been fatigue.'"

9. Juan José Iturriberry, "El piano y otras manías uruguayas" [The Piano and Other Uruguayan Obsessions], *Marcha* (Montevideo), December 17, 1971, 24–25.

10. Viglietti, 176.

11. Pujol, 35.

12. Born in Logroño, Spain, in 1891 and died in Buenos Aires in 1950.

13. On December 15, 1939, he used, in two of the three parts of his concert, an "electrophonic guitar" invented by Horacio Paganini, owner of a Montevideo music business.

14. Born in Durazno, Uruguay, in 1901 and died in Montevideo in 1973.

15. Viglietti, 238.

16. Scherping, 10–17. Carlevaro was habitually imprecise when alluding to his age. He was actually twenty when he first met Segovia.

17. The relationship between Segovia and Carlevaro, first that of a teacher and student and later one of friendship, has been analyzed in depth in Escande, *Abel Carlevaro: Un nuevo mundo en la guitarra.*—*Trans.*

18. María Esther Gilio, "Esa increíble mano derecha" [That Incredible Right Hand], *Brecha* (Montevideo), July 14, 2000, 32–33.

19. Dessent and Maiztegui Casas, "El pensador de la guitarra" [The Guitar's Thinker], *Posdata* (Montevideo), August 24, 1995, 65–68.

20. Born in Montevideo in 1905 and died in the same city in 1988. In some ways a self-taught guitarist, he is considered one of Uruguay's most influential guitar teachers.

21. Alcázar, *The Segovia–Ponce Letters*, 182.

22. Sofía Puig Madriguera, interview by the author in her home, October 4, 2005. The accident of the hydrogen-filled zeppelin *Hindenburg* (making its first transatlantic flight with passengers traveling from Frankfurt, Germany, to New York City) took place on May 6, 1937, while it was attempting to land at the airstrip of the Lakehurst (New Jersey) Naval Air Station, just across the Hudson River from New York. The widespread expectations generated by its arrival drew many reporters and photographers, who captured the tragedy in still photos and newsreel film. The recorded eyewitness account was broadcast over the radio the next day, and the famous newsreel account was shown in movies around the world in the coming days. Thirty-five of the ninety-seven passengers and crew died, along with one person on the ground. The accident ended the airship era.—*Trans.*

23. Ortiz Tirado was a physician and a famous Mexican singer; he was born in 1893 and died in 1960. After he developed an active operatic tenor career, the new medium of

radio led him to enter the world of popular romantic music in his country, in which he was considered the best of his era.

24. Anton Giulio Bragaglia (1890–1960), an Italian theater director, filmmaker, photographer, essayist, and journalist.

25. What Segovia probably means by "entrepreneurial spirit" is that there were those who wrongly gambled that the Republican government would score an early victory over Franco's Nationalist troops.—*Trans.*

26. Alcázar, *The Segovia–Ponce Letters*, 164.

27. Pérez Mondino, n.p.

28. Ibid.

29. Pedro Duval's article, mentioned in the last chapter, makes note of the Theme and Variations by Frescobaldi, a Minuetto by Rameau, and a Ciaccona by Pachelbel as being among the transcriptions of works originally written for harpsichord. At the same time, a letter from the guitarist to Villa-Lobos states that he was practicing three of the Brazilian composer's Etudes—Nos. 5, 7, and 8—with plans to include them in the concerts during this tour.

30. The incident was reported in the *Journal de Genève* on October 23 under the headline "Terrible Accident in Versoix: A Son of the Famous Guitarist Segovia Is Burned Alive," with a follow-up the next day entitled "After the Terrible Versoix Accident" providing more details.

31. E-mail from María Rosa Puig to the author, April 16, 2009.

32. At the Beethoven Hall, in Berlin.

33. A reference to the lawyer Aparicio Méndez. In Uruguay and other Latin countries, lawyers are usually referred to by the title of "Doctor" (of jurisprudence).—*Trans.*

34. Today, María Rosa insists that she never studied guitar and that it was actually very difficult to study music at home. Both she and Sofía say that "[Segovia and Paquita] were the artists, and nobody else could make music there. Besides, the piano or the guitar could always be heard." It is possible that those studies Paquita alludes to were nothing more than an early attempt that later failed. It has not been confirmed, but the teacher mentioned could be Abelardo Rodríguez, who also worked as manager of the Palacio de la Música (a commercial establishment that imported instruments and sheet music, and with which Segovia had close ties). Abel Carlevaro once said that Segovia, during the weeks following their first meeting at the Parque Hotel, had gone to see Pedro Vittone (Carlevaro's first guitar teacher) about the possibility of lessons for one of his stepdaughters.

35. The school that Paquita's daughters attended in Montevideo, still in existence. Interestingly, it is Protestant, not Catholic.

36. Actually, Don Andrés went to Paris on the night of December 18 and returned to Geneva on the morning of December 21. It is probable that during those two days in Paris, Segovia met with Ida Presti (1924–1967), who then—like the recently

deceased Leonardo—was thirteen. This was Segovia's only visit to the French capital in 1937. In an article about Presti, published by *Classical Guitar* magazine (May 1992), Eleftheria Kotzia writes, "Segovia himself said, when she was 13, 'I have nothing to teach her—she should not accept the advice of any other guitarist.'"

37. Alcázar, *The Segovia–Ponce Letters*, 183.

38. There are two interesting facts to observe in the identification document: it carries the birth date of February 21, 1893 (in spite of the fact that the family always celebrated Segovia's birthday on November 11), and the authority that signed the document, as assistant police chief and director of divisions, was Carlos Mascaró Reissig, brother of the then-president of the Centro Guitarrístico del Uruguay, Pedro Mascaró Reissig.

Chapter 11. Montevideo—Fruitful Isle of Stability

1. While not certain today, it is believed to have been a gallbladder operation.

2. Albert Spalding (1888–1953) was a famous American concert violinist and teacher who gave the world premiere of Samuel Barber's *Violin Concerto* in 1941.—*Trans.*

3. Otero, *Mario Castelnuovo-Tedesco*, 66.

4. According to Paquita's diary, that happened on January 10 while Segovia was giving concerts in San Remo before continuing on to Bologna.

5. Hans von Bülow (1830–1894) was a German pianist, conductor, and composer. He premiered the Liszt E-flat Major Piano Concerto and Tchaikovsky's Piano Concerto No. 1.—*Trans.*

6. The great opera composer Richard Wagner (1813–1883) seduced and eventually married Bülow's wife, Cosima (the daughter of Franz Liszt), in a famous scandal of the nineteenth century. Bülow later stated, "If it had been anyone other than Wagner I would have shot him!"—*Trans.*

7. This visit took place on the night of January 14, after Segovia's concert at the Bianca Hall of Florence. He had returned from Bologna on the early hours of January 11, on January 12 they would both have lunch with the Castelnuovo-Tedescos, and on the January 13 they traveled to Rome for another concert by Segovia.

8. This seems like another case of stereotyping by the pianist of her Jewish hosts.

9. Madriguera, 107–9.

10. Alcázar, *Segovia–Ponce Letters*, 187. Segovia describes in detail the orchestration that Castelnuovo-Tedesco had arranged for accompanying the guitar.

11. Ibid., 186.

12. He was born in Montevideo in 1894 and educated in the Royal Conservatory of Naples and the Imperial Academy in Berlin. At the age of twenty he was already a substitute cello teacher in the Berlin academy.

13. City in the Department of Colonia, located seventy-five miles west of Montevideo on the Río de la Plata, and presently called Nueva Helvecia (New Switzerland). Its first settlers, in the nineteenth century, were Swiss immigrants.

14. Smith, 124.

15. The Spanish Phalange started out as a fascist party in the 1930s. Franco combined it with the Carlist movement to create the sole and official conservative political party during his thirty-six-year dictatorship.

16. On April 19, 1939, *La Vanguardia* (Barcelona) published a list of donations received at the "4ᵗʰ Military Region, for deposit in the National Treasury." It says that "162 British Pounds Sterling, 840 French Francs and 50 Gold Dollars" were deposited in the name of Andrés Segovia.

17. This comes from the recorded version of an informal conversation between Abel Carlevaro and the participants of a course given by Alfredo Escande on May 30, 1992, in Montevideo.

18. Miguel Ángel del Pino Sardá (1890–1973) was one of the most famous portrait artists of the early twentieth century. He was from Seville, Spain, but fled to Buenos Aires during the Spanish Civil War and lived there for approximately thirty years before returning to Seville a few years before his death.—*Trans.*

19. Concert pianist and orchestra conductor, born in Valencia, Spain, in 1895. He lived in the United States from 1928 until his death in 1980. Iturbi went to Montevideo several times; this occasion was on the last week of May 1939. Paquita and Segovia hosted him at their house, and at the beginning of June part of the family traveled to Buenos Aires to attend one of his concerts at Teatro Colón.

20. In reality, *Chôros No. 1* was composed in 1920, four years before the two musicians met in Paris, and dedicated to the famous Brazilian pianist and composer Ernesto Nazareth (1863–1934).

21. Alcázar, *The Segovia–Ponce Letters*, 187.

22. E-mail from María Rosa Puig to the author, March 19, 2006.

23. Interview by the author with Sofía Puig at her home, August 4, 2003.

24. Located on the downtown corner of Mercedes and Andes Streets, it was the site of the Teatro Urquiza, which was reconditioned with the best techniques of the time to produce a modern hall suitable for both symphony and chamber music concerts. The auditorium was completely destroyed by fire in 1971 and rebuilt and totally modernized in 2009.

25. Botet, 11.

26. *La Mañana* (Montevideo), October 29, 1939, n.p. The Vivaldi referred to is the Concerto in B Minor for Four Violins and Orchestra, Op. 3, No. 10.

27. This epic pursuit and eventual battle was similar to the more famous hunt of the *Bismarck*, Germany's battleship, in the North Atlantic in May 1941. Hitler personally ordered Hans Langsdorff, captain of the *Admiral Graf Spee*, to fight his way

from Montevideo to Buenos Aires. Refusing to risk the lives of his men, Langsdorff sank his ship and later committed suicide rather than risk dishonor. His men were imprisoned in Uruguay and repatriated to Germany in 1946.—*Trans.*

28. Argentinean poet and novelist who was born in Brussels in 1914. His family settled in Buenos Aires when he was young; he immigrated to Paris in 1951, in protest of the Perón government, and lived and worked there for the rest of his life, dying in 1984.—*Trans.*

29. This short story is part of the book *Final del juego* (End of the Game), published in 1956.

30. Alcázar, *The Segovia–Ponce Letters*, 194.

31. Andrés Segovia, *Manuel M. Ponce: Notas y recuerdos*, 13–14.

32. Francisco Curt Lange (b. Germany, 1903; d. Uruguay, 1997) was a musicologist who had settled in Uruguay in his youth. He founded the Discoteca Nacional (National Sound Recordings Library), which belonged to SODRE, in 1930 and directed it until 1948. In 1940 he created the Instituto Interamericano de Musicología (Inter-American Institute of Musicology), through which he organized a great number of musical activities in various parts of the continent. In particular, he was the promoter of Villa-Lobos's visit to Montevideo in October 1940.

33. Alcázar, *The Segovia–Ponce Letters*, 194.

34. Ibíd., 194.

35. Andrés Segovia, *Manuel M. Ponce: Notas y recuerdos*, 14.

36. Traditions that are not religious, as a result of the marked nonclerical makeup of the Uruguayan government, but designed to promote internal tourism and festive events associated with livestock, the main component of domestic production in the country. Since the beginning of the twentieth century, the official name for Holy Week in Uruguay has been Semana de Turismo (Tourism Week).

37. Residential zone of Montevideo that contains a park, various sporting areas, and a section called La Rural (The Countryside), in which the agricultural expositions and the Creole shows, mainly those in the horse coliseum, are held during Tourism Week.—*Trans.*

38. Alcázar, *The Segovia–Ponce Letters*, 198.

39. Ponce must have seconded Segovia's support of Franco; Castelnuovo-Tedesco, however, feared (unjustly, as it turned out), that the Spanish dictator might duplicate the anti-Semitic policies of Hitler and Mussolini.—*Trans.*

40. Ibid.

41. Segovia tells Ponce in one of his letters that del Pino came to Montevideo repeatedly to paint portraits for many wealthy people there.

42. Alcázar, *The Segovia–Ponce Letters*, 204.

43. Interview by the author of Sofía and María Rosa Puig at Sofía Puig's home, October 18, 2005.

44. Sofía Puig Madriguera, interview by Ramón Mérica aired on November 23, 1993, on the program *En vivo y en directo*, Radio Sarandí (Montevideo).

45. Interview by the author of Sofía and María Rosa Puig at Sofía Puig's home, October 18, 2005.

46. Interview by the author with Sofía Puig at her home, August 4, 2003.

47. Alcázar, *The Segovia–Ponce Letters*, 207. It is possible that Segovia is referring to alternative cadenzas that Ponce may have written for one or more of the Beethoven piano concertos.—*Trans.*

48. Andrés Segovia, *Manuel M. Ponce: Notas y recuerdos*, 14.

49. In French in Ponce's manuscript.

50. Alcázar, *The Segovia–Ponce Letters*, 208–209.

51. The complete letter, occupying pages 210–12 of Alcázar's book, cannot be completely understood outside the context of this full story, and is recommended for further reading.

52. The so-called Embajada Artística Brasileña (Brazilian Artistic Embassy), headed by Villa-Lobos, was made up also of Arminda Neves d'Almeida, Ruth Valladares Correa, Gazzi Galvao de Sá, Arnaldo de Azevedo Estrela, José Vieira Brandao, Iberê Gomes Grosso, and Oscar Borgerth.

53. Arminda was born in 1912 and died in 1985. Although she had been in a romantic relationship with Villa-Lobos for several years, the composer did not appear to introduce her officially as his spouse, as he was not divorced from his first wife. In Paquita's diary she says that the composer arrived with "two other people from his entourage." And when Segovia clarifies Arminda's signature in the note he sends Ponce on that same day, he writes: "A woman from the Cultural Embassy who accompanies Villa-Lobos."

54. It is based, as is the case with all the letters Segovia sent to Ponce, on Alcázar's collection. There is, however, an error in the order of the material. The short letter no. 102 is placed chronologically between a letter dated September 12 and another one dated October 5. However, it is actually a page written on October 20 and later added to the letter of October 22, as is clear from the sequence of events being narrated here. What Alcázar considers illegible are the signatures of Gazzi Galvao de Sá and Arminda d'Almeida, along with Arminda's note in Portuguese saying, "I will never forget your magnificent concerto."

55. It is interesting to note that Segovia says in his letter, "He came to the house with six preludes dedicated to me." Segovia's counting is always confusing, so it is not possible to say with certainty that six preludes were presented instead of the now-published five. At no time does Segovia say that Villa-Lobos left him a copy of any of those preludes. It is easy to assume that the composer refrained from giving Segovia a copy when he perceived his cool attitude; he seemed to be more concerned with refuting the Brazilian's musical ideas and comparing them with those of Ponce and Castelnuovo-Tedesco than with paying attention to the compositions Villa-Lobos

was trying to show him. In the end, the Five Preludes were officially dedicated "to Mindinha" ("Little Mindy," the composer's nickname for Arminda) rather than Segovia—probably because of the Spaniard's initial lack of interest.

56. Some excerpts from that letter: "The music was terrible, especially that of Villa-Lobos," and "raucous, discordant, and brutal noise," when he comments about the music played by the Brazilian delegation. Referring to the preludes that Villa-Lobos showed him: "Deadly boredom," "vulgar preludes," and "they made me want to laugh."

57. Alcázar, *The Segovia–Ponce Letters*, 206.

58. Ibid., 215.

59. See Escande, *Abel Carlevaro: Un nuevo mundo en la guitarra*.

60. Interview by the author with Sofía Puig at her home, August 4, 2003. According to Sofía, during those first years of classes Segovia asked himself if Abel Carlevaro did not follow his advice strictly because he did not want to or because he could not. That distance between maestro and student started after Carlevaro's visit with Villa-Lobos, and was complete once Segovia realized that the correct answer was the first one. Quietly, and in the issues that had to do with music and the guitar, Carlevaro kept doing what he wanted, even against his maestro's advice. During the visit that Eduardo Fabini and Carlevaro made to Segovia and Paquita in April 1939, Don Andrés told the Uruguayan composer: "You have to leave Abel alone, because he does it all."

61. "Fue magnífica la recepción de ayer en lo de Segovia-Madriguera" [The Reception at the Segovia-Madrigueras' Yesterday Was Magnificent], *La Mañana* (Montevideo), October 28, 1940, n.p.

62. Alcázar, *The Segovia–Ponce Letters*, 216–217.

63. Ibid., 219.

64. In a previous letter, Segovia had suggested to Ponce that the cadenza of the third movement be less poetic and more brilliant, keeping in mind that the finale is, "for the majority of the ignorant public, like the high Cs of the tenor or the trills of the soprano." And, he added, "There are those who go just for that."

65. Alcázar, *The Segovia–Ponce Letters*, 226.

66. Ibid., 233.

67. Ibid., 236.

68. Ibid., 240–41.

69. He is referring to the Mexican ambassador in Uruguay.

70. Alcázar, *The Segovia–Ponce Letters*, 248.

71. Ibid., 252.

72. José María Fontova, "Fueron ovacionados en una audición A. Segovia y P. Madriguera de Segovia" [A. Segovia and P. Madriguera de Segovia Were Applauded at a Concert], *Noticias Gráficas* (Buenos Aires), August 16, 1941, n.p.

73. In the period of Porfirio Díaz, president of Mexico from 1876 to 1880 and again from 1884 to 1911 (when he was considered a dictator). He was forced from power by the second Mexican Revolution and fled to France, where he died in exile in 1915.—*Trans.*

74. Otero, *Manuel M. Ponce y la guitarra*, 100.

75. Roberto Lagarmilla, "Andrés Segovia: Grato e ilustre huésped" [Welcome and Illustrious Guest], *El Día* (Montevideo), August 12, 1979, 31.

76. With "world premiere" in parentheses. In the biographical sketch of Segovia included in the program, the date of the guitarist's birth is listed, curiously, as February 18, 1894—not February 21, 1893, as was already being used for his Uruguayan document of identification, nor November 11, which he continued to celebrate with his Montevideo family.

77. Chapultepec ("Grasshopper Hill" in Indian dialect) is the large wooded park of Mexico City. Ponce's sketches—*Early Morning, Daytime Stroll*, and *Fantastic Full Moon*—depict Chapultepec at three different times of the day.—*Trans.*

78. A romance poem about the revolt in 1568 commanded by the Moorish leader Aben Humeya (1520–1569) against Spain's King Phillip II, in reaction to the harsh treatment of the Muslim population of Andalusia.—*Trans.*

79. "El concierto sinfónico del sábado" [Saturday's Symphony Concert], *La Mañana* (Montevideo), October 1, 1941, 7.

80. R. E. L., "Andrés Segovia estrenó el Concierto del sur" [Andrés Segovia Premiered the *Concierto del sur*], *La Mañana* (Montevideo), October 5, 1941, 9.

81. "Fue clamoroso el triunfo de Paquita Madriguera en el SODRE" [Paquita Madriguera's Success Was Resounding at the SODRE], *El Diario* (Montevideo), October 12, 1941, n.p.

82. "Manuel Ponce dirigió ayer su segundo concierto" [Manuel Ponce Conducted His Second Concert Yesterday], *La Mañana* (Montevideo), October 12, 1941, n.p.

Chapter 12. From South to North—The Agitated Journey from Success to Crisis

1. The South American soccer tournament between the ten Spanish and Portuguese-speaking countries of the Confederación Sudamericana de Fútbol (South American Soccer Confederation). In recent years, the tournament has invited two additional countries from outside the confederation.—*Trans.*

2. Gilson Antunes, "Entrevista Ronoel Simoes" [Interview with Ronoel Simoes], conducted in 1994 and published, in Portuguese, in *Fórum Violao Erudito* at www.oocities.org/vienna/waltz/3039/ronoel.html, October 2008.

3. In a total of twelve days that Segovia spent in Rio de Janeiro on this trip, the only meeting with Villa-Lobos was on this occasion. There is no information in Paquita's

detailed diary of any visit to his house or that they ever paid any attention to music composed by the Brazilian for the guitar. The Montevideo brush-offs must have been fresh in Villa-Lobos's memory, although not so much as to cause him to neglect the basic rules of courtesy—the composer had been feted with a reception at Segovia's home, so he responded with a restaurant dinner. It is most likely that Segovia was aware of the fact that two of those preludes that Villa-Lobos took to Montevideo in 1940, which—according to one of Segovia's letters to Ponce—were originally dedicated to the Spanish guitarist, had been published in February 1941 by the Brazilian magazine *Musica Viva* with the dedication "to Arminda Neves d'Almeida."

4. The Polish-born concert violinist Henryk Szeryng (1914–1988) became a Mexican citizen in 1946.

5. Alcázar, *The Segovia–Ponce Letters*, 260–61. The letter was dated December 13, 1943.

6. Alexander Uninsky was a Russian-American concert pianist who was born in Kiev in 1910. He won the 1932 Chopin Competition in Warsaw and died in Dallas, Texas, in 1972.

7. "Sociedade de Cultura Artística" [Society of Artistic Culture], *Diario Popular* (Pelotas, Brazil), July 12, 1942, n.p.

8. Enio de Freitas Castro, "Paquita Madriguera," *Diario de Noticias* (Porto Alegre), July 17, 1942, n.p.

9. Alcázar, *The Segovia–Ponce Letters*, 261.

10. "Paquita Madriguera en la A. Wagneriana" [Madriguera in the Wagnerian Association], *Noticias Gráficas* (Buenos Aires), August 8, 1942, n.p.

11. Many of these would be published later by the two publishing houses of Ricordi and Antigua Casa Nuñez in Buenos Aires.

12. Born in Santiago de Chile in 1893, Carvajal was brought to Montevideo to conduct the SODRE Symphony Orchestra in two concerts during that month of August.

13. "Armando Carvajal ofreció un buen concierto sinfónico" [Carvajal Gave a Good Symphonic Concert], *La Mañana* (Montevideo), August 16, 1942, n.p.

14. "P. Madriguera—A. Carvajal," *La Tribuna Popular* (Montevideo), August 16, 1942, n.p.

15. "Paquita Madriguera brindó en La Filarmónica una noche de arte" [Paquita Madriguera Offers a Night of Art at the Philharmonic], *La Gaceta* (Tucumán), October 18, 1942, n.p.

16. "Paquita Madriguera y Andrés Segovia fueron aclamados en La Filarmónica" [Paquita Madriguera and Andrés Segovia Were Acclaimed at the Philharmonic], *La Gaceta*, October 20, 1942, n.p.

17. "A. Segovia nos habla de Abel Carlevaro" [A. Segovia Talks to Us About Carlevaro], *La Mañana* (Montevideo), November 9, 1942, n.p.

18. Fishing port and tourist resort located south of Buenos Aires on the Atlantic Ocean, just beyond where the Río de la Plata joins the sea. It is Argentina's seventh-largest city today.—*Trans.*

19. In a way this can be regarded as a significant turning point in the student–teacher relationship between Carlevaro and Segovia. After the "consecration concert" of the previous year ("consecrating" each of them for different reasons, in response to their respective roles), Carlevaro performed this major premiere of an important work for guitar and orchestra—very obviously independent of the Spanish maestro's influence. And it received unanimous praise from the critics. One of the reviews, signed by the eminent musicologist Lauro Ayestarán, stated: "Seldom have we heard playing so clear and with such penetrating musicality. Undoubtedly we are before a performer of excellent quality who honors our musical environment."

20. The Italian guitarist, composer, and editor Angelo Gilardino wrote about this in the booklet of a CD dedicated to works for guitar by Santórsola (*Guido Santórsola*, performed by Antonio Rugolo and the Paul Klee Quartet [STR 33777, Stradivarius, 2007]): "The writer [Gilardino] of these notes was also a witness to this bittersweet relationship between Santórsola and Segovia when the Uruguayan maestro visited Italy in 1974 and was the guest for a few days of this then-young Italian guitarist. While the composer openly criticized and expressed his complete disapproval of Segovia's choice of repertoire and his interpretive guidelines, he also dedicated to and sent Segovia a new composition for guitar—at that same time! It was clearly a conflicting attitude that annoyed the composer, but for which he had not been able to find an unambiguous resolution" (p. 6).

21. On April 3, 1943, the manager Ernesto de Quesada received a note from his American colleague Sol Hurok confirming that Segovia was guaranteed a minimum of ten concerts in the United States for a period beginning on November 1, 1943, and ending on January 31, 1944.

22. An Uruguayan narrator, dramatist, and politician (1898–1968), Zavala Muniz was the creator of the Comedia Nacional and headed the board of directors of SODRE between 1948 and 1951.

23. Here Lange is referring to the orchestra conductor Theo Buchwald, who was born in Vienna and immigrated to Peru. He became the first permanent conductor of the National Symphony Orchestra in Lima in 1938, a post he held until his death in 1960.

24. Just a month earlier, on April 6, 1943, Chile had experienced an earthquake of magnitude 8.2 in Ovalle, two hundred miles north of the capital.—*Trans.*

25. Here the reference is to the Chilean composer Domingo Santa Cruz (1899–1987).

26. This letter is numbered 122 in the Alcázar compilation. Segovia only indicated the month and the year next to his signature. His sentence "Paquita gave a splendid performance of the Concerto by Grieg a couple of days ago" allows us to determine the exact date of the letter.

27. J. A. O. C., "Segundo concierto sinfónico en el Municipal" [Second Symphony Concert in the Municipal], *El Mercurio* (Santiago de Chile), May 10, 1943, n.p.

28. Typed letter on letterhead from the Hotel Crillon in Santiago de Chile and dated May 13, 1943.

29. Born of Russian immigrants in 1914 in Buenos Aires, he developed a brilliant career in Europe and the United States from early childhood. He died in Vienna in 2004.

30. Ramón I. Alvarez, "Nos visitó Abel Carlevaro, que mañana se presentará nueva-mente en el SODRE" [Carlevaro, Who Will Perform Again Tomorrow at the SODRE, Visits with Us], *La Razón* (Montevideo), August 9, 1944, 7.

31. Alcázar, *The Segovia–Ponce Letters*, 261.

32. Paricutín, two hundred miles west of Mexico City, was the site of the sudden appear-ance and eruption of a volcano right under the feet of an Indian farmer sowing his field on February 20, 1943. This spectacular event drew scientists from around the world to witness and record the growth of a new volcanic mountain, which reached a height of about 160 feet the day following its initial eruption and was about 1,100 feet high a year later, when Paquita and her companions made their excursion to see the phenomenon. It finally reached a height of about 1,400 feet. It has shown no further activity since 1952.—*Trans.*

33. Madriguera, 70.

34. The reference is the northeastern Brazilian state of Bahia, located on the Atlantic Ocean. Being the center of the former slave trade, its culture and cuisine are a rich blend of African and Brazilian traits. Although Olga Coelho was born in the Amazon region when her father was working there, her family is from Salvador, the capital of Bahia, and she spent most of her childhood there.—*Trans.*

35. Luis Antonio Giron, "A soprano insaciável" [The Insatiable Soprano], *Caderno fim de semana* [Weekend Notebook], *Gazeta Mercantil* (São Paulo), May 4, 2001. All quotations in this section from Coelho are from this interview.

36. An upper-middle-class neighborhood of Rio de Janeiro.—*Trans.*

37. Born in 1882, Vargas was the dictatorial president of Brazil from 1930 to 1945. He was then elected by the people to serve from 1951 until a military coup forced him from office and caused him to commit suicide in 1954. He was very instrumental in the government-appointed music-education career of Villa-Lobos in the 1930s and 1940s.—*Trans.*

38. The Graf Zeppelin was a German hydrogen-filled airship, similar to the *Hindenburg*, the fatal crash of which the three Puig Madriguera girls witnessed in New Jersey in 1937.—*Trans.*

39. *Guitar Review* published an announcement referring to the previous year: "In Octo-ber, the Gaspar Coelhos (she is Olga Coelho, the famous Brazilian soprano and guitarist) announced the birth of their son, Miguel, on the 21st of that month." *Guitar Review* 8 (1949): 46.

40. For example, *Neblina* (Mist), published in *Guitar Review* 12 (1951): 25.

41. Zanon, 30–31.

42. Gilardino, 28.

43. Orchestra conductor who was born in Vienna in 1890 and died in Zurich in 1956. He lived in Argentina from 1938 until the end of World War II.

44. Segovia gave a concert in that country on March 22. According to three eyewitness accounts given to Richard Stover and mentioned in his book *Six Silver Moonbeams*, the second encounter between the Spanish maestro and the great Paraguayan guitarist-composer Agustín Barrios would have occurred around this date. Barrios died four and a half months later in the Salvadoran capital.

45. "El concierto de Paquita Madriguera" [Paquita Madriguera's Concert], *La Prensa Libre* (San José), March 21, 1944, n.p.

46. Juan Pablo Muñoz Sanz, "El recital de Paquita Madriguera en el Teatro Sucre" [Paquita Madriguera's Recital in the Teatro Sucre], *El Comercio* (Quito), April 23, 1944, n.p.

47. That letter, numbered 127 in Alcázar's compilation, should have been placed immediately after no. 123. The ones numbered 124, 125, and 126 were written later from the United States in 1946. Letter no. 124, which has no visible date, must have been written a few days after January 13, 1946, when Segovia played the *Concierto del sur* at Carnegie Hall. The letter numbered 125 was written on February 18 of that year, in San Francisco, when he was on his way to Seattle.

48. Alcázar, *The Segovia–Ponce Letters*, 270.

49. The Teatro Municipal of Lima was inaugurated with the name Teatro Forero on July 28, 1920.

50. *El Comercio* (Lima), May 18, 1944, n.p.

51. It is probable that during these months Segovia prepared his famous version of *Twenty Studies for Guitar by Fernando Sor* (Los Angeles: Edward B. Marks, 1945).

52. "Hoy ofrecerán su último recital Andrés Segovia y Paquita Madriguera" [Today Segovia and Madriguera Will Play Their Final Concert], *La Capital* (Rosario), July 16, 1944, n.p.

53. A. E. T., "Segovia dio ayer su última actuación" [Segovia Gave His Last Concert Yesterday], *Crítica* (Buenos Aires), July 25, 1944, n.p.

Chapter 13. Montevideo and Buenos Aires— Poles of a Shifting Crisis

1. Mauricio Müller, "El recital de Paquita Madriguera" [Paquita Madriguera's Concert], *El País* (Montevideo), June 8, 1945, n.p.

2. On July 15 in Buenos Aires, Segovia signed a presentation statement for Abel Carlevaro that was practically identical to the one he had written in 1942 to introduce

him to the Montevideo public. The text, with Segovia's autograph, was included in the printed program for Carlevaro's concert at the Teatro Odeón in the Argentinean capital eight days later. Segovia's initial reluctance to fulfill this promise to sponsor and present his student to the Argentinean audience was another factor in the deterioration of their relationship, and it gave rise to some arguments between them. To exacerbate the situation, aside from Carlevaro's visit with Villa-Lobos and the premiering of some of the Brazilian composer's works, the young guitarist would be performing, and thus competing, on the same stage where Segovia played his regular concert series in Buenos Aires.

3. "Con Paquita Madriguera obtuvo la Filarmónica un nuevo éxito" [The Philharmonic Has Another Success with Paquita Madriguera], *La Gaceta* (Tucumán), October 1, 1945, n.p.

4. Vladimir Bobri was Segovia's closest friend in New York City, as Papas was in the U.S. capital. Bobri was born Vladimir Bobritsky in Ukraine in 1898 and immigrated to the United States after fleeing the Russian Revolution. He was a successful professional artist and an amateur guitarist who helped found the New York Guitar Society in the 1930s and its sporadic but quality publication, *Guitar Review*, in the late 1940s. Bobri served as editor and art director at various times for *Guitar Review* and designed the covers for many of Segovia's Decca LP recordings. He also wrote and published, with the maestro's collaboration, *The Segovia Technique* (New York: Collier Books, 1972; reprint, New York: The Bold Strummer, 1990). A fire broke out in his Rosendale, New York, home (about eighty-five miles north of New York City) in the autumn of 1986; Bobri and his wife escaped, but he dashed back in to save his guitar collection and was killed.—*Trans.*

5. Smith, 135.

6. "Homenaje a Enrique Granados" [Homage to Granados], *Marcha* (Montevideo), June 28, 1946, n.p.

7. Lauro Ayestarán, "Ayer se ofreció en el SODRE un bello homenaje a Granados" [SODRE Offered a Beautiful Homage Yesterday to Granados], *El País* (Montevideo), July 11, 1946, n.p.

8. Roberto Lagarmilla, "Tomas Mayer dirigió nuevamente la OSSODRE—Paquita Madriguera intervino como solista" [Mayer Directs the SODRE Symphony Orchestra Again—Madriguera Acts as Soloist], *Mundo Uruguayo* (Montevideo), September 26, 1946, n.p.

9. "Un espléndido festival artístico en el SODRE" [A Splendid Artistic Festival in the SODRE], *El Bien Público* (Montevideo), October 12, 1946, n.p.

10. María Rosa and Sofía Puig Madriguera, interview by the author at Sofía's home, October 18, 2005.

11. Madriguera, 199.

12. Alcázar, *The Segovia–Ponce Letters*, 271–72. It was probably on this occasion that Segovia moved several guitars and three boxes of papers (among them many valuable

manuscripts that would take more than fifty years to surface when they were auctioned in London) to the home of Aparicio Méndez.

13. María Rosa and Sofía Puig Madriguera, interview by the author at Sofía's home, October 18, 2005.

14. He is referring to the orchestra conductor Vladimir Shavitch (born in Russia in 1888; he later became a naturalized U.S. citizen and died in 1957). He had conducted the orchestra in the premiere of *Campo*, by Eduardo Fabini, at Montevideo's Teatro Albéniz on April 29, 1922.

15. Alcázar, *The Segovia–Ponce Letters*, 272.

16. Ibid.

Chapter 14. Beatriz

1. Alcázar, *The Segovia–Ponce Letters*, 186.

2. The Signoria were the ruling members of medieval and Renaissance Florence.—*Trans.*

3. Letter dated January 3, 1939, Florence.

4. Alcázar, *The Segovia–Ponce Letters*, 256.

5. Paquita kept a meticulous record in her notebooks, month by month, of all the letters sent, and it is striking that in all of 1948 she did not write a single letter to Segovia.

6. María Rosa Puig Madriguera, e-mail to the author, December 11, 2005.

7. Letter written around April 8, 1949. Easter Sunday that year was on April 17.

8. María Rosa's son.

9. Paquita Madriguera, letter to María Rosa Puig Madriguera, Buenos Aires, August 29, 1949. A *zamba* is a dance from the northeastern region of Argentina.—*Trans.*

10. Sister Gertrudis de San José, sister of Segovia's mother, was a cloistered nun in a convent in Málaga from her early youth. She turned seventy-eight the year this letter was written. Her correspondence with Paquita is abundant and allows the reconstruction of some aspects of the family life. Sister Gertrudis died in March of 1955.

11. She refers to the debt generated by her presence in the convent and for the funeral of Segovia's mother. In another letter she explains that "the Reds" took her entire dowry [during the Spanish Civil War].

12. María Rosa Puig Madriguera, e-mail to the author, March 19, 2006.

13. A seaside neighborhood suburb of Montevideo, just east of Pocitos. —*Trans.*

14. Casal Chapí was born in Madrid in 1909 and died in the same city in 1977. He was a Republican who exiled first to the Dominican Republic and then to Montevideo (1950–56), where he was the artistic director of the SODRE Symphony Orchestra for a while.

15. Letter dated August 16, 1952.

16. The Palio di Siena is a horse race run twice a year, on July 2 and August 16, in the Piazza del Campo in Siena. The competition has its origins in the fourteenth century. In the modern version, which dates from 1656, ten horses from the city's seventeen wards compete in a rough-and-tumble race of three laps around the plaza. This spectacle and the events in the days leading up to it jam the city with tourists.—*Trans.*

17. Segovia had returned to play in Spain in 1952 for the first time since Franco came into power, and he was now worried about how the North American managers would react, since thirteen years earlier they had closed the doors to him for his statements in support of Franco.

18. This explains why everything Segovia left behind in Barcelona was not lost when they fled the Civil War. Paquita's uncle Ramón Rodón (Mamá Paqui's youngest brother) was the one responsible for saving those things until Segovia's return sixteen years later.

19. The reference is to the Spanish portrait artist Miguel del Pino, a friend of Segovia's since his youth.

20. This is a sarcastic play on words by Olga, because "playing the bass" is a saying in Spanish and Portuguese that means "acting stupid."—*Trans.*

21. Letter of October, 16, 1952, typed (as are almost all of Paquita's letters). Following the signature she added a phrase that could well explain the hostility of the words Segovia received from his Brazilian girlfriend, through del Pino's letter, while in Barcelona. Referring to an Argentinean magazine that had published some photos of Segovia with Paquita and Beatriz, taken during his recent visit to the Río de la Plata, Paquita wrote: "Olga must have seen the pictures in the *Atlántida* and must be furious. Now it's her turn to put up with it!"

22. María Rosa Puig Madriguera, e-mail to the author, November 29, 2005.

23. Traditionally the fifteenth birthday party (*la quinceañera*) is considered a young lady's introduction into society.

24. Due to the difficulties that Juan Perón's government in Argentina was creating for those wanting to travel to Uruguay at that time, Paquita wanted a Spanish passport to facilitate her movements between the two countries.

25. Paquita was in Buenos Aires. That Segovia would include a letter for her in the envelope for María Rosa, who lived in Montevideo, indicates that he did not want whoever delivered his correspondence to the post office to know that he was writing to Paquita. Also, the postscript leads one to believe that he wanted to be sure that an eventual response from Paquita or her daughter was not going to be intercepted by someone else. Many years later, in the last stage of his life, and after both Paquita and Beatriz had died, Segovia continued to use those precautions and other special codes in correspondence with his Uruguayan stepdaughters.

26. The reference is to Beatriz's godfather, Aparicio Méndez.

27. This is probably a reference to Paquita's scheduled trip to Montevideo. It was a gift from Segovia so that she could spend a few days with Beatriz before going to Europe. It is also possible that he is referring to the official Spanish passport that had been requested, without which it would have been impossible to cross to Montevideo because of the restrictions imposed by Perón's government

28. Segovia elaborates on this in a long letter he wrote to María Rosa the following April 1954.

29. The "Cholo" mentioned is María Rosa's husband.

30. Sol Hurok, Segovia's concert manager in the United States.

31. This again refers to the travel restrictions imposed by the Argentinean government at that time.

32. Paquita had finally gone to Spain on October 26, 1953, and would return to Río de la Plata on January 15, 1954.

33. The emphasis could be a clarification, for both Beatriz and her mother, that he would not be accompanied by Olga, as well as a reply to the Paquita's demands that she herself accompany her daughter.

34. Saying that he is "alone" could well be another message for Paquita.

35. Earlier underlined emphases in original.

36. This remark is a reference to the plans Segovia was making with the collaboration of Mamá Paqui in 1952.

37. María Rosa Puig Madriguera, e-mail to author, December 11, 2005.

38. U. F. Zanni, "Palacio de la Música—La pianista Paquita Madriguera y la Orquesta Municipal" [Palace of Music—The Pianist Paquita Madriguera and the Municipal Orchestra], *La Vanguardia Española* (Barcelona), October 31, 1953, n.p.

39. Emphases in the original.

40. He is referring to his ties to Olga Coelho.

41. The last two emphasized passages appear to be his fear of the threats he read in front of Mamá Paqui. Segovia had problems with the music managers in the United States during the Spanish Civil War and feared that Olga, who had been living in New York for many years, had developed strong connections in that field.

42. Remember that Segovia had written to Beatriz seven months earlier, on September 7, that this trip "will resolve a lot of things for me."

43. What Segovia is saying in this seemingly contradictory sentence is that he was "alone from Olga" for nineteen days, and, in spite of his attempts to keep her away from the hospital (his "negative gesture"), she showed up anyway, and he "stopped being alone."—*Trans.*

44. Interview by the author, November 23, 2007.

45. The Asociación Latinoamericana del Libre Comercio (Latin American Free Commerce Association), which a few years later would become ALADI (Asociación

Latinoamericana de Integración [Latin American Integration Association]). It had its headquarters in Montevideo.

46. María Antonia Iglesias, "Andrés Segovia," *Los Españoles* (Madrid) 23, March 8, 1973, n.p.

47. María Rosa Puig Madriguera, e-mail to the author, November 26, 2007. Also confirming this is López Poveda's biography, *Andrés Segovia: Vida y obra*, which on page 399 shows the guitarist on an intense twenty-five-stop concert tour of the United States from November 2 through December 16 of that year.

48. He is referring to the government of General Juan D. Perón.

49. Similar to *nadie* and *nada*, which in Spanish mean "nobody" and "nothing," respectively.

50. Lambretta was a popular line of lightweight Italian motor scooters, similar in design to the better-known Vespa. They were manufactured from 1947 until 1972, when economical small cars replaced their need. They were also manufactured in several South American countries, including Argentina.—*Trans.*

51. The word *papa* is used in Latin America for "potato," while Spain uses *patata*. In Spain *papa* means "pope," so you can imagine the reaction when Beatriz asked for an order of "fried popes"!—*Trans.*

52. The lunch hour in the Río de la Plata area, as in northern Europe and the United States, is at noon, while in Spain they have their main meal around 2:30 P.M. and a lighter meal after 9 P.M.—*Trans.*

53. Otero, *Mario Castelnuovo-Tedesco, su vida y su obra para la guitarra*, 119.

54. Enrique Larroque, "El recuerdo de Granados" [The Remembrance of Granados], *El Hogar* (Buenos Aires), July 19, 1957, n.p.

55. Whose paternity, as we have read, the singer attributed to Andrés Segovia.

56. María Rosa Puig Madriguera, e-mail to the author, December 11, 2005.

57. Born in Germany in 1912, Heinrich moved with her family in 1926 to Argentina, where she died in 2005. Her signature, followed by Bs As (for Buenos Aires), appears below each photo on the mat, and the year (not seen here) appears in the mat's lower right-hand corner.

58. Since Enric lived in New York, as did Segovia and Olga at this time, he is probably excusing himself from writing in order to remain reserved on the subject.

59. Since this is the only mention in the letter of a social event with her father, the "other people" could mean or include Olga, and Beatriz is being discreet.

60. "Dado" was the nickname of a former boyfriend, named Eduardo, of Beatriz. They had a brief romance at the time of this letter.

61. María Rosa Puig Madriguera, e-mail to the author, December 11, 2005.

62. A typical Spanish breakfast ending a late-night celebration during the holidays.—*Trans.*

63. British Overseas Airway Corporation (BOAC) was the British state airline for overseas flights at the time and was the first airline in the world to use passenger jets. In 1974 it merged with British European Airways (BEA), the state airline for domestic and European flights, to form British Airways.—*Trans.*

64. María Antonia Iglesias, "Andrés Segovia," *Los Españoles* (Madrid) 23, March 8, 1973, n.p.

65. The ceremony took place on the tiny British territory of the Iberian Peninsula. At that time all marriages in Spain had to be performed in the church, which, like Spanish law, did not recognize divorce.

66. "Boda en la diplomacia" [A Diplomat's Wedding], *La Mañana* (Montevideo), August 23, 1963, n.p.

67. Sofía Puig Madriguera, interview by the author at her home, November 2007.

68. Abel Carlevaro made the following entry in a notebook in which he wrote down his artistic activities of 1967: "Friday March 3—recital at the home of Dr. Jorge Giucci in honor of Beatriz Segovia Madriguera. Works by Haydn, Sor, Bach, Villa-Lobos, Carlevaro, and Albéniz."

69. Hector Mario Artucio (d. 2005) was Uruguay's minister of education and culture in 1979 under President Aparicio Méndez.

70. Lars Fagerström sent an e-mail to the author on August 26, 2010, saying that Segovia never expressed any such anger toward him. He added, "Andrés and I were good friends before and after the death of Beatriz. We stayed in contact by letter up to his death in 1987."

71. Michael Lorimer, e-mail to Charles Postlewate, February 26, 2011.

Chapter 15. Epilogue—The Compass Continues Pointing South

1. Both María Rosa and Sofía Puig Madriguera emphatically insist that in those August days of 1979, Segovia appeared to be more concerned about getting Paquita's death certificate than about the concert in honor of his daughter. Divorce was not legal in Spain until 1981, after the Franco dictatorship and the installation of the new democratic monarchy. Since Segovia was divorced from Paquita, his marriage to Emilia Corral Sancho in 1962 was not recognized under Spanish law. By showing that his second wife had died and he was a widower, he would be able to legalize his third marriage.

2. There is excellent visual evidence showing Segovia shortly before the death of his daughter. The documentary *Segovia in Los Olivos* was filmed by Christopher Nupen during that European summer of 1967, when the guitarist could not even imagine the tragedy that would take place just a few weeks later.

3. Sofía Puig Madriguera, interview by Ramón Mérica aired on November 23, 1993, on the program *En vivo y en directo*, Radio Sarandí (Montevideo). In a conversation this author had with her and her sister María Rosa (October 18, 2005), Sofía

confirmed that fact and said that Segovia's request was also made during their last visit at his Madrid home. Sofía's words were, "Andrés, crying, was asking us to take him to Montevideo, that he did not have the money to go."

4. The photo, taken in Barcelona in 1933, is reproduced on page 36.

5. Escande, *Abel Carlevaro: Un nuevo mundo en la guitarra*. Chapter 12 presents the entire surviving correspondence, which is part of Carlevaro's archives, between both guitarists.

6. The letter is undated but was stamped May 27, 1969 by the post office. The entire paragraph is marked by a lateral handwritten note that says: "Read this paragraph to María Rosa, if you get to talk to her. THANK YOU."

7. María Rosa Puig Madriguera, e-mail to the author, December 16, 2006.

8. A mountain ski-resort town about forty miles northwest of Madrid. —*Trans.*

9. Andrés Segovia was given the hereditary title of Marquis of Salobreña by Spain's King Juan Carlos on June 24, 1981. The title has been passed on to the maestro's youngest son, Carlos Andrés. Salobreña is a small village, five miles east of Don Andrés's vacation home of Los Olivos, with a tenth-century Moorish castle on a hill that overlooks the Mediterranean Sea.—*Trans.*

10. Whoever was taking the dictation and typed the letter probably misunderstood and wrote "directions" instead of "digressions."

11. López Poveda, *Andrés Segovia: Síntesis biográfica*, 11–12.

12. In March 2010, almost a year after the present book was first published in Spanish, the two-volume biography that López Poveda had spent four decades preparing was published. This substantial work partly rectifies those omissions and makes reference to Segovia's relationship with Paquita Madriguera and his link to Montevideo. Though quite incomplete in this area, it is more extensive and detailed than the biographical synthesis. I can report with great satisfaction that after the appearance of *Don Andrés y Paquita* an important section of the Segovia Museum in Linares was dedicated to the guitarist's Montevideo period. It now exhibits important photos of Paquita, her daughters, and the country estate of El Campito, as well as materials that have to do with the pianist's brilliant artistic career—all ornamented with the flags of Spain and Uruguay.—*Author.*

13. Segovia's stay in Montevideo began in April 1937, but it is difficult to say exactly when it ended. Perhaps it is closer to the truth to say that it lasted about a decade.

14. Sofía Puig Madriguera, interview by Ramón Mérica aired on November 23, 1993, on the program *En vivo y en directo*, Radio Sarandí (Montevideo).

15. Donal Henahan, "Andrés Segovia Is Dead at 94," *New York Times*, June 4, 1987, A1.

Bibliography

Alcázar, Miguel. *Obra completa para guitarra de Manuel Ponce* [Manuel Ponce's Complete Works for Guitar]. Mexico City: Conaculta y Ediciones Étoile, 2000.

———. *The Segovia–Ponce Letters*. Columbus, OH: Editions Orphée, 1989.

Blanco Ruiz, Carlos. *La proyección internacional de Francisco Calleja* [The Future International Image of Francisco Calleja]. La Rioja, Spain: Instituto de Estudios Riojanos, 2003.

Botet, María Emma. "Apuntes sobre la última visita de Segovia a La Habana" [Notes About Segovia's Last Visit to Havana]. *Guitarra* (July 1945). Reproduced in *Clave* 2–3 (2003): 43–44.

Caetano, Gerardo y José Rilla. *Historia contemporánea del Uruguay* [Contemporary History of Uruguay]. Montevideo: Fin de Siglo, 1994.

Cancela, Gladys. *La guitarra y su magia* [The Guitar and Its Magic]. Montevideo: Editorial Goes, 1973.

Carlevaro, Abel. *Mi guitarra y mi mundo* [My Guitar and My World]. Heidelberg: Chanterelle, 2006.

Clark, Walter Aaron. *Enrique Granados: Poet of the Piano*, New York: Oxford University Press, 2006.

Colonna, Maurizio. *Chitarristi-compositori del XX secolo* [Guitarist-Composers of the Twentieth Century]. Padua: Franco Muzio Editore, 1990.

Cortázar, Julio. *Final del juego* [End of the Game]. Buenos Aires: Editorial Sudamericana, 1956.

De Andrade Muricy, José Cândido. *Villa-Lobos: Uma interpretação.* [Villa-Lobos: An Interpretation]. Rio de Janeiro: Ministerio de Educação, Serviço de Documentação, 1961.

De La Guardia, Ernesto. "La guitarra a través de los tiempos: Origen e historia de la guitarra" [The Guitar Throughout Time: Origin and History of the Guitar]. *La Guitarra* (July 1923): 3–10.

Dessent, Daniel, and Lincoln Maiztegui Casas. "El pensador de la guitarra" [The Guitar Thinker]. *Posdata* (August 24, 1995): 65–68.

Dieu, Lionel. "Entretien impromptu avec Abel Carlevaro" [Impromptu Interview with Abel Carlevaro]. *Les cahiers de la guitare* (first trimester 1991): 13–17.

Duval, Pedro. "Andrès Segovia nell'America del Sud" [Andrés Segovia in South America]. *La chitarra* (September 1937): 67.

———. "L'attività di Andrea Segovia" [The Activity of Andrés Segovia]. *La chitarra* (October 1937): 73–74.

Escande, Alfredo. *Abel Carlevaro: Un nuevo mundo en la guitarra* [Abel Carlevaro: A New World in the Guitar]. Montevideo: Editorial Aguilar, 2005.

García Lorca, Federico. *Obras completas* [Complete Works]. Madrid: Editorial Aguilar, 1963.

Gilardino, Angelo. "Heitor Villa-Lobos, genio ribelle che divenne maestro e profeta" [Heitor Villa-Lobos, Rebel Genius Who Becomes Teacher and Prophet]. *GuitArt Special* 13 (2007): 7–29.

Godoy, Sila-Szarán, Luis. *Mangoré: Vida y obra de Agustín Barrios* [Mangore: Life and Works of Agustín Barrios]. Asunción: Editorial Ñandutí, 1994.

González de Amaro, Elizabeth. *Agustín Barrios: Patrimonio de América* [Agustín Barrios: Heritage of America]. Montevideo: Author's Edition, 1994.

Gran Enciclopedia del Uruguay [Great Encyclopedia of Uruguay]. Montevideo.: El Observador, 2002.

Horn, Guy. "January 8, 1928: The Moment of Truth for the Classical Guitar in the United States." *Soundboard* 20, no. 3 (1994): 17–19.

Kotzia, Eleftheria. "Wish You Were Here: Ida Presti, 1924–1967." *Classical Guitar* (May 1992): 11–18.

López Poveda, Alberto. *Andrés Segovia: Vida y obra* [Andrés Segovia: Life and Works]. Jaén: Universidad de Jaén, 2009.

———. *Andrés Segovia: Síntesis biográfica*. Linares, Jaén: Tipografía Predilecta, 1987.

Madriguera, Paquita. *Visto y oído* [Seen and Heard]. Buenos Aires: Editorial Nova, 1947.

Mangado, Josep María. *La guitarra en Cataluña, 1769–1939* [The Guitar in Catalonia, 1769–1939]. London: Tecla, 1999.

Milton, John W. "Granados and Goya: Artists on the Edge of Democracy." Paper presented at the conference "Music in the Time of Goya, and Goya in the Time of Granados," University of California, Riverside, February 25, 2005. http://www.cilam.ucr.edu/diagonal/issues/2005/milton.html, accessed December 15, 2011.

Mora Guarnido, José. *Federico García Lorca y su mundo* [Federico García Lorca and His World]. Buenos Aires: Editorial Losada, 1958.

Nahum, Benjamín. *La época Batllista, 1905–1929* [The Batllista Period, 1905–1929]. Montevideo: Ediciones de la Banda Oriental, 2007.

———, Angel Cocchi, Ana Frega, and Yvette Trochon. *Historia Uruguaya: Crisis política y recuperación económica, 1930–1958* [Uruguayan History: Political Crisis and Economic Recovery, 1930–1958]. Montevideo: Ediciones de la Banda Oriental, 2007.

Otero, Corazón. *Canto obstinado* [Stubborn Song]. Victoria, British Columbia: Trafford, 2008.

———. *Manuel M. Ponce y la guitarra.* Mexico City: Edamex, 1997.

———. *Mario Castelnuovo-Tedesco: Su vida y su obra para guitarra* [Mario Castelnuovo-Tedesco: His Life and Work for the Guitar]. Mexico City: Ediciones Musicales Yolotl, 1987.

Pérez Mondino, Cecilia. *Margarita Xirgú en Montevideo durante la Guerra Civil española* [Margarita Xirgú in Montevideo during the Spanish Civil War]. Montevideo: CIDDAE, 2005.

Persia, Jorge de. *I concurso de cante jondo: Edición conmemorativa, 1922–1992* [First Flamenco Competition: Commemorative Edition]. Granada: Archivo Manuel de Falla, 1992.

Pinnell, Richard. *The Rioplatense Guitar.* Westport, CT: The Bold Strummer, 1991.

———. "Segovia in Exile: Protagonists and Projects of the Montevideo Period (1936–1947)." *Guitar Review* 110 (1997): 1–8.

Prat, Domingo. *Diccionario de guitarristas* [Dictionary of Guitarists]. Buenos Aires: Casa Romero y Fernández, 1934.

Pujol, Emilio. *La guitarra y su historia* [The Guitar and Its History]. Buenos Aires: Casa Romero y Fernández, 1930.

Scherping, Rüdiger. "Der Weg des Mensches ist der Mensch selbst" [The Man's Journey Is the Man Himself]. *Staccato* (January–February 1998): 10–17.

Segovia, Andrés. "I Meet Villa-Lobos." *Guitar Review* 22 (1958): 22–23.

———. "Manuel M. Ponce: Notas y recuerdos" [Manuel M. Ponce: Notes and Memories]. *Guitar Review* 7 (1948): 13–14.

———. *Segovia: An Autobiography of the Years 1893–1920.* New York: Macmillan, 1976.

Segovia, Carlos Andrés. "Algunos datos y reflexiones sobre la biografía de Andrés Segovia, su formación intelectual y sus ideas políticas" [Some Data and Reflections about the Biography of Andrés Segovia, His Intellectual Formation, and His Political Ideas]. http://guitarra.artepulsado.com/guitarra/reflexiones_segovia.htm (February 2006), accessed December 15, 2011.

Simoes, Ronōel. "The Guitar in Brazil." *Guitar Review* 22 (1958): 6–7.

Smith, Elisabeth Papas. *Sophocles Papas: The Guitar, His Life.* Chapel Hill, NC: Columbia Music, 1998.

Stover, Richard D. *Six Silver Moonbeams: The Life and Times of Agustín Barrios Mangoré.* Clovis, CA: Querico, 1992.

Torrellas, A. Albert. *Diccionario de la música ilustrado* [Illustrated Dictionary of Music]. Barcelona: Central Catalana de Publicaciones, 1928.

Usillos, Carlos. *Andrés Segovia*. Madrid: Servicio de Publicaciones del Ministerio de Educación y Ciencia, Dirección General de Bellas Artes, 1973.

Viglietti, Cédar. *Origen e historia de la guitarra* [Origin and History of the Guitar]. Buenos Aires: Editorial Albatros, 1976.

Wade, Graham. *Segovia: A Celebration of the Man and His Music*. London: Allison & Busby, 1983.

Wade, Graham, and Gerard Garno. *A New Look at Segovia: His Life, His Music*. Pacific, MO: Mel Bay, 1997.

Zanon, Fabio. "Olga Coelho 1909–2008, Obituary." *Classical Guitar* (July 2008): 30–33.

Zárraga, Miguel de. "España en Nueva York, la más grande pianista del mundo" [Spain in New York, the World's Greatest Pianist]. *Blanco y Negro* (Madrid), September 2, 1917, 14.

Index of Names